Reese Ryan writes sexy, emotional love stories served with a heaping side of family drama.

Reese is a native Ohioan with deep Tennessee roots. She endured many long, hot car trips to family reunions in Memphis via a tiny clown car loaded with cousins.

Connect with her on Instagram, Facebook, Twitter or at reeseryan.com

Join her VIP Readers Lounge at bit.ly/VIPReadersLounge.

A former job-hopper, **Jessica Lemmon** resides in Ohio with her husband and rescue dog. She holds a degree in graphic design, which is currently gathering dust in an impressive frame. When she's not writing supersexy heroes, she can be found cooking, drawing, drinking coffee (okay, wine) and eating potato chips. She firmly believes God gifts us with talents for a purpose, and with His help, you can create the life you want.

Jessica is a social media junkie who loves to hear from readers. You can learn more at jessicalemmon.com

A REUNION OF RIVALS

REESE RYAN

ONE LAST KISS

JESSICA LEMMON

MILLS & BOON

First Published in Great Britain 2020
by Mills & Boon, an imprint of HarperCollinsPublishers,
1 London Bridge Street, London, SE1 9GF

A Reunion of Rivals © 2020 Roxanne Ravenel
One Last Kiss © 2020 Jessica Lemmon

ISBN: 978-0-263-27929-0

0720

Printed and bound in Spain
by CPI, Barcelona

A REUNION
OF RIVALS

REESE RYAN

To the amazing readers in the
Reese Ryan VIP Readers Lounge on Facebook:
thank you for your continued support.
I appreciate you all so much.

To Jennifer Copeland: thank you for
recommending the perfect Robert Frost poem.

To readers Cassandra Hunt,
Nalria Wisdom Gaddy, Julie Eichelberger-Ford
and Nicole Trudeau Westmoreland: thank you
for the peach drink recommendations.
I can't wait to try all of them.

One

Max Abbott had a king-size headache and a serious case of jet lag. After spending seven days in Vegas on a business trip that ended with the three-day-long bachelor party of a college friend, he was grateful to be back in Magnolia Lake—his small Tennessee hometown nestled in the Smoky Mountains.

He'd drunk way too much and slept far too little. And this morning, his thirtysomething body was clearly protesting his twentysomething antics over the weekend.

Max was the marketing VP of King's Finest, his family's world-renowned distillery. So he usually made a point of arriving in the office ahead of his team. But today he was so exhausted he could barely see straight. If it hadn't been for his father—Duke Abbott, the company CEO—calling an emergency meeting this morning, he would've stayed home and slept it off.

Instead, he lumbered into the office still wearing his Saint Laurent shades at ten thirty—half an hour before the scheduled meeting. Just enough time to check in with his assistant.

"Good morning, chief." Molly Halloran glanced up from typing furiously on her keyboard.

He removed his shades, squinting at the light pouring in from the nearby windows.

"Sheesh!" she exclaimed in a voice reminiscent of Lucille Ball's in *I Love Lucy*. "Must've been *some* weekend."

"It was." Max parked his butt in the chair in front of Molly's desk, not willing to expend the additional energy to take the dozen or so steps to his office. "And good morning to you, too, sunshine."

"Can I get you some coffee? You're going to need it if you don't want to look like the stiff in *Weekend at Bernie's* the rest of the day." She bounced out of her seat and moved toward the coffeemaker before he'd even grunted his response.

Molly's brutal honesty was one of the reasons he valued her so much. And if it caught him in the chin with a right hook every now and again, so be it.

He pulled out his phone and checked his text messages and email to see if anything pressing required his attention.

There was nothing that couldn't wait until he was fully conscious, which, at this rate, might be in a day or two.

Max thanked Molly when she handed him a black mug engraved with the white King's Finest Distillery logo. He set his phone on her desk and wrapped his hands around the warm cup, inhaled the fragrant black liquid and took his first sip of coffee of the day. He released a small, contented sigh, his eyes drifting closed momentarily.

"We've got twenty minutes to go over everything." She tapped on the fitness wearable on her wrist. "That takes into account the five minutes you'll need to walk to the conference room."

Brutally honest and extremely efficient.

"Fine." He took another swig of coffee, set his mug down and opened the notes app on his phone. "Shoot."

"Your father is being tight-lipped about this meeting." She lowered her voice, her blue-gray eyes shifting away from him. "But last week, while you were gone, he asked me and Emily to compile everything you and Zora had on your proposal to add fruit brandies to the KFD lineup."

That woke him up more than the bulletproof coffee had.

Three years ago, his grandfather, Joseph Abbott, the founder of King's Finest Distillery, had proposed that the company begin making fruit brandy. His father had been opposed. In a compromise, they'd spent a small mint to set up separate stills and bring in a brandy distiller. The company began experimenting with making small batches of fruit brandy, using the excess, overly ripe fruit supplied by his grandfather's best friend, who owned an orchard just outside of Knoxville.

The brandy they'd produced was damn good. So for the past two years, Max and his sister, Zora, the company's VP of sales, had been trying to convince their father to move forward with bringing a KFD brandy to market.

His father agreed that the quality was outstanding. Still, he hadn't been ready to commit to expanding the company's basic product line beyond the limited-edition moonshines they'd rolled out in honor of the company's jubilee three years ago.

He would pick the day I feel like I've been run over by a truck to discuss this.

"Print me a copy of everything you have on—"

Molly shoved a binder with colored tabs in his direction. "That's everything. Oh, and I took the liberty of updating the projected sales numbers. I also created a quick summary of the key selling points. It's on page one."

Note to self: get Molly that limited edition Star Wars electric pressure cooker she's been eyeing for her birthday.

She finished briefing him on the materials, then urged him in the direction of the conference room, armed with a fresh cup of coffee, promptly at five minutes to eleven,.

At least now he more closely resembled a fully functioning human being.

Max entered the room and slid into his usual chair beside Zora.

"Glad you could join us," his sister whispered, elbowing him in the ribs. "I thought we might need to send someone to revive you."

"Ha-ha." He didn't look in his sister's direction. Instead, he focused on the older man seated on the other side of the table whose snow-white hair and beard contrasted his dark brown skin. "Good morning, Mr. Bazemore."

"Morning, Max." A wide smile spread across Dixon Bazemore's face as they both rose to their feet and shook hands. The old man had been the owner of Bazemore Orchards longer than Max had been alive. "Good to see you, young man."

"You, too, Mr. B." Molly's instincts about the reason for the meeting had been right. Why else would Dixon Bazemore be here? Still, he asked, "What brings you to see us today?"

"We'll go over everything during the meeting," Max's father interjected. "We're waiting for one more person."

Max glanced around the table. All of the members of the executive committee were present. His grandfather and father. His brothers Blake and Parker, the operations VP and CFO, respectively. Blake's wife, Savannah—the company's events manager. Zora, him and his father's admin, Lianna, who was there to take notes.

"Who are we—"

"I'm sorry. I got a little turned around finding my way back here from the parking lot. But I've got your portfolio, Grandad."

Max snapped his attention in the direction of the familiar voice. He hadn't heard it in more than a decade, but he would never, *ever* forget it. His mouth went dry, and his heart thudded so loudly he was sure his sister could hear it.

"Peaches?" He scanned the brown eyes that stared back at him through narrowed slits.

"Quinn." She was gorgeous, despite the slightly irritated

flare of her nostrils and the stiff smile that barely revealed her dimples. "Hello, Max."

The *good to see you* was notably absent. But what should he expect? It was his fault they hadn't parted on the best of terms.

Quinn settled into the empty seat beside her grandfather. She handed the old man a worn leather portfolio, then squeezed his arm. The genuine smile that lit her brown eyes and activated those killer dimples was firmly in place again.

Max had been the cause of that magnificent smile nearly every day that summer between his junior and senior years of college when he'd interned at Bazemore Orchards.

"Now that everyone is here, we can discuss the matter at hand." His father nodded toward Lianna, and she handed out bound presentations.

"As you can see, we're here to discuss adding fruit brandies to the King's Finest Distillery lineup—a venture Dad, Max and Zora have been pushing for some time." Duke nodded in their general direction. "I think the company and the market are in a good place now for us to explore the possibility."

"Excellent." His sister beamed. "Would this be a permanent addition to the product lineup?"

"I'll only commit to a limited-edition trial." Duke frowned slightly. He always did what was best for their family-owned distillery. But Zora—the youngest and the only girl in a family of four boys—was still his "princess," and his father hated disappointing her. "But if the numbers support it, as with the special-edition moonshines we introduced a few years ago, I'm willing to discuss making the line permanent."

"Bourbon is what we're known for," Parker, also known as Negative Ned, chimed in. "Won't adding other liquors to the lineup dilute our brand?"

Parker wasn't being argumentative. He was painstakingly methodical and questioned everything. It was the way his intricate mind worked.

Zora rolled her eyes and folded her arms, not bothering to hide her annoyance. "Pepsi sells several types of soda, water, tea, juice and energy drinks. It hasn't damaged their reputation as a top beverage company."

Parker thought about Zora's words for a moment, then nodded sagely. He scribbled on the ever-present pad in front of him and pushed his glasses up the bridge of his nose. "Good point. Go on."

Duke fought back a chuckle, then continued.

Max should have been riveted by the conversation. After all, this project was one he'd been fighting for over the past thirty months. Yet, it took every ounce of self-control he could muster to keep from blatantly staring at the beautiful woman seated directly across the table from him.

Peaches. Or rather, Quinn Bazemore. Dixon Bazemore's granddaughter. She was more gorgeous than he remembered. Her beautiful, deep brown skin looked silky and smooth.

The simple gray shift dress she wore did its best to mask her shape. Still, it was obvious her hips and breasts were fuller now than they'd been the last time he'd held her in his arms. The last time he'd seen every square inch of that shimmering brown skin.

Zora elbowed him again and he held back an audible *oomph*.

"What's with you?" she whispered.

"Nothing," he whispered back.

Maybe he wasn't doing such a good job of masking his fascination with Quinn.

Max opened his booklet to the page his father indicated. He was thrilled that the company was ready to give their brandy initiative a try, even if it was just a test run.

He understood why Mr. Bazemore was there. His farm

had been providing the fruit for the brandy and would continue to do so. But that didn't explain the presence of his ex.

Quinn shifted in her seat beneath Max Abbott's heated stare. She refused to glance in his direction. She wasn't here to flirt with the handsome-as-ever Max Abbott. She'd come to King's Finest Distillery for two reasons: to help save her grandfather's farm and to build a case study for the consultancy she'd launch as soon as the farm was on stable ground again.

It was a venture she'd mused about as an undergrad. But she'd settled into a comfortable public relations career instead. Until six months ago, when she'd found herself out of a job and unable to work in her field within a fifty-mile radius of her home in Atlanta.

With no immediate plans, she'd packed up her condo and accepted her grandfather's invitation to their family farm just outside of Knoxville, where she'd spent her summers as a kid.

Just until she figured out her next move.

The excitement of helping her grandfather establish important strategic partnerships revived her interest in her forgotten venture. So she'd dusted off her business plan, plugged in the holes and improved on it. Now she needed to build her portfolio while she waited out the remaining six months of the non-compete clause in her employment agreement with her former PR firm. Then she'd return to Atlanta and launch her new practice.

This proposed partnership with the world-renowned King's Finest Distillery would be the cornerstone of her growing portfolio. So if that meant pretending not to be affected by the man who'd broken her heart and crushed it into minuscule pieces without so much as a backward glance, she'd suck it up and do just that.

If Max could behave as if that summer between them had never happened, so could she.

Duke was explaining that they would begin the venture with apple-, peach-and cherry-flavored brandies, and that all of the fruit would be sourced from Bazemore Farms.

Quinn's heart swelled when everyone in the room applauded. She was relieved no one had objected to making her grandfather's farm the sole source for the fruit. It was a sweet deal for the farm, which had been struggling in recent years. Partly because of a shift in the market and how difficult it had become to get solid, reliable help at a price the farm could sustainably afford. Partly because of the shady accountant who'd taken over the books after her grandmother's death several years ago.

"This will be a co-branded product, something we've never done before. A partnership that was brokered by Dixon's lovely granddaughter, Quinn." Duke gestured toward her. "She's here in her capacity as an executive of Bazemore Farms, but she's also a collaboration expert. We had a fine chat last week about some of her innovative ideas for quickly getting this venture to market. Quinn."

"Thank you, Mr. Abbott." Quinn stood, pulling a stack of presentations from her bag. She walked around the table, placing one in front of each person as she explained how she'd created lucrative partnerships between clients in the past.

"As a rep at one of Atlanta's most prestigious PR firms for the past eight years, I…" Quinn stammered, unsettled by the jolt of heat that surged through her when Max's eyes met hers as she handed him a copy of the presentation.

It was her nerves, *not* Max Abbott, that had caused her words to come out in a jumble.

Despite the silent outrage in the widened eyes framed by thick, neat brows, the man was still devastatingly handsome. He was a little older and his shoulders were a bit broader.

But he looked essentially like the boy she'd fallen in love with that one passionate summer. The last she'd spent with her grandparents before going off to college. The summer Max had been an intern, living and working on the farm.

That was more than a decade ago. Time had treated him well.

"I've handled sensitive public relations campaigns for some of the biggest names in fintech," she continued.

"We already have a PR person," Parker interrupted, shoving his glasses up the bridge of his nose.

"You have a college student who handles social media, your newsletter, and the occasional press release." Quinn maintained her warm smile. Duke had warned her Parker would be a tough nut to crack, and that Max and Zora might be insulted by the idea of bringing her on to execute the project that had been their baby. "But a project of this magnitude requires a dedicated, experienced professional who'll get vendors and consumers excited about the new product line. Just as Savannah did for the company's jubilee and the associated release of limited-edition moonshines a few years ago."

Savannah smiled approvingly, and Parker nodded in agreement, silenced for the moment.

"If you'll turn to page five, we can quickly review a rundown of how I'm proposing to help King's Finest and Bazemore Farms make the most of this joint venture."

"You're bringing in someone else to execute our proposal?" Max ignored her completely, asking the question of his father instead. "Zora and I are fully capable of—"

"Speak for yourself, big brother." Zora turned her chair toward him before their father could respond. "I have a lot on my plate. We've seen a real uptick in our international sales and domestic market share in regions outside of the South since the jubilee. I'm traveling extensively over the next few months. I can't add another thing to my to-do list right now. Neither can my team. As long as we're consulted regularly, I'm all for bringing someone else on to do the heavy lifting."

Quinn exhaled quietly, and her racing heart slowed in response to Zora's encouraging nod.

"And you've had your hands full with the expansion of our marketing efforts," Duke reminded him. "So it would be better to have someone wholly dedicated to the project."

Max's nostrils flared, and a streak of red bloomed across his forehead and cheeks. He opened his mouth to object further, but his grandfather cut him off.

"Let Quinn finish her presentation, son. Then we can discuss any concerns privately and make our final decision." Joseph Abbott nodded in her direction. "Please continue, Quinn."

She smiled gratefully at the older man she'd always called Grandpa Joe, then inhaled deeply, smiled broadly and put on the presentation of her life.

She'd won over Joseph and Duke Abbott, the company's founder and CEO. Zora and Savannah were also on board. Blake, she couldn't quite read but Parker and Max definitely required convincing. So that was what she would do.

In this room, in this moment, Max Abbott wasn't her first love, her first real kiss, her first…*everything*. He was a skeptical company executive, not unlike the dozens she'd encountered before in her career.

Despite whatever else Max might be feeling toward her—curiosity, animosity, maybe even attraction—he was a sensible individual. And like every other Abbott at the table, she knew he wanted what was best for King's Finest.

She just needed to convince him that she was the best person for the job. And convince herself that working with her ex wasn't her worst idea ever. Her entire future was riding on it.

Two

Max groaned quietly as Quinn finished her presentation. He'd sifted through her proposal and listened carefully, ready to poke holes in it and rip it apart. But the plan was solid, and Quinn had suggested useful partnerships he and Zora hadn't considered.

Still, this project was *his* and Zora's baby. They'd taken their grandfather's request to add flavored brandies to the lineup seriously. Had worked with him to develop it. Worn their father down until he'd agreed to invest in the stills and bring in an expert brandy distiller. Revisited the topic at *every* damn quarterly meeting for the past two years. So for his father to just hand off the project to his ex of all the goddamned people on the face of God's green earth... Yeah, it felt a hell of a lot like a solid knee in the nuts. Even if no one in the room besides him and Quinn were aware of their romantic history.

But his father was right. He and Zora had their hands full with all of the additional business King's Finest was doing. Much of it could be credited to the efforts of his sister-in-law, Savannah, who'd become their de facto PR person since she'd joined the company three years ago. Savannah handled event management for both the distillery and the renovated barn on the edge of his parents' property, which they rented out for weddings and other events.

The company's event and tour business was booming

now. But Savannah was six months pregnant with her and Blake's second child, and their two-year-old son was already a handful. The last thing his sister-in-law needed was another project.

"Well, what do you think?" Grandpa Joseph beamed. Dixon and Quinn had been dispatched on an hour-long tour of the King's Finest Distillery while the Abbotts formally debated the Bazemore Farms proposal. "That one's a sharp cookie, eh?" His grandfather chuckled. "I remember the first time I met Quinn. She was about three years old and she had more questions than any kid that age I'd ever encountered besides Zora." He grinned at his only granddaughter.

"I love the plan she put together for us." Zora thumbed through the document Quinn had prepared. "Having her handle all of this is a godsend. And she's got the right personality for the job. She didn't skip a beat or get frustrated with Parker's myriad questions or Max's pushback." Zora raised an eyebrow at him. "And I love her suggestions for finding new ways to partner with state and local vendors."

"Excellent. Blake, how about you?" Duke asked Max's eldest brother, the heir apparent to the King's Finest CEO-ship.

"I love everything about the plan." Blake tapped the cover of the presentation. "I like Quinn, and I know the distributors will like her, too. If she can do half of what she's presented here, I'm sold."

"Parker?" Duke turned to him, as if prepared for the worst.

Parker scanned the data again. "The numbers look good. If you're sure we can do this without compromising our position in the bourbon market…" He shrugged. "I'm fine with moving forward on a trial basis. Say…six months once it goes to market. If sales are good, we can talk long-term."

"Sounds fair." Duke nodded, then turned to him. "And what say you, Max?"

Max released a quiet breath. Every eye in the room was focused on him. Quinn's plan was flawless; he had no legitimate reason to object to it.

So what was he going to say?

That he didn't want to work with her because it would be a constant reminder that he'd been a complete dick to her thirteen years ago?

"The plan is fine…okay, it's good," he amended in response to everyone's guffaws and raised eyebrows. "It's damn good. I'll give you that. But this is *our* company." He tapped the table with his index finger. "*Our* project. A project we're doing in memory of Savannah's grandfather Martin. Don't you think *we* should be the ones to handle it rather than bringing in an outsider?"

Had that come off as spoiled and elitist as it sounded in his head?

God, I hope not.

"Seriously, dude? *She's not one of us,*" Zora mimicked him in a whiny, low voice. "*That's* the best you can do?"

Everyone at the table laughed.

"You gotta admit, that argument is weak sauce, bruh." Blake chuckled. "Quinn is an experienced professional and she and Mr. B are good people."

"And I know she's not technically family, but I wouldn't exactly call her an *outsider*, either," Grandpa Joe added, sounding a little hurt by the dig. "I've always been quite fond of the girl. Considered her an honorary granddaughter."

"I know, Gramps. And I didn't mean anything by it." Max sighed and scrubbed a hand down his face. "I guess what I'm saying is that I have a lot of time and energy invested in this project. So the idea of relinquishing complete control of it isn't sitting well with me."

"I can respect that, Max." His father nodded sagely as

he rubbed his whiskered chin. He leaned forward on one elbow. "What can we do to make you more comfortable with Quinn running point on the project?"

Translation: This is *happening, son. You've been out-voted.*

"I want to be the point person on this project internally," Max said definitively. "And it should be clear that Quinn reports to me."

"Done." His father shrugged. "That'll leave me more time to golf. Anything else?"

"I plan to be as involved in the project as my schedule permits." Max folded his hands on the table in front of him. "And I need to have the option to terminate the agreement early should I find just cause."

Duke stroked his chin as he silently contemplated Max's request. He nodded begrudgingly. "Agreed, but I get the final say on such a drastic action."

"Perfect." Grandpa Joe slapped the table and chuckled. "Lianna, order us some lunch. We've got reason to celebrate. And make sure to break out the good mason jars so we can all sample a little of that brandy."

Just peachy.

He'd be working closely with the one ex who had it out for him. The stiff smile she'd given him when he'd used her nickname made it obvious she was still harboring a grudge that would impede their working relationship. This project was too important to his grandfather and their company. He wouldn't permit his past mistake to interfere with family business. He'd handle this the way he handled every other business problem: by facing it head-on.

That meant clearing the air with Quinn the first opportunity he got.

The Bazemores had returned to the conference room where a selection of pastas from a local Italian restaurant awaited them. They'd shared a meal with the Abbotts and sampled the peach, apple and cherry brandies. All of them were remarkably good.

Max's father and grandfather had invited Dixon to join them for a celebratory round of golf and, doubtless, more drinking. Parker had left to walk Cricket—his fiancée Kayleigh Jemison's golden retriever. That left Zora, Quinn, Blake and Savannah, who were seated at the table chatting after the meal.

Quinn was mooning over the adorable photos of Max's nephew, Davis, on Blake's phone.

Max had waited patiently, not actively joining in the conversation, instead staying engaged and nodding or chuckling whenever warranted. He needed a moment alone with Quinn.

He glanced at the text message that flashed on his watch: The league wants to talk sponsorship in an hour. We need to review notes.

For the past several months he'd been working on a sponsorship deal with the Memphis Marauders professional football team. Turning down the call wasn't an option. But he didn't want to put off clearing the air with Quinn, either.

If they were going to work together, they needed to start off with a clean slate.

Max stood abruptly and everyone in the room turned toward him. He cleared his throat. "Hey guys, I need to speak with Quinn for a moment...*privately*," he added, for the benefit of his sister, who'd shrugged.

Blake and Savannah exchanged a puzzled look.

"Yeah, sure." Blake stood, helping his wife up.

Savannah rubbed her growing belly. "It was a pleasure to meet you, Quinn. Lianna will give you my contact information. I'd love to meet for lunch later this week."

Blake and Savannah left, hand in hand. Zora folded her arms.

"Zora." Max gave her his *I'm not bullshitting right now* voice. A voice he'd had to employ often over the years with his little sister.

"Fine." Zora stood, then looked at Quinn. "As long as you're okay with this."

"It's fine, but thank you, Zora." Quinn smiled politely as she stood, gathering her papers. A clear sign that she was leaving, too.

Zora shot Max a warning look and breezed out of the room.

As soon as the door closed behind his sister, Quinn turned to him and scowled. "Why would you give everyone the impression something is going on between us?"

He tried not to take her words personally, but damn if it didn't feel like she'd kicked him in the teeth wearing a pair of steel toe boots.

There was a time when her greatest desire had been for them to go out on a proper date and let the world see them together. Rather than sneaking around and hooking up in his shabby little loft over the barn or in the bed of his truck, parked beneath the stars.

Heat stung his cheeks as he jammed his hands into his pockets. "They probably assume I want to talk about the project or catch up with an old friend."

He pretended not to notice the way she pressed her lips together and furrowed her brows when he referred to them as *friends*.

Damn. Is there a draft in here?

The chilly vibe coming from his ex was all too real.

"And I really would love to catch up at some point. But first, I need to tell you just how sorry I am."

"No." She shook her head, her tousled beach waves swinging gently.

He curled the fingers still shoved into his pockets into tight fists. Max couldn't help remembering how he'd sifted the soft strands through his fingers as she had lain in his arms. And the dreamy way she'd gazed up at him after they'd made love.

There was nothing remotely romantic about the frosty look Quinn cast in his direction from beneath her long, thick eyelashes.

"No, you won't allow me to apologize to you, or no, you're not willing to accept my sincere apology?" He sat on the edge of the conference table.

"Both." Quinn folded her arms, her expression neutral. Despite the iciness that slid over his skin in response to her answer, her tone and expression betrayed no anger. "A—I don't want your apology. B—There's no need for it."

Heat spanned his forehead. Max had imagined having this conversation with Quinn dozens of times. He'd envisioned anger, forgiveness and lots of incredibly hot makeup sex. What he hadn't foreseen was Quinn standing here calm, callous and completely out of fucks to give.

Not that he didn't deserve it.

"I appreciate you saying that, Quinn. But I'd feel better if—"

"No." Her voice vibrated with thinly veiled anger this time and her eyes narrowed. "You don't get to do this."

"I don't get to do what? Apologize?" Max was genuinely stunned by her refusal.

"You don't get to absolve yourself of guilt this way." Quinn raked her fingers through her hair and tucked a few strands behind her ear. "It's been thirteen years. If you didn't see fit to apologize before now, I can't imagine that your apology is sincere. So let's not do this, *please*."

The soft, pleading tone with which she ended her request reminded him of how she'd uttered his name during those sultry summer nights.

Max winced and swallowed hard. His hushed tone matched hers. "You have every right to be angry with me, Quinn."

"I wasn't angry, Max. I was hurt." Her stony expression faltered momentarily. "By the end of that summer you'd proclaimed your undying love for me. Then as soon as you returned to campus you broke up with me via a one-sided, two-minute phone call. For months, I wondered what I'd done wrong. I finally realized that it wasn't anything I'd done." She shrugged, her smile returning. "You were just an ass. A handsome, charming one. But an ass nevertheless."

"On that we can agree." He sighed, folding his arms.

She flashed the triumphant half smile he remembered so well.

"If there's nothing else, I should go." She lifted her bag onto her shoulder. "We can meet in the morning to strategize, if that works for you."

"Are you staying at the farm?" he asked.

"I am," she said in a tone that made it clear she felt the question too personal. "Why?"

"You have nearly an hour drive to get here." He walked her toward the door. "So you name the time."

"Ten o'clock?"

"See you then." His heart thudded as he watched her slip out the door.

He'd screwed up by walking away from Quinn the way he had. Now those chickens had come home to roost.

Max groaned quietly as he sank onto a nearby chair. He and Quinn would only need to work closely together at the outset of the project. After that, they could work together remotely, when necessary. He could certainly keep it together for a few months.

Shit.

It was the same lie he'd told himself when he'd first laid eyes on Quinn that summer.

Just look at how that turned out.

Three

Quinn changed her outfit for the third time this morning. It was unlike her. She was organized and decisive. With her planner on hand, she was always ready for the day ahead. But she hadn't slept well last night. It didn't help that she'd drifted off while reviewing her notes for her upcoming meeting with Max.

He'd seemed disappointed to discover that her proposal was a good one. He'd clearly been expecting her to flop. And if she did, Max would no doubt be ready to pull the plug on their project. So there was no room for failure, fear or hesitance. She had to show up today at Max's office with her game face on. Make it clear that she knew *exactly* what she was doing.

This deal meant too much to her grandfather's farm and to her future. So she wouldn't allow herself to be intimidated by the fact that Max clearly didn't want her there. Nor would she be distracted by Max's good looks, his charm or the fact that when his eyes met hers she still felt…*something* for him.

When she'd seen him yesterday, a jolt of electricity had rocketed up her spine. His dark eyes had seemed to peer straight through her, like armor-piercing rounds shredding her flesh, despite the mental suit of armor she'd donned before she'd stepped into the room.

The truth was that she hadn't gotten lost on her way back

to the conference room that morning. She'd simply needed a moment to compose herself before she came face-to-face with Max again.

It'd been thirteen years since she'd seen Max Abbott, more than a third of her thirty-one years. Enough time to give her distance and perspective. Enough time to realize that Max Abbott hadn't been as important in the overall scheme of her life as her teenage brain had once believed.

Yes, he'd been her first love, and over that long, hot summer she'd allowed herself to believe that Max was the alpha and omega of her romantic life. That there would never be another man for her.

Quinn laughed bitterly. *God, you were naive.*

Unfortunately, she hadn't learned her lesson after Max. She'd still wanted to believe that people were inherently good and could be taken at their word. Her most recent ex had finally cured her of her Pollyanna-ish misconceptions.

The cold, hard fact was that there were a lot more liars in the world than there were people she could count on. But her grandfather was firmly in the latter camp. She wouldn't disappoint him by allowing her inconvenient history with Max to sabotage this deal.

Quinn followed the smell of pancakes, bacon and coffee down the stairs. Her grandfather stood over the sizzling cast-iron pan with a spatula in hand.

The memory of her grandmother—vibrant and beautiful until the day she died—standing there in the kitchen, cooking in that pan, with that spatula, flashed through Quinn's brain. Her mouth curved in a faint smile, though her chest suddenly felt heavy.

"You've got her smile, you know." Her grandfather's voice startled her from the daze she'd fallen into.

"I know." Quinn's smile deepened. She set the heels she was wearing today by the kitchen door. "And I love that I'll always have that connection to her."

She didn't bother to ask how her grandfather knew she'd been thinking of her grandmother. It was hard not to enter what had been Lydia Bazemore's domain and *not* think of her.

"Maybe you'll have a little girl someday with that same smile." Her grandfather winked, chuckling when she rolled her eyes and groaned in response. "Hey, an old man can dream."

"Hate to break it to you, Gramps, but there are zero prospects of a great-granddaughter on the horizon. At least not from me." She kissed her grandfather on his stubbly cheek. "I can't speak for Marcus and Mavis," she said of her younger twin siblings.

"I don't think the world is ready for the progeny of Marcus or Mavis." Her grandfather laughed, and she did, too.

Her younger brother and sister were hyperfocused science geeks who lived in their own little world. A world she never quite fit into. They were just five years younger than she was, but with the emotional distance between her and her younger siblings, it might as well have been five light-years.

The two of them were more like their parents—both scientists working in academia—than Quinn would ever be. At the dinner table with her family, she'd always felt like the answer to one of those *Sesame Street* skits: *Which one of these doesn't belong?*

"One day." He smiled. "Just not today." Her grandfather nodded toward the coffeemaker. "Grab yourself a cup of coffee and have a seat. I know you have to get out of here soon."

Quinn didn't argue. Instead, she poured herself a cup of coffee and added creamer from the fridge. Then she pulled out one of the yellow-vinyl-and-chrome chairs from beneath the chrome and yellow Formica table. Her grandparents had owned the vintage set for years, and, despite its age, it was in excellent shape. She sank onto the chair.

Her grandparents had always been frugal and sensible, saving up for when they'd leave the farm to their children or grandchildren and then travel the world. But none of their children or grandchildren had ever taken an interest in owning the farm. And then her grandmother had died suddenly of a stroke a few years ago, leaving her grandfather devastated.

Since Quinn had come to stay with him a few months ago, he'd been the happiest she'd seen him since the death of her grandmother. Maybe it was because her smile reminded him of his beloved wife's. Or maybe it was because it had given him a new purpose—fussing over her.

Her grandfather brought their plates to the table and they settled into their usual morning rhythm. Only there was nothing usual about this morning. Today she would return to King's Finest, where she and Max would start working together on this project.

"You must've had a good time at the country club yesterday." Quinn put a forkful of the buttery pancakes in her mouth and chewed.

"We did." He nodded. "And I would've told you all about it, but you were knocked out when I got back. I put all of your paperwork on your desk and draped one of your grandmother's quilts over you." He sipped some of his coffee. "You haven't crashed like that since the day you first arrived here from Atlanta. When you were so stressed-out it was like you were all tied in knots."

There was an odd stretch of silence between them as he nibbled on his bacon and she ate her pancakes.

"You seemed tense in the meeting yesterday." He peered at her over his coffee cup. "Particularly with Max." He set his cup down and folded his arms on the table, his dark eyes assessing hers. "Everything okay between you two?"

"Of course." Quinn drank long and deep from her coffee mug before lowering it. She forced a smile much bigger and brighter than the occasion called for. "Why wouldn't it be? I haven't seen him since I was eighteen."

One of her grandfather's wiry eyebrows seemed to levitate. He frowned. "You remember *exactly* how long it's been since you've seen the boy?"

Quinn froze, her smile still in place.

"It was the summer before I went to college." She stuffed more pancakes in her mouth and chewed.

"But there's no bad blood between you two, right? I mean, you got on well enough the summer he interned for me, but if there's something I need to know—"

"There isn't." Quinn placed a hand on her grandfather's forearm. Her voice was firm as she met his gaze. "Everything is fine."

"You're sure? Because I sensed some tension on his side of the table, too. When you walked in that door, it was like the boy had seen a ghost."

It'd felt that way for her, too, though she'd had the advantage of expecting that ghost and bracing for it.

"Well, like I said, we haven't seen each other in… what…?" She made a show of counting in her head. "Thirteen years. That's bound to surprise someone, right?" She laughed nervously. "As for the tension… Look at it from Max's perspective. He's the VP of marketing and I come waltzing in the door with my fancy plan. To him, it must feel like a challenge to his authority. Like I'm saying I can do his job better than he can. But it's not about that. It's about this single joint project and how we can make it amazing by thinking more broadly about opportunities for collaboration."

Her grandfather nodded and sighed—a sure sign he wasn't convinced of her explanation for the tension he'd noticed.

"Well, you don't want to be late on your first day." He stood, collecting his dishes. "Leave everything when you're done. I'll clear the table."

Quinn ate the last of her bacon and finished her coffee. "Thanks, Gramps." She got up, pushed her chair under the table and kissed his cheek again. "I'll keep you posted on how things go today. But don't wait up for me. By the time I drive back from Magnolia Lake, it'll probably be pretty late."

He stopped running the water in the sink and frowned. "You know I believe in doing things face-to-face rather than on the phone or those video calls. But I hate that you'll be on the road so much."

"I know, but it won't be forever. Just until we get everything sorted out and in motion."

"Still, it's an hour each way. Maybe we should rent a place for you in Magnolia Lake for a few months."

"Things are already tight around here." Quinn hated bringing it up. Her grandfather felt bad enough about being so distraught over the death of his wife that he hadn't noticed the accountant he'd hired to manage the books—something her grandmother had handled—was robbing him blind.

It had been Quinn's distinct pleasure to throw the guy out on his ass and report him to the local sheriff.

"I know." He nodded solemnly. "But I'd never forgive myself if something happened to you. So keep an eye out for a room or apartment you can rent short term. I'll ask around at the senior center—"

"Not necessary." Quinn shook her head vehemently. She'd end up staying in some creepy room filled with dolls or cats or hooked up on a blind date with someone's worthless grandson.

No thanks.

"I'll handle it. You just worry about sticking it to them

in the next Scrabble tournament." Quinn grinned at her grandfather.

Her grandfather raised his fists and shuffled his feet as he bobbed and weaved, doing his best Muhammad Ali imitation. "This time, I'm gonna take every last one of those suckers out."

Quinn laughed. Her grandfather was still smarting over his second-place finish in the last tournament. "I know you will, Grandad."

She got into the Honda her younger brother had gifted her when the lease for her expensive import had ended. Here in rural Tennessee, she couldn't get anywhere without a reliable car, and she'd never learned to drive her grandfather's truck—a stick shift.

It was a long drive, and she used the time to review the plan in her head while listening to something soothing and upbeat.

Prepare the plan. Don't worry about the man.

That would be her motto as long as she worked with Max. Still, she couldn't help thinking about how handsome he looked. Or how incredible he smelled. The heat she'd felt standing so close to him when the two of them were alone. His pained expression when she wouldn't accept his apology.

She shut her eyes and sighed. It didn't matter if she was still attracted to him. It didn't matter that her memories of that summer had come roaring back to her in her sleep, as vivid as the day they'd occurred. Her summer fling with Max was a part of her distant past. And that was exactly where it would stay.

Four

Max glided into the office well ahead of his usual start time, but not early enough to beat his assistant.

"Mmm…doughnuts." Molly's eyes danced with excitement when she caught a glimpse of the small box in his hand. "Did you get—"

"A bear claw for you?" He grinned, holding up a separate bag in the same hand as his cup of coffee. "Of course."

She thanked him, accepting the bag. Molly tilted her head as she scanned him for a moment.

"What is it?" He looked down at his shirt. Had he spilled coffee on it?

"You look…nice," she said. Only Molly Halloran could pay someone a compliment and still make it sound like an accusation.

"That's a good thing, right?" He unlocked his office door. "Besides, I'd like to think I look nice every day."

"You do." She trailed him into the office. "But today it feels like you *tried* to look good, and you went a little heavy on the cologne. So I'm guessing this is for the benefit of Ms. Bazemore." Molly stated the facts as if they were the elements of a math equation. Two plus two equals four. She studied his expression, then nodded. "You're definitely into her."

Max wouldn't debate Molly's conclusion, and neither was there reason for him to give it credence. "Remember what we talked about, Mol. Use your deductive powers for good. Not to analyze my romantic interests."

"Right," Molly took a bite of her bear claw as she contemplated his words. "The doughnuts were a nice gesture, since you obviously aren't happy about having to work with her on this project." She put the rest of the bear claw back in the bag and closed it. "I'm going to get one of those cake stands of your mother's from the break room. It'll make a nice display."

"Sounds great. Thanks." He settled behind his desk and took a deep breath, glad for a few minutes alone with his thoughts.

It'd been nearly twenty-four hours since he'd seen Quinn Bazemore again, and his head was still swimming. The memories of their summer fling had kept him up all night, tossing and turning.

He hadn't thought about Quinn in so long. And now he couldn't think about anything else. There had been something so authentically joyful about her. He couldn't ever recall laughing and grinning more than he had during those few months.

Max remembered the first time he'd laid eyes on her that summer. He hadn't seen Quinn since she'd been ten and he'd been thirteen. He'd been stunned that the annoying little chatterbox in pigtails had grown up to be the sexy, long-legged temptress in front of him. And yet, he'd feigned a complete lack of interest and maintained his distance.

Their grandfathers were close friends. Getting involved with her could only mean trouble.

But she'd been flirtatious, persistent, funny and just so damn... Quinn. She'd cut through his resolve to ignore her like a hot knife slicing through whipped butter.

How could he *not* have fallen for her?

Quinn had been gorgeous with her dark brown skin and her thick, black hair pulled back in a single braid. She was bright and amusing. Thoughtful and opinionated. Hopeful yet pragmatic. She'd stimulated his curiosity about the world beyond his privileged purview more than anyone or anything else had. He'd loved seeing the world through her eyes and debating all manner of issues with her.

And there was something mesmerizing about her brown eyes. He still remembered the first time she'd gazed at him like he was everything she'd ever wanted. It was one of those nights she'd snuck up to his loft with leftovers in tow and they'd played video games while debating which male tennis player would win the US Open that year.

She'd been right, as she so often was.

Max sighed softly. He'd felt incredibly lucky to be the object of Quinn's admiring gaze. He'd also felt unworthy of it. But when she'd leaned in and pressed her mouth to his, he'd been an absolute goner. One kiss was all it had taken to get him completely addicted to the sweet taste of her mouth. To the lush feel of her soft curves pressed against him.

The look Quinn had given him when he'd called her *Peaches* at yesterday's meeting was the complete opposite of how she'd regarded him when he used the affectionate moniker back then. Max knifed his fingers through his headful of short curls and groaned quietly. He would never forget the fleeting look of abject disgust in the same brown eyes that had once shone with deep affection.

A knock at the door startled Max.

"Quinn." He stood suddenly, tipping over his cup of coffee. The dark brown liquid spread, soaking the papers on his desk, including the presentation he'd been reviewing.

Not a good look, man.

"Sorry, I didn't mean to startle you." Quinn dropped her bags near the door and quickly scanned the room. She spotted a stack of napkins on the small table in the corner of his office. Quinn grabbed a handful and blotted the mess while he stood there, frozen, staring at her. "I realize I'm a few minutes early, but your assistant was away from her desk, so I just knocked. I didn't mean to—"

"You're fine," he said. He swallowed hard, his cheeks heating as his rogue eyes quickly scanned her deliciously curvy form, highlighted by the fitted skirt and blouse she wore. "I mean…*it's* fine." He finally sprang into action, grabbing a handful of napkins and dabbing at the wet papers. "I shouldn't have been sitting here daydreaming."

"Garbage can?" Quinn asked.

He grabbed the trashcan from beneath his desk and held it up so she could drop the wet napkins into it. "I've got this."

"I don't mind." Her gaze met his momentarily. "After all, I feel partly responsible."

"You shouldn't," he said. *"Really."*

Molly rushed into the room with the sparkling-clean glass-domed cake stand.

"Sorry it took me so long, but I had to wash this. It's been sitting on top of the refrigerator for a few months and—" She stopped short when she noticed Max wasn't alone. "Oh, you must be Ms. Bazemore."

"It's Quinn." She moved toward Molly with her hand extended and a warm smile on her face.

She's even more beautiful than she was that summer. How is that even fucking possible?

"It's a pleasure to meet you…"

"Molly. Molly Halloran." His assistant shook Quinn's hand. "It's a pleasure to meet you, too."

"I'm afraid that I'm to blame for this mess. I startled Max when I came in just now," Quinn said. "Would you have something I can clean it up with? Disinfectant wipes, maybe?"

"No worries. I'll take care of it, Ms.…Quinn." Molly shifted her gaze to Max and gave him a *what happened?* look. "Can I get you some coffee or maybe a doughnut?"

Molly set the cake stand on the small table in the corner and then used the wax paper to carefully arrange each dough-nut on the glass stand.

"Is that raspberry jelly–filled?" Quinn pointed to one of the doughnuts.

"It is." Max remembered how much she'd loved them.

Quinn momentarily glanced up from beneath her thick lashes before returning her attention to the assortment. She picked up the raspberry jelly–filled doughnut and took a bite.

"It's delicious. Thank you," she muttered through a mouthful. "That was thoughtful of you."

He exhaled quietly and shoved a hand in his pocket. It was his peace offering since she wouldn't allow him to apologize for how he'd ended things between them.

Molly quickly cleaned up the mess, promised to reprint the ruined documents and left the room.

"Have a seat, please." Max pulled out the closest chair for Quinn, then took his own across from her.

She put down her partially eaten doughnut and wiped the powdered sugar from her hands and mouth with a nap-kin. She reached into her bag and pulled out two binders: one thick, one thin.

"I thought we could start by going through the plan I laid out yesterday. You can tell me what works for you and if there's anything you object to. Then we can establish an agenda for the next six months."

Six months. He gritted his teeth.

Max had managed to get through more than a decade without running into Quinn even once, despite the friend-ship that their grandfathers shared. And now he was being forced to work with her for half a year.

Peachy.

"Excellent idea," he said. "Because I'd like to make a few amendments."

He didn't intend to insult her; this was business, not personal. His first obligation was to his family and King's Finest. If Quinn couldn't handle that, he needed to know now.

"Amendments?" Quinn frowned. "Like what?"

Molly brought Max a fresh cup of coffee and the newly printed copies. She was gone as quickly as she'd entered the room.

"You were saying?" Quinn's posture was stiff.

"You've suggested that we have representation at numerous domestic and international distributor conventions."

"Yes?"

"It's a great idea, in theory," he said. "In reality, the plan feels too ambitious. It represents quite an investment of resources for a six-month trial period. And it would spread me and Zora too thin. We already have a lot on our plates."

"Fair point on the budgetary considerations." She opened her planner and made a few notes. "I know you and Zora are busy. That's why I'm here. I didn't expect either of you to attend the listed events."

"Then who would represent…wait… *You'd* be the lone representative of King's Finest at all of these events?" He pressed his back against the chair. "This distillery is my family's legacy. We don't just sell spirits, Quinn. We sell the storied history of this place…of this family. And, no offense, but yesterday was the first day you've ever set foot in this building. I'm not comfortable sending someone who isn't an Abbott out to represent our family and my grandfather's legacy."

"Grandpa Joe didn't seem to have a problem with it." She folded her arms over her ample chest and his heart beat faster in response.

He dragged his eyes back up to meet hers. "I doubt he realized that you intended to fly all over the world as the sole representative of our family." He folded his arms, too.

"I discussed this very idea with him." Quinn pursed

her lips as she put her elbows on the little table—narrowly avoiding squishing her doughnut. "He didn't express any doubts. After all, I'm an experienced public relations professional, and I've represented billion-dollar organizations."

"I don't doubt your abilities, Quinn. But this isn't an impersonal corporation. Here, everything we do, we take it extremely personally." He tapped his index finger on the table. "Because the King's Finest name is on every single bottle we sell. We're all keenly aware that with each transaction, the crack of every single seal, our family's name and reputation is on the line."

"I can appreciate why this is such a sensitive subject for you." Quinn seemed to make a pained effort to keep her voice even and her expression calm. "However, you seem to forget that my family's name will be on those brandy bottles, too. I have just as much invested in the success of this project as you do. Perhaps more. Because if this venture doesn't deliver results, King's Finest will scrap it and move on. My grandfather might never get another high-visibility opportunity like this again."

"Your job is to protect your grandfather's interest. I respect that. But I need someone on hand whose first interest is this distillery."

Her frown deepened. "You don't believe I'm capable of being equally invested in both our interests?"

"I wouldn't know, Quinn." He shrugged. "We knew each other for one summer thirteen years ago."

"And whose fault is that?" she snapped, then shook her head and inhaled deeply. "No, we're not doing this. We agreed not to revisit the past."

"We didn't *agree*, Quinn. You insisted on it." He pointed out, leaning forward with his arms on the table. "But we need to talk about what happened back then."

"Why? It has no bearing on this project."

"Doesn't it?" He searched her face. "We're less than an

hour in and it's already become an issue. Yet, you won't allow me to apologize for my behavior back then."

"Because it isn't—"

"I remember every single word you said yesterday, Quinn, believe me." He held up one hand. "I strongly disagree."

"Is discussing our past a prerequisite for the deal?" she asked.

"Of course not."

"Then I respectfully decline." She looked away, her voice faint. "Sorry I snapped at you—it was a gut reaction, and I apologize." Quinn shifted her gaze back to his. "It's out of my system now. *Really.*"

Was he supposed to believe that all of the pent-up anger she'd apparently been harboring had evaporated in an instant? Did she honestly believe that herself?

"That wasn't fair of me." Quinn stood, leaning against the wall behind her. "But you're not being fair, either."

He cocked a brow. "How so?"

"You're arbitrarily rejecting the key component of my plan. And before you claim that you aren't—" she raised a hand to halt his objections "—we both know that you were the only one in that room yesterday who didn't want me working on this project."

She huffed, taking her seat again. "I realize it must be… disappointing to have an outsider work on your pet project. But Max, I'm *really* good at what I do. I'm not asking you to take my word for it. I'm just asking for a fair shot to prove I can deliver everything I promised."

"I know you probably think I'm being an ass just for the hell of it." Something in his chest tightened. "I'm not, Quinn. My fiduciary responsibilities to King's Finest come before any personal relationship—"

"You think I'm asking you to do me a favor because

we spent one summer together over a decade ago?" She laughed bitterly.

"Aren't you?" He didn't see what was so funny.

"You expect favors of friends," she said. "We aren't… that. And if you'd consider the plan objectively, you'd see the benefits for King's Finest." She tipped her chin defiantly, her eyes meeting his. "I'm not asking for a personal favor here. I'm asking you to do what's in the best interest of King's Finest, *despite* whatever personal feelings you might have about me."

He hated that she believed he harbored ill feelings toward her. Nothing could be further from the truth. True, he hadn't been eager to work with her. But that was because he hadn't wanted a daily reminder of his blunders where Quinn was concerned, not because he had ill will toward her.

He'd be happy to tell her that if she wasn't so insistent on not discussing their past.

Besides, he would've objected to allowing *anyone* outside of their family represent the company's interests. Especially someone he hadn't worked with before.

And if there was any resistance to Quinn specifically, it wasn't because he resented her. It was because he wouldn't blame her for resenting him, and he couldn't allow his past blunder to jeopardize King's Finest. Giving Quinn the power to impact the distillery's reputation left him feeling more vulnerable than he was comfortable with.

Max picked up the document and reviewed all the trade shows that Quinn had suggested the company attend. He took his pen and circled five of the domestic listings. "I'm already attending these." He circled three international events. "Zora is attending these." Max put a question mark by two others. "I'll consider these, based on the results of the first three conferences." Finally, he struck a line through the remaining events. "These are off the table for now." He put his pen down and sat back in the chair. "How's that for compromise?"

"Sounds fair." She took the list and read it over. "But where does that leave me? Your father appointed me to take the lead on the project. How can I do that if I'm not attending any of these?"

Max groaned quietly, already regretting what he was about to suggest. "You can accompany me to the first event."

"So… I get to do what? Play Vanna White? Maybe hold up a bottle of brandy while wearing a sparkly dress?" Quinn folded her arms, her leg bouncing.

Was it crazy that he could see that in his head?

"No, of course not." He cleared his throat. "You'd be there to observe and learn."

"Max, I'm not your summer intern. I'm a public relations *expert*," Quinn reminded him. "I don't claim to know everything, but please don't treat me like some clueless novice."

He sighed. "I need to ensure that these trips will provide an acceptable return on investment and that you can handle representing the distillery."

"Then give me a fair shot at demonstrating that." She leaned forward. "You're making your decision based on the first three domestic conferences. So I should attend all three of them."

Quinn stared at him, as if daring him to reject her reasonable suggestion.

He nodded begrudgingly, extending one hand across the table. "Deal."

Max tried to ignore the electricity that tickled his palm when Quinn placed her much smaller hand in his and shook it. The first time he'd held her hand that summer flashed through his brain.

Quinn yanked her hand from his and stood abruptly. "Thank you for giving the plan an honest chance. And for the doughnut. I won't take up any more of your time this morning. I'll get started on some ideas for marketing collateral. I'll need samples of your past marketing campaigns to ensure the look and message are consistent."

"My team will make sure it is." He stood, too. "Molly will get you anything you need. The first event is in a few weeks. Do you think we can turn everything around by then?"

"Absolutely." Quinn didn't hesitate for a moment. He admired her confidence. She glanced at the small antique watch on her wrist. "I'm meeting with Zora later today, and having lunch with Savannah. They'll help bring me up to speed. And I learned quite a bit on the distillery tour we took while you decided our fate yesterday." She flashed a teasing smile.

"I'll need to review whatever you come up with, and we can bring more of the marketing team in on this to ensure everything is done right and on time," he said as she gathered her things.

"Of course. I'm your partner in this project, Max—not your enemy or rival," she assured him.

"My dad brought you in to head up a project I've been working on for nearly *three years*, Quinn. Maybe it doesn't feel like a competition to you, but it sure as hell feels that way to me," he said gruffly, then quickly changed the topic. "Molly will book your travel, so be sure to give her the necessary info."

"I will. Thank you." Quinn lifted her bag onto her shoulder and raked her fingers through her hair, tugging it over one shoulder.

Max froze for a moment, his eyes drawn to the elegant column of her neck. He'd once trailed kisses down the delicate skin there. Traced a path there with his tongue. He swallowed hard. His pulse quickened, and his throat was suddenly dry.

"I'll have something for you to review by Friday," Quinn said, snapping him out of his brief daze.

"Great. Let's meet first thing Friday morning." His parents' fortieth anniversary party was on Saturday. Savannah was in charge of the arrangements. Still, he expected to get roped into last-minute preparations. "Oh, and Molly will show you the temporary workspace that's been set up for you."

Quinn thanked him, then left to meet with Molly.

Max returned to his desk to work on the football sponsorship deal still in negotiation. But no matter how much he tried to erase all thoughts of Quinn, the vision of her in that fitted skirt and top just wouldn't leave his brain.

Quinn had obviously written off their past as if it had never happened. Why couldn't he do the same?

Five

Quinn gave Molly the information she needed to make her travel arrangements, then settled into her temporary workspace. She appreciated having her own dedicated space to work. Unfortunately, it provided a direct line of sight to Max's office.

She groaned quietly, then made her way toward the executive floor bathrooms. Standing in front of the mirror, she pressed her hands on the cool granite counter and sucked in a deep breath, her eyes drifting closed momentarily.

Quinn should be proud of herself. She'd shown no visible reaction when her hand had touched Max's—despite the bubbling brew of emotions that had come flooding back to her. She'd forgotten how much larger his hands were than hers. And she'd been drawn in by his enticing masculine scent.

After all this time, just being near Max still made her belly flutter and her temperature rise. Had he noticed the beading of her nipples or how her breath caught? The way her hand trembled in his?

How could something as innocent as a handshake evoke such vivid images and visceral sensations?

Quinn couldn't help thinking of the little touches and stolen kisses they had sneaked in whenever they could on the farm.

The secrecy had made the relationship exciting. It was

something for just the two of them. And yet, she'd been bursting to tell someone how giddy and wonderful she felt. Like she was floating in a bubble of contentment. She'd fallen for Max. Hard. And she hadn't been able to imagine going back to a life without him.

Quinn opened her eyes slowly and sifted her fingers through her hair. What she'd felt for Max had been a stupid teenage fantasy. She'd believed him when he professed to love her. When he said he couldn't imagine his life without her, either.

Despite how things had turned out, she couldn't regret being with Max. She regretted her naivete in assigning that chapter in their lives more meaning than it held for him.

Quinn had been the one to pursue Max. She'd barreled right through Max's initial warning that he wasn't looking for a relationship, determined to change his mind. By the end of the summer, it'd seemed as if she'd succeeded.

Until she'd received the call that made it clear she hadn't. She'd stood there stunned long after Max had ended the call. Gutted by a deep, soul-racking pain that had ripped her to shreds.

Eventually, she'd moved on, putting that summer behind her. So why couldn't she look into those dark, brooding eyes without a shiver running down her spine? And why did the timbre of his deep voice still do things to her?

Why didn't matter. She just needed to hold it together for the few months it would take to get this project off the ground. Then they would go their separate ways, and she could put Max Abbott right back where he belonged. In her rearview mirror.

Max sent his last email at the end of what felt like an unbearably long week.

Thankfully, his second meeting with Quinn earlier that morning had gone well. He'd kept their contact during the week minimal and focused on his other projects, allowing Zora and Savannah to bring her up to speed.

The football sponsorship deal was grinding forward, even if it was happening at a snail's pace. And his week had been filled with a series of conference calls. At least he'd gotten a chance to spend some time with his two-year-old nephew, Davis, whom he adored.

Spending time with the precocious little guy was the highlight of any day.

He and Davis had been eating lunch and watching *Bubble Guppies* in the conference room when Savannah had joined them with Quinn in tow.

Quinn had been just as taken with his nephew as he was. Which only made her even more endearing. It'd barely been a week and it seemed that his entire family was enamored with Quinn Bazemore.

Despite being busy with work, he was still preoccupied with thoughts of Quinn.

After all this time, he was as affected by her now as he'd been at twenty-one. When he'd fallen head over heels for her.

Max quietly groaned, thinking of those lush lips and the enticing curve of her hips.

He couldn't pinpoint exactly what it was about Quinn that drove him to distraction. But he was still captivated by her. His heart raced and his pulse quickened when he was around Quinn. And his dreams had been fueled by vivid memories of the intimate moments they'd shared.

"This is more serious than I suspected." Zora startled him when she slid into the chair on the other side of his desk.

"Didn't hear you come in." Max cleared his throat.

"That's because you were in a daze. I called your name twice," she informed him.

"Oh. Well, I was reviewing the day in my head," he stammered.

Zora leaned forward with her elbows on the edge of his desk. "How about we *not* do this thing where you pretend you weren't sitting here thinking about Quinn and let's skip to the part where you tell me what's really going on with you two?"

Max rubbed his jaw and sat back in his chair, narrowing his gaze at the nosiest of his siblings. He'd managed to avoid this conversation all week. Until now. "There's nothing to tell."

"Then why did you freak out when Quinn walked into that conference room?"

"You're being melodramatic. I didn't 'freak out.' I was simply surprised to see—"

"Your ex?" Zora grinned.

"Quinn," he continued, ignoring her accusation. He was prepared to walk the superthin tightrope between lying and just not telling his nosy-ass sister something that clearly wasn't her business. "Because I hadn't seen her in years, and last I heard, she was living in Atlanta."

"So you've been keeping tabs on her since that summer you interned at Bazemore Farms." Zora seemed pleased with herself for extrapolating that bit of information.

"Gramps mentioned it in passing." He shifted his gaze back to his computer and started to shut it down.

"You were floored when you saw Quinn. And you were surprisingly hard on her plan."

"Can you blame me? This project is a big deal. It's Grandpa Joe's way of honoring the last wishes of Savannah's grandfather. Plus, I get the feeling there's a lot riding on this deal for Mr. Bazemore. Maybe you don't feel the pressure of all of those expectations, but I do. So, of course, I'm reluctant to turn the reins for this project over to a virtual stranger."

He shut his laptop and slid it into his bag.

"Quinn isn't a stranger. She's a family friend and an experienced public relations professional. And the way you called her *Peaches*, it felt like you'd had a more intimate relationship." Zora's voice was gentler. "There's no crime in that. But if you still have a thing for her—"

"I don't," he insisted.

Being one of five kids in an outspoken family, it was par for the course that they gave each other a hard time. But Zora's words had definitely struck a nerve, and they both knew it.

Zora stared at him, neither of them speaking.

Finally, Max spoke. "Look, I know you're just looking out for this deal—"

"And you. Because whether you want to talk about it or not, it's obvious you feel *something* for Quinn. Don't let those feelings cloud your judgment." Zora stood. "Let Quinn work her magic."

Damn his nosy little sister and her insightfulness.

"I won't jeopardize this product launch, Brat. Promise." He'd invoked her childhood nickname, which she liked about as much as Quinn liked Peaches.

"You'd better not." She pointed a finger at him, but then her expression softened. "And be careful, Max. You're in deeper than you realize. You both are."

"Everything is just fine with me and Quinn, I assure you." He stood, lifting his bag onto his shoulder. He'd had enough of his little sister's lecture.

"Great." Zora walked him to the door. "Because I invited Quinn to Mom and Dad's anniversary party."

Max turned to his sister, panic flaring in his chest as he locked the door behind them. "Why?"

"I thought it would make Quinn feel welcome." Zora shrugged. "But she seems reluctant to attend. I think she feels like she'd be crashing our family party. Or maybe she's worried she won't know anyone besides us and her grandfather."

"Then maybe it's better if she doesn't come." Max shrugged as they walked toward Zora's office.

"Or maybe you could invite her," Zora prodded. "I put you down for a plus-one, but you never did RSVP with one. So there's an extra space beside you that—"

"If I recall, you and Cole have unused plus-ones, too. No one is bothering either of you about it."

"Dallas is coming as my plus-one."

Dallas Hamilton—Zora's best friend since kindergarten—was a self-made millionaire. He'd started his craft furniture business by fiddling with scrap pieces of wood in his family's run-down barn. Despite his mother's best efforts, Dallas and Zora's relationship was still platonic.

"And I know Cole hasn't RSVP'd." It was one of the many things about his youngest brother that irritated him. "That would be far too considerate."

Zora stopped him just outside of her office. "When are you going to stop being so hard on Cole? He chose not to join the family business. So what? You act like he's committed a crime against humanity."

"Grandad created a legacy for *all* of us." Max waved his hand around the impressive office space that had been expanded and remodeled over the years. "But Cole just blew it off. He's always felt the need to buck the system."

"Yes, Cole is doing his own thing, and he's damn good at it. It's obviously the thing he was meant to do."

"That isn't the point."

"Isn't it? Because what Grandad wants for us more than anything is that we're happy and successful in life. Cole has found that. He's the premier home builder in the area. Why can't you just be happy for him?" Zora poked a sharp finger into his bicep that would likely leave one hell of a bruise.

Maybe he deserved it.

"Ready to shut it down? If so, I'll walk you to your car."

The shift in topic was his clear signal that their discussion about Cole was over.

Max leaned against the door frame while his sister gathered her things. He toyed with her suggestion to invite Quinn to his parents' anniversary party.

A part of him wanted to spend time with Quinn socially. But the part of his brain that was fully functioning when it came to Quinn Bazemore recognized that it was a horrible idea.

"You should reconsider inviting Quinn to the party," Zora said as they left the building and headed into the executive parking lot. "We're working on a really short timeline on this project. You two need to be in sync, and you need to learn to trust each other. This party is the perfect opportunity for you to get reacquainted in a relaxed setting."

"No, Zora," he said firmly as they arrived at his sister's car. "End of discussion." He folded his arms and stared down his scheming little sister, who was clearly amused by his resistance to her not-so-subtle matchmaking.

She squeezed the car door handle and the doors unlocked. "I reserve the right to resume this line of questioning at a later date."

There was that one year of law school Zora had taken, rearing its head again.

"And I reserve the right to ignore it." Max gave his sister a one-armed hug. "Good night, Brat. Drive safe."

Zora laughed as she slung her bags into the back seat and slid in behind the wheel. "You, too."

Max shook his head as he watched his sister drive off. Then he walked toward his SUV.

The only other person as invested in his love life as his sister was their mother. Iris Abbott had been trying to marry her kids off since long before Savannah had arrived in town.

But with Blake married to Savannah, Parker engaged to Kayleigh, and their second grandchild on the way, his mother had eased off on pressuring the rest of them.

Zora was obviously still on mission—as long as she wasn't the person being matched.

Six

Quinn stepped out of her car and handed her keys to the valet. She smoothed down the front of the floor-length, pale blue, one-shoulder Marchesa gown that she'd blown a mint on and had never gotten to wear.

She lifted the hem of the dress so it wouldn't drag on the ground. Quinn felt slightly ridiculous walking into a barn in a floor-length gown with a small train. But Zora had stipulated that the event was black-tie, and this was the only dress she'd brought to Knoxville that seemed dressy enough for it.

"You look beautiful, sweetheart." Her grandfather extended his arm. "If your grandmother could see how much you look like her right now." He chuckled softly. "She'd be pleased as punch."

"Thanks, Gramps." She sucked in a quiet breath and surveyed the large building with its weathered exterior. Bright, festive strings of fairy lights adorned the top of the structure, providing a warm contrast to the cool gray exterior. Strings of hanging white bulbs led up the pathway to the open barn door.

The decor inside was simply breathtaking. Glamorous, but with a nod to the rustic surroundings. Swaths of cream-colored fabric hung from the ceiling, as did several beautiful chandeliers. The tables were draped in rich, sumptuous fabrics. Yet the centerpieces and table decorations evoked the mountains and the nature that surrounded them.

Mason jars of various sizes were adorned with burlap and lace and overflowing with small bouquets of flowers. The table runners were accented with sprawling greenery that ran the length of each table. There were glass bottles in a kaleidoscope of colors and lanterns filled with candles all throughout the space. And the chair backs were topped by chiffon hoods in a dusty rose with ruffled embellishments.

"This place is incredible, Gramps. Did Savannah do all of this?" It was a visual feast.

"She sure did. Before Savannah came along, this was just a run-down barn—a little too rustic." Her grandfather chuckled. "Since the renovation and decor upgrade, they've easily tripled their event income." He nodded in Savannah's direction. "She's a savvy businesswoman, and so are you. You'll show 'em."

"Thanks, Gramps." She squeezed his arm. He always seemed to know when she needed a shot of confidence.

A woman whom Quinn recognized from Savannah's staff took their names and gave them their table assignments.

After they greeted a few of her grandfather's friends, they parted ways. Quinn pressed a fist to the knot in her stomach. Suddenly she wished she'd taken Zora up on her offer to rearrange the seating chart so she could sit with her grandfather.

But the truth was she wouldn't be here if it hadn't been for the series of frantic text messages she'd received last night.

I need a plus-one for my parents' anniversary party.

To which she'd responded, I'm sure you'll have no problem finding someone.

True. LOL. But this is a family event, so I'd rather hang out with someone I have zero interest in.

Your "bedside" manner sucks. No wonder you can't find a date.

Also true. You should take pity on me.

This was followed by the Puss in Boots puppy dog eyes GIF.

Not fair! You know I can't resist a good Shrek GIF!

Besides, there'll be free food and booze plus party favors. And my charming company, of course. Come. PLEASE.

I'm thinking you got in line twice when egos were handed out. But the free food and booze sounds tempting. What kind of party favors are we talking?

Guess you'll have to come to find out.

She hadn't responded, but on the third, increasingly desperate request, she'd given in. The texts had made her laugh, plus she was half-asleep by then, so she'd let her guard down and accepted the invitation. But as she scanned the open space, she didn't see Mr. It's-Definitely-Not-A-Date anywhere.

"Quinn, you look gorgeous." Savannah said as she approached, wearing a long, flowing, wrap gown in a sumptuous red fabric. A sash was tied just above her belly. Her hair was braided in an elaborate updo that completed the goddess look. "I didn't realize you'd changed your mind about coming tonight."

"It was a *really* last-minute decision." Quinn fought back

the urge to touch her hair and make sure her hasty updo was still in place. "I hope it's okay that I'm here."

"Of course, it is." Savannah nodded at someone over Quinn's shoulder and held up her index finger before turning back to her. "I have to take care of a few things before we get started, but I trust that you know where you're seated?"

"I do. Go. We'll catch up later." Quinn's hands trembled slightly as she surveyed the room filled with people. "I could use some of that free booze right about now," she muttered under her breath as she moved toward the bar at the back of the room.

"Quinn, you came after all." Zora gave her a genuine hug that eased some of the tension in her shoulders. "I didn't realize you'd changed your mind."

"Your brother is persuasive and persistent," Quinn said.

Zora's eyes lit up. "Well, good for him. I'm glad he was able to talk you into joining us." She scanned the crowd, then waved at someone on the other side of the room.

Quinn turned to the bartender and ordered a glass of white wine. When she turned around again, she met a familiar stare.

"Hey." Max's gaze drifted down the length of her body before returning to her face.

"Good evening, Max." Beneath his stare, Quinn felt self-conscious in the dress, which exposed her back, one shoulder and a bit of cleavage. "You look…handsome."

"Thanks." He smoothed down his beautiful purple necktie—the perfect complement to his white shirt and charcoal-gray tuxedo, accented by a purple pocket square. "And you look…incredible." Max gestured toward her, then cleared his throat. "But I'm surprised to see you here. Zora said you passed on the invite."

"What do you mean you're surprised to see her here?"

Zora gave Max the strangest look. "Quinn said you invited her."

"No, *I* invited her." As Cole joined them, he signaled for the bartender to give him a refill, then set his empty glass on the bar and leaned in to give Quinn a bear hug. Finally, he released her. "Thanks for rescuing me tonight. I know it was last-minute. I owe you one."

"Cole, *you* invited Quinn?" Zora's eyes went wide.

"Who else would've invited her?" Cole gave Zora a quick hug and acknowledged Max with a slight head nod.

Zora stared at Cole, then shifted her attention to Quinn. "I didn't realize that you two were—"

"Friends," Quinn volunteered quickly, so there would be no misunderstandings. "Cole and I became friends about four years ago. We ran into each other in Atlanta one weekend when Cole was in town visiting friends."

"Wow. I did *not* know that. Did you, Max?" Zora elbowed her brother, who was staring at the two of them as if Quinn had just declared that they'd been abducted by aliens.

"Uh…no," Max said, still staring at her. He turned to his brother. "Cole, how is it that you never mentioned that you and Mr. Bazemore's granddaughter were such good friends?"

So now I've been bumped down to "Mr. Bazemore's granddaughter." Fine.

The more distance between them the easier it would be for them to work together for the next few months.

Cole thanked the bartender for his drink and shoved money in the glass tip jar.

"Just never came up, I guess." He shrugged. "Funny story, though. Quinn and I hooked up at a speed dating event."

Oh, God. He had to tell the story, didn't he?

"You two dated?" Deep grooves formed across Max's forehead.

"No, we did *not*." Quinn paused, allowing that clear statement to sink in before continuing. She shot her friend a warning look and Cole smirked. Quinn turned back to Max and Zora. "*Hooked up* probably isn't the best word choice. Once we started talking, we each recognized who the other was and—"

"She shut me down immediately." Cole chuckled, as if the concept of a woman not being interested in him romantically was remarkable. "What was it that you said exactly?"

Quinn's cheeks stung under the heat of Max's and Zora's stares. She sighed quietly. "I believe I told you that you had a better chance of being hit by a meteorite than you did of getting me into bed."

Cole laughed as hard as he had the night she'd said it. She and Zora couldn't help laughing, too. But Max clearly wasn't amused by their friendship meet-cute.

"I knew right then that we were going to be friends. After the event, we went to this amazing burger joint, then we went out dancing. It was honestly the best time I'd ever had in Atlanta." Cole draped an arm over her shoulder. "Since then, we've kept in touch."

"I'm impressed, Quinn. You're probably my brother's first platonic female friend since middle school," Zora said. "Maybe there's hope for you after all, Cole." She slipped her arm through Max's. "Well, there are a few things we should take care of before the festivities start. Excuse us."

Zora, in her elegant white jumpsuit with a low-cut back, guided Max to the other side of the barn. Quinn couldn't miss the tension in his jaw and shoulders or the narrowing of his gaze as he glanced back at her.

Did Max honestly have the nerve to be angry about her friendship with Cole?

She certainly wasn't trying to make him jealous by being

here with his brother. Cole had blown up her phone with text messages, asking her to be his guest for the event. And they were *just* friends.

Max watched his mother practically float through the room after the big surprise reveal. The presentation had begun with all of the siblings sharing some of their parents' history as a couple. Then they'd shared some of their favorite parenting stories. But then his brother Parker's fiancée came out to deliver the big surprise. King's Finest had purchased Kayleigh Jemison's building as a gift to their mother, Iris.

The building, home to Kayleigh's jewelry design business and consignment shop, was once owned by his mother's family. They'd run a small, family-style restaurant there until it had gone out of business when Max's maternal grandfather had been swindled out of a bundle of cash and he lost the place.

Their mother had mused about opening a family restaurant in memory of her father's legacy. As a surprise to her on her wedding anniversary, the Abbotts had decided to fulfill their mother's dream by buying the building and turning it into a family restaurant associated with the distillery.

The unexpected bonus was that Kayleigh and Parker had resolved a decades-long feud and become engaged during the course of the negotiations.

It had been surreal to see how moved Parker—who rarely exhibited emotion—was over Kayleigh's speech. And how tenderly he'd hugged and kissed his fiancée when she was done.

Max would've bet the house that Parker would end up as that crotchety old uncle who never married and yelled at the neighborhood kids to get off his lawn. But now he and Kayleigh were engaged, and Kayleigh had moved into Parker's house with her golden retriever—whom Parker doted on.

It was a shocking turn of events no one in their family had seen coming.

Cole would clearly be the old player who chose not to marry. He'd still be dating half the women at the nursing home at ninety.

So maybe Max had been demoted to eternal, grouchy bachelor status. Standing alone in the corner, scowling, he was off to a great start.

From where he stood, he could easily see Quinn.

"You okay, big brother?" Zora handed him a glass of punch.

"Why wouldn't I be?" he asked after thanking her for the drink.

"Because you evidently feel something for Quinn and now… Well, she's here with Cole instead. Which wouldn't have happened had you asked her yourself, like I suggested."

Max gritted his teeth, wishing he'd taken his sister's advice. Still, he wouldn't admit as much to Zora. It would only further encourage her to stick her nose where it didn't belong.

"Quinn and I are coworkers, just like we were the summer I interned at the farm," he said. *True.* "And she has every right to be here with her grandfather, Cole, or anyone else on the guest list." Max shrugged. "It's none of my business, *or yours*, who Quinn is seeing."

"Then why are you standing here lightweight stalking her?" Zora shook a finger to head off his objection. "Not up for debate. I saw you watching them just now."

Shit. Had he become *that* guy? The one who didn't know when to let go and move on?

Zora carefully sipped the red punch so she wouldn't get it on her white jumpsuit. "Are you buying this story about Cole and Quinn just being friends?"

Max sucked in a quiet breath, then sighed. "I hope so.

Because if there's more to it and Cole screws up and upsets her, he could throw a wrench into this whole operation. There's a lot at stake here for all of us."

"I know," Zora agreed. "But if they are together, I'm happy for them. I just hate that it'll make you unhappy."

Max draped an arm over his sister's shoulder and sighed. He appreciated her support, even if it would be wiser not to say so. He glanced over to where Cole and Quinn had been sitting, but they were gone. Where they'd gone was none of his business.

"C'mon, Brat. We should check in with Mom and Dad."

"Mom and Dad are fine. They're showing off out on the dance floor. We should join them." She put down her punch and his, then tugged him onto the dance floor without waiting for his response.

Max followed his sister. This was a celebration of his mother and father's forty amazing years of marriage and the incredible family that had resulted from it, for which he was grateful.

Time to stop pouting and at least make a show of having a good time.

Today was about his parents, not him and his regrets.

Seven

Quinn had danced with Cole, her grandfather and his stable of widowed or divorced friends. The sparkly four-inch, open-toe sandals she was wearing were killing her feet and she was pretty sure there would be indentions from the straps across her instep. But it had been an amazing night.

She'd worried that she would feel like an intruder during this momentous occasion. Instead, the Abbotts made everyone in the room feel like they were family. It'd been a lovely evening filled with love. But what had stayed with her most was Kayleigh's speech.

I am so grateful to have my best friend and the love of my life back. I'm thankful that we were able to break down the wall we'd erected between us. That we didn't allow our misguided pride to keep us from the thing we needed most: each other.

When Kayleigh said the words, tears had filled Quinn's eyes and her focus had shifted involuntarily to Max, who met her gaze.

Had Kayleigh's words made him think of her, too?

"Lost in thought?" Cole, her dance partner, leaned in to be heard over the music.

"I was thinking about Kayleigh's speech."

"It was beautiful, huh? I'll admit, she *almost* got me." He chuckled, nodding toward Parker and his fiancée dancing together. "I'm thrilled for them."

"They seem happy and incredibly in love." Quinn stole one more glance at the couple. Kayleigh's curly red hair was twisted up in a bun with a few curls hanging free.

"Switch partners?" Zora asked. She was dancing beside them.

Quinn studied Max's face. He looked as mortified by the prospect as she felt. This obviously wasn't his idea.

"If Quinn doesn't mind." Cole looked to her.

She took a step backward and her heel caught in the hem of her dress. Before she could fall and make a scene, Max was there, his arms encircling her waist.

"I've got it from here." Max's gaze locked with hers.

Quinn nodded to let Cole know she was okay with the switch. She and Max danced together in silence for a few moments before she finally spoke.

"Thank you. My shoe got caught in the back of my dress."

"I noticed." Max's tone was flat and unreadable. "You didn't twist your ankle, did you?"

"No. Just battered my pride." Her face still stung with embarrassment over the near miss.

"Have I told you how amazing you look tonight?" he asked after a beat of silence between them.

"You have." Quinn couldn't help the slow smile that tightened her cheeks. "But it's just as nice hearing it the second time."

Max leaned down and whispered in her ear. "Good. Because it bears repeating. You look sensational."

Quinn's cheeks and chest warmed. She gave silent thanks for the melanin that masked the flush of her skin. Especially in a dimly lit room like this one. But she had no mechanism to disguise the erratic beating of her heart, which Max could no doubt feel through his fingertips pressed to her back.

"Thank you." One of her hands rested on his upper arm.

Even through the fabric of his tailored tux, she could feel the impressive bicep. "But why do I feel like I'm not going to like whatever you're about to say next?"

Max halted momentarily. Tilting his head, he studied her. He lowered their joined hands and resumed their movement. His posture stiffened.

"This thing with you and Cole…"

"You mean my *friendship* with Cole," she corrected him. Now her body tensed. "What of it?"

"Seems odd that neither of you have mentioned it before."

Tension trailed up her shoulders and into her jaw. "And when exactly would I have shared that with you, Max? Before this week, we haven't seen or talked to each other in years."

"I realize that, Quinn, and you may not want to hear it, but I regret that. I regret *how* things ended," he clarified.

"So you don't regret unceremoniously dumping me, just that you were a jerk about it." She met his gaze. "Got it."

"It's not that simple, Quinn." He frowned. After a few moments of uncomfortable silence, he said, "We met twice this week. You didn't mention your friendship with Cole either time."

"I didn't mention any of my other friends, my parents or my siblings, either," she noted calmly. "Because those weren't social meetings. They were business meetings, so we discussed business. Because despite this dance, that's the extent of our relationship."

She stopped, extracting herself from his grip. "Thank you for the dance, but it's been a long night and I have a long drive ahead of me. It's time I say good-night to everyone."

"Quinn, I didn't mean to upset you." He lightly gripped her wrist, pinning her in place. "Wouldn't you be suspicious if I'd showed up at your office in Atlanta and claimed to have a four-year-long friendship with your younger sister?" His pleading tone begged her to be reasonable. "Wouldn't you find that *odd*?"

"Why is it so hard for you to believe that my relationship with Cole is purely platonic? Do you sleep with *every* woman you meet?" She yanked her arm from his grip.

"No, but my brother does." He folded his arms over his broad chest. "Or didn't Cole mention that?"

"Maybe your brother isn't prepared to get involved in a long-term monogamous relationship. But at least he communicates openly and honestly with the women he's involved with. Call me old-fashioned, but I admire that in a man, whether he's a friend or a lover."

Max cringed when she used the word *lover*. It seemed that the very thought of her and Cole together evoked a physical reaction.

If she were a better person, perhaps she wouldn't have taken the slightest bit of delight in the discomfort the thought evidently caused him.

"You don't know my brother the way I do, Quinn. He doesn't do relationships. Whatever this is between you two…he's only going to hurt you."

"Maybe you don't know your brother as well as you think you do." She poked a finger in his chest and did her best not to react to the firm muscles she encountered. Instead, she focused on being indignant on her friend's behalf. "Cole's right. You underestimate him and you don't respect his choices. That's a shame. Because despite everything, he still looks up to his big brothers, including you."

"I'm sure Cole has made me the bad guy in all this, but—"

"Do you honestly think we spend our time together discussing you?" Quinn asked with a humorless laugh. "Spoiler alert—we don't. Get over yourself, Max."

Quinn made her way across the crowded dance floor

and returned to the table where her grandfather and most of the Abbott family were assembled.

She forced a smile and slid into the seat beside her grandfather. Leaning in closer so that only he could hear her, she asked, "Ready to head out? We have a long drive home."

"Actually, there's been a change of plans." He smiled. "The celebration continues tomorrow with brunch at Duke and Iris's place. You and I are invited. Then Joe and I are going fishing tomorrow afternoon with a few friends."

"You're driving all the way back here tomorrow morning?" Looking at her wrist, she checked the thin, delicate antique watch that had once belonged to her grandmother. "It's already so late."

"Which is why I'm staying in one of Joe's spare rooms at the cabin. Don't worry, he's got an extra room for you."

Spend the night with Gramps at his buddy's bachelor pad? Hard pass.

"That's generous of Grandpa Joe," Quinn said. "But I don't want to encroach on your buddy time. I'll just drive back to Knoxville tonight and come back and get you tomorrow afternoon, after you guys have gone fishing. I'll bring the cooler."

"You're not coming to brunch?" Cole slid into the empty seat on the other side of Quinn. He set a small mason jar of peach cobbler and a sculpted glass bowl filled with vanilla ice cream in front of her. "You should definitely come to brunch. The spread is going to be amazing."

Warm peach cobbler and homemade vanilla ice cream?

Cole knew her weakness and was prepared to play dirty. She stared at the cobbler but didn't touch either dish.

"Listen to Cole, sweetheart." Her grandfather got up from his chair and patted Cole on the shoulder before sauntering back onto the dance floor at the invitation of an insistent older woman Quinn didn't recognize.

"Your grandad is right." Cole nudged her with his shoulder. "You should come to brunch tomorrow."

"It sounds nice," Quinn admitted. He handed her a spoon, and she broke down and tried a little of the miniature cobbler with a spoonful of the ice cream. "That's really good."

Not *quite* as good as hers, but still delicious.

"I'm pretty sure there'll be more at brunch tomorrow," he teased in a singsong voice as he dug into a small mason jar of apple crisp.

"By the time I get back to Knoxville tonight, it'll be really late. Then I'll have turn around and come right back here."

"So stay here," he said, as if the solution should be evident.

"I'm not up for a sleepover with our grandfathers at Grandpa Joe's cabin," she muttered through another spoonful of food.

"Don't knock it till you've tried it. Give those two a bottle of top-shelf bourbon and they'll tell you anything you want to know. Actually, way more than you ever wanted to know or can mentally unsee." Cole chuckled.

"That's gross and it proves my point." She nearly choked on her cobbler, laughing. "I'll pass."

Savannah, Blake, Parker and Kayleigh, who'd all evidently tuned into her and Cole's conversation, burst into laughter, too.

"Sounds like Gramps and Mr. B," Blake said.

"So don't stay with the notorious GPs." Cole shrugged, using his and Quinn's shared nickname for their grandfathers. He took another bite of apple crisp. "Stay at my place instead."

There was a collective gasp at the table, which Cole was either oblivious to or chose to ignore.

Maybe she misunderstood him.

"Do you have a rental place in town?" Quinn knew that Cole owned property at the beach in Charleston, but he'd never mentioned having local property aside from his home.

"No. But I do have a guest room, and you're welcome to it." He shoved another spoonful of apple crisp into his mouth, blissfully ignorant that everyone at the table was staring.

"Or you could stay with me. I have a spare guest room, too," Zora offered.

Cole finally seemed to notice he had everyone's attention. He shrugged. "My place is closer."

"She's *not* staying at your place, Cole." The entire table turned toward the source of the gruff voice. Max stood behind them, his hands clenched at his sides.

"As long as she's safe—and she will be—why the hell do you care where Quinn sleeps tonight?" Cole glanced over his shoulder at Max. His expression was neutral, despite the tension evident in his tone. "Who died and made you either of our fathers?"

"No one thinks they're anyone's daddy." Zora glanced cautiously between her brothers. "I think maybe Max just feels Quinn might be more comfortable staying with someone—"

"She barely knows?" Cole raised an eyebrow.

Everyone at the table turned to look at her. Quinn's face was heated as she glanced around. Max was fit to be tied. Cole seemed to straddle the line between being mildly annoyed and gleefully irking his brother. Zora seemed desperate to play peacemaker. Savannah, Blake, Kayleigh and Parker were all riveted by the conversation, as if they were watching a messy reality TV drama.

Quinn stood suddenly, careful not to trip on her dress this time. "Thank you both for the invitation. I don't want to inconvenience either of you. It would probably be best if I just headed home."

"I have a suggestion," Kayleigh spoke up, drawing everyone's attention. "I do have a rental unit in town. Now that the building officially belongs to King's Finest, I won't be renting out the unit anymore. Construction doesn't begin for at least another month, right, Cole?" She looked at her future brother-in-law for confirmation. He nodded begrudgingly. "So why don't you stay there tonight, Quinn?"

"That's a great idea, babe." Parker squeezed her hand. "In fact, the place is just going to be sitting empty for the next month. So you're welcome to use the place rather than commuting back and forth to Knoxville every day."

"That's an excellent idea, Parker," Zora said. Blake and Savannah agreed.

"You're sure?" Quinn was still on the fence about spending the night in Magnolia Lake. However, using the place as a crash pad for the next month would be ideal. The drive back and forth each day was exhausting. "I'd have to pay you, of course."

"No, you don't," Blake insisted. "Like Kayleigh said, it would just be sitting empty."

"But not the entire building," Kayleigh clarified. "My shop is on the first floor, and we won't be moving it for a few weeks." Parker's fiancée pulled a pen out of her crystal-studded Alexander McQueen clutch with its signature skull and knuckle-duster clasp. She scribbled on a napkin, then folded it and passed it to Parker, who handed it to Quinn.

There was an address and two six-number codes.

"The building and the apartment have key code locks. That's all you'll need to get in. I can walk you through the place if you'd like," Kayleigh said.

"No, I'll be fine. Thank you, Kayleigh."

"Will you need clothes? I'm sure I have something you could borrow. We could swing by my place and take a look," Zora offered.

"I have a change of clothing in my workout bag in the trunk, but thank you, Zora," Quinn said absently.

I guess I'm really doing this.

With her overnight arrangements settled, the conversation returned to its normal ebb and flow. But as Max took his seat, there was still a hint of tension between him and Cole.

"You're not upset that I passed on staying with you, are you?" Quinn whispered, nudging Cole.

"No, of course not. I'm just glad you'll be at brunch tomorrow." He flashed that million-dollar smile, the one she could never resist reciprocating. "I have to do something for my dad, but I'll be ready to leave in an hour or so. If you don't mind waiting that long, I'd be happy to do a walk-through with you at Kayleigh's place."

"No need. I'm exhausted, so I'm leaving in a bit. Thanks anyway."

"Then text me once you're settled, so I know you're okay." Cole hugged her, then left the table.

Max peered at her for a moment, then got up and left the table, too.

Quinn sighed softly.

You don't owe him an explanation. Just let it go.

But the hurt look on Max's face tugged at her chest for reasons she couldn't explain. Or maybe she could. But the truth was simply too painful to bear.

Eight

"Cole!" Max hadn't meant to call his brother so loudly, but he was seething with anger as he waited patiently for Cole to finish talking to their parents.

Cole glanced at him and rolled his eyes before stalking over. He folded his arms, his legs planted wide.

"What is it now, Max? Is this our quarterly conversation where you accuse me of being a self-interested ingrate who isn't toeing the family line?"

"Can we talk?" Max refused to acknowledge his brother's flippant remark.

"Isn't that what we're doing?" Cole raised a brow.

"Privately," Max said. He turned and walked toward the back office, near the restrooms. Max used his keys to open the door and they went inside.

"Are you deliberately trying to sabotage this deal with Bazemore Farms?" Max sat on the front edge of the desk.

"Why on earth would you ask a dumbass question like that?" Cole's nostrils flared.

Max forced himself not to react to his brother's raised voice. "Then let me rephrase the question. What the hell is going on with you and Quinn?"

"First, I don't see how that's any of your business. Second, Quinn was pretty clear about it. She and I are friends. We have been for a few years."

"You never mentioned being friends with Dixon Bazemore's granddaughter. Not once." Now Max's voice was slightly elevated.

"I didn't mention it to you," Cole said. "But then our conversations pretty much consist of *this*. You calling me on the carpet like I'm still twelve. I'm not. I'm thirty-three fucking years old, Max. And last I heard, Duke and Iris Abbott are my parents. Not you." He jabbed a finger in his direction.

Max ground his back teeth, his muscles tensing. He and Cole were what his late grandmother referred to as Irish twins, born just under twelve months apart.

Yet, Cole and Zora had always been closer.

"Maybe try not acting like a horny teenager all the time," Max said. "Show a little self-control, as adults do. Like by not taking every single woman you meet to bed. Especially when she's the granddaughter of Grandpa Joe's closest living friend."

Projecting much?

Yep, he was a total hypocrite for that one.

If he got taken out by a lightning strike right this moment, he couldn't even complain. He legit had it coming.

"I am *not* sleeping with Quinn." Cole stabbed his finger angrily at the air in front of Max's face. "Because, as I already told you, she shot me down. I respected her decision then, as I do now. I haven't made a move on her since then."

"Really? Because you two seem *overly* familiar. You keep putting your hands on her. Hugging her. Whispering in her ear. Draping your arm over her shoulder."

"Is that what you've been doing all night? Spying on me and Quinn? Dude, you seriously need to get a life…or get laid. Maybe both." Cole smirked in a way that made Max want to grab him by the collar.

"I have a life. And right now, this joint brandy project with Bazemore Farms is at the center of it. So I need you to back off of Quinn before you blow up the entire deal and cause irreparable damage to Gramps's relationship with Dixon Bazemore," Max said.

"I realize you always think the worst of me," Cole said. A hint of anger and maybe hurt glinted in his brother's dark eyes. "But Quinn told you herself we're just friends. Are you calling her a liar, too?"

"It's not that I think the worst of you, Cole. It's that I expect better. Being an Abbott means something, you know."

"You don't think I know that?" Cole laughed bitterly. "None of you ever let me forget it. But you don't get to define what being an Abbott means for me," he said without a hint of apology. "Now, you want to tell me what this is really about? Because this is extra, even for you."

Cole's voice faded at the end of the sentence and then his eyes widened with realization. He rubbed his chin. "Oh."

"Oh…what?" Max asked casually, despite the subtle quickening of his pulse.

"I've seen this movie before. You're into Quinn. That's why you want me to back off." Cole paced the floor. He stopped, then turned to him abruptly. "No, it's more than that. That summer you worked at Bazemore Farms… The two of you were together, weren't you? *That's* why Quinn shut everything down between us the moment she realized I was your brother."

Max closed his eyes. His cheeks and forehead burned with heat.

Seriously, you had one job, asshole.

He'd promised to keep his relationship with Quinn under wraps. That he'd *never* kiss and tell. Even if she hadn't kept her side of the bargain, it'd been important to him that he kept his promise to her. But watching Cole with Quinn all night… His jealousy had circumvented his better judgment.

What conclusion did he expect Cole to come to after his full-court press about his brother's relationship with Quinn?

Cole was a lot of things. Stupid wasn't one of them.

"You've been spending too much time with Zora," Max said. "I'm just trying to protect our family's interest here. Something you seem to care very little about."

Flames seemed to shoot from Cole's dark eyes as he stepped forward, his hands clenched at his side.

"This isn't about me or this brandy deal. It's about you wanting Quinn. I'm guessing you screwed up with her back then."

Max wouldn't look at Cole, unwilling to confirm or deny his brother's accusation.

"First, Parker thinks I'm making a move on Kayleigh. Now you think I'm screwing Quinn. News flash—I'm *not* that guy. You'd think my own damn brothers would realize that."

Max raised his head and met Cole's intense stare. There was genuine pain in his brother's voice and expression.

Guilt churned in Max's gut. "You're right. Quinn and I were involved back when I worked on the farm. No one else knows."

Max's head spun with all of the complicated emotions he'd felt for Quinn that summer. Emotions he'd buried and thought were long dead until Quinn Bazemore sashayed into that conference room earlier that week and turned his world upside down. It had unearthed a complicated mixture of feelings: affection, admiration, desire, love, guilt and pain.

"But this isn't about how you felt about her back then, is it? You're still into her." There was pity in Cole's voice rather than the resentment that had been there moments earlier. When Max didn't respond, Cole added, "Let me help you out—that wasn't a question."

"I'm not discussing this with you," Max said.

"And I'm tired of you guys projecting your bullshit on me." Cole shoved a finger in his direction again. "If you want another shot with Quinn, man up and tell her. If you're not willing to do that, then leave her the fuck alone. Because you never deserved her anyway."

Max had no argument. Quinn did deserve better.

"Quinn is special, Max. I don't have many friends like her. So make up with her. Don't make up with her. Whatever. But I won't give up my friendship with Quinn just because you're pissed that you screwed things up with her a lifetime ago. So get your head outta your ass and either shoot your shot or get over it. *Period*."

Cole left the office, slamming the door behind him.

Max closed his eyes and heaved a sigh. God, he hated it when Cole was right.

He sucked in a deep breath, his mind buzzing with all of the things he'd wanted to say to Quinn and all the reasons he shouldn't say them. Starting with the fact that she clearly didn't want to hear them.

Quinn wouldn't even let him apologize. So how could he possibly tell her the truth? That he'd never stopped caring for her. That he'd do anything to hit Rewind and do things differently.

She wasn't ready to hear his truth, and he had no right to impose it on her to assuage his own guilt. He'd screwed up, so he had to take the L.

The words of his high school football coach echoed in his head.

Don't force it, son. Read the field and take whatever the defense gives you.

That was exactly what he needed to do.

Stop behaving like a possessive asshole and accept the small olive branch Quinn has extended.

He needed to find Quinn now.

Nine

Quinn handed her ticket to the valet, and the man left to retrieve her car. Suddenly a familiar voice called her name.

She turned to find Max jogging toward her with an intense look on his face.

Her heart raced. "Is my grandfather okay?"

"Sorry, I didn't mean to alarm you. Mr. B is fine. I just…" He cleared his throat, then shoved his hands into his pants pockets. "You're not familiar with the area, and since half the town is here tonight, downtown will be pretty deserted."

"I don't expect I'll have any problem finding the place," Quinn said.

"Still, I would feel better if someone…" He cleared his throat again. "I would feel better if I saw you home and made sure everything was okay." He straightened out his cuff links.

"Are you concerned about my safety, Max? Or are you worried that I'll meet up with Cole afterward?" Quinn folded her arms, irritated that Max obviously didn't believe there was nothing going on between her and his brother.

"I'm concerned about you, of course." He lightly gripped her elbow and guided her to a spot a few feet away from the valet stand where the two remaining valets had turned their attention toward them. "About earlier, what I said about you and Cole. I'm sorry. I was way out of line. Forgive me?"

She studied the handsome features that had always intrigued her and the dark, piercing eyes that stared back at her. Eyes she'd gotten lost in many a night during that long, hot summer.

Quinn released a quiet sigh and nodded. "Okay."

"Okay, you forgive me for being an ass earlier? Or okay, I can see you to Kayleigh's place tonight?"

"Both." One side of her mouth curved in an involuntary smile. "But I'm leaving now. Don't you need to be here until the end of the party?"

"I'll come back after I see you home." He dug his valet ticket out of his inside jacket pocket and handed it to the valet. "Pull out to the edge of the property and wait. Then you can follow me into town."

"Okay," Quinn agreed.

When the valet returned with her car, she reached into her purse to tip the kid, but Max waved her off and tipped him generously. She thanked him, then drove to the edge of the property and waited.

A small part of her was eager to be alone with Max in that apartment. The same part of her that had relished being in his arms again on that dance floor.

Max was her distant past. That crazy, hot summer they shared was a fantasy they'd both awakened from once they'd returned to the reality of their daily lives.

He'd obviously put it out of his mind. Why couldn't she do the same?

Maybe because what they'd shared had evidently meant more to her than it had to him. Max was her first love, and she'd fallen hard for him.

She'd been so sure they'd shared a deep, unbreakable bond. But Max had forgotten her the moment he'd put her grandfather's farm in the rearview mirror.

She should take notes and do the same.

They could work together. Be friendly. Even share an

occasional dance. But she wasn't a starry-eyed eighteen-year-old anymore. She understood how the world worked. That people didn't always mean what they said…what they promised. Not even the people who'd promised to love you.

Quinn's attention was drawn to the headlights that flashed in her side view mirror. Max pulled beside her in his SUV and indicated she should follow him. She did, though she'd already plugged the address into her phone's GPS app.

They went back past the distillery, then followed the undulating road to a one-lane bridge that led them into downtown Magnolia Lake. Max pulled his black SUV into a parking lot next to an older block of buildings. She parked beside him as he rummaged for something in the back of his truck.

Their cars were the only two in the lot. Suddenly Quinn was grateful Max had insisted on seeing her here. The area did feel deserted. And aside from the dim lighting in the front window of Kayleigh's store, the building looked abandoned.

Quinn grabbed her gym bag from the trunk and slammed it shut, then gathered the bottom of her dress in her other hand, not wanting a repeat of her earlier clumsiness.

Max had what looked like a T-shirt draped over his shoulder. He reached for her bag.

"I've got it," she insisted.

"Your hands are already full." He indicated where she held up the hem of her dress. "And I don't mind. Really."

Quinn handed the bag off to him as they moved toward the side entrance of the building. From her bag she retrieved the napkin with the codes and punched in the six digits for the main door.

Max opened the heavy door and they stepped inside. The sound of her heels clicking against the wooden floor echoed in the narrow stairwell. When they reached the apartment door, Quinn entered the next six-digit code. The decor in the cozy little one-bedroom apartment was absolutely adorable. Nothing extravagant, but the kind of place she could easily imagine spending the next few weeks.

They walked through the space, and Max dropped Quinn's gym bag at the foot of the bed.

"That reminds me," he said. "If you need anything, Zora said give her a call. I assume you have her cell number."

"I do."

Quinn tossed her clutch on the bed and released the bobby pins in her hair that had been killing her all night. She shook her hair loose and raked her fingers through it, sighing with relief. When she looked up, Max was staring at her.

"Is there anything else?" Quinn asked.

"No." Max shook his head and took a step backward. "Actually…yes." He snatched the garment he was carrying off his shoulder. "I had a clean T-shirt in my gym bag. I thought you might need something to sleep in."

He held out a white T-shirt with the words King's Finest Distillery, Magnolia Lake, Tennessee printed on it in black lettering.

"Thank you." She accepted it, noticing how the soft, cotton had already taken on a subtle hint of Max's cologne.

They stood in silence, the air around them heavy with all of the words that neither of them would allow themselves to say.

For the briefest moment, she wished Max would lean down and kiss her. Satisfy her growing curiosity.

Had his kiss really been as amazing as she remembered? Or had she just been a misguided young woman with so little experience that any kiss would've seemed memorable?

Max's phone rang. Heaving a quiet sigh, he pulled the phone from his inside pocket and checked the caller ID before sliding it back into place. His expression was un-readable.

Was it a woman calling him this late in the evening?

After all, if it had been a member of his family, wouldn't he have answered the phone, as he had many times before in her presence?

So what if some woman was calling him at Netflix-and-chill hour? What business was it of hers?

"I have to go," Max said. "Lock up after me."

Quinn followed Max back through the apartment won-dering about the identity of his mystery caller.

Was it someone she'd met at the party tonight? Some-one who worked at the distillery? Or maybe someone who lived nearby? Maybe that was the real reason he left the party early.

"Good night, Quinn." His intense gaze shot straight through her, sending tingles down her spine and heating her skin. "Guess I'll see you tomorrow."

"At noon, right?" she asked, then added, "Wait, I don't know where we're meeting for brunch."

"At my parents' place. It's at the end of the same road where the barn is. I'll text the address to you." He pulled out his phone and tapped on the screen.

"You have my cell phone number?" She was surprised. They hadn't exchanged numbers.

"I maintain a list of contacts for my entire team," he said casually, without looking up. "While we're collaborating on this project, that includes you and Mr. B." He slid the phone back into his pocket. "The contact list was part of the packet you received during our first meeting."

"Of course." Quinn tucked her hair behind her ear, em-barrassed that she'd read more into the fact that Max had saved her number in his phone. "The list is in my portfolio."

"Good. See you tomorrow."

Quinn watched as Max trotted down the stairs. She

locked up behind him and returned to the bedroom where they'd stood together moments ago.

She kicked off her shoes, stripped out of the gorgeous, pricey dress—a reminder of what almost was—and removed her makeup. She slipped on the white T-shirt that smelled faintly of Max. The soft, brushed cotton caressed her naked skin, abrading her already taut nipples and making her fully aware of the throbbing between her thighs.

Max hadn't kissed her, hadn't laid a hand on her there in the apartment. Yet, just being near him, her body ached for his touch.

Squeezing her thighs together, Quinn sucked in a deep breath and released it, trying to ignore the shiver that ran down her spine.

She slid beneath the covers, her body exhausted and ready for sleep. But her anxious mind won the battle. Quinn tossed and turned most of the night, inappropriate thoughts of Max filling her head.

Ten

Max stood by the bar in his parents' outdoor kitchen, quietly surveying the small crowd of friends and family. His mother was still over the moon about her anniversary gift and the prospect of establishing a new restaurant in the same space where her family's diner once stood.

"Mom hasn't been this giddy since Davis was born." Zora sipped her sweet tea.

"She was pretty happy when she learned that Savannah and Blake were pregnant again." Max nodded toward his sister-in-law, who stood on the other side of the space rubbing her protruding belly as she chatted happily with Quinn.

Quinn.

Aside from a cursory greeting when she'd first arrived, he'd tried his best to ignore her. But he couldn't seem to resist stealing glances at her.

She wore a basic, sleeveless minidress. But the cut of the dress gently hugged her full breasts, round bottom and curvy hips. The hem grazed her thighs and highlighted her toned muscles. And the deep turquoise color popped against her dark brown skin.

Her hair was twisted at the nape of her neck. Just a few strands hung loose near her temple, giving him an unobstructed view of her face. Quinn's broad smile was as bright as the midday sun. And something about the sound of her laughter filled his chest with a warmth that reminded him of those nights when she'd snuck to his loft over the barn to hang out with him.

"She's stunning, isn't she?" Zora commented quietly.

"Savannah?" He sipped his tea to cool the heat rising in his neck. "Yes, pregnancy definitely agrees with her."

"You know who I'm talking about." Zora could barely stifle a giggle. "The last time I saw that forlorn a look, it was when Cricket was staring at the pork chop in Davis's hand," she said, referring to Kayleigh's golden retriever.

Note to self: stop staring at Quinn like a lovesick fool.

Max finished his glass of tea and set it down on a nearby table with a thud.

"Actually, I was just keeping an eye on Savannah. She's probably uncomfortable out here in the heat. I'll take her a glass of tea."

He excused himself, retrieved two glasses of sweet tea from the beverage table, then made his way to Savannah and Quinn.

"I thought you ladies might like some refreshments," he said with a smile as he approached them.

"Yes!" Savannah proclaimed, fanning herself with one hand as she reached for the glass with the other. "Thanks, Max. You're a sweetheart." She took a long drink from the glass.

"How about you, Quinn?" Max held up the other glass.

"Sure. Thanks." She flashed an obligatory smile. That brought the total number of words she'd spoken to him so far today to four.

Savannah excused herself to go and check on Davis, who was playing with his cousin Benji's twins, Beau and Bailey. The kids got along well, but occasionally someone didn't want to share. Right now, that was Davis.

Max and Quinn stood in silence as she slowly sipped her tea and looked anywhere but at him.

"How was the apartment?" he asked. "Did you sleep well?"

"The apartment is perfect." She turned to face him. "Grandad is thrilled I won't be making that long drive back and forth every day. We're grateful to your family for providing it. That'll buy me time to find another place before Cole begins demolition."

Why was the mention of his brother's name like a bucket of ice water being poured over his head?

"I'm glad. And I'm sure we can help you find something else between now and then," he said.

"It was nice seeing Benji again." Quinn nodded toward his cousin and his fiancée, Sloane Sutton—the mother of their twins. "He has a beautiful family and he's done well for himself."

Benjamin was a tech genius who'd moved to Seattle, where he'd developed a healthcare tech app that he'd sold for more than two billion dollars a couple of years ago. And he and Sloane—Benji's older sister's best friend and his long-time crush—had hooked up at Blake and Savannah's wedding. Which had resulted in the twins and eventually their engagement.

Benji and Sloane's wedding was in a few weeks. After their honeymoon in Greece, their little family would spend a year in Japan while Benji oversaw a project for the company that had purchased his app. After that, they planned to settle down in Magnolia Lake where Cole was building a custom home for them.

"The marriage bug is hitting your family hard," Quinn teased. "Pretty soon, you and Cole will be the lone bachelors. Unless of course…"

"No, I'm not seeing anyone." He restrained a smile. "If that's what you're asking."

"I wasn't, at least not for the reason you're probably thinking," she said quickly.

He folded his arms, amused. "And just what do you think I'm thinking?"

She pressed a hand to her forehead and groaned. "God, this is awkward, isn't it?"

"It is." Max chuckled. "I was pretty shocked to see you come waltzing into the conference room that day, but the truth is it's good to see you again."

She sank her teeth into her lower lip and nodded. "It's good to see you again, too, Max."

He held her gaze, neither of them speaking. This time, the silence didn't feel uncomfortable.

"Zora," he said finally. "You forgot that Zora is still single, too."

"Is she, though?" They both turned toward where Zora sat on a sofa with Dallas, the two of them laughing. The corners of Quinn's mouth quirked in a soft smile. "I've been watching them for the past two days, and they behave like a couple if ever I've seen one."

Max studied his sister and her best friend. "I've mentioned as much to Zora before. She insists that what they have is a classic bromance. She just happens to be a girl."

"Cute explanation." Quinn laughed. "I'm not buying it, but it's cute just the same. Then again, dating must be tricky when you live in a small town *and* have four older brothers."

"Guess I hadn't really thought about that." Max rubbed the back of his neck as he watched Zora and Dallas. "But my sister is no pushover. She has never had a problem standing up to any of us. That includes my parents and my grandfather."

"I don't doubt that." Quinn smiled. "That doesn't mean she doesn't care what you all think. You're her family, and you're important to her. Of course, she wants your approval. The same goes for Cole."

"I doubt Cole much cares what any of us think." Max glanced over at his younger brother, who was playing with the kids. "Not everyone has that luxury. Some of us have obligations to fulfill."

He looked at Quinn and couldn't help the tinge of jealousy that arose at the sweet smile on her face as she watched Cole with the children.

"Children are an excellent judge of character, and they adore him," Quinn said. "He's a good uncle and a good friend." She turned back to Max. "In fact, he seems to get along well with everyone except you. And if you don't think that bothers him, you don't know your brother very well at all."

"Did Cole ask you to talk to me about—"

"Your dysfunctional relationship?" She laughed bitterly. "You must know Cole's much too proud for that. I doubt he's even willing to admit to himself how much it bothers him that nothing he does is right in your eyes."

"That isn't true." The accusation stabbed at Max's chest and heightened the guilt he already felt.

Yes, he was hard on his brother, but it was because he loved him and wanted the best for him.

"Cole is very good at what he does. Family or no, we wouldn't have engaged his services to renovate the barn or the restaurant if he wasn't the best man for the job," Max said. "And the house he built for our parents—" Max gestured toward it "—I honestly haven't seen finer craftsmanship anywhere."

"Maybe tell him that sometime." Quinn smiled softly, then sighed. "I'd better see if my grandfather needs anything. Thank you again for seeing me home last night."

He nodded. "Anytime, Quinn."

Max couldn't turn his gaze away from Quinn as she walked over to where their grandfathers were gathered with some of the other older folks in town. Sloane's grandfather, Atticus Ames, was among them. He bounced his great granddaughter on his knee, much to Bailey's delight.

Quinn was beautiful and no less opinionated than she'd been that summer when they'd debated everything from sports to politics.

Now, as then, Quinn didn't pull any punches. She had no qualms about calling him out on his bullshit, a trait he admired in business and personal relationships.

Max thought he'd eradicated the feelings he'd once had for Quinn. Instead, they'd clearly burrowed deeper, lying in wait for the opportunity to reemerge.

Every moment he spent with Quinn rekindled those feelings and stoked the fire he'd worked so hard to extinguish.

He'd spent a single summer with Quinn Bazemore. So why was it so damn hard to let go of their past?

Eleven

It was the beginning of a new week and Max found himself in another mandatory, impromptu meeting. This one had been called by his brother Parker—the company's chief financial officer. Max sat at the conference table with his father and grandfather, Parker, Blake and Zora, waiting for Parker to explain why he'd called this meeting when they were already inundated with work and exhausted from the previous weekend's festivities.

Parker pulled a stack of documents out of a manila folder and handed one to each of them.

Max read the title of the document aloud. "'Merit-based Succession vs. Birth-Order Succession in Family-Owned Businesses.' Parker, what the hell is this?"

Everyone else turned toward Parker, but Max glanced at Blake—next in line to become CEO of King's Finest. There was no anger or confusion in Blake's expression. Only keen interest.

"Well, Parker?" Their grandfather frowned. "What exactly is this about?"

Parker pushed his glasses up the bridge of his nose. "If you'd turn to the introduction I've prepared on page one—"

"I don't want to read a prepared statement, son." Their father dropped the document onto the table with a thud without opening it. "If you're proposing what I think you're proposing, you'd damn well better have the balls to explain it yourself."

"All right." Parker set the document down.

He looked at their grandfather, then their father. Finally, his gaze settled on Blake with a hint of apology in his expression. It was a look they'd rarely seen from Parker before he'd started dating Kayleigh. His sister had teased that Kayleigh had sprinkled fairy dust on Parker and made him a real boy with real feelings.

That wasn't exactly true.

Parker had always been keenly aware of his own feelings, and still completely ruled by logic. Emotions didn't factor into his decisions. And he'd been a little too straightforward for his own good. Parker was still that person. His love for Kayleigh had simply shown him the power and usefulness of emotions like love and compassion. And he'd been making an effort to empathize with the people around him. So the pained look on Parker's face was alarming.

"Blake, you are a phenomenal operations manager. The efficiency with which you run the floor and the way you handle the staff… I'd venture that no one else at this table could handle either as well as you do," Parker said.

"Thanks, Park. That means quite a bit coming from you." Blake leaned back in his padded leather chair, his eyebrows lowering as he regarded his brother warily. "But?"

Everyone in the room turned back to Parker, as if they were watching a tennis match.

Parker cleared his throat and shoved his glasses up on his nose again. "You strictly adhere to company standards, and you ensure that your team does, too. It's one of the reasons King's Finest is known for producing some of the best bourbon on the market. But the soft center that makes you a great boss and an exemplary husband and father would be your Achilles' heel as the CEO."

"Seriously, Parker? That's what you're going with?

Blake doesn't have an asshole mode, therefore he isn't tough enough to run the company?" Zora stared daggers at their brother.

"That's bullshit," Max said, taking up Blake's cause. "You just said yourself that no one else could run production the way Blake does. By your own logic, doesn't it follow that if he runs operations so well, he'll also run the entire company well?"

"Not necessarily." Parker shrugged, shoving his hands in his pockets. "How many great players in basketball or football turn out to be substandard coaches or GMs? You're not going to sit there and tell me that you think your all-time favorite basketball player is a good general manager, are you?"

"Point taken," Duke said gruffly. "But it's a hell of a leap to say the same about your brother with no evidence to substantiate your claim."

"And that proof would come at what expense, Dad?" Parker asked. "Should we wait until the company is in decline before we declare that the experiment is a failure?"

Everyone at the table was outraged on Blake's behalf. Yet he just stared intently at Parker with an unreadable expression.

"You act as if King's Finest is struggling. We can afford to absorb a misstep or two," their grandfather said, then turned to Blake. "Not that I'm saying it would be a misstep to appoint you as CEO, son."

"It's okay, Gramps." Blake put a reassuring hand on their grandfather's shoulder.

"That's true," Parker acknowledged. "But we have the potential to achieve even more if we take a more aggressive approach."

"What's the upside of adopting a riskier approach when we're already seeing phenomenal results?" Zora demanded.

"That's the same thing we all thought initially when Savannah came to the company with her ideas about expanding our market share," Blake said quietly. "But she was right and the uptick in sales we've seen in the past three years is directly tied to the fact that we took a risk and adopted her suggestions."

"A project Blake encouraged us to take on," Max reminded Parker.

"True," Parker acknowledged. "But would Blake have had as favorable a view of Savannah's proposal if it hadn't been delivered by a beautiful woman to whom he was attracted?"

Blake stood abruptly and slammed his hand on the table. "If you want to question my leadership ability…fine. Do it. But don't bring my wife into this discussion. This has nothing to do with Savannah."

"That isn't a slight against Savannah." Parker held up a hand. "I hold her in the highest regard, as both my sister-in-law and as the event manager here. We're damn lucky to have Savannah as an employee and part owner of the company."

Parker inhaled deeply, then released a quiet sigh. "You don't have that killer instinct, Blake. Which makes you a great brother and a fine husband and father. But when it comes to our highly competitive industry, it's a fatal flaw."

"The liquor business has always been cutthroat, whether it was legal or not. Running moonshine was dangerous business back in my father's day," their grandfather said, referring to the company's namesake—his father, King Abbott. "And surely you don't think it was easy for me, as a black man, to enter into this business fifty-three years ago."

"Of course not, Grandad," Parker said. "Every single person at this table appreciates the sacrifices you made to start this company and establish a legacy for all of us. But we live in very different times. Everyone and their mother is starting a craft distillery these days. And some of the products are remarkably good. I'm not saying we need to regard the other companies out there as the enemy, but we have to take a focused, straightforward approach if we want to achieve our goal of being the best. That's the goal you established when you started this company fifty-three years ago. I take that seriously. And I've proven my willingness to make hard sacrifices on behalf of the company."

"So now you're trying to leverage the fact that you were willing to play fake fiancée to Kayleigh in order to acquire her building?" Zora asked, her jaw dropping.

During the acrimonious negotiations to convince Kayleigh to sell her building, Parker had agreed to pose as her fiancé at the wedding of her ex's younger sister. Which had led to Parker becoming Kayleigh's actual fiancé.

"Really, Park?" Max laughed. "You're the one who came out ahead in that deal."

Everyone at the table chuckled.

"Definitely," Zora agreed. "Kayleigh is the best thing to ever happen to you, Parker. Plus, she took you on an all-expenses-paid trip to a tropical island. So don't try to spin this like you're some self-sacrificing martyr."

"She *is* the best thing that's ever happened to me, and I'm incredibly grateful to have her in my life," Parker admitted. "But I had no idea things would end up this way. I did something extremely uncomfortable for the greater good of the family and the future of this company."

"This is all a bunch of nonsense, Parker." Their father's face and cheeks were flushed, and his voice was strained. "I'm sorry that you somehow feel wronged because you weren't the firstborn, but that's just the way it is."

"That's not exactly true, either, son." Their grandfather chuckled, rubbing a hand over his thinning gray hair.

"What do you mean, Dad?" Duke asked.

"You were an only child." Joseph shrugged. "Not much competition there. You always knew that I was going to hand the company off to you. But what if you hadn't been an only child? What if you'd been second or third in line? Maybe you'd see Parker's argument differently."

The room grew quiet as they considered his grandfather's words.

They'd simply accepted that as firstborn, Blake was the one who'd be named CEO. Max had no doubt his brother would make a good CEO. But was he the *best* choice? It was a question he'd never considered. None of them had, except Parker, apparently.

"All right, Parker. Maybe you're right." Blake tapped the table, drawing everyone's attention. "This isn't some royal dynasty where birth order determines destiny. Nor do I want there to be any question about whether or not I deserved the position of CEO. I put a hell of a lot of thought into every hire I've ever made for this company. And I've never hired anyone—including Savannah—who I didn't feel was the absolute best candidate for the job. I care enough about Grandad's legacy to insist that the same care and effort be given to deciding who will one day replace Dad at the helm of this organization. So I agree that the decision should be merit based. And whatever choice Dad and Grandad make, I'll stand behind it."

The entire room fell silent. But no one seemed more surprised by Blake's concession than Parker.

"Now, if you'll excuse me, this marshmallow of a man has work to do." Blake stood, pushing his chair beneath the table and leaving the room.

They all sat in stunned silence, staring after him.

Did that mean Parker would be appointed the new company CEO? Max never had any qualms about working for Blake. But working for Parker? He wasn't sure who'd want to strangle his brother first—him or Zora.

Parker's mouth curved in a faint smile, as if he'd already achieved victory.

Zora folded her arms and stared Parker down. "If this is going to be a merit-based decision, that means the CEO–ship is open to any of us. That includes Max and me."

"Max lacks the killer instinct, same as Blake," Parker said flatly. "You have it in spades." He shook a finger in her direction, and she smiled proudly. "But while I struggle to figure emotion into the equation, it's nearly impossible for you to leave emotion out of any decision. With you, *everything* is personal."

"You're playing the emotion card because I'm a girl. How original," she said mockingly.

"No, I'm stating a fact because you're a hothead. The moment someone upsets you, you're ready to key their car." Parker stared at her.

He isn't wrong.

"I might think it, say it, dream about it. Maybe even threaten it. But I haven't keyed anyone's car to date," Zora argued.

They all stared at her and Duke raised an eyebrow.

"Okay, there was that one time. But that mofo totally deserved it."

The room erupted into laughter before it settled into an eerie quietness again.

"This is something your grandfather and I hadn't considered." Duke glanced over at their grandfather. "So we'll need to discuss the matter ad nauseam." He stood, picking up the document Parker had prepared. "Don't expect a decision on this anytime soon." He pointed at Parker, then glanced around the room. "And no matter what, we're a family first. I hope all of you will keep that in mind. Greed and ambition have been the downfall of entire societies. They can easily destroy a family and a company like ours."

"Yes, sir," Max said. "We won't forget that. But if we are making the choice based on merit, Zora and I should be a part of the discussion, too. Regardless of what Parker thinks." He narrowed his gaze at his brother.

"Wouldn't have it any other way, son."

"I do have one question," Zora said to Parker. "This idea that you should be the CEO instead of Blake… Is Kayleigh behind it?"

They all regarded Parker carefully. He and Kayleigh were engaged now, but before then Kayleigh had hated their father, mistakenly believing he'd swindled her mother out of property once owned by her maternal grandfather.

She now knew the truth. Duke had been an anonymous benefactor to Kayleigh and her sister at the request of her now deceased mother. They'd embraced Kayleigh as part of their family. But maybe some residual animosity had prompted her to push Parker into making this power grab.

"No," Parker said adamantly. "This is something I've been thinking about for at least a year. I wanted to do my research first. Then I was looking for the right time to bring it up. Seemed like *after* the anniversary party would be wise."

Max stood. He'd heard all he needed to hear. He said goodbye to everyone and made his way back to his office.

"Ah…there you are, boss. The meeting didn't go too well, huh?" Molly's observation was more of a statement than a question. "Anyway, Quinn dropped by. She wants to know when you two can meet to go over some marketing ideas she has for your first event in two weeks."

Max grunted. Before, he'd been irritated that he had to relinquish control of his pet project to someone else. And now that he had just as much of a shot at becoming CEO as any of his siblings, he resented having to share the spotlight on a project that could sway the decision his way.

He rubbed the back of his neck. "Tell her I'm busy today. Maybe we can meet tomorrow afternoon."

Molly frowned. She knew his schedule better than he

did, so she was well aware that he could spare Quinn an hour or two. But she didn't challenge him on it. She nodded, instead. "Will do. Can I get you anything?"

"No, thanks." He forced a smile and closed the door behind him.

His father had been clear that working with Quinn wasn't an option. But maybe he could change his mind.

Twelve

Quinn drove into town for lunch. Frustrated with Max's sudden lack of communication, she needed fresh air and a change of scenery.

She'd been working on the project furiously and had lots of exciting ideas to pitch to Max. But he'd been nearly impossible to reach all week.

Something is definitely going on with him.

Every time she'd tried to phone him her call rolled over to voice mail. When he was in the office, his door was closed. And Molly, who'd previously known her boss's schedule to the nanosecond, seemed utterly confused about when or if the man would ever have time to meet with her again.

Max was clearly avoiding her, and she intended to find out why.

As she entered the Magnolia Lake Bakery, Quinn inhaled the aroma of the delicious peach tartlets they served. She'd definitely be having one or two of those.

"Quinn!" Savannah grinned. "Kayleigh and I were just leaving. I'm sorry we missed you."

"Me, too." Quinn said. "I would've enjoyed the company."

Quinn studied Savannah's warm smile, her brain churning. She needed help tackling the situation with Max, and she wasn't comfortable going to Duke, Grandpa Joe or her grandfather. It felt too much like tattling. But this deal was important to her family, and she wouldn't allow Max to sabotage it.

"Savannah, if you have a few minutes, I'd love to pick your brain about something," Quinn said.

"Of course." Savannah didn't hesitate. "Let's grab a seat. My back is killing me."

"And that's my cue to leave." Kayleigh smiled. "Besides, I have orders to fill and lots of packing to do."

Kayleigh hugged Savannah and bade them both goodbye before heading to her shop on the other side of Main Street.

"What's going on?" Savannah asked as soon as they'd settled into a booth near the window. "Have you run into a problem planning the marketing materials?"

Quinn explained her dilemma with Max.

"It's like he's become a totally different person in the past few days," Quinn said, wrapping up her concerns. "I'm not sure what I've done to tick the guy off."

"It isn't you, Quinn, so don't take it personally." Savannah's hazel eyes suddenly seemed sad. "There's a lot going on at KFD right now, and everyone is kind of on edge."

That tracked with what she'd noticed over the past few days. It wasn't just Max who seemed distracted. Zora and Blake seemed stressed. Duke and Grandpa Joe hadn't been around that much. Only Parker seemed unaffected by whatever was bothering the rest of the family.

"Max probably just needs time to sort through what's going on. You might actually miss the silence once things are back to normal," Savannah joked.

"Everything is okay with Duke and Grandpa Joe, I hope."

Savannah wasn't going into detail, and she respected that. After all, she had secrets of her own.

Everythang ain't for everybody to know.

Her grandmother's words rang out clear in her head.

"Yes, they're both fine," Savannah assured her.

"Good." Quinn was relieved. She genuinely liked both men. "And I get what you're saying about Max needing time. The problem is we haven't got much of it. Our first trade show is coming up soon."

Savannah frowned. "That is a problem."

She checked her watch, then climbed to her feet. "I have a meeting with a bride and her family at the barn, so I have to run. But I'd give Max until the end of the week. If he hasn't come around by then, do whatever it takes to snap him out of it. If you need reinforcements, I'm prepared to ride shotgun." Her warm smile returned.

Quinn thanked Savannah, hugging her as they parted ways. Then she ordered lunch, including a double order of peach tartlets.

She realized that Savannah's allegiance was to the Abbotts. But Quinn liked her, and trusted that Savannah would keep her word.

So she'd take her advice and give Max a few more days to sort out whatever the hell was going on with his family. Then she'd put her foot down and do what she had to do to get this project back on track.

Because she needed to protect the interest of *her* family. And she wouldn't allow Max Abbott to get in the way of that.

Max was searching the file cabinet beside his desk for a document he needed when his cell phone rang.

Quinn.

He sighed, letting the call roll over to voice mail.

The three voice mails she'd left in the previous days made it clear she was beyond pissed.

Max wasn't exactly avoiding Quinn. He just didn't have anything new to report. Or rather, he didn't have anything he was ready to report to her since their last conversation.

And since he'd been considering campaigns that went in a completely different direction from her idea, he needed to have everything in order before they spoke again.

It was after 5:00 p.m. on a Monday and it was turning out to be another long week.

There was a light tap on his closed office door.

"Come in, Molly," he called without looking up from the file cabinet.

The heavenly floral and citrus scent that wafted into his office indicated it wasn't Molly who'd entered.

Max turned around to see Quinn standing by his desk with one hand propped on a cocked hip and one eyebrow raised.

"Hello, Max." She folded her arms. "I realize that you're busy, but we need to talk."

"Hey, Quinn." Max cleared his throat and smoothed down his tie. "We do. I realize that. But now isn't the best time."

"Now is *never* the right time with you, Max." Quinn inched closer. "It's been over a week since we've had any traction on this project. Our first event is coming up soon, and there's a lot we still need to work out."

"Your concerns are valid, Quinn, and I promise to address them. But right now just isn't the best time."

"Look, Max, blowing me off in our personal lives, that's your prerogative. I accepted it and moved on. Blowing me off on this project is reckless and unprofessional." Her words came flying at him with increased speed and indignation. "This isn't about what happened between us. Or you being mad that Cole and I are friends. Our family legacies are at stake here, and I—"

"Good evening, Quinn." Zora stood up from the little table where she'd been sitting, blocked from Quinn's view.

"Oh, my God." Quinn's eyes widened. She pressed her fingertips to her mouth. "I didn't realize you two were in a meeting. I would never have… I'm sorry." She returned her attention to him. "Max, we can continue this discussion some other time."

"No, stay." Zora's tone was warm and understanding. She placed a gentle hand on Quinn's shoulder. "We were just chatting. Nothing urgent. It sounds like the two of you need to talk. It's been a long day, and I'm ready to head home. Good night, Quinn. Good night, Max."

Zora gave Max a knowing glance, one that urged him to talk to Quinn. Something she'd been vocal about the past few days.

Don't shut her out, Max. Just tell her the truth. She'll understand.

Max clenched his hands in his lap as the door closed behind his sister.

There was a moment of heavy, awkward silence between them. Clearly, Quinn still hadn't recovered from the embarrassment of Zora having heard her entire rant. And he wasn't ready to say what he needed to say. But time was their enemy. He couldn't put off this conversation any longer.

Max shot to his feet and shoved one hand in his pocket. He gestured with the other for Quinn to take Zora's vacated seat and joined her at the table.

"I'm sorry." They both spoke at once, each seemingly surprised by the other's apology.

"I'm sorry I barged in on your meeting with Zora," Quinn said. "I would never have done that intentionally, and I certainly wouldn't have said the things I did about our past and about you and me and Cole. I assume she didn't know about any of it." Quinn tucked her hair behind her ear.

"Zora's part-time job is minding the business of everyone else in the family," Max said, only half-joking. "No, she didn't know, but she did suspect there was something between us."

"Which I just confirmed." Quinn groaned. "God, that was idiotic of me." She shook her head, then suddenly narrowed her gaze at him. "But I wouldn't have felt compelled to take such drastic action if you hadn't been acting like such a—"

"Ass?" He chuckled at her surprised reaction.

"I was going to say *child*." She folded her arms. "But I'll defer to your word choice because it's also accurate."

"I deserve that," Max admitted, dragging a hand down his face. "Which brings me to the fact that I'm sorry, too. I know it seems I've been avoiding you for the past few days…"

"And you're going to tell me you haven't been avoiding me?" She arched her eyebrow and crossed one leg over the other.

His attention was drawn to the smooth brown skin of her toned legs revealed below the fitted, knee-length black skirt. Max was sure his heart was suddenly beating faster.

"Okay, so I have been avoiding you," he admitted. "Mostly because my mood hasn't been conducive to conversation. Nothing against you personally."

"Mostly," she repeated the word. "So tell me about the part that does have to do with me personally."

He walked to the window overlooking King's Lake—the sole source of water for their world-renowned bourbon.

Quinn followed him to the window. "Everything seemed fine between us and then suddenly it wasn't."

He turned toward her. "Everything *is* fine between us. I've been contemplating whether it's the best use of resources for both of us to be working on the project."

Quinn's eyes widened and her mouth fell open. She clutched at her stomach, as if his words had caused her physical pain.

He hated being the cause of more pain for Quinn. But

he hadn't created this situation; Parker had. He was simply trying his best to play the hand he'd been dealt.

"We've been through all of this," she reminded him. "My being here isn't a commentary on how competent you are at you job, and this isn't a competition."

He folded his arms over his chest as he studied her.

Damn, she's beautiful.

His breathing became shallow as he tried to ignore her delicious scent and the electricity that rolled up his spine being this close to her.

He couldn't help remembering how good it had felt to hold her in his arms again on the dance floor at his parents' party.

"Maybe it isn't a competition for you, Quinn. But it is for me."

"I don't understand." She stepped closer, tipping her chin so their eyes met. "Who is it that you feel you're competing with? Certainly not me."

"No." He kneaded the knot at the back of his neck. Zora's words echoed in his ears. *Tell her the truth. She'll understand.* "I find myself in competition with my siblings."

"For?"

"Cone of silence?" he asked.

A slow smile spread across her lovely face, deepening the dimples he'd been obsessed with that summer. It'd given him a thrill to make her smile or to be the source of her unique laugh. "You're invoking *Get Smart* right now?" she asked. "Really?"

"Really, Agent 99." He leaned in closer, one side of his mouth curved in a smirk.

The familiar nickname prompted a giggle from her. The tension in his shoulders eased in response to the infectious sound, which invoked a kaleidoscope of fond memories. His chest ached with both deep want and gut-wrenching regret.

"Okay," she said begrudgingly, her wide brown eyes

filled with curiosity. "Consider the cone of silence invoked." She gestured over her head, as if she was pulling a plastic dome down over it. "Now, tell me why you're being weird all of a sudden."

"Last week, Parker essentially declared that he should be the next KFD CEO." Max's shoulders tensed.

"Who did you expect to succeed your father as CEO? Blake?"

"Yes, because he's the oldest," Max confirmed. "But Parker believes the appointment should be merit based and that it should go to him."

"How did Blake take Parker's proposal?" Quinn asked.

"Better than Zora and I did," he admitted with a shrug.

"Neither of you anticipated being named as your father's successor, so why'd you take Parker's challenge so personally?"

Max ran a hand over his head and sighed. "Parker acts as if the only logical choice is between appointing Blake because he was born first or appointing Parker because he believes that he deserves it. As if Zora and I don't even warrant consideration."

Quinn nodded sympathetically. Her sincere expression was like warm water sluicing over the knotted muscles in his neck and back. A balm that soothed the anger and resentment the entire ordeal had stirred in him.

"I understand why that would be upsetting. After all, you're both an integral part of the organization," she said. "Did you tell Parker how that made you feel? Why you objected to him presenting the situation that way?"

Max turned to look at the placid waters of King's Lake. "We made it clear that if the decision is going to be merit based, it should be open to everyone. Grandad seemed to agree, and my father is considering it."

"That explains why the mood has been tense around here, but it doesn't explain why you seem upset with me."

"I'm not." He turned toward her again. "I'm sorry if I gave you that impression."

"Then why did you suddenly shut me out like I'm the enemy?" Her eyes searched his.

"If the decision is based on who has the biggest impact on the company…" His gaze dropped momentarily from hers and he shrugged. "I've been working on this project for a long time. Long before you got involved. And it's an excellent opportunity for me to demonstrate my value to our organization in an immediate, tangible way."

"You're dismissing me from the project? I thought you liked my proposal. Your entire family approved it."

The hurt in her voice brought back the day he'd called to end their relationship.

Why, Max? Was it something I did? Something I said?

The guilt of that day never seemed to leave him. It retreated to the recesses of his mind and heart, but it was never far-off. Always prepared to rear its ugly head again.

Today that guilt was front and center.

He was disappointing Quinn, again. And now, just as then, she was blaming herself when the culpability was all his.

"I do like your proposal." Max placed a gentle hand on her arm, drawing her gaze back to his again. "You're brilliant, Quinn. There's no doubt about that. Honestly, I've come up with dozens of different takes on this thing, and none of them have surpassed yours."

She sucked in a deep breath and her panicked expression transformed to one of pure bewilderment. "Then I don't understand. Why are you dismissing my proposal? Dismissing me?"

"I never planned to dismiss you from the project. I just hoped to come up with a better plan. A different direction that I would run point on." His thumb absently caressed her arm through the fabric of her sleeve. "It was a mistake, and I'm sorry for being such a jerk."

"Good." Quinn nodded. "Because if your goal is to impress your father and prove you're just as deserving of consideration, I can help you." She stepped closer and tugged on his tie, a teasing lilt in her voice. "I'm not your rival, Max. But I can be a damn good partner. If we work together, we'll impress both our families, and we'll each get what we want."

Her sweet scent filled his nostrils, and he could feel the heat radiating from her flawless brown skin. He couldn't help being mesmerized by this woman. If she asked him right now, he would've given her just about anything.

"Partners?" Quinn's eyes danced and her dimples were in full effect. She extended a hand.

"Partners." He shook her hand.

The sensation of her warm, soft skin against his stunned him, like an unexpected jolt of electricity. Max stood frozen as her eyes searched his.

Quinn slipped her hand from his and stepped backward. She turned toward the speaker mounted high on the wall. Music drifted down quietly from it.

She turned back to him. "'Make It Last Forever.'" A slow smile spread across her face. "Gosh, I remember every word of every song on that Keith Sweat album," she mused.

"I was definitely going through a Keith Sweat phase at the time." Max chuckled at the fond memories. "But c'mon, it's an R & B classic."

"True," she agreed. "And it would be more accurate to say you were going through an eighties and nineties R & B phase." Her eyes gleamed as she listed the artists he'd been obsessed with that summer. "Wow. That feels like forever ago. Come to think of it, you were supposed to make me a mixtape, which I never got."

He stared at her for a moment with his hands shoved in his pockets, debating his next move.

Would she consider him sweet and sentimental? Or would he come off as a pathetic sap?

Max rubbed his stubbled chin and sighed.

Fuck it.

He walked over to his desk, rummaged in the lap drawer and pulled out a plastic case. He handed it to her.

"You've got to be kidding me." She accepted the compact disc—a relic from their past.

"I made the CD, as promised." He sat on the front edge of his desk. "I just never got the chance to give it to you."

"You kept it all this time?" She stood in front of him.

"I probably remember that summer more fondly than you do. But seeing you again after all this time threw me for a loop," he admitted. "I found the disc at my parents' place over the weekend in a box of my things from college. I couldn't bring myself to throw it out." He shrugged. "I brought it here to upload it to my computer."

Quinn stared at him, blinking. She seemed stunned.

"Why are you telling me this?" Her words came out in a rough whisper.

"I don't know." His heart beat rapidly. "I know you don't want to talk about our past." The sound of his own blood rushing filled his ears. "But it's all I've been thinking about lately. I messed up, Quinn. I hurt you, and I am so sorry for that."

"I should go." She turned to leave, but he caught her hand in his.

"I'm sorry if that upsets you. I thought you deserved to know that if I had the chance to go back and do things differently, I would. You have no idea how much I wish that were possible."

Quinn turned back to him, her eyes searching his before she put the jewel case down on his desk.

She was rejecting his gift. Rejecting him.

He should've kept his mouth shut.

"I appreciate your apology. Now, for the sake of this deal, I propose that we let go of the anger and guilt we both seem to feel about what happened that summer." She shrugged. "Maybe we could just hug it out and agree to move on. I hear that's what adults do."

Her sensual lips quirked in a half smile.

"I'd like that." Max grinned. Relief eased the tension in his chest. He opened his arms wide and she stepped forward, looping her arms around his neck as he hugged her waist.

Max allowed Quinn to dictate the physical interaction between them, grateful she'd at least given him the chance to apologize. She held onto him much longer than he'd expected.

Quinn had always given the best hugs. That hadn't changed. He welcomed the heat and the comfort of her embrace, unable to bring himself to be the first to pull away.

Finally, she dropped her arms from his neck. Rather than pulling away, Quinn cradled his face, caressing his stubbled cheek with her thumb as her gaze met his.

There was something so warm and comforting about her soft gaze. Without thought, Max grasped the hand that caressed his cheek and kissed her palm, then her wrist.

Quinn's hand trembled slightly, and she sank her teeth into her lower lip as she leaned in, eyes closed.

Max erased the sliver of space between them, tasting her full, sensual lips. Arms locked around her waist, he tugged her closer. His heart beat wildly in response to the sensation of her luscious curves crushed against his hard chest. He swallowed the sound of her soft sighs with his hungry kiss.

Since Quinn had come back into his life, he'd often found himself wondering what it would feel like to hold her in his arms and kiss her again.

His fantasies hadn't even come close to the reality.

He glided his hands down her back and over the full, round bottom, as firm and plump as the ripe, juicy summer peaches Bazemore Farms was so famous for. Max pulled her tighter against him, reveling in the sensation of her body pressed to his.

Quinn parted her lips on a sigh, and he slid his tongue between them, deepening their kiss. He savored the warm, sweet cinnamon taste of her velvety tongue. Her kiss was hotter and sweeter than he remembered. He honestly didn't think he'd ever get enough of it.

"You know, Max, I was thinking that… Oh, shit. Sorry." Zora had barged into his office unannounced.

Why hadn't he thought to lock that damn door?

Quinn slipped out of his arms and moved toward the window. With her back turned to them, she straightened her blouse and raked her fingers through her hair.

Max heaved a sigh as he glanced down at his lap. *Major hard-on situation.* Standing was not an option.

"What is it, Zora? I'm kind of busy."

"Obviously." She cast an amused glance in Quinn's direction.

"I thought you were leaving." He tried to keep the annoyance with his little sister out of his voice. After all, it wasn't unusual for them to pop into each other's offices. Though the circumstances were clearly different this time.

"I should go," Quinn said suddenly, hurrying past both of them toward the door. "Good night."

"Quinn!" he called after her. She didn't break her stride.

Max groaned, running a hand over his head.

"Sorry, I didn't realize you were entertaining company." Zora's expression was a mixture of contrition and amusement.

"How about knocking next time, Brat?" Max suggested. "And do me a favor—"

"I won't say anything to anyone. I promise," she interrupted. "I'll tell Quinn that myself, if you'd like."

"No, I should talk to her," he said, finally comfortable enough to stand. Nothing killed the mood like your little sister walking in on you. "What did you need?"

"It's nothing urgent. We'll talk tomorrow." She turned to leave. "Good night, Max."

He sighed, his eyes drifting closed at the soft click of the door behind his sister.

That went sideways fast.

Max honestly hadn't intended to kiss Quinn. He'd imagined it, ruminated over it and fantasized about it, without actually planning to do it. But once he held Quinn in his arms again, it was clear he'd never really gotten over her. That he wanted the chance to fix things between them.

Until Quinn had leaned in for a kiss, he hadn't believed that another chance with her was possible. After all, she'd insisted on behaving as if the intense summer they'd shared had never even happened. It had been driving him insane, because he could hardly think of anything else.

Max waited a beat and then followed the carpeted path to Quinn's desk. She wasn't there. She'd evidently fled the building, not just his office.

Hopefully, she hadn't encountered Zora on her way out.

Suddenly the ladies' room bathroom door opened, and Quinn appeared. Her brown eyes went wide, then she glanced around the space as if she expected another of his siblings to pop up.

"Zora's gone. For real this time," he said with a small smile, hoping to inject some humor into the situation and relieve the anxiety she was obviously feeling. "And I'm pretty sure everyone else is already gone. Parker and Blake don't stay late at the office much these days."

Her only response was a sigh of relief as she circumnavigated him and went to her desk. She pulled her purse out of the large bottom drawer and hitched it on her shoulder.

"I'd like to meet tomorrow morning to discuss the upcoming trade show." Her eyes didn't meet his. "If you can make the time."

"Of course, I can," he said, then leaned in closer and lowered his voice. "I realize how awkward that was in there." He jerked a thumb over his shoulder in the general direction of his office. "But you don't need to rush off."

She glared at him with fire in her eyes. As if that was the most ridiculous thing she'd ever heard.

Whatever progress he and Quinn had just made had been erased in an instant.

Thirteen

"You shouldn't have followed me out here." Quinn scanned the space around them. Her heart was still racing. "Isn't it bad enough that your sister just walked in on us kissing?"

Technically, he'd kissed her. But she'd leaned in first. And the hug that precipitated the kiss had been her idea, too.

Quinn cringed. How could she have done something so stupid?

"We need to talk." Max's firm voice shook her from her panicked daze. "We can have the conversation here or in the privacy of my office," he added when she didn't respond.

Quinn huffed, then turned and followed Max back to his office. He closed the door behind them.

"This is a really bad look, Max." Quinn's cheeks flamed, and her pulse raced.

She'd lost it. She'd kissed Max right there in his office. And it hadn't felt like some random, isolated act. She'd felt like that starry-eyed girl falling for Max all over again. Which was crazy. Because she wasn't naive enough to fall for Max again. He'd shredded her heart to pieces once. Wasn't that enough?

Been there and done that. Spoiler alert: it does not end well.

Falling for Max Abbott again would only lead to another

broken heart. And this time, she'd deserve it. Because experience had taught her better.

"No one is here except us," he assured her.

"It doesn't matter, Max." Quinn's head suddenly
throbbed and her throat felt dry. "Zora saw us together."
Quinn pressed a fist to her belly, her stomach in knots.
"By the time we arrive here tomorrow morning, both of
our families will know."

Her grandfather would be monumentally disappointed
in her. Duke and Iris would never take her seriously again,
and they certainly wouldn't refer her to any of their friends
and business associates. And she could forget using her
work here as a case study, which had been a critical piece
of this for her.

Quinn squeezed her eyes shut and took slow, measured
breaths. If only she could rewind the clock fifteen minutes.
Before she'd gotten dreamy and nostalgic while listening to
the unofficial soundtrack of that summer and remembering their first kiss. She opened her eyes and blinked back
the tears she refused to let fall.

"I really screwed up." She shook her head.

"Zora won't say anything," Max assured her. "She promised me," he added, in response to her incredulous expression. "And she'd never give Parker that kind of ammunition
against either of us. So you don't need to worry, Quinn.
This isn't a big deal."

Quinn wished she could believe that. But even if Zora
didn't tell anyone else, *she* knew. Even if she never mentioned it, the other woman would be judging her.

"Maybe your sister has walked in on you making out
with a business associate before." She could barely contain
the bitterness rising in her chest as the old wounds resur-
faced. "But it's a first for me, and for me this could have
very real consequences."

"What's that supposed to mean?" He frowned but didn't

acknowledge her dig about him making out with other women in his office.

"It means my future is very much at stake here." Quinn smacked a hand to her chest. "I don't have the luxury of being an Abbott. For a moment, I allowed myself to forget that."

"I'd never stand by and let you take the fall for something I was clearly complicit in." Max sat on the edge of his desk again. "That goes for what happened just now and this entire project. Whatever happens, good or bad, we're partners in this. I'd never let you take the blame for me."

An eerie chill ran down Quinn's spine and she clenched her fists at her sides. She'd heard nearly the same promise before. The moment she'd chosen to believe it was the moment her career had begun to unravel.

She wouldn't fall for it again. *She* was the only person she could trust to safeguard her future.

"I kissed you, and I shouldn't have." Quinn didn't acknowledge his insistence that they were partners and that he'd protect her. "I lost my head momentarily. It won't happen again." She forced herself to meet his wounded gaze. "It *can't* happen again."

Deep wrinkles formed above Max's furrowed brows. He folded his arms and sighed. "If that's what you want, Quinn."

"It is." She tipped her chin, hoping she conveyed more conviction than she possessed at the moment. That her tone didn't betray her disappointment at how easily he'd acquiesced. As if she and the kiss really were no big deal for him. Already nearly forgotten.

"All right, Quinn. This is strictly a business relationship. Nothing more. And maybe, if I work really hard at it, I can pretend that summer never happened, too." His tone was biting.

Max had obviously been more perturbed by her refusal

to discuss their past than she realized; nonetheless, it had been a good decision. Just look what had happened the moment she allowed herself the luxury of fondly revisiting their past.

Keeping their relationship strictly professional was in the best interest of her career and her heart—regardless of what her body wanted.

Because, even now, she wanted Max to kiss her again. She wanted to invite Max back to her place and get reacquainted with every inch of his body. To spend the rest of the night making love to him. She longed for the taste of his mouth, and her body ached for the pleasure of his touch.

She sucked in a deep breath, forced an uneasy smile and turned to leave.

"Wait." He held up the CD with *Mixtape for Peaches* scribbled on it in black permanent marker. "You forgot this."

A tiny piece of her heart crumbled, seeing those words and remembering the friendship and intimacy they'd once shared. A part of her wanted all those things with Max again, even knowing that revisiting the past would only lead to more disappointment.

"I appreciate the thought, Max. I really do. But maybe it's better if we leave the past in the past and focus on the future of this project. We both have a lot riding on it." She placed a gentle hand on his forearm and forced another smile, despite the electricity that filtered through her fingertips where her skin touched his. "I'll see you in the morning."

"Good night, Quinn." His voice sounded achingly sad.

She slipped out of his office, closing the door behind her.

It was better this way. Eventually, Max would realize it, too.

Quinn made her way to her car and took the narrow road toward town. She was angry with herself, and her eyes burned with tears. If anyone was aware of the consequences of mixing business and pleasure, it was her.

At the PR firm she'd worked for in Atlanta, she'd fallen for her boss's son. He'd pursued her for more than a year, and she'd finally given in. After a year of dating, he'd asked her to marry him.

She'd accepted Melvin Donaldson's proposal and blown a mint on that Marchesa gown for their engagement party. But the week before the party, she'd walked into his office and discovered him seated at his desk, his pants unzipped and his secretary on her knees in front of him.

Quinn had dumped the lying, cheating bastard and tried to focus on doing the job she loved. Rather than being ashamed of his own behavior, he'd insisted she was making a big deal over nothing. That his encounter with his secretary hadn't meant that he didn't love her. He'd just been stressed and blowing off steam. And he'd been furious that she'd "humiliated" him by calling off their engagement after the party invites had already gone out.

Once it had become clear she wouldn't go back to Melvin, her corporate nightmare began. After being named Employee of the Year two of the previous three years, suddenly Melvin and his father, Oscar Donaldson—the head of the firm—found fault with everything she did. One by one, she'd been taken off the larger, more prestigious accounts. Worse, the Donaldsons had maligned her character to clients who'd complained about her being removed from their accounts. Finally, they'd manufactured cause to fire her. Her only recourse had been to quietly resign.

Embarrassed by the whole ordeal, Quinn hadn't told her grandfather the real reason she'd left the firm. Nor had she admitted the full extent of what had happened to Cole. Only her college roommate, Naomi, knew the truth. She'd called her friend in tears the day she'd been forced to resign.

Naomi had wanted her to hire a lawyer, and her friend was prepared to trash the firm online. She'd even suggested that Quinn talk to a reporter. Quinn decided she had suffered enough humiliation.

Even now, she hated herself for having been too much of a coward to stand up for herself. But she had no desire to become a poster girl for workplace romances gone wrong. And if she was being honest, she blamed herself for going against every instinct that had warned her not to get involved with Melvin.

She could still remember her father's words when she'd told her parents she was dating the boss's son.

Never crap where you eat, sweetheart. It won't end well.

Boy, had her father been right.

Quinn pulled into the parking lot of Kayleigh's building. She walked down the street to Margot's Pizzeria and ordered the personal-sized Hawaiian pizza Kayleigh and Parker had recommended so highly. Then she returned to the apartment with a piping-hot pizza in hand.

She'd agreed to let go of her anger over her and Max's past and just move on. And that still stood. But she wouldn't make the same mistake again. Especially not with a man who'd already let her down in the past.

Max had quickly agreed to her terms. So why had his easy and immediate acquiescence filled her with a deep sadness she couldn't quite explain?

It didn't matter. She just needed to get over herself and let go of the past. Her career and her grandfather's farm depended on it.

Max spent another hour working in his office with Vivaldi's *Four Seasons* playing softly in the background after Quinn left. He'd needed to switch from the mixtape of old-school R & B that he'd been playing incessantly for the past week. Nearly every one of those songs reminded him of cherished moments with Quinn that summer.

Maybe it's better if we leave the past in the past.

Quinn's words replayed in his head, like an old vinyl record with a deep scratch.

He'd quickly agreed to her request because Quinn was right. Neither of them could afford the distraction of trying to safely navigate the land mines of their past.

So why did a little voice in his head and the knot in his gut call BS on his agreement to let go of the past and move on?

What right did he have to be crushed by Quinn's refusal to explore what their kiss had meant? After all, he'd been the one who'd initially rebuffed her.

Quinn's rejection was a karmic dish of justice served cold.

Yet, he couldn't help the deep ache in his chest. How could Quinn walk away from a second chance for them so easily when he couldn't stop thinking of and wanting her?

He'd been young and stupid. Mostly, he'd been overwhelmed by the intensity of his feelings for Quinn. In her he saw his future set in stone: marriage, a home, kids.

All of the things neither of them had been ready for.

He wasn't the man Quinn deserved then. Maybe he still wasn't, but he wanted to be everything she deserved and more.

All of the things that had frightened him back then—thoughts of marriage and family—still seemed overwhelming. Yet, he found himself wondering if he and Quinn would have had all of those things together if he hadn't broken up with her.

Max dragged a hand down his face and sighed. He'd made his choice back then; now he had to live with it. Despite his growing feelings for Quinn, he'd respect her wishes and keep their relationship strictly professional.

He now regretted his decision to have Quinn accompany him to the trade show in San Francisco.

This trip would put his resolve to the ultimate test.

Fourteen

Quinn sat across from Zora in a booth at the Magnolia Lake Café. She politely waited for the other shoe to drop.

She'd made it all the way to Friday without anyone mentioning the kiss that Zora had walked in on. But when Zora insisted on treating Quinn to lunch today, she knew it was only a matter of time before Max's sister brought it up.

Instead, Zora had shown her photos her best friend, Dallas, had sent from his trip to Sweden. And she'd revealed some of their plans for the family-style restaurant they would be opening across the street.

When Quinn had finally started to relax, Zora pushed aside her empty plate and folded her hands on the table. "So about you and Max…"

Quinn nearly choked on a forkful of chicken potpie. She gulped down some water.

"Sorry, I didn't mean to startle you." Zora looked genuinely concerned. "I just wanted to say that I appreciate how awkward it must be for you and Max to work together. I don't know what happened between you two in the past, but you obviously have feelings for each other."

Quinn poked at the flaky crust and tender chunks of chicken with her fork. She shrugged. "It was a really long time ago, Zora."

"Didn't seem so long ago." Zora could barely contain her grin.

Touché.

"It's a mistake neither of us intends to repeat."

"Or maybe you two have been given a second chance at this."

"I didn't come here to reignite an old flame. I'm working with Max, despite our past. This is a golden opportunity to expand the reach of both of our families' companies."

"No one thinks you came here for Max," Zora assured her. "But if my interruption the other day derailed whatever might be going on with you two, I apologize. I like you, Quinn. And I can see why Max does, too."

"That's kind of you, Zora, and I appreciate it. But I'm sorry to disappoint you. There isn't anything happening between me and Max. That kiss was a one-off. We just got caught up in the moment."

"I respect that." Zora nodded. "But I also realize that a big family like ours can be a lot to deal with. Admittedly, a few of us are a little extra." She raised her hand slowly, and they both laughed, easing the tension. "So if your feelings for Max ever do change, know that I'm rooting for you two." Zora smiled. "Now, unless you decide otherwise, we'll never speak of this again." Zora locked her lips with an imaginary key, then tossed it over her shoulder.

Quinn grinned. Zora was extra, but she couldn't help liking Max's nosy little sister. She was well-meaning and obviously loved her brothers.

"Zora, Quinn." Benji approached the table holding his daughter, Bailey.

Quinn had gotten to know Benji and his fiancée, Sloane, a little at the anniversary party and brunch. They were a sweet couple with adorable one-year-old twins.

"Hi, Zora." Sloane, carrying their son Beau on her hip, leaned down and hugged the other woman. "Hi, Quinn." She surveyed their empty plates. "I wish we'd arrived earlier. We could've eaten together. That is, if you two don't mind eating with two ravenous toddlers who get more food on their bellies than in them." Sloane tickled her son's stomach and the boy doubled over with laughter.

"That would've been fun." Quinn jiggled Bailey's little foot, clad in a sparkly pink ballerina flat that complemented her pink tutu dress. The toddler giggled, burying her face in her father's shoulder.

"We were about to leave, but we can watch the twins while you get your order. And you can have our table." Zora glanced around the packed eatery.

"Thanks." Sloane handed Beau to Zora. The little boy was mesmerized by her dangling earrings.

Benji handed Bailey off to Quinn, and he and Sloane promised to return as quickly as possible.

"The twins are adorable." Quinn tickled Bailey, and the little girl laughed.

Spending time with the twins and Savannah and Blake's son, Davis, made her wish she had nieces and nephews of her own to spoil.

"And they're the sweetest children," Zora said wistfully as she tapped a finger on Beau's nose. "They make me want children of my own."

"The kids all adore you, and you're so patient with them," Quinn said. "You'd be an incredible mom."

"Now, I just need to find the right guy…or not," Zora said with a mischievous grin. "As my gram always used to say, there's more than one way to get a pickle in the jar."

Quinn burst out laughing as she bounced Bailey on her knee. "Wait, are you considering going to a sperm bank?" Quinn covered Bailey's ears and mouthed the last two words.

"Why not?" Zora shrugged. "I want kids now. What if the right guy doesn't come along for another ten years? Or what if I'm not able to have kids anymore when and if he does?"

"You've given this a lot of thought, haven't you?" Quinn moved the salt and pepper shakers beyond Bailey's reach.

"I've been thinking about it for at least six months." Zora kissed the top of Beau's head. "I honestly don't know why I just told you that. Please don't say anything. My family will freak out. I'm prepared to handle the flak, if I decide to go that route. But there's no point in riling them up when I'm still undecided."

"It's not my place to say anything." Quinn smiled reassuringly. "So this stays between us."

"Thank you." Zora seemed relieved. She jingled her car keys, then gave them to Beau so he'd let go of her earring.

Quinn admired Zora's clarity about what she wanted. Max's sister was outspoken and unapologetically direct, but Quinn liked her. And she'd grown increasingly fond of Max and his family.

She smoothed back the little girl's curls, bound by a frilly headband dotted with fabric flowers.

What would her little girl look like? Quinn couldn't help smiling but shook off the thought.

Zora's baby fever was contagious.

"You two are officially relieved of babysitting duty." Benji rolled up highchairs for the twins and helped load the kids in them. "And Quinn, Sloane dropped your invitation to our wedding in the mail yesterday."

"That's generous of you, but I don't want to throw off your seating arrangement." Quinn hated that they'd felt obligated to invite her.

"We want you there," Sloane insisted with a warm smile.

Quinn graciously accepted, then she and Zora said their goodbyes.

On the ride back to the office, they discussed Quinn and Max's upcoming trip to San Francisco. But like a silent movie playing in the background, her kiss with Max played on a loop in Quinn's head.

Maybe she couldn't get her brain to cooperate, but she had full control of her other body parts. This time there would be no reminiscing and she'd keep her hands and lips to herself.

Fifteen

Max sat up and leaned against the headboard, reaching for his cell phone on the nightstand in his darkened San Francisco hotel room. He checked the time and groaned.

Not quite six and he'd gotten very little sleep, despite turning in early.

He and Quinn had arrived the previous afternoon. They'd checked in at the trade show, set up the King's Finest booth, attended a mixer for sponsors, then enjoyed a lovely meal together at the premium steakhouse in the hotel.

Despite their rough start and the unexpected kiss, they'd managed to get back on track. Their collaboration had gone smoothly for the past week. They were finally working in sync toward a common goal, which also served their individual agendas.

With their unique creative styles and different approaches to problem solving, they complemented each other well. Max was proud of the campaign they were building.

By all accounts, he should've slept like a baby.

Instead, he'd been restless, tossing and turning the entire night. Not because he was nervous about the trade show. He simply couldn't stop thinking of Quinn. Wanting her.

She'd looked beautiful in a simple tan suit yesterday. The slim pants were tapered at the ankle, highlighting her strappy, nude-colored, high-heel sandals. The crisp white shirt she wore beneath it provided the perfect contrast to her gleaming brown skin.

He couldn't help wondering if Quinn's hair, worn in glossy beach waves combed to one side, was as smooth and silky as it appeared. And he couldn't stop remembering how luscious her full lips had felt when he'd kissed them or how firm her plump bottom had been when it filled his palms.

The thing that had kept him awake the most was the question that constantly churned in his brain.

What would've happened if Zora hadn't interrupted them?

The only topic that had gotten more rotation in his Quinn-preoccupied brain over the past weeks was how different their lives might be now if they'd stayed together back then.

He and Quinn had agreed to stick to business, and they'd both kept their word. They'd fallen into a relaxed rhythm and gotten comfortable enough with each other to talk about their families and fill each other in on their pasts. They discussed pop culture and current events. They'd even become comfortable enough with each other to joke around a bit.

The easy, familiar relationship they were building wasn't unlike the relationships he'd established with his assistant Molly and other members of his team. Yet, it clearly wasn't the same. No matter how much he tried to convince himself otherwise.

Max groaned and placed his feet on the floor.

No use staring at the ceiling for another hour.

He might as well do something constructive with his time.

Their first meeting today was with a buyer for a nationwide restaurant management company—JRS. They were meeting with the rep before the trade show opened. Getting up this early gave Max a couple of hours to swim—a great way to calm his nerves and get his head on straight.

When he got to the pool downstairs, he tugged his shirt over his head and tossed it onto a lounge chair with his towels and his phone before stepping beneath the poolside shower. But before he could get into the pool, his phone alerted him to a text message.

He picked up the phone.

Quinn.

He obviously wasn't the only one up early this morning.

Can we go over the presentation before we meet with JRS?

He typed in his response: At the pool. About to swim laps. Meet you at the buffet for breakfast at eight?

Three little dots appeared, signaling that she was typing her response: Eight is perfect. Meet you there.

Max slid his phone beneath his T-shirt, put on his waterproof audio player and turned on his old-school hip-hop playlist. He stepped off the deck, plunging into the cool water. Kicking off the tiled wall, he went directly into swimming laps.

Hopefully, an hour of swimming would silence the disquieting chatter in his head and prepare him to spend the next ten hours with Quinn—pretending he didn't want more than just a business relationship with her.

Quinn walked out of the coffee shop on the first floor of the hotel after ending her call with the rep from JRS. He'd rescheduled their appointment. She immediately dialed Max's cell.

No answer.

Not surprising, given that he'd texted her to say he was at the pool swimming laps. The phone rang several times, then rolled over to voice mail. Quinn was about to leave a message when a sign indicating the direction of the pool caught her eye.

She ended the call without leaving a message.

She'd once heard Parker say he didn't believe in coincidences. Maybe he was onto something.

If she left Max a voice mail, he might not get it for another hour. Someone else might have booked the JRS rep's remaining time slots by then. And if they missed their opportunity today, they might not get another.

It had sounded like the rep was hungover and too tired to make their early meeting. The man was evidently a partier. They needed to pin him down before he was either booked or too buzzed for a productive meeting.

JRS was the big fish she'd come here to bag. It was an account King's Finest Distillery didn't already have, and it would be a real coup for her and Max if they could get their new brandy and KFD's other products into the long list of JRS-managed restaurants.

Rather than heading toward the bank of elevators and returning to her room, Quinn followed the signs that directed her to the pool where Max was swimming laps.

She was going to the pool because it would be quicker if she simply strolled down there and nailed down a time with Max. It definitely wasn't because she was hoping to see him emerging from the pool half-dressed.

God, what if he's wearing a Speedo?

She would *never* be able to unsee that.

Quinn followed the signs to a bank of elevators that provided access to the pool and workout room. Hopefully, Max's text about going swimming hadn't been cryptic code for *I hooked up with some chick at the bar last night and I'm busy.*

A knot tightened in her stomach. It pained her to think of Max with someone else. But what right did she have to be jealous?

Quinn shook the thought from her head as she exited the elevator and made her way toward the wall of windows, cloudy with condensation.

She used her key card to enter the pool area. Only a few people were there. A hotel employee who was restocking towels greeted her warmly. There were two lap swimmers; one of them was Max.

Perfect.

Now she wouldn't have to traipse all over the hotel hunting him down in five-inch heels. She'd worn her open-toe Jimmy Choo platform sandals again today partly because they complemented her tan-and-black blazer and black knee-length skirt so well. Partly because Max hadn't been able to take his eyes off them yesterday.

Quinn stood motionless and watched him swim freestyle from her vantage point on the pool deck. She would've been content to sit there with a peachtini and watch him for hours. However, she needed to focus on her reason for coming here, and it wasn't to gawk at Max Abbott.

She walked over to the shallow end and waved to get his attention.

"Quinn?" Max didn't look happy about her intrusion as he tugged the red-and-black waterproof headphones from his ears.

He stood, rising above the shallow water that came up to his hips, and wiped the water from his eyes. Her gaze was drawn to the tattoos on his muscular chest.

Those were new. He hadn't had any ink on his brown skin that summer. She remembered their conversation about it like it was yesterday.

They'd been lying on an old blanket in the middle of a field, staring up at the stars that dotted the darkened sky.

She'd sat up suddenly and turned to him. "When I'm in a serious relationship and I *know* he's the one... I want to get matching tattoos. Maybe instead of rings." She'd only been half-joking.

At the time they'd kissed, had even made out a little, but they hadn't slept together or committed to each other in any way.

Max had chuckled, turned over on his side and traced a finger up her thigh, exposed by her tiny frayed jean shorts. "What tattoo would you get?"

Quinn had thought for a moment, then the perfect idea popped in her head. "I'd get a few lines from one of my favorite poems in a really pretty font."

"Wouldn't it be more significant if the poem was meaningful to the other person?" he'd asked.

She remembered so clearly how something about his answer had warmed her chest. In that moment, she'd truly believed Max Abbott was *the one*. That they'd forever be friends and eventually lovers.

She'd been wrong.

At eighteen, Quinn had been a dreamy teenager with a ridiculous crush while Max had been a man, three years her senior. Only a year away from joining his family's company.

"Quinn, what are you doing here?" Max's question brought her back to the present with all the ease of falling off a soft, dreamy cloud and crashing to the hard, dry earth.

Well, it's good to see you, too, Boo.

Max's chilly reception was a punch to the gut after she'd gotten lost in such a sweet memory. Quinn forced a smile, as if she was completely unfazed by his sour expression and brusque response.

"Martin, the JRS rep, canceled our scheduled meeting this morning. I'm pretty sure he was hungover from last night."

"Okay?" Max folded his arms over his chest, accentuating his toned pecs and triceps. The move prompted her to peer more closely at the tattoo on the left side of his chest that he seemed to be intent on shielding from her.

"We need to reschedule the meeting, hopefully for later today. Marty gave us a few options. I wanted to see which time works best for you so I can get back to him as soon as possible, before someone else books our spot." She spoke quickly, the words tripping from her tongue so she could quickly let him return to his moment of peace. Still she couldn't take her eyes off the black ink etched into his brown skin.

Her eyes widened suddenly, and she sucked in a quiet breath. A chill ran the length of her spine. Quinn pressed her fingertips to her lips, her hand trembling.

She didn't consider herself vain or self-absorbed. And maybe she was making a self-aggrandizing assumption, but...

"Whatever time you pick is fine," he said gruffly. "Just tell me when and where."

"Let's take the one-o'clock spot. We can treat him to a pricey lunch before the show officially kicks off at three," she said absently. "Can I ask you something, Max?"

"Sure." There was apprehension in his voice, as if he anticipated her question. "Give me a sec."

Max climbed out of the pool, then asked the attendant for a couple of towels. He dried himself off before draping the towels over his shoulders. But she'd already seen the tattoos.

The letters QB were tattooed over his heart. Beneath that were a few lines of a poem she'd been obsessed with that summer: Robert Frost's "Stopping by Woods on a Snowy Evening."

The woods are lovely, dark and deep,
But I have promises to keep,
And miles to go before I sleep,
And miles to go before I sleep.

The lines of poetry were bordered by a rendering of woods in black ink.

"Is that…" She pointed at the tattoos. "Did you—"

"Yes." His voice was low.

There was only the sound of little splashes of water as the other swimmer continued his laps. Quinn stared up at Max, waiting for further explanation.

He offered none.

She pressed her fingers to her mouth, ruining her carefully applied lip gloss.

"How long have you had these?" she finally asked.

"Since a few months after we broke up."

Her gaze snapped up to his. She scowled.

"*We* didn't break up. You *dumped* me." She pointed at each of them in turn, underscoring her words. "With no real explanation, no discussion. So I'm having a really hard time understanding—"

"Maybe we should talk over there." Max turned and walked toward the lounge chairs at the far end of the pool.

Quinn followed him and stood with one hip cocked and her arms folded. "Why?" she asked impatiently. "Why would you have my initials and a quote from my favorite poem carved into your body *after* you dumped me? Who does that?" Her voice was unsteady and louder than she'd intended.

"I can only imagine all of the things that must be going through your head right now." He pulled on a white King's Finest T-shirt. "We can talk about this as much as you'd like but preferably not here." He glanced in the direction of the man in the pool and the attendant. Both seemed to be paying close attention to them now.

Quinn lowered her voice but ignored his request to take the conversation elsewhere. "I just need to know why you'd do this *after* it was over. In all these years, you never once tried to contact me."

"That isn't true." There was a pained expression on his face. He sighed and shook his head. "Not that it matters now."

"Of course, it matters. At least, it matters to me. So tell me… When was it that you reached out to me? Because I haven't received so much as a text message from you."

"That's because you changed your phone number." He folded his arms. "Couldn't have been more than a month afterward."

Quinn stood frozen, her heart beating harder.

She'd gotten a new phone a few weeks after Max had broken up with her. She'd decided to remove any temptation to call him and any anxiety about whether or not he'd call her. So she'd requested a new number and made a point of not transferring Max's contact info to her new phone.

But he would only know how quickly she'd changed her number if he'd tried to call her not long afterward.

"Our grandfathers have been best buddies since before either of us was born." She folded her arms defiantly, proud of her comeback. "If you'd really wanted to contact me, you would've found a way to do it."

"We managed to keep our relationship under the radar that summer," he said. "But how long do you think that would've lasted if I'd rung up your grandparents and asked for your new phone number?" Max raked his fingers through his damp hair and sighed. "You didn't want anyone to know about us, and I agreed. The last thing I was going to do was tip off your shotgun-toting grandfather that I'd spent the summer eating at his dinner table and secretly banging his granddaughter."

Now Quinn glanced around to see if anyone else could hear their conversation.

"You knew where I went to school. You could've written to me there."

"Do you *really* not know?" Max narrowed his gaze and stepped in closer.

"Do I really not know *what*? That my ex tagged his chest with my initials and favorite poem *after* he decided he wasn't that into me after all?"

"I *never* said I wasn't into you. If anything, I was too into you and it scared the shit out of me." He huffed. "I loved you, Quinn. But it felt like too much too soon. We were so young." Max rubbed the scruff on his chin. "I panicked and backed away. Within a month I realized I'd made a huge mistake. I tried to call you, but you'd changed your number. I couldn't go to your grandfather without breaking my promise to you. So I decided to go see you in person. I realized how royally I'd fucked up. I needed some grand gesture to prove to you how much I loved you and wanted you back."

He sighed heavily, as if reluctant to continue.

"I remembered what you said about the tattoos. That it was what you'd do once you were sure you'd found the person you wanted to be with for the rest of your life. So that's what I did. Then I hopped into my truck and drove all the way from my campus in Florida to yours in Virginia."

"Then why didn't I see you?" Quinn asked.

"I went to your dorm room and your roommate answered."

"My roommate?" She poked a thumb to her chest. "You must've gone to the wrong room. If you'd come to our dorm room, my roommate—"

"Nora… Natalie…" He frowned, trying to recall the name.

"Naomi." Quinn's heart plummeted to her stomach, then thumped so loudly that the sound filled her ears. Her chest felt heavy, like a tombstone lay on it.

The one she was going to erect after she murdered her college roommate.

"Naomi, right." Max snapped his fingers. "That was her name. Strawberry blonde with grayish blue eyes, about yay high." He leveled his hand just below the earphones hanging around his neck.

Quinn felt dizzy. Her head throbbed and her mouth was dry. "You met Naomi?"

"Fierce little thing." He chuckled bitterly. "Part pretty little coed, part pit bull, and a thousand percent protective of you."

Quinn couldn't have described Naomi better herself.

"She obviously knew exactly who I was and that you never wanted to see or hear from me again. Naomi hated my guts and she had no qualms about telling me *exactly* what she thought of me."

Max had definitely met her friend. She could only imagine how the encounter had gone. Quinn understood why Naomi would've hated Max. But why hadn't her friend told her that Max had driven up from Florida to see her?

"What did Naomi say?"

"I believe her exact words were, 'Fuck off, you fucking fucker, and leave my friend alone. She's finally happy again now and the last thing she needs is for you to pop 'round and fuck with her head, again.'" He said the words in a feigned British accent reminiscent of her friend's.

Naomi always did enjoy a good f-bomb.

"You'd gone to all the trouble of getting my initials tattooed on your skin and you let a five-foot-three-inch sprite run you off." Quinn folded her arms and tipped her chin defiantly.

"No." He sounded incredibly sad. "I told her I needed to hear it from you. That if you told me you didn't want to see me again, I'd walk away and never bother you again."

"And?"

He gathered his things from the lounge chair and shoved

his cell phone into the pocket of his swim trunks. Then he turned to her and sighed.

"Naomi said you were out doing some other guy, and that she didn't expect that you'd be back anytime soon."

"And you believed her?"

Quinn hadn't dated anyone seriously for more than a year and a half after Max. But Quinn could easily imagine her roommate telling him such a lie to bruise his ego. Her overprotective friend would've tried to cut Max deep with her words after spending the previous two months nursing Quinn's broken heart and trying to cheer her up.

At the end of the two months, Quinn had promised herself and her friend that she wouldn't waste another moment of her life mooning over Max Abbott. That she never wanted to hear from or see Max again.

Naomi, evidently, hadn't trusted that Quinn would stick to her resolution when presented with the chance to see Max again. Instead, she'd made the decision for her. Quinn and Naomi had remained best friends, though Quinn had gotten a job in Atlanta and Naomi was now a married mother of two running her own kiddie clothing business in California. In all the years since college, her friend had never once revealed that Max had come to campus to see her.

"No, I didn't believe her." Max rubbed the back of his neck. "I hung around, parked outside of your dorm. If you didn't want to see me again, I would've respected that. But I wanted to hear it from you."

"So why didn't you ask me?"

"I saw the guy bring you home, and I saw him kiss you. I realized Naomi was right. You'd moved on, and you deserved better." Max's mouth twisted and deep wrinkles spanned his forehead.

Quinn thought back to that time in her life. She hadn't been seeing anyone. Maybe Max had mistaken someone else for her. She was about to tell him as much when she remembered the one guy who had kissed her around that time—Naomi's cousin, Rick. The guy her roommate had tried desperately to hook her up with. That explained why Naomi hadn't told her about Max's visit.

She didn't owe Max an explanation, but she had some choice words for her friend.

"Getting those tattoos before you knew if we'd get back together... That was—"

"Dumb?" he volunteered.

"I was going to say risky as hell," Quinn said. "You had no idea how I'd react or if I had, in fact, moved on."

"I realized what a gamble my grand gesture was." He patted his chest where her initials were carved into his skin. "That there was a good chance you still wouldn't forgive me. But I needed to show you how much you meant to me. And even if we never got back together, I guess I wanted to hold on to you in some small way." He rubbed at the tattoo through his shirt.

Quinn frowned, tears burning her eyes. She turned away from Max, abruptly changing the subject. "I should go make sure everything is ready."

"I'll walk you to the elevator." Max gestured toward the door.

Quinn nodded and went with him.

"How did you explain the tattoos to your friends and your family?" she asked after they had stepped into the elevator.

"I'd had them for a few years by the time anyone in my family saw them." Max punched each of their floor numbers. "I played the backup quarterback position for my school's football team. They assumed that was what the QB stood for, and I didn't correct them. As for the poem... Turns out I'm a fan of Robert Frost's poetry, too. More people have those words inked on them than you probably think."

"The way you ended things between us so abruptly without explanation... It seemed like what we'd shared never really meant anything to you. That I meant nothing to you. But—"

"You meant *everything* to me, Quinn." Max swallowed hard, his Adam's apple bobbing. "And it terrified me. I'm sorry I was a dick about it. I should've just been honest with you about how I was feeling, but—"

Quinn planted a hand on Max's chest, lifted onto her toes and pressed her lips to his—salty from the pool. She slipped her hands beneath the damp T-shirt and glided them up the strong muscles of his back.

Max backed her against the elevator wall, his tongue eagerly seeking hers. His hands glided down her body, gripping her bottom and hauling her against him. She could feel him hard against her belly.

The robotic voice alerted them that they were approaching their first stop—Max's floor.

He pulled his mouth from hers, both of them breathless as his dark gaze drank her in. Her mouth curved in a half smile.

She sank her teeth into her lower lip as she dragged her manicured nails over his skin. "Invite me to your room, Max," she breathed.

His eyes danced with excitement momentarily. Then he frowned and heaved a sigh.

"I think you know how much I'd like to take you up on your offer, Quinn." He twirled a strand of her hair around his finger, focusing on it rather than her eyes. "But I don't want you to regret this the way you regretted that kiss in my office. You were adamant about it never happening again."

Shit. She *had* said that, and at the time she'd meant it.

"That was before I knew the whole story." She pressed a palm to where her initials were inscribed on his skin.

The elevator jerked to a stop and the doors slid open, accompanied by the announcement of the floor number.

"I would *love* for you to come to my room, Quinn," he whispered, pressing a fleeting kiss to her lips. "But I never want to see the pain and disappointment in your eyes that I saw there after Zora interrupted us. I hurt you before. I won't do it again. So think about it. Make sure this is what you want. I'm in room 1709."

Max gave her another quick kiss and exited the elevator.

Quinn squeezed her eyes shut, her heart racing and her head still spinning from Max's kiss as the elevator continued its ascent to the twenty-fourth floor. She'd never been more confused about what she wanted than she was right now.

Her heart and body wanted to be with Max. But her brain reminded her that he'd let her down before and warned her that, if given the chance, he'd let her down again.

Sixteen

Max held the razor beneath the running water, then tapped the handle on the side of the sink before returning it to its carrying case. He preferred the look of a five-o'clock shadow, but he'd decided to shave this morning.

There was a knock at his hotel room door. *Good.* After his shower, he'd requested additional towels. He was barefoot and wearing only a pair of pants slung low on his hips. Max pulled on a short-sleeve shirt, quickly buttoned it and opened the door.

"You asked for fresh towels?" Quinn held up the stack of towels as if it was a silver platter. Her sensual mouth curved with an impish smirk that brought out her dimples. She broke into laughter. "Don't worry. I tipped the housekeeper. Is it okay if I come in?"

"Of course, thanks." He accepted the towels from her and stepped aside to let her in, still a bit stunned she was there.

It'd been nearly an hour since he'd left Quinn in that elevator. As much as he'd hoped she'd come to his room, he'd assumed that she'd renewed her resolve not to get romantically involved. He'd even tried to convince himself that it was for the best. But now he hoped like hell that she'd changed her mind. Still, he wouldn't presume that was why she was here.

Max put the towels away. "What's up?"

"I contacted Marty. He's good with meeting us for lunch

at one. He wants to go to the seafood place downstairs. You're not allergic, are you?"

"No." He gestured for her to have a seat in the living room. "The seafood restaurant at one is fine."

Quinn sat in the chair and he sat on the end of the couch nearest her. Neither of them spoke right away.

"It was nice of you to deliver the message," he said. "But you know you could've just called me or sent a text, right?"

Quinn nibbled on her lower lip, looking like a kid who'd gotten busted with a hand in the cookie jar. "I suppose that's true."

"So why'd you really come down here, Quinn?" He wanted to be clear about his intentions. And he needed her to be clear about hers, too.

Quinn set her purse on the small table beside the sofa and stood in front of him. She stripped off her jacket and dropped it on the chair she'd vacated. Her beaded nipples poked through the thin fabric of her camisole.

She slid her skirt up just enough to allow her to straddle him. Her knees dug into the sofa on either side of his hips.

"There is one other reason I wanted to see you." She captured his mouth with a soft, teasing kiss.

"I'm trying *really* hard to respect the boundaries you established, Quinn." His voice was a tortured whisper, which she seemed to relish. Like it fed the ravenous, seductive beast inside her. Something he remembered all too well. "You aren't making this very easy for me."

"Maybe I've changed my mind," she whispered between kisses to his jaw that sent blood rushing below his belt.

Quinn hadn't done anything like this since the summer she'd worn Max down, convincing him to give in to the attraction between them. Mostly because she'd won the battle yet lost the war. In the end, once she'd fallen for Max—heart and soul—he'd walked away.

Just as her mother had warned her.

Men only want fast girls for one reason. They have no intention of ever taking them home to their mothers.

Now here she was, the pull of Max Abbott so strong that she was ignoring her mother's advice again. She'd spent more than a decade being the "good girl." Being pursued rather than going after what she wanted. And what had it gotten her?

She'd ended up alone. Without a job. Her reputation tarnished.

This time she'd get what she wanted: sex with no strings attached. Then they could both just walk away.

"*Maybe* won't cut it, baby." Max held her chin between his finger and thumb, forcing her to meet his gaze. "You need to be sure."

Quinn's heart thudded in her chest as she grabbed her purse from the side table. She stuck a trembling hand inside and produced a small, overpriced box of condoms. "I went to the drugstore and got these." She waved them. "So yes, I'm sure."

Her cheeks and face flamed with heat. She'd never felt more vulnerable.

What if he says no?

The few seconds of silence that elapsed as he studied the box in her hand with furrowed brows were agonizing. Quinn swallowed hard, her pulse racing.

She was about to tell Max that she'd temporarily lost her mind, and he should disregard everything she'd said and done that morning. But then Max slid his arms around her and squeezed her bottom, pulling their bodies closer. His hardened length against her sensitive flesh sent a shiver of pleasure up her spine.

Max pressed his open mouth to hers, his tongue seeking hers in a kiss that was hungry and impatient. Heat spread throughout her body, emanating from every place he touched her—even through their clothing.

He tightened his embrace, his large hands on her back, crushing her breasts and sensitive nipples against his hard chest. She moved her hips, moaning into his mouth at the intense pleasure as she dragged her sensitive clit along the outline of his hardened shaft through the thin material of their clothes.

Max gently bit her lower lip before going in for a deeper kiss.

Her skin tingled, as if tiny licks of fire scampered across her flesh. Max Abbott was an excellent kisser. But now, just as then, he seemed hesitant to take things to the next level.

She'd come this far. *No turning back now.*

Quinn tugged up Max's shirt and skimmed her hands over the dusting of hair on his belly. As they continued the kiss, she slowly unbuttoned his shirt, starting from the bottom. Then she slid it from his shoulders, revealing the tattoos.

She broke their kiss, allowing herself the luxury of admiring the artwork. She traced the letters with her fingertip, applying only the lightest pressure.

QB. Her initials. Followed by her favorite lines from the poem she'd read to him that summer. Both tattoos had been there nearly the entire time they'd been apart.

Quinn pressed a soft kiss to those letters, brushing her lips over the words of poetry inked on his skin. Then she flicked his nipple with her tongue. He sucked in a deep breath, his muscles tensing.

Max speared his fingers into her hair, dragging her mouth to his again. Slipping his hands beneath the hem of the camisole, he tugged it over her head, then dropped it onto the floor. He fumbled with the clasp of her bra, releasing it and gliding it off her arms.

"Fuck," he muttered softly. His appreciative gaze trailed down her exposed torso, and her belly tightened in response.

She gasped in surprise when Max suddenly flipped her onto her back on the sofa and slid down her body. Taking one of the already ultra-sensitive nubs into his warm mouth, he grazed it with his teeth.

Quinn murmured softly in response to the sensation— part pleasure, part pain. She dug her fingers into his soft curls, gripping his hair as she arched her back in a greedy plea for more.

Max's mouth curved in a sensuous smile as his hooded gaze met hers. He shifted his attention to her other nipple, licking and teasing it with his tongue. Pleasure radiated throughout her body, her sex pulsing. Aching for his touch.

Gliding his hand down her side and beneath the short, black skirt, Max cupped the damp space between her thighs. He tugged aside the fabric, plunging a finger inside her as his thumb caressed the slick, hypersensitive bundle of nerves.

She trembled, unable to hold back quiet moans as he circled her clit with his thumb. Max slipped another finger inside her as he continued to lick and suck her sensitive nipple.

The symphony of varying sensations sent Quinn floating higher and higher, the intensity building until she'd reached a crescendo. She cried out in intense pleasure, her body shuddering and spent, yet craving more.

Her chest heaved with rapid, shallow breaths that left her slightly lightheaded.

Max trailed kisses up her chest and neck. Kissed the side of her face. Finally, he pressed a lingering kiss to her mouth. He stood, retrieving the box of condoms. His gaze held hers as he extended his open palm.

"Are you still with me, Quinn?"

Maybe this was a really terrible idea, but being with Max felt amazing. And maybe she shouldn't, but she trusted Max to be discreet.

Standing on unsteady legs, Quinn nodded and placed her hand in his, following him to his bed.

Seventeen

Max hadn't yet mastered the fine art of resisting Quinn. Not when she'd been a smoking-hot college-bound freshman who had her sights set on him. Not now that she was a mature, incredibly beautiful woman who knew exactly what she wanted in the boardroom and was willing to go to the mat for it.

Then again, maybe his inability to resist her was because he wanted the same thing she wanted: to have her in his bed. Which was where she now lay.

He joined her in the bed and kissed her, relishing the sweet taste of her mouth and the feel of her soft lips. The glide of her tongue against his. Their kiss was feverish and hungry. Reminiscent of the desperate need they'd both felt that first time…so long ago.

Max was already on the edge, having watched her fall apart in his arms. He'd always loved the sweet little sounds she made, indicating that she was close or that she wanted more.

What was it about Quinn that had always made him feel a complete loss of control?

He glided his hands along the soft, smooth skin of her back. Inhaled her divine citrus scent and the smell of coconut wafting from her dark hair. Her quiet moans as they kissed ignited a raging fire inside him.

"You are so fucking sexy," he muttered against her lips.

Max trailed kisses down her jaw, down her neck, through the valley between the glorious mounds of her full breasts, then down her belly. His gaze locked with hers. "I haven't stopped thinking about you since the day you waltzed this perfect ass into our conference room."

"Same." A wide smile lit Quinn's brown eyes as she slid her fingers into his hair. There was something so intimate about the gesture. "By the way, the look on your face that day—priceless."

"I'll bet." He pressed another kiss to her stomach as he glided the zipper down the side of the black skirt that had been tempting him all morning. Quinn lifted her hips, helping him slide the garment off. He took a moment to admire the gorgeous brown skin of her full hips and curvy thighs.

Quinn's belly rose and fell with shallow breaths as he laid kisses just above the waistband of her black panties. She gasped softly when he tugged the material down just enough to plant soft kisses on her hip bone.

The scent of her arousal teased him. Made his dick hard as steel. He was desperate to finally be inside her. Yet he wanted to savor every moment with her.

Max dragged the damp fabric down her hips and off her legs. He spread her open with his thumbs and pressed a kiss to the glistening pink flesh between her thighs. He reveled in the salty sweet taste of her desire as his tongue traced the pink slit and lapped at the sensitive, swollen flesh.

Quinn shuddered. In a silent plea for more, she angled her hips, permitting him better access.

Max gladly obliged. He licked and teased her sex, then sucked on the distended bundle of nerves until she cried out. Her legs trembled and the space between her thighs pulsed.

He'd imagined this since the day she'd walked through the door of that conference room and set his world on fire, reminding him of all the things he'd tried so damn hard to forget. That he'd had the most amazing woman in his life, and he'd walked away from her because he'd been a coward. Terrified that one or both of them would regret committing to each other at such a young age. But the only thing he'd ever really regretted was letting Quinn go.

Max stripped off his remaining clothes and tore into the box of condoms, quickly ripping one from its foil packet and rolling it up his shaft. He teased her, pressing the head to her entrance before slowly pushing inside her warm, tight sheath.

He groaned at the searing pleasure of her flesh enveloping his, then slowly glided inside her until he was fully seated.

"God, Quinn, you feel so amazing," he growled, his voice so gruff he barely recognized it.

He leaned down and captured her open mouth in a kiss. Quinn dug her fingers into his back, her hips lifting to meet each stroke. He swallowed her soft murmurs as he moved inside her until she cried out with pleasure again. Until he followed her over the edge.

Max collapsed onto his back beside Quinn, both of them breathing heavily. An awkward silence descended over the room momentarily. When his breathing evened out again, Max rolled onto his side and planted a soft kiss on her lips. He sifted his fingers through her glossy strands of hair.

"No regrets?" It would kill him inside if Quinn regretted, even for a moment, what they'd just shared.

"None." A shy smile animated Quinn's dimples. She grazed the letters on his chest with her thumb and kissed him again.

Max discarded the condom, then crawled into bed. He cradled Quinn in his arms, with her bottom nestled against him, and kissed the shell of her ear. He'd be content to lie with this woman in his arms and not leave this room for the next three days. Until he'd convinced her that this time, things would be different. That he'd never hurt her again.

* * *

Max blinked, looking up at the brown-skinned goddess calling his name.

Quinn, who was fully dressed, shoved his shoulder again. "Max, you have to get up. We're scheduled to meet Marty in forty-five minutes and I still have to go to my room to shower and change." She put on an earring, which he vaguely remembered her losing at some point when they'd made love again.

"Wait…we're still planning on meeting the JRS guy for lunch?" He rubbed an eye as he propped himself up on his elbows. "I thought we were gonna spend a few more hours in bed." He tugged at the hem of her skirt.

She slapped his hand playfully. "There will be plenty of time for that later. Right now, I need to ensure that you're awake and that you'll be there on time. Remember, JRS is the white whale we came here for. Everything else is gravy."

"To be fair, he canceled on us first." Max dragged himself to a seated position, back pressed against the headboard.

"Max." Quinn used the same warning tone his mother had when he was a kid.

"Fine. But shouldn't we at least… I don't know." He rubbed the sleep from his eyes again. "Shouldn't we at least talk about what happened before you run off."

"It's a little late for a conversation about the birds and the bees." She dragged her fingers through her hair.

"I'm not talking about that and you know it."

"Then we're fine. I'm not a virgin this time."

"Which, to be fair, I had no idea about before the fact," he reminded her.

"I know." She smiled. "I'm just saying that while I have no regrets about what happened here, I also have no delusions that this is about anything more than sex for you... for us."

Wait...what?

Had he given her the impression that sex was all he wanted? Or was she making it clear that's all she wanted from him?

Either way, if that's the way you want to play this, sweetheart, fine.

"Good talk, Quinn."

"Look, this was fun, Max. No..." She shook her head, then gazed up dreamily. "This was...intense, and you were amazing. It took me back to that summer when everything between us felt so perfect. Everything was great until I tried to make it more than it was."

"And what was it, Quinn?" It was a sincere question. Because he knew what it had been for him: the best damn summer of his life—until he'd screwed up and lost the perfect girl.

"A summer fling. That's what it was then, and that's what this is now. Two old flames feeling a little nostalgic and reliving the past," she said. "But this time, we keep things simple and be honest with each other about where this is going. That way, no one gets caught up in their feelings or has any false expectations."

She leaned down and kissed him. "You still with me, Max?" She smirked.

Damn. She was using his line on him. But if this was the only way to keep Quinn in his life—in his bed—then he'd accept her terms. *For now.*

"Okay, Quinn." Max sighed. "What are the rules of engagement?"

Quinn sat on the edge of the bed and crossed her legs. She propped her chin on her fist, her foot bouncing, as she contemplated his question.

"The first rule of a secret summer fling is we don't talk

about our secret summer fling—to anyone. Second, we only see each other on our business trips. Third, no overnights. We end the night in our own beds. Fourth, when we complete this project, we walk away. We both get closure and there are no hard feelings."

"Sounds like you've given this a lot of thought." He sifted a few strands of her hair through his fingers. "But things are never quite that simple. What happens if one of us doesn't want to walk away?" he asked.

She frowned, her nose crinkling. "We cross that bridge if we come to it," she said. "But there should be no expectations of anything beyond what I've outlined. Deal?"

"Deal," Max agreed. "But after the trade show today…"

She pressed a lingering kiss to his mouth and smiled. "Meet you back here then."

Max watched as she sashayed from his bedroom and into the main space where she retrieved her purse, then left his suite.

Heaving a sigh, Max got out of bed and hopped in the shower again.

He would play by Quinn's rules. But he looked forward to getting her to break each and every one of them. Because this time he had no intention of walking away so easily from the woman whose initials were branded on his skin.

Eighteen

Quinn sat cross-legged on the sofa in Kayleigh's rental apartment, exhausted after the conference in San Francisco. She hadn't realized how much walking was involved when attending a trade show. Then there were the early-morning meetings and the late nights spent in either her or Max's hotel room.

She and Max had spent nearly every waking hour together. When they weren't working, they'd shared meals, watched movies and spent lots of time discovering new ways to bring each other pleasure. All of it—except for a few meals—had taken place in private. The only thing they hadn't done together was sleep. At the end of the night, she either returned to her room or sent him, begrudgingly, back to his.

Quinn couldn't help smiling as she hugged her knees to her chest. Her week with Max had been incredible.

They'd bagged the deal with JRS and gotten preorders from a slew of other clients, both current and new King's Finest buyers. The trip had been an all-around success.

So why was the time she'd spent with Max the thing she remembered most fondly? Quinn tried not to think too deeply about the reasons. *Why* didn't matter. Her stay in Magnolia Lake was temporary. She wasn't looking for a serious relationship and neither was he.

Her cell phone rang, and she couldn't help hoping it was Max.

She checked the caller ID.

Wrong brother.

"Hey, Cole. What's up?"

"Hey, Q. I know this is really, *really* last-minute…"

"I already don't like where this is going." She put Cole on speakerphone and went to the kitchen to make a snack. "Spit it out, Abbott. What do you need?"

She opened the fridge and took out fruit and cheese.

"I need you to be my plus-one, again," Cole said.

"For Benji and Sloane's wedding this weekend?"

"Yes. Say yes, *please*," he said. "I have three women dropping hints about being my date for this thing. I honestly just want to go, celebrate with my family and have fun."

Quinn put the fruit in a colander and rinsed it, then set it on the counter. "I'm surprised you want a date. I thought wedding receptions were a player's playground."

"I resent the term *player*. I'm up-front with every woman I've ever been with about not wanting anything serious. Plus, weddings might be great for hookups, but they also get women thinking about their own weddings. Like I said, I don't ever lead anyone on. So you'd be doing me a favor. We go as friends. I can enjoy the evening without anyone thinking that I'm going home with them or, worse, that I'd be their best bet for a wedding of their own."

"You're kind of a drama king. Anyone ever tell you that, Cole?" She sliced the apple.

"Only because I'm misunderstood." She could hear the grin in his voice. "Speaking of misunderstandings and drama… Us going to this thing together won't create any static between you and Max, right?"

The knife slipped and she cut herself. Blood oozed from her fingertip and dripped onto the cutting board.

"Shit."

There was a knot in the pit of her stomach.

The first rule of a secret summer fling is we don't talk about our secret summer fling—to anyone.

Had Max broken rule number one already? No, he wouldn't have talked to Cole about them. Had Zora broken her promise and told Cole about the kiss she'd seen? Or was Cole just fishing?

Relax.

"What's wrong?" Cole's voice was laced with concern.

"The knives here in Kayleigh's rental are surprisingly sharp. I sliced my finger." Quinn turned on the water and rinsed the cut beneath the faucet until the bleeding stopped. She cleared her throat. "Why would Max care about me going to Benji's wedding with you?"

Cole didn't respond right away.

"That was the vibe I got between you two at my parents' anniversary party," he said. "Max was… I guess the best word for it would be *territorial*."

Quinn breathed out a quiet sigh of relief.

They had agreed to keep things casual and not tell anyone. So going to Benji and Sloane's wedding with Max wasn't an option. No doubt, that was why he hadn't asked her to go with him, even though he knew Sloane had invited her.

Besides, Max knew that she and Cole were nothing more than friends.

"Max will be fine," she said. "The real dilemma is what am I going to wear?" Maybe Kayleigh had something in the shop downstairs that would work. "Never mind, I'll figure it out."

"So you'll come?" There was a lilt in Cole's voice whenever he convinced her to do something out of her comfort zone.

"I obviously have zero compunction about crashing your

family's events, so why not?" She shrugged. "This time, I've actually been invited."

She glanced at the open but unanswered invite to Benji and Sloane's wedding on the counter.

"Awesome. That's the good news," he said. "The bad news is we're ahead of schedule on the restaurant project. Construction begins within the next two weeks. Which means—"

"Kayleigh and I both need to be out by then." Quinn sighed.

It looked like she'd be back to making that long daily commute again in a couple of weeks.

She made arrangements to meet Cole at the event on Saturday. He was in the wedding party, so even though she'd be his plus-one, she wouldn't see him until well into the reception.

Hanging out with Cole would be fun, and it would give her an excuse to see Max despite the rule she'd established about not seeing each other while they were in town. The truth was that she missed spending time with him. And she hated seeing Max around the office but pretending there was nothing between them.

Quinn picked up her phone again and typed a text message.

Hey, Max. Just an FYI. Cole asked me to be his plus-one at Sloane and Benji's wedding.

Three little dots showed up on the phone almost immediately. But after five minutes, there was still no message. Quinn put down the phone and went back to preparing her snack.

An hour later Max's single-word response came through.

Okay.

That was all he had to say?

But what exactly did she expect Max to say?

Don't go with my brother. Come with me instead.

Maybe he would've, if she hadn't insisted that they keep the relationship secret and not see each other in town.

You can't have it both ways, babe.

Quinn cursed to herself, grabbed her phone and wallet, and headed down to Kayleigh's shop.

Max watched as Benji and Sloane greeted some of their guests. He couldn't be happier for his cousin and his new bride.

Sloane was beautiful in a simple, strapless, ivory wedding gown. Her short pixie haircut was adorned with a crown made of fresh flowers.

Benji was a tech billionaire who could've easily afforded a huge, lavish destination wedding. But he and Sloane would've been content to get married by the justice of the peace.

Benji and Sloane considered the wedding to be the public formalization of what they already were: a family. The small, elegant ceremony and reception were simply concessions to their families. After their honeymoon, Benji, Sloane and the twins would spend a year in Japan. So it was the last time their entire extended family would be together until Parker and Kayleigh's wedding—scheduled for soon after Benji and Sloane's return.

Max had tried to stay in the moment, celebrating with his family. But he'd been distracted the instant Quinn walked in the door. She was stunning in a pale pink, backless dress with a beaded top. The ethereal, knee-length overlay made it seem as if Quinn floated around the room.

Still soaring after the incredible time they'd had together in San Francisco, Max was completely taken with her.

He could get accustomed to spending time with Quinn.

She was brilliant at her job, and people loved her. She was affable yet persuasive. Fun to be around, and she had the best laugh. And though she was generally thoughtful and careful, there was a side of Quinn that was audacious and slightly uninhibited. He'd enjoyed every moment they'd spent together, and he was eager for their trip to Chicago in a few weeks.

But waiting three whole weeks to spend time with Quinn again didn't sit well with him. Being this close to her now only heightened his hunger for her.

Max had agreed to Quinn's terms, and he understood her hesitance to go public with their relationship while they worked together. But it didn't mean he had to like it.

As he watched Quinn dance with Cole, both of them laughing, he cursed himself for not sending his original text message. Or any of the ten messages he'd composed then deleted before finally sending his lame, one-word response.

Okay.

He definitely was *not* okay with Quinn being here with Cole. Max didn't care if the two of them were just friends. He wanted Quinn to be here with him. And only him.

Max had typed several variations of that message before finally deciding that coming off as jealous, possessive or downright needy would only scare her off.

He went with Option B instead: Just play it cool.

As if Quinn being here with his annoying younger brother was no big deal. Which now felt like the second dumbest idea he'd ever had. The decision his younger self had made to break up with Quinn definitely ranked first.

"Ask her to dance." Zora nudged his shoulder. "It's a wedding reception. There's nothing weird about that."

"Maybe." Max sipped his glass of bourbon neat.

Just the thought of holding Quinn in his arms again brought back vivid memories of their week together. Reminded him of how much he wanted her in his bed.

But sitting there watching Cole and Quinn together was another form of torture. He wasn't sure which was worse.

Max finished the last of his drink, then excused himself from the table before heading onto the dance floor.

He approached Cole and Quinn. "Mind if I cut in?"

"Only if you let me lead," Cole said.

Quinn broke out in her melodic laughter.

Max couldn't help laughing, too. "I meant I'd like to dance with Quinn, smart ass," he said before turning to her. "If you don't mind."

"Not at all." Her brown eyes danced.

Max took her hand and slipped an arm around her waist. They danced in silence for a few moments. "You look gorgeous, Quinn."

"Thank you." Her broad smile revealed the depth of her dimples. "You look pretty dashing in your tux."

He cradled her in his arms as they moved together, his hand pressed to the smooth, soft skin of her bare back. The sensation reminded him of how he'd skimmed his hands over her bare skin as she lay naked in his arms just a few days ago.

Max inhaled the familiar scent of coconut and citrus as he leaned in, whispering into her hair, "God, I've missed you."

She looked up at him. One corner of her mouth curved in an almost shy smile. "Me, too."

It was a small win. The first step toward making his case for breaking rule number two.

"I'm looking forward to Chicago," he said.

"For business or personal reasons?"

"Both," he admitted. "But I've been thinking—"

"Quinn, Benji had a brilliant idea," Cole appeared beside them suddenly with Benji in tow. "The cabin will be empty while he and Sloane are away."

"We'd rather have you stay there than for the place to sit empty," Benji explained.

It was a wonderful offer, though she doubted she could afford to rent the cabin of a tech billionaire.

"That's kind of you and Sloane, Benji. But I don't know if—"

"You'd be doing us a favor." Benji grinned. "You need a place to crash in town, and we could really use a house sitter while we're away." He shrugged. "I consider it a fair tradeoff."

Quinn agreed, thanking Benji for his generosity.

Max was glad Quinn would be staying in town once construction started on Kayleigh's building. But he hadn't finished his conversation with Quinn and couldn't help resenting his brother's awful timing.

Or maybe Cole had timed the situation perfectly.

Max assessed his younger brother coolly, but as usual, Cole was completely unfazed.

He forced a smile through clenched teeth, then put a discreet hand on Quinn's waist and leaned in to whisper in her ear. "Catch up with you later?"

Her brown eyes offered a quiet apology for the interruption. "Of course. Thank you for the dance."

Max nodded and walked away, heaving a quiet sigh. But if his past with Quinn had taught him anything it was not to give up so easily. He'd find another opportunity to make his proposal.

Quinn said goodbye to the bride and groom and to all of the Abbotts.

As she approached the valet stand, Max called her name.

"Leaving already?"

"It's been a long week," she said.

"True," Max agreed. "Mind if I walk you to your car instead?"

Quinn glanced over at the valet, who looked at them expectantly. She returned her gaze to Max. "It's a beautiful night. A short walk would be nice."

Max held out his hand and she gave him her ticket, which he used to retrieve her keys and get the location of her car. He extended his elbow to her and she slipped her arm through his.

It was a common, courteous gesture. But something about it felt warm and intimate, sending a small shiver up her spine.

"So we were talking about how much we enjoyed this past week together in San Francisco and how much we're looking forward to spending time together in Chicago," he repeated.

"All true," she agreed.

"But Chicago isn't for another three weeks, which feels like an eternity," Max said. "So I propose we nix rule number two. Because I'd *really* like to take you back to my place tonight, Quinn. We could spend the rest of this weekend in my bed."

"I'll admit that sounds intriguing, but this is a rather small town, Max." She glanced around the parking lot, suddenly conscious of whether anyone might overhear their conversation. "We agreed to be discreet about this. Hooking up here in town seems imprudent. Like we're asking to get caught."

Max stopped and turned to her. "Fortunately, my place is on the edge of town. Which is why it's the place my family is *least* likely to stop by unannounced. And once you move into the cabin… It's even farther out of town."

Quinn hiked an eyebrow.

"Seems you've given this idea quite a bit of thought."

"I've given *you* a lot of thought, Quinn." His voice was low and gruff as his dark eyes searched hers. "In fact, I haven't been able to think of much else."

His words, uttered so sincerely, filled her chest with warmth and short-circuited her brain.

But then, something about Max Abbott always had.

"It's already late tonight, but maybe I could come by your place sometime tomorrow."

One side of Max's mouth lifted in a crooked half smile. "I'll text you my address."

He saw her to her car. After the intimacy they'd shared over the past week, it seemed odd for him not to hug or kiss her goodnight. A part of her wanted him to—despite the risk.

Quinn released a quiet sigh as she drove away from Max, still standing there in the parking lot.

Do not fall for Max Abbott again.

But even as she repeated the warning in her head, it was clear that her heart had a mind of its own.

Nineteen

Quinn climbed back into Max's bed and cuddled against his broad chest. She traced her initials inscribed over his heart: something she often found herself doing absently as they lay together after making love.

They'd returned from the trade show in Chicago—another successful outing—and she'd moved into Benji and Sloane's cabin. But this Saturday evening, they were at Max's town house on the outskirts of Magnolia Lake. And he was unusually quiet.

Quinn lifted onto her elbow and stroked the whiskered chin that had sensitized her flesh as he'd kissed his way down her body earlier.

"There's obviously something on your mind tonight. Do you want to talk about it? Or would you prefer some space? If so, it's okay. I understand."

Max clamped a hand on her wrist. His dark eyes locked with hers. "What do you want, Quinn?"

Something about the question felt heavy and meaningful. He wasn't asking about her career. He was talking about them.

"You." The immediate, genuine response surprised her. Made her feel exposed. "*This*, I mean," she clarified.

"You've got me." He cradled her jaw, tracing her cheekbone with his thumb. "So now what do you want?"

"I don't know." She shrugged, keeping her tone light. "What do you want?"

"This isn't about me. This is about you being comfortable with asking for whatever you want." He pressed a lingering kiss to her lips. "Demanding whatever it is you need. You deserve that, Quinn. And any man worthy of you would be willing to give that to you."

"You're proposing we play a naughty game of Simon Says?"

He chuckled. "If it's easier to think of it that way."

Tempting. She swallowed hard, her skin on fire with the possibilities. A vision of this beautiful man on his knees worshipping her body flashed through her brain. "You're saying I should take control during sex? What brought this on?"

Max dragged a thumb across her lower lip. "Being with you is incredible, Quinn. But sometimes it feels like you're holding back. I don't want you to feel like you need to do that with me. You should say or do whatever feels good for you. Ask for whatever you need from me."

"Maybe you haven't noticed, but you do a pretty damn good job of anticipating what I want and what I need." She kissed him again. "I assure you—I have no complaints."

"I'm glad to hear it." Max trailed a finger along her collarbone, and she trembled slightly at his touch. "But I want this to be just as amazing for you as it is for me."

"In my experience, men don't take instructions in the bedroom very well. They consider it an attack on their manhood."

"Ah, you've been with one of those guys." He sighed. "The dumb, selfish fucks who never learn to please a woman because they're too concerned about getting off themselves. They don't realize how much better the experience would be if they'd learn to *thoroughly* please their partner."

Max brushed back her hair and tucked a few strands behind her ear. "If a dude gets upset because you're telling him what does or doesn't feel good to you, run. Because he's not just selfish in the bedroom. He's selfish about everything."

"God, that's true." Quinn sat up, scooting back against the headboard. She cleared her throat. "So all of the *skills* you've acquired… Never mind."

Quinn felt her cheeks getting warm as she smoothed the comforter over her lap. It was none of her business what Max had done in the years they'd been apart.

"Yes." He sat up beside her. "I learned by listening and observing, but also by asking." He stroked her cheek.

"What you've done and with whom…is none of my business."

Max's expression was suddenly serious. "Ask me anything you want to know, Quinn."

There was something so sincere in his gaze. Butterfly wings fluttered in her stomach. Her heart felt as if it might burst. She wasn't supposed to be falling for Max Abbott. She wasn't supposed to be feeling any of what she was feeling right now.

Quinn's breath hitched. "Make love to me, Max. Now."

Desire. That was the emotion she should focus on. Not whatever it was that made her feel like her heart might beat right out of her chest.

There was a momentary sadness in his expression. Her tactic wasn't lost on him. He'd wanted to do an emotional deep dive. She wanted sex, plain and simple.

"That's a command, not a question," he said.

"You said I should ask for whatever I want."

He chuckled, a grin spreading across his incredibly handsome face. "I did, didn't I?"

Max retrieved a strip of condoms from the nightstand and reached to turn off the bedside lamp.

"No." She stilled his hand, her heart racing as he met her gaze. "Leave the light on."

Max's eyes widened momentarily. Then a knowing grin curved the edges of his sensual mouth. "Yes, ma'am."

"And Max?" She trailed a hand down his stomach and cupped his growing erection.

"Yes?"

"How sturdy would you say this headboard is?" Quinn asked with a smile.

"Fuck," he whispered. "This is going to be one hell of a night, isn't it?"

It was, and she was going to enjoy every single minute of it. Because as good as things were between them, their little affair had a built-in expiration date. In a few months she'd leave Magnolia Lake, and eventually she'd return to Atlanta. But this time she'd walk away without expectations or regrets.

Max's eyes fluttered opened. An involuntary smile crept across his face. His night with Quinn had been beyond amazing. It was a reel that would replay in his head until the end of time. He reached for Quinn, but she was gone.

Rule number three: no overnights.

Max wasn't sure which he found more exasperating: being kicked out of Quinn's bed or waking to discover that she'd disappeared from his.

He grabbed his phone and checked the time. Apparently, great sex promoted sound sleep. He'd slept right through his alarm. Now he needed to hurry if he didn't want to be late for another Monday morning meeting.

Max climbed out of bed and headed for the shower, hoping the day would end better than it had started.

Twenty

"Nice of you to join us, son," Duke Abbott teased as Max slid into the leather chair beside Zora.

"Sorry, I…overslept." Were his cheeks as bright red as they felt? His sister's knowing grin provided a clear answer.

Max avoided Zora's gaze. "So what's this about?"

"Your grandfather and I have discussed Parker's proposal. We've decided that selecting the next CEO based on merit is a reasonable request," his father said.

"You're naming Parker as the next CEO?" Zora asked.

"We haven't decided who will be the next CEO." Duke gave Zora a pointed look. "We've simply decided the title will be earned, not inherited. I'm sure we can all agree that's fair."

Parker shoved his glasses up the bridge of his nose and grinned. As if the crown had already been placed atop his peanut head.

"You can wipe that self-satisfied smirk off your face, Parker. You're not the only one who has a shot at this." The words left Max's mouth before he could rein them in. He was already cranky about waking up to a cold, empty bed after the night he and Quinn had shared. Now this. "So get over yourself and maybe take the self-righteousness down a notch."

"Maybe use that same energy you're coming at me with to step up your game," Parker suggested smugly.

Something in Max's head snapped. He jumped up and his chair tumbled backward, crashing to the floor. Max made his way toward Parker, who was sitting at the opposite end of the table from their father, like he was already king of the court.

Zora and his grandfather were calling Max's name, and Blake had rounded the table and stepped between him and Parker.

Blake braced his large hands on Max's shoulders. "Park is just trying to get a rise out of you, Max. No one here is questioning your abilities."

Max was still staring down Parker, who seemed oddly confused by the entire ordeal. As always, Parker said whatever popped into his head—the things most people mused about and didn't say aloud. It was difficult for him to know when to let thoughts just simmer in his brain rather than saying them.

Parker was making an admirable effort to do better in that regard when dealing with his fiancée. It would be nice if he tried a little harder where his family was concerned, too.

"Max, what's gotten into you, son? You've never allowed your brother to get to you like this before," his father said.

When Max turned to respond, he noticed his grandfather clutching the back of his head.

"Gramps, are you okay?" Max asked.

"Suddenly got the worse headache of my life." The old man wavered, as if dizzy. "Think I've got a touch of…"

Grandpa Joseph slumped over onto the table, unable to finish his sentence.

Quinn had forgotten how therapeutic cooking could be. She'd loved spending time in the kitchen with her grandmother before a massive stroke had taken her from them.

She'd been cooking for three days straight in Benji and

Sloane's state-of-the-art kitchen. A pot roast was going in the slow cooker. A ham was cooking in one of the ovens. A pot of collard greens cooked on the stove. And the surface of the granite countertop was dusted with flour and covered in strips of pie crust for the peach cobbler she was making.

Three days ago, she'd been floating around the office on a high after an amazing night with Max. Suddenly, an ambulance had come and taken Max's grandfather away. Everyone at the distillery was still stunned.

The indomitable Joseph Abbott had had a stroke caused by a blood clot, and he'd been hospitalized for the past three days, surrounded by his family.

She'd talked to Cole, who'd kept her updated on their grandfather's condition, and Zora, who'd mentioned that first day that they were eating God-awful food from the hospital cafeteria. Since then, Quinn had made it her mission to feed the Abbott family home-cooked meals, which Cole transported to the hospital. She'd probably cooked more in the past three days than she had in the past three years.

Quinn was grateful Joseph Abbott had chosen to work with Bazemore Farms, and she'd grown incredibly fond of the Abbott family. She was glad she could be there for them in some small way during such a stressful time. But more than anything, she wanted to be there for Max.

According to Zora, he blamed himself for his grandfather's stroke, despite the doctor's assurance that it was better that it happened at the office because they'd quickly gotten him medical assistance.

She'd tried calling Max, but he hadn't answered his phone. Nor had he responded to her text messages. He'd sent her a single email authorizing her to make any necessary decisions on his behalf regarding the brandy campaign—including representing King's Finest at the next trade show. And he'd copied his father, Zora and his assistant on it.

Quinn picked up her phone and reread the email for the fifth time. As if the terse business message might reveal something more. Like how Max was doing or if he needed her. Which was ridiculous.

She'd been the one who'd insisted on keeping their relationship a secret and on keeping it casual. What right did she have to be hurt by the fact that Max was clearly shutting her out now?

Quinn checked on the ham and greens, then typed out a text message to Zora.

How is Grandpa Joe?

Same.

How are all of you doing?

We're all holding up as best we can. Cole is trying to lighten everyone's spirits, but we're all on edge. Max is taking it especially hard. Still thinks this is his fault, though we've learned Gramps had a couple of mini strokes before this. Max hasn't slept much. Mom sent him home to get some sleep about an hour ago.

Give my love to Grandpa Joe and to everyone.

Will do. Thanks. We're all a wreck. You've been a godsend. Hugs

Quinn put down the phone, her heart breaking for Max. She could only imagine the guilt he was feeling. Max adored his grandfather. They all did. No wonder he'd taken it so hard.

Maybe Max wasn't ready to let her in or talk about what was bothering him. But hadn't she been the one who'd erected a wall around her heart first?

Max was simply following her lead.

She had laid out the rules. Rules meant to protect her heart and keep her from getting in too deep. But little by little she'd grown attached to Max and his family anyway. He'd been hinting at wanting more and trying to get her to open up to him. He'd even invited her to join him for Sunday night dinner at his parents' home—as a friend. But she'd maintained emotional distance, determined not to be hurt again.

Now it was Max who was keeping his distance. Reminding her of the casual nature of their relationship. They were business associates and fuck buddies. Not the person you turned to in a crisis.

It was what she thought she wanted. So why did she feel such a deep need to be there for Max? And so powerless because he wouldn't let her?

Maybe it was because the wound still felt so fresh from her own grandmother's death and her father's medical emergency just a few years ago. She'd allowed her emotions to cloud her judgment, let down her defenses and gotten involved in ill-advised relationships.

Was that what she was doing again?

Quinn washed her hands at the sink and returned to assembling the peach cobbler. She needed to focus on doing what she could to help the family. Especially since her own grandfather was in Arizona visiting his ill older brother. So she was making sure the Abbotts were well-fed and that their plans for the introduction of the new brandies continued to move forward.

It had been a long, somber day at the office, and she'd been cooking since she'd returned to the cabin. As soon as the ham and the cobbler were done, she'd turn in for the night.

Quinn preheated the second oven then hopped into the shower.

Afterward, she slipped on a short, vintage silk kimono she'd purchased at a little shop in Toronto a few years ago. There was something soothing about the brilliant turquoise hue and luxurious material with its colorful embroidery.

She returned to the kitchen to put the cobbler in the oven. Then she saw headlights approach, flashing through the front windows. She peeked outside.

Max.

He parked his SUV and got out.

Quinn's heart thudded in her chest. Had something happened since Zora's last text message?

She opened the front door, startling Max as he bounded up the stairs.

Lines creased his forehead and shadows hovered beneath dark eyes filled with sadness. He stepped inside, closing the door behind him.

"Max, is everything all—"

He captured her mouth in a hungry kiss that stole her breath and stoked the heat between her thighs.

She leaned into the kiss, parting her lips to give him access as his tongue sought hers. Lost in his kiss, everything faded away except his clean, woodsy scent and the warmth and solidity of his hard body.

Finally, Max pulled his mouth from hers, his chest heaving as he cradled her face in his large hands. His eyes met hers, as if there was something he needed to say, but he couldn't.

Oh no. No, no, no.

Quinn swallowed hard, panic filling her chest. She gripped the back of his T-shirt, terrified of the words Max couldn't bring himself to say.

REESE RYAN   169

"Baby, what is it? What's happened?" When he didn't answer, she prodded gently, "Tell me, Max. I'm here. Whatever you need, just—"

"*You*, Quinn," he said in a breathless whisper. "I need you."

He kissed her again, swallowing her gasp of surprise as he glided his hands down her body and lifted her.

Quinn hooked her legs around his waist. Gave into the comfort of his fiery kiss. Pushed aside the nagging questions about what his words meant beyond this moment.

He needed this. Needed her. And whether he was seeking solace in the arms of his lover or the luxury of losing himself to a few hours of passion, tonight she wanted to be that for him. To be a source of shelter from the storm brewing behind those dark eyes. Even if it was only for a little while.

Max carried her to bed. He toed off his shoes and stripped off his shirt, revealing the tattoos she'd kissed more times than she could remember.

The space between her thighs pulsed at the sight of this man's broad chest and toned body. His jeans hung low on his hips and her eyes were instantly drawn to the ridge beneath his zipper and then to the hungry gaze in his dark eyes as he climbed onto the bed, still wearing his jeans.

Max untied the sash of her silk robe. A wicked smile lit his dark eyes upon discovering she wore only panties beneath it. He pressed a sensuous kiss to her lips before trailing slow, tender kisses down her body. He seemed to relish each shudder of anticipation.

Hooking his thumbs in the waistband of her panties. he dragged them down her legs, dropping the scrap of fabric on the floor.

The hunger in his eyes made her belly flutter and something deep in her chest bloomed like a flower welcoming rays of sunlight. What she felt for Max wasn't just desire.

It was need and something more. Something she was afraid to give voice to—even in her own head.

When Max lapped at the sensitive nub between her thighs, all speculation about what tonight meant faded to the recesses of her mind. Her back arched and she clutched at the bedding as the sensation built with each stroke of his tongue.

He slid two fingers inside her, working them until her quiet whimpers ascended to desperate little pleas. Until body trembling, legs quivering and back arched, she tumbled over the edge, his name on her lips. Pleasure exploded in her center and radiated from her core, leaving her on a dreamy wave of indescribable bliss she'd only ever experienced with Max.

He crawled up the bed a little and laid his head on her stomach, his hand bracing her hip. Both of them were silent as she lay there with her eyes closed and her heart rate slowing. She placed a gentle hand on his head.

"Is it okay if I ask about Grandpa Joe now?"

Quinn wasn't being flippant or judgmental. She understood how Max must feel. She'd always appreciated inquiries about her father when he was ill, but there were times when she'd needed the mental reprieve of *not* discussing her father's health. Not being reminded that his life was teetering on the edge.

"Didn't leave much time for talk, did I?" Max's reserved chuckle vibrated against her skin. He kissed her belly. "The old man gave us quite a scare. But he got treatment quickly, and they expect him to make a complete recovery."

"It's okay to be overwhelmed by what happened, Max. I know how terrifying it is to almost lose someone you love." Quinn stroked his hair. "My dad suffered a heart attack a few years ago. He had to have triple bypass surgery. We'd just lost my grandmother a couple years earlier, so it was one of the scariest moments of my life."

Suddenly the timer blared in the other room.

"My peach cobbler." Quinn shot up. "Actually, it's *your* peach cobbler. I promised Zora I'd make one for your family, so I'd better not burn it."

Quinn slipped from beneath him and gave him a quick kiss before making a dash to the adjoining bathroom to freshen up.

"I won't be long." She slipped her robe back on. "But when I return, I don't expect to be the only one naked."

Max grinned. "Yes, ma'am."

Quinn hurried to the kitchen to get the cobbler out of the oven. It wasn't quite brown enough. But if she returned to a naked Max, there was a good chance she wouldn't make it out of the bedroom again. So she spent the extra ten minutes there in the kitchen jotting down her to-do list for the next day in her planner. And she tried not to overanalyze the words Max had uttered when he'd first arrived, the desperation in his eyes when he'd said them or the way they'd seemed to reach into her chest and squeeze her heart.

You, Quinn. I need you.

She shook the thought from her mind as she removed the ham and perfectly golden brown peach cobbler from the ovens and turned them off.

Quinn hurried back to the bedroom.

Max's jeans were on the floor, and he was in bed. His head was buried in the pillow as he snored softly.

She sighed, disappointed they wouldn't get to finish what they'd started.

Don't take it personally. The man has barely slept in three days.

Then there was the sheer mental exhaustion that accompanied anguish and guilt.

Quinn stood there frozen for a moment as she watched him. Max was an incredible man. A man she was definitely falling for. Or maybe she'd just never stopped loving him. Quinn pressed a soft kiss to Max's forehead and pulled the covers up over him. She stared at the empty space beside him.

Rule number three: no overnights.

It had been a hard rule. No exceptions. But wouldn't it be strange if she went to the guest room and left him alone here?

Quinn groaned quietly. Neither solution was perfect. But waking Max up and sending him home would just be plain cruel. Besides, if she was being honest, a part of her had always wondered what it would feel like to wake up with Max in her bed.

It seemed she would find out. Though this wasn't quite the scenario she'd imagined.

Twenty-One

Max woke the next morning, unsure of the time. He definitely wasn't at his own place. And though he was exhausted, he felt as if he'd been asleep for hours.

Rolling onto his back, he threw an arm across his forehead as he stared at the high ceilings with their exposed beams.

Benji and Sloane's cabin.

He glanced at the empty space beside him in bed, and the events of the previous night came rushing back. He'd crashed and burned spectacularly when Quinn had gone to the kitchen.

As desperately as he'd wanted to be with her, his body had won the battle. The sheer exhaustion of being at the hospital around the clock for the past three days had taken its toll, and he'd dozed off, breaking rule number three.

No overnights.

Unlike their decision to start seeing each other while in town, this wasn't something they'd discussed.

Not okay, Max.

He hadn't done it on purpose. But then again, maybe subconsciously he had. Because he'd wanted to spend the night with Quinn since that very first night at the hotel in San Francisco. And now things felt... different between them. Or maybe he was just projecting his own feelings onto Quinn.

Either way, he owed her an apology. First, for falling asleep before they'd actually gotten to the deed. Secondly, for staying over when it wasn't something she'd agreed to. And though he should probably just be content with their arrangement, a growing part of him needed to know where things stood between them. But first, he needed a shower. And he hoped to God there was a spare toothbrush around here somewhere.

After Max showered and got dressed, he followed the heavenly scent of bacon and waffles to the kitchen. Quinn was in that sexy little kimono again, but this time she wore a nightgown beneath it. Her hair was pulled into a messy topknot.

God, she was gorgeous. His mouth tugged into an involuntary grin.

How amazing would it be to wake up to this woman every morning?

Quinn gave him a sheepish smile, her brown eyes glinting in the sunlight. "Morning, sleepyhead."

"Sorry about that." Max dragged a hand down his face. "I don't sleep this late normally, and I know we don't do sleepovers…ever," he added.

Quinn flipped the bacon over on the griddle. "You don't normally spend three days straight awake at the hospital, worrying about your grandfather's health, either. So there's that." She returned her attention to the stove, but there was tension in her voice.

Was Quinn minimizing his breaking of their no sleepover rule because she genuinely felt it wasn't a big deal? Or was it because it was a *huge* deal and she'd rather tiptoe around the subject than address what it might mean for both of them?

Max settled onto a bar stool. "I can't thank you enough for how you've taken care of my family. The food has been amazing and having home-cooked meals has been a source of comfort for us during all of this. I hadn't had your cooking since—"

"Since I helped my grandmother fix meals for the farmhands that summer." Her smile turned sad. "My repertoire has expanded considerably since then. Waffles?"

"Please." He pushed up his sleeves.

She handed him a mug of piping hot coffee and gestured toward the cream and sugar on the counter.

Quinn joined him at the kitchen island where they ate bacon and waffles with peach cobbler flavored syrup in near silence. Neither of them seemed eager to discuss last night.

"Thank you for breakfast. Everything was delicious." Max patted his stuffed belly and stood once they were done eating. "Let me get the dishes."

"I've got it." She stood, too, waving him off.

Max sank back onto his bar stool and cleared his throat. "About last night—"

"Last night was fine." She moved their dishes to the sink. "Fantastic, in fact," she added with an almost shy smile. "I certainly have no complaints."

"Good to hear." He forced a small smile, uneasy about the wall she seemed to be erecting this morning. "Still, it was rude of me to fall asleep."

"Extenuating circumstances and all that."

Max walked over and slipped his arms around her waist. She smelled like summer peaches and sunshine and everything that was good about the summer they spent together. He nuzzled her neck.

Holding Quinn in his arms now didn't feel like revisiting the past. It felt like a glimpse into his future. But rather than dissolving into giggles or climbing him like a tree— her usual responses to him kissing the sensitive spot where her neck and shoulder met—Quinn's shoulders stiffened.

Max turned her in his arms and studied her face.

Was she angry with him?

"Look, Quinn, I know how this must seem… Me showing up at your door so late last night and then taking you straight to bed. But don't think that I—"

"If this is the part where you try to convince me that you didn't come here just for sex—don't. That's the very nature of our little arrangement." She smirked, returning to the dishes. "I'm obviously fine with that."

"True, but last night was about more than that—"

"You're under a lot of stress right now." She shrugged. "Sometimes, we just need the comfort of human connection to get us through those times."

She was minimizing what they'd shared last night. As if it was just a meaningless hookup.

It hadn't been.

And as hard as she was trying to convince herself otherwise, Quinn realized it, too. But then, being with Quinn had never felt inconsequential to Max. And despite the nature of their current arrangement, he doubted that any of their encounters had ever felt insignificant to her, either.

"Admittedly, once I saw you in this little robe," he teased, tugging at the silken material, "all bets were off. But I honestly didn't come here to take you to bed, Quinn. I came here because I really needed to see you." He lightly gripped her wrist to stop her from frantically scrubbing a pan.

The pan fell to the bottom of the sink with a clang.

"*Why* did you need to see me, Max?" She turned to him, nibbling on her lower lip. Despite asking the question, she seemed apprehensive about his answer.

His shoulders tensed and his heart beat double time.

Just tell her.

Max sucked in a deep breath, then slowly released it. "The past few days, I watched Blake and Parker at the hospital with Savannah and Kayleigh. They're both damn lucky to have them in their lives."

He hooked a finger in the sash of her robe and tugged her closer. She braced her hands on his chest to steady herself as she gazed up at him.

"Suddenly, I realized that all the things I've been feeling about us lately… I want that with you, Quinn. You're the only woman I've ever been able to imagine a future with. It scared the shit out of me that summer because neither of us was ready for it. But we're in a different place in our lives now. I'd like to see what the future has in store for us."

Quinn blinked; her lashes were wet. She seemed apprehensive. And the five or ten seconds of silence felt like an eternity to Max.

"That's incredibly sweet, Max." Quinn freed herself from his hold and swiped a finger beneath her teary eyes. "But this is a really emotional time for all of us and—"

"You think this is just some knee-jerk reaction to my grandfather's stroke?" Max asked.

"I'm not discounting your feelings," she said carefully. "But I can't risk mine on something that might only *seem* real to you now."

"If you're not interested in a relationship, I promise to respect that, Quinn. But if this is because—"

"I don't know if I can do this with you again." She blurted out the words suddenly, finally meeting his gaze for a moment before pacing the kitchen floor. "With a no-strings arrangement, there are no expectations, so no one gets hurt. But what you're proposing…that raises the stakes in a way I'm not sure either of us is prepared for."

Max rubbed absently at the ink on his chest. His wounded heart beat furiously beneath the long-healed skin.

Maybe she was right; he'd timed this poorly. But it didn't change how he felt.

Max placed his large hands on her shoulders to halt her

frantic pacing. "You're telling me that this is really just about sex for you—nothing more?"

"I'm saying that I need to be sure of my feelings and yours," she said.

"I *am* sure of what I feel for you." He cupped her cheek, his heart racing as she looked at him expectantly.

Say it. Now. Before you lose your nerve.

Max swallowed hard, his eyes not leaving hers. The corners of his mouth curved in a soft smile.

"I'm in love with you, Quinn, and I don't want to hide that anymore. I want to be with you and only you because you are the most amazing woman, and I am so damn proud of you. My heart belongs to you. It always has. I want everyone to know I'm yours and that you belong to me." He pressed a soft kiss to her lips. "Is that clear enough?"

Her brown eyes were wide and glossy with tears. She searched his face as if trying to determine the answer to a question she had yet to ask.

Quinn stood frozen, her heart swelling with emotion and her eyes brimming with tears. There were so many things she needed to say, but where did she even begin?

"Talk to me, babe. Please." Max rubbed a hand up and down her arm, as if trying to warm her. "Tell me what's going on in that brilliant mind of yours."

Wringing her hands, Quinn walked over to the front windows overlooking the lake. The sunlight filtering through the window warmed her skin. She took a deep breath, then sighed, turning back to face him.

"There's something I need to tell you. Something I should've told you before now."

"Okay." Max kept his voice even, but worry lines spanned his forehead. He extended a hand to her. "Let's sit down and talk."

Quinn put her hand in his and he led her to the sofa in

the great room. He squeezed her hand, as if to encourage her, but waited patiently for her to speak.

She turned toward him and met his gaze.

"Last year, I was engaged to a man I worked with. He was my boss's son," she admitted quietly. "The engagement didn't last very long, but that beautiful Marchesa gown I wore to your parents' anniversary party…it was a splurge for what would've been my engagement party."

"What happened?" Max frowned, gently caressing the back of her hand with his thumb.

"I ended it when I discovered him with his secretary. He felt I was overreacting. His father, who owned the firm, agreed. Neither of them took my rejection well. I stayed on, tried to be professional, like none of it had ever happened. But they held a grudge and eventually pushed me out of the firm. Due to a non-compete clause, I had to wait at least a year before I could work in the industry there again. That's the real reason I left Atlanta."

Quinn's cheeks stung and a knot tightened in her gut from the sheer humiliation of reliving that entire ordeal. One she should've seen coming.

She wiped angrily at the hot tears that leaked from the corners of her eyes. "Just like that, I flushed my career down the drain."

"I'm sorry you had to endure that, Quinn. But you're not to blame for what happened."

"Aren't I?" She tugged her hand from his and smoothed loose strands of hair before securing the knot atop her head. "I should never have gotten involved with my boss's son, and now I…" She sighed, letting her words trail off.

"And now you're afraid you're making the same mistake by getting involved with me." Max rubbed his chin. "So it's not just our history I'm battling. It's your history with him, too."

She shifted her gaze from his without response.

"Quinn, look at me." Max took her hand in his again, meeting her gaze. "I know I hurt you, and I am *really* sorry. I was young and stupid, and I had a lot to learn. I don't blame you for being wary about getting involved with me again. But sweetheart, I'm *not that* guy you were engaged to. I'm not even the guy I was thirteen years ago. Hurting you is the single biggest regret of my life, Quinn. We've been given another chance at our happy ending. There's no way I'm going to screw this up again. I promise you that."

She wanted to believe she could trust Max and that he wouldn't hurt her again. Because she wanted to be with him, too. She'd mused over the idea. Fantasized about what a real, adult relationship between them would be like. But the cautious part of her that had erected a fort around her heart was still terrified of taking the leap.

Once bitten, twice shy.

"I know you want an answer right now, Max, but—"

"No pressure, beautiful. I understand now. Take whatever time you need." Max stood, giving her a half smile. "Thank you again for breakfast. I'd better get back to the hospital."

"Thank you for last night." Quinn flashed a playful grin, hoping it masked the uneasiness she felt. She lifted onto her toes and pressed a tame kiss to his lips.

Max cradled her face and deepened their kiss, filling her body with heat and making her wish they could pick up where they'd left off last night.

Suddenly, he broke the kiss and released her.

Quinn's body protested. Her nipples throbbed and there was an insistent pulse between her thighs.

He lifted her chin gently, so their eyes met. "I'm sorry for what you went through in Atlanta, Quinn, and I'm glad you felt comfortable enough to share that with me. But that asshole's loss is our gain. I'm grateful you've come back into my life. These past few months have been so special for me, Quinn. I hope they have been for you, too."

Max pulled away, not waiting for a response. He shifted the topic instead. "You mentioned a care package you wanted me to take back to the hospital."

"Yes, right." She pulled the cardboard box neatly packed with all of the food she'd prepared out of the stainless steel refrigerator. Then she watched as Max loaded up his SUV and drove away. She sighed, missing him already.

Quinn checked her phone. She had a conference call soon with one of the vendors they'd met in Chicago.

Her personal life was a complicated mess, but at least the joint brandy project—though still in its infancy—had already hit a homerun. They'd inked a deal with JRS to carry the KFD line, including their brandies, in all of the restaurants they managed nationwide.

After tasting the product, vendors were clamoring for it and preorders already far exceeded even their most ambitious projections. Duke had indicated that they needed to discuss the possibility of expanding the facilities so they could increase production.

In a few more months, she would turn the project over to Max to be handled in-house, so she could go back to concentrating on the farm and on developing her own consultancy. News that should've thrilled her. But the thought of walking away from Max made her chest ache.

This was supposed to be purely physical and just for fun. No hearts involved.

So much for her simple plan.

She hadn't expected Max would spend the night. She certainly hadn't anticipated that he'd declare that he loved her and wanted a future with her. But Quinn had lain awake after nights with Max wondering if things could work out between them this time or if she was just setting herself up for more heartbreak. She'd had more than enough of that.

Fear is a piss-poor decision-maker. Don't ever make a decision strictly out of fear.

More of her grandmother's wisdom, which she'd invariably heeded in her career. But was she brave enough to follow her advice when it came to her heart?

Twenty-Two

Quinn paid the cashier for two caramel vanilla lattes and found an empty table in a secluded area of the hospital cafeteria. She slid into the chair and wrapped her hands around one of the steaming hot paper cups. A group of women in white jackets and colorful scrubs sat a couple of tables away.

Work had kept her preoccupied for the past two days. But not busy enough to prevent her from obsessively reflecting on her conversation with Max at the cabin. In quiet moments, his words echoed in her head. She could recall nearly every word, every gesture, every expression he'd used. She remembered that he'd smelled of her soap. His mouth had tasted like rich caramel-pecan bourbon coffee and there was a hint of the peach cobbler syrup she'd brought from Georgia by the case on his sensuous lips.

I'm in love with you, Quinn.

I want to be with you and only you.

I want everyone to know I'm yours and that you belong to me.

Those phrases had replayed in her head again and again for the past two days as she'd sorted through her jumble of emotions, confronted her immobilizing fears, and contemplated the realities of a future with Max Abbott—the man she'd first fallen in love with in that misty haze of being a wide-eyed college freshman.

"Quinn, hey." Max looked handsome but tired as he approached the table. He wore a button-down shirt and a pair of broken-in jeans.

"How's Grandpa Joe doing?" She resisted the urge to bound out of the chair and wrap her arms and legs around him. It'd only been two days since she'd seen him. Yet she'd missed him desperately, and she had been counting the hours until she would see him again.

"Gramps is good, all things considered. Full of fire and ready to blow this joint. He'll probably outlive us all." Max seemed to debate whether he should hug her. But he sat down in the chair opposite her and folded his hands on the table instead. "Thanks for meeting me here. They're running a battery of tests on Gramps, and I wanted to be here for them."

"I thought maybe you could use some coffee." She slid the paper cup toward him.

"Thanks." He gripped it but didn't take a sip. His attention was focused on her. "You wanted to talk?"

"I do." Quinn widened her nervous smile and tucked her hair behind one ear. She extended her hands across the table, palms open.

Max relaxed his cautious smile. His dark eyes seemed hopeful as he took her hands.

After all of the nights they'd spent together over the past few months, his touch still made her skin tingle and sent chills up and down her spine.

"The other day, when you said that…" Quinn stumbled over the word. She'd repeated Max's declaration in her head again and again, but this was the first time she was saying the words aloud.

"That I'm in love with you?" he offered, a smirk curving one side of his mouth. He was barely able to contain his amusement and seemed to get a kick out of being the one on the offensive this time around.

"Yes." She took a deep breath before meeting his gaze again. "It was a really beautiful moment. But when you compared what you wanted with me to what Blake and Savannah have... I'll admit it freaked me out a little."

"It kind of freaked me out to realize it." He brushed his lips over the back of her hand. "But it's the truth. We've already missed so much time together, Quinn, and I know that's my fault," he added quickly. "But I don't want to miss another minute with you. I want you in my life, in my bed. I want you to be my plus-one. And I want you beside me at those Sunday night family dinners. To quote Roger Troutman, I want to be your man. Plain and simple."

Quinn laughed at his mention of yet another song he'd played for her that summer. Her vision blurred with tears. "Good. Because I love you, too, Max. And I want all of those things with you, too."

"God, I'm glad to hear you say that." He stood, rounding the table and pulling her into a tight hug. Max breathed a sigh of relief that gently rustled her hair. "When I didn't hear anything from you the past couple of days... I'll admit I was a little worried." He chuckled. "But I would've waited for as long as it took to hear those words." He gave her a quick kiss, his gaze lingering on her lips.

"We should get out of here before we're thrown out for making out in the hospital cafeteria." Quinn's cheeks warmed as she glanced around at the people staring at them.

"Good idea. Besides, Gramps is really looking forward to seeing you," Max said. "Walk back with me?"

She nodded and they grabbed their lukewarm coffees and linked hands as he led her toward a bank of elevators. Max pushed the button.

"In case it wasn't already obvious, you're invited back to my place for part two of our sleepover. We have some unfinished business, and I've been thinking of creative uses for that peach cobbler syrup." Quinn smirked.

"Ooh…not fair." He tugged her onto the elevator once the door opened and pushed the button for the fifth floor. "You're not the one who'll have to hide a raging hard-on from his entire family."

He backed her up against the elevator wall and kissed her, both of them trying not to spill their coffee. They got off on the fifth floor and he pulled her aside before they entered a set of secure doors. "Before we walk through those doors, you need to understand what you're getting yourself into," he said ominously.

"Okay," she said apprehensively. "Let's hear it."

He drank most of his cooled coffee then discarded the cup.

"My brothers will tease us mercilessly. My sister will try to push us down the aisle. And my mother will start dropping hints about grandchildren in a month or two, tops."

"You're exaggerating, Max." Quinn laughed, relieved. "Besides, I adore your family, and I'm prepared for whatever they dish out, as long as we're in this together."

"Don't say I didn't warn you." Max kissed her, then pulled away. He stared at her for a moment, a blissful smile animating his face. "By the way, not a proposal, but if I haven't already made it clear, I have every intention of marrying you, Quinn Bazemore."

"You'd better." She grinned. "Otherwise, good luck explaining to some woman why my initials are inked on your chest. *Awkward.*"

"Good point, and that reminds me, we need to talk about which of my favorite poems you should incorporate in your tattoo," he teased, barely able to restrain his grin.

The two of them broke into laughter as they walked through the doors and into a private family waiting room, hand in hand.

Iris's brows furrowed with confusion and she whispered loudly to Duke, "I thought Quinn was Cole's girlfriend."

His father responded, "I think Cole did, too."

Cole shot them both a death stare and shook his head. "No one in this family ever listens to me."

He stood and hugged Quinn, then he shook his brother's hand. They'd been making more of an effort to get along since Quinn had been spending time with both of them. "About time you two knuckleheads figured this out. And absolutely no pressure, but it would be nice to have someone else in this family besides Zora who actually gets me."

"I thought you said Zora would be the one pushing us down the aisle," Quinn whispered to Max loudly.

Zora bounded out of her chair and launched herself at Max, hugging him and then Quinn. "We can tag team the whole wedding thing," she said to Cole.

Max and Quinn settled into chairs next to each other amid the questions and excitement of his family. They were all inquisitive and teasing, but also warm and welcoming, making her feel like she was already one of their own.

Maybe she and Max had taken the long route to get here, but she was exactly where she'd always wanted to be.

* * * * *

ONE LAST KISS

JESSICA LEMMON

For those of you who
believe in second chances.

Prologue

Five and a half years ago, New Year's Eve

"Daddy," Gia Knox said from between clenched teeth. But her father, busy bragging on her as per his usual, wouldn't be dissuaded. His current brag was her graduating the Massachusetts Institute of Technology with honors, and the impressive work she would soon do at the family company, ThomKnox.

"She inherited her brains from me, of course." Jack Knox gave his only daughter a wink and wrapped an arm around her.

"Don't be silly, Jack," Gia's mother, Macy, interjected. "Everyone knows our daughter inherited her intelligence from me. Let's leave these kids alone. We're ruining their fun."

Macy whisked Jack away so suddenly, Gia was left alone with one of the most talented web designers in the company. She shuffled her feet as best she could in black Louboutins, clasping her hands in front of her black glittery skirt. By the time she was fiddling with her long beaded necklace over her sequined top, she realized she was having a rare awkward moment.

"Sorry about that," she muttered to the man before her. "They're proud. Anyway, it's great to meet you, Jayson."

"Cooper," he said, the deep timbre of his voice glancing off each one of her ribs. "No one calls me Jayson."

"Well, then I definitely won't call you Cooper. I pride myself in being unique." She'd meant the quip to be a cute conversation salve to the embarrassing display by her dad, but it came out sounding flirty. And Jayson responded.

"You, Gia Knox, are definitely unique." His smile twitched beneath a trimmed neat goatee before vanishing. That half smile was completely attractive. Disarmingly so. All of him was. He had broad shoulders and wore a suit well. She'd surreptitiously checked him out more than once while her father was rattling off her GPA.

Jayson's thick wavy dark hair was cut professionally and close, but his facial hair lent him an air of mystery. And those eyes. Blue and piercing, she'd bet they didn't miss a thing.

"Well, then, Jay," she said, testing the new nickname and receiving an eyebrow arch in response, "you'll either be enchanted or disappointed to hear I'm joining the tech team."

"Enchanted," he answered without hesitation. "Definitely enchanted."

"Sixty seconds!" Her brother Brannon called out, blowing into a noisemaker and earning a round of cheers and applause. Nearly every employee of ThomKnox was present at the New Year's Eve celebration, including Gia's family since they *were* ThomKnox.

Partygoers followed Bran's lead and pressed in toward the center of the ballroom, leaving Jay and Gia to watch them go.

"The moment we've all been waiting for," she said as the crowd began a sloppy midnight countdown at the thirty-second mark. "A bunch of employees making out at the stroke of the new year."

This time when her gaze clashed with Jayson's, it stuck. She found herself unable to look away. The moment his eyes left hers they took an inventory of her mouth.

She felt the brush of his gaze the way she might have felt his hand. Or his lips. It was intimate. It was heady. He had her thoroughly distracted and totally off-kilter. She'd had one glass of champagne, no more, but felt as if she'd polished off a bottle and then someone had hit her over the head with it.

Had she ever met a guy and felt this much *longing*? And what was it about *him*—but she knew. Jayson was as charmed by her as she'd been by him. Rarely was attraction ever that equal.

At that second—and the three that followed—she imagined satisfying her longing and kissing Jayson Cooper. Lifting to her toes and pressing her mouth to his. He smelled good from where she stood, and she'd bet he was absolutely intoxicating close up.

There's only one way to find out.

Jayson, his gaze trickling back up to hers, leaned forward the slightest bit.

Then a red-haired woman who was even shorter than Gia and wearing a skirt that was a lot tighter than Gia's, crashed into him.

"Cooper, come *on*! We'll miss the countdown!" The redhead bounced as she wrapped both her arms around one of his. Her headband bobbed, the words *Happy New Year* waving. "Hi," she chirped. "I'm Shelly."

"Gia Knox." Gia shook the other woman's hand, feeling the loss of Jayson's attention when he rigidly looped his arm around his date's waist.

As if summoned, Gia's boyfriend, Tom, approached. "There you are."

Tom leaned in to kiss her cheek and she pasted on a plastic smile.

"It was nice to meet you, Jay," Gia called as Tom pulled her toward the crowd. Jayson nodded, his frown slight but visible, as Shelly towed him to the middle of the room.

Gia and Jay watched each other as the countdown continued, as more and more distance separated them and more and more people came between them.

Three.

Two.

One.

"Happy New Year!" the crowd shouted as silver and gold confetti rained down on the ballroom.

"Happy New Year, baby," Tom said to Gia and then captured her mouth in a kiss. She pushed aside the inconvenient—and possibly insane—attraction she felt toward Jayson and focused on her date. But Tom's kiss barely registered on her *oh, baby* scale. Her heart wasn't racing the way it was a moment ago. Her stomach wasn't clenched in delicious anticipation as it had been a moment ago.

She leaned into the kiss, determined to bury that errant blip of lust. She was soon going to be working with Jayson Cooper, and indulging in anything, especially a fantasy, wasn't a great start to her career at ThomKnox.

That night became a night she never ever forgot. Not because of Tom or the party or the tepid New Year's kiss. No, the most memorable part of that night was meeting a handsome, blue-eyed stranger that, little did she know at the time, would soon become her husband…and soon after that, become her *ex*-husband.

One

The technology department was a big, open bullpen-style seating area with Jayson Cooper in the mix with his brethren. Gia, who'd worked in tech for years, had recently had a title update. She'd taken over as chief marketing officer after she and Jayson divorced. Her office was still on this floor, off to the side, with windows so she could look out on all of them.

Jayson didn't used to mind her being nearby.

Now, though, he *minded*.

It was closing in on a year and a half since their divorce. Moving on was difficult when the woman you were to move on *from* was directly in your line of vision day after day.

He was being looked after by a woman who'd refused to let him look after her during their entire marriage. What good was a husband whose wife refused to let him care for her?

No good, that's what.

He and Gia worked well together for their sakes as

much as the sakes of their coworkers. They gave each other crap—the good-natured kind—at work and made sure to always end the day on a positive note. It'd been working… for a while.

He thought he knew how to protect and love a woman, but when it came to Gia Knox-Cooper, he'd been at sea. She was independent and headstrong and rarely if ever met him halfway. He'd known that about her going into their marriage but had expected things to change after the "I dos." Each of them had only grown further apart. Which was why their divorce had been a blessing. He understood now that were better separate.

Taylor Thompson, soon to be Taylor Knox as she was the fiancée of Royce Knox, swept into the department and past Jayson's desk.

"Coop, can you pop into Gia's office with me for a second?"

"Sure thing." He rose and followed Taylor, who was dressed smartly in a no-nonsense black dress, her dark blond hair pinned at the back of her head. She was second in charge as COO of the company, professional and spunky and exactly what Gia's oldest, most rigid brother had needed in his life. She'd sprung a pregnancy announcement on Royce last year, and now those two were to be wed. With better results, Jayson hoped, than his marriage to Gia.

Anyway, their wedding ceremony would likely include their daughter, born right after Addison and Brannon Knox's wedding six months ago. Or, as Jayson liked to think of it, the night when he *nearly* lost his damn mind and slept with his ex-wife.

In her office, Gia was leaning back in her leather executive chair, her long dark hair spilling over her petite shoulders. Her red dress one that would make Jessica Rabbit weep with envy.

Gia was petite, curvy and hiding a beautiful body beneath that frock. It was a body he'd brought to the pinnacle of euphoria time and time again. If physical compatibility equaled a successful marriage, they'd still be together.

Taylor slapped two cream-colored notecards onto the desk and two pens on top of them. "Fill these out. Each of you."

Gia and Jayson exchanged glances before Gia picked up one of the cards to examine it more closely. "It's filled out, Tay."

"So's mine," Jayson said, picking up the other card. His name was right there. *Jayson Cooper* and beneath it, the box "attending" was marked with an X.

Taylor snatched the card from him and pointed at the blank area beneath it. "This reads 'Plus-one, yes or no' and there is a line there for a name for the seating chart."

Taylor handed the card back to him. "Yes," she said and then snapped her gaze to Gia. "Or no. This isn't twenty questions. It's *one*. I don't care what the answer is, but I need a final headcount for the caterer."

He narrowed his eyes at Gia and she mimicked his reaction.

"I'm a yes," she answered cheerily, marking the box with a flourish. "But as my date's a celebrity, he'd rather not have the catering staff know his name." She handed over the card, her smile forced, Jayson guessed, for his benefit.

"Really?" Taylor asked, proving this was news to her. "We'll talk later. What about you, Coop?"

"Same situation," he answered, marking the yes box. "Ironically."

Gia crinkled her nose, but he kept his gaze trained on Taylor.

"There. Now was that so hard?" Taylor offered a saccharine-sweet smile and then spun on one heel and left the office.

"Holy Bridezilla," Gia said once she was gone. "She's

my best friend and I love her, but *yikes*." Then she looked at him. "I didn't know you had a date."

"I didn't know you had a date, either." Going for casual, he tucked his hands in his pockets and waited.

Silence invaded for a few uncomfortable seconds while she examined her fingernails.

"Well, I didn't want to attend my other brother's wedding and have a repeat of what happened at Bran's." She then fidgeted with a pen. "That was a mistake."

Her pulling him into a spare bedroom at the mansion and kissing him so hard he saw stars was a *big* mistake and she wasn't the only one who thought so. Since then he'd had trouble keeping his mind on work and keeping their above-board banter from crossing into sexual territory.

His mind returned again and again to the way she'd tasted that night—like champagne, and a woman he hadn't had a sampling of for too long. If there was one essence he was powerless against it was the rare and intoxicating flavor of his ex-wife.

They'd made out hot and heavy, hiding in the spare guest bedroom after the wedding. Her dress was rucked up to her waist while she plunged her hand down his pants. The memory of the heat, the *want* and the sheer high of being able to take her where she needed to go was a memory that hadn't faded for him in the least.

He clasped his hands in front of his crotch to hide his reaction, and forced his thoughts on what had interrupted them that night.

Taylor's going-into-labor screech.

There. Thinking of that helped quell the lust.

"I didn't realize you were seeing anyone," Gia said, obviously fishing for details. Details she wouldn't get since Jayson didn't actually have a date. He guessed now he'd have to find someone. A celebrity apparently, since he'd coat-tailed Gia's story with a story of his own. He sure as shit wasn't admitting he lied to save face.

"It's new," he answered. "I didn't realize you were seeing anyone either." He'd stayed similarly single. Work kept him busy, but even if it hadn't he had no interest in a relationship. Once bitten...

Last fall he'd attended Bran's wedding alone, not thinking a thing of it. Jayson was still considered family outside of the office. Bran and Royce were like brothers. That said, even if he'd had one, bringing a date to a Knox family gathering would have been strange for him and stranger for his date.

It hadn't occurred to him until now that Gia might have a date for *this* wedding. He'd assumed she was following the same unwritten rule: no bringing dates around the ex.

Guess not.

"The tablet update is nearing release," he said, guiding the conversation back to the safe, neutral ground of Thom-Knox. Where he and Gia were concerned, work might well be the last frontier of neutral territory. They'd had their differences in the past—namely him working hard to make her happy and her resisting his every effort—but here they had the same goal.

ThomKnox was the number one priority in their lives. They'd always do what was best for the company.

And, in this case, he thought as he took a seat to tell her about the latest software update in detail, the best thing for the company was Gia and him getting along.

Together or not.

Two

Six months ago at Bran's wedding

This is crazy.

You're crazy.

We're both crazy!

But oh, did Jay taste good. Really damn good. After being without sex for so long, Gia was beginning to worry about ill effects. She'd gone on a few random dates over the summer, since not dating would be admitting she wasn't over her ex, but each of those dates had ended with a good-night kiss that had only made her think of Jayson Cooper. So while he was totally over her, evidently she was still affected by him.

Case in point.

His tongue, though. Who could deny how good he was with it? Either tangling with hers or gliding down her neck. He suckled on her pulse point while his fingers lifted her dress to do what he was best at: pleasure her.

Fingers in her panties, he slipped along her folds, driving her wild. She moaned into his mouth. He kissed her harder, trying to quiet her. Possibly the only part crazier than carrying on with him was doing it in her parents' vineyard mansion after her brother's wedding. When she saw the guests filtering outside, either to leave or enjoy cocktails around the fire, she'd rushed him into the nearest spare room.

No one had noticed them missing. Nor would they if she could keep her *moaning* to a minimum. A challenge, given his touch was sending her into an orgasmic stupor.

It didn't take long.

She gripped his shoulders hard, pulled her mouth from his and came. She allowed herself a breath or two before her hand was shakily finding its way to his pants. She had his belt undone, zipper down, and was cradling several inches of his budding erection when it happened.

A scream of pain shattered the air—coming from the back patio and from, she guessed, a very pregnant Taylor.

Jayson snapped his mouth from Gia's, blinking hard as if trying to focus. She held her breath and listened. A going-into-labor Taylor shouted again.

Talk about a buzzkill.

"Damn," he said, which is probably what Gia would have said had she been able to speak after her powerful release.

And, oh, was her orgasm a good one. She'd been in charge of her own pleasure since she and her ex went kaput. It was irksome to be reminded of what she'd been missing.

"Get dressed, G," he said, his raspy voice dancing along her nerve endings. He moved her hand out of his pants, flashed her a smile that made her knees weaker, and then kissed her palm.

"What did we do?" she muttered. There was no good end to this night if they slept together, intellectually she'd known that. Yet look how close they'd come to actually sealing the deal!

What was she thinking?

She *wasn't* thinking. Plain and simple…

Gia, chin in her palm, eyes unfocused and gazing into the distance, blinked back to reality.

Her blue cheese–stuffed-olive dirty martini was half gone, but then she'd arrived at the bar early on purpose. She hadn't intended on daydreaming about her ex-husband, or reminding herself that she'd been without an orgasm of that caliber in over six months. She'd arrived early and drunk down half a martini for one reason: she needed to bolster her confidence before meeting her celebrity date.

Blinking the bar into focus, she sucked in a breath and blew it out. Other couples dotted the room, drinks in front of them, the low candles on the table setting the tone: romantic. Why did she choose someplace this romantic? She should have invited him to coffee…

Denver "Pip" Pippen, skateboarding superstar and hot cult god, was about to be interviewed for the role of a lifetime: to be her date to Royce's and Taylor's wedding.

Not that he knew that.

No, she hadn't had a date when she'd marked the RSVP card. But, with Jayson standing there looking as gorgeous and distracting as ever, she realized that attending another wedding without a date could land her in the guest bedroom with him again.

That.

Could not.

Happen.

She'd found Pip's profile on Divinely Yours, a dating app for the wealthy and elite. Not quite A-listers, but not D either. The app was recommended to her about a year ago by a well-meaning friend. At the time she'd shrugged it off, too focused on the ThomKnox tablet launch to dream of throwing herself to the wolves on a dating app. But after filling out Taylor's RSVP card under duress, Gia decided that the dating app might not be the worst idea ever.

Tonight, she'd find out.

She spotted Denver the moment he breezed through the entrance. He carried with him a certain amount of charisma that turned more than her head. As the hostess walked him over, Gia tested her own reaction. She'd seen photos, and videos, online, but this was Denver Pippen in the flesh. That was always a different experience.

His longish dark blond hair was messy and wavy. He wore a baggy T-shirt and jeans—casual but designer, and Converse sneakers. He shot her a smile that took up most of his face in the most charming way imaginable.

Yes. He'd do nicely.

"You must be Pip," she said, offering her hand.

She hadn't expected a demure kiss to the hand and wasn't disappointed. Instead he said her first name, dragging it into a prolonged "Jee-ahh" and kissed her on the cheek.

When he backed away she noticed the silver scar on his eyebrow, and another on his upper lip. She knew from videos of his skateboarding stunts that Denver also had plenty of scars on his upper arms and calves. Somehow, on him, the messy hair and scar combo worked.

"Fancy place." His lazy speech was half surfer dude and half stoner.

"I ordered already. I'm terribly impatient." She fingered the stem of her martini.

"Rad." He flagged down a waitress and ordered a beer. He was polite and brought forth a genuine smile from the waitress. *Nice.* Had he been rude, Gia would have had to leave and gone back to square one. He was doing well so far.

"So, ThomKnox. Computers. Cell phones. All that techy stuff." He wiggled his fingers as if he were talking about sorcery instead.

"That's the gist of it."

"What's your jam over there?"

"I run the marketing department."

"Rad."

She sipped her martini, hiding a smile. *Rad*, indeed. She'd always thought that with her MIT degree she'd be *running* the tech team, but that position had gone to Jay.

Her father had assured her that Jayson was the right fit, and that he'd preferred Gia to be in a higher position, one of more prestige at ThomKnox. But when Jack's own CEO position had come up for grabs, Gia was content to let her brothers duke it out. Literally, as it were.

Newly divorced, she'd cashed in on another interest and opted to run Marketing instead. On good days she stood behind her decision to nurture her need to lie low. On bad days, she wished she'd insisted on taking over the department she loved.

Pip rapped his knuckles on their table to the beat of the music and drew her from her musings. With her eyes, she traced the scars on his hands.

"How did skateboarding become a passion?" she asked.

"My dad bought me a board when I was twelve. He used to do it. He was killer. Once I landed my first big jump, I was hooked." He held up one injured hand, where his middle finger bent at an unnatural angle. "Never deterred by danger."

"I guess not." From what she'd read on his Wikipedia page, Denver Pippen had broken bones. A lot of them. "Once I crashed, I'd be done. I'm not much of a risk taker."

She winced at the truth behind that admission, recalling the way she'd ducked out of the tech department after the divorce. She'd loved her job, but after she and Jayson split she couldn't bear to be "under" his authority another second. She needed space, and while she didn't have it in physical form, since her office was still on the tech floor, at least they weren't quibbling over who ran the weekly meetings.

"Why would you risk ruining those beautiful brains?" Denver flipped his palm over and motioned for her hand. Intrigued, she slipped her hand into his. Rough. Calloused. "I looked you up. MIT, smarty-pants. You're the prize Knox. So why'd you swipe on my mug on Divinely Yours?"

Good question. She'd waded through a sea of billionaires, millionaires, actors and video game creators. Pip was wildly different from someone she would normally choose—different from who anyone would choose for her. Pip was a guy who would be a good short-term solution to a problem. Since she wasn't ready to submerge herself entirely into the dating pool, she figured he'd be a perfectly good date to the wedding. He wouldn't have the wrong impression about how serious they were, and he'd likely walk away without looking back.

Instead of telling him he was a convenient solution, she went with a more palatable answer. "I liked your face."

He grinned. It was a handsome face.

"I like your face, too, *Jee-ahh*. So what's up? Drinks on a Monday at six o'clock? This screams trial." He drank from his beer glass. "What's the real gig?"

He was sharper than he wanted others to believe. And direct.

She lifted an eyebrow. "Now who's the smarty-pants?"

His laugh was a low, rolling chuckle.

She held on to the stem of her martini glass and told him the truth. "I need a date for my brother's wedding. It's next Saturday."

"And you thought of me?" Humor radiated off him. "You want to piss off your parents or make someone jealous?"

She wasn't trying to make Jayson jealous. Nor did she care if her parents were upset by her attending solo or with a date. What she did care about was the seemingly undeniable lure of her ex-husband.

The way Jay could look at her from across a room and make her heart skip a beat and her brain forget their checkered past. An innocent, polite dance at the last wedding reception had turned into more when his hand moved to her lower back and he'd laid his lips against her ear.

She couldn't let that happen again.

"A bit of both," she lied to her date.

"I'm your guy." Pip held up his beer glass in a toast.

He wasn't, not permanently, but he'd fill a much-needed void. Smiling, Gia tapped her glass with his.

Three

The woman lying in the sand was tall, given the way her limbs splayed attractively into a pose as she leered at the camera lens.

Gia's claim she was dating a celebrity had given Jayson an idea. He'd called his stepbrother, Mason, later that day and, as luck had it, learned that Mas had a photoshoot scheduled with a supermodel.

Cha-ching.

Mason squatted in the sand in front of the woman and gave her commands like "sultry, now sweet, give me a smile" while the shutter clicks from his camera fired.

Jayson had heard enough teasing over the years to last a lifetime. *Mason and Jayson, are you two twins or something?* The answer was obvious just by looking. Jayson had a wider, thicker build than his brother. Mason was tall and slim, with an added four inches of height. They'd both had goatees years ago, but Jayson had abandoned his. Now he either shaved or didn't and those were the only two options.

"Beautiful, Natasha," Mason praised the model as he lowered his camera. *Beautiful Natasha* was an apt nickname. The bikini-clad goddess with sand stuck to her boobs had graced many a magazine. She was on the cover of last year's *Sports Illustrated* swimsuit edition. This year she'd been replaced on the cover, but was still featured inside, and today she was shooting her own calendar.

Landing *the* Natasha Tovar was a big win for Mas. He'd started his career taking family portraits, made a brief foray as a wedding photographer—Jayson and Gia's wedding, actually—and then Mason had stumbled into shooting models, which was harder than one might imagine in California.

"We have it?" Natasha brushed sand from her supple body before slipping on a white "robe," for lack of a better term.

Jayson could see right through it and when the cups of her bikini top wet the robe, they were a pair of fluorescent orange globes he had trouble looking away from.

"Who's this?" She toweled her hair and walked every inch of her mostly legs body toward Jayson.

"This is my brother, Jayson Cooper. Goes by Cooper." Mason slanted a glance from Natasha to Jayson, his eyebrows winging upward as if to say *I told you she was perfect.*

"Nice to meet you, Cooper." She extended a hand, which he accepted. She left sand in his palm. She didn't introduce herself and Jayson figured it was because she didn't have to. He possessed a penis therefore he should know who she was. She excused herself and walked up the beach toward a trailer.

"She's putting that wiggle into her walk for you," Mason said. He thumbed through some of the shots on his Canon while the lighting guy left behind his umbrellas and reflector panels to seek out the food truck parked in front of the more populated part of the beach. "You hungry?"

"Always," Jayson said.

"That food truck sucks—" Mason tipped his head to indicate the direction his lighting guy went "—but I brought Chester's homemade tamales."

Jayson's stomach roared. Mason's husband made the best tamales on the planet. "I am not above eating half your lunch. Especially if Ches made it."

"He's a keeper." Mason smiled.

At eighteen years old, after he graduated high school, Mason had come out officially. Jayson's response? A nonchalant shrug. He couldn't have been less surprised.

Mason's father, Albert, was alarmed, which helped Jayson realize that his stepfather rarely paid attention to life outside of work. But, Albert was also a good man and, while it took him longer, he accepted that his son was gay. Jayson's mom, Julia, was as unsurprised as Jayson. She'd helped Albert realize the truth: Mason was still Mason, no matter who he loved.

Anyway, that was ancient history. Mason and Chester had wed two years ago and were now like any boring married couple. Or, what Jayson thought a boring married couple should be like. He and Gia hadn't made it to "boring."

The brothers split a pan of tamales—thankfully, Mason had two forks—while sitting on a piece of driftwood watching the waves crash on the shore. Not a bad way to spend an afternoon.

"Can't believe you drove all this way to meet her. You must be desperate," Mason said around a final bite.

Jayson tossed his fork on the empty pan and swiped his teeth with his tongue. How to respond to that? Mason knew Jay needed a wedding date—an impressive one—but Jay hadn't told him why.

He hadn't shared with his brother that he'd brought Gia to orgasm six months ago and since then she'd shut him out like it'd never happened. It wasn't unlike right before their divorce hearing, when they'd had car sex. Unplanned, mind-blowing car sex. Then, five days later, Gia showed up at court with ice in her veins like she hadn't felt the earth move.

But mind-blowing car sex could not a marriage save. Whenever they were arguing, and that became more and more often near the end, she claimed she couldn't be with someone who "controlled" her. Jayson, whose real father had controlled their household with fists and fear, never reacted well to that accusation.

"Want to tell me why you need a supermodel as your wedding date?" Mason asked.

Well. What the hell.

"Gia is bringing a date to her brother Royce's wedding. I'm not showing up alone."

"How mature."

"Gia and I almost had sex not that long ago, Mas." Jayson shook his head. "Could have set us back years. Plus, the guy's famous. I had to step up."

"Famous?"

"Denver Pippen," Jayson said through his teeth. Apparently, Gia had met him for cocktails and things went well. Not that Jayson had been lurking around the office, but okay, he'd been *sort of* lurking. And he'd heard Gia excitedly telling Taylor that her date was going to be none other than skateboarding legend, Denver "Pip" Pippen.

"He's hot," Mason said. "That sports drink commercial where he leaps those cars…"

"Not helping." Jayson stood, frustrated. "What could Gia possibly have in common with a guy who's broken nearly every bone in his body? She's all brains and he pounds his into the pavement."

"And you thought Natasha would make her as jealous as you are." Mason smirked.

"I'm not jealous of that joker-smile idiot." He frowned, considering. "But if I see him kiss Gia, I'm going to give him a new scar."

Mason laughed. "It's past time you *both* got out there, Coop. You've been out of the game for a while."

"Thanks for the reminder." He pushed a hand through his hair. "It's not easy to date when your ex-wife is in your social circles."

Mason gave his brother the side-eye. "You two *stay* in each other's circles. You still act married. Divorced people move on. You two moved sideways."

Jayson shook his head, but he wasn't committed to it. Mason had a point. It wasn't easy to move on when the wound was fresh.

"I'm moving on now," Jay said, simply because he needed to say it out loud.

"Good. I've been priming Natasha today about your arrival. Told her you were hot and single. Then I mentioned that you were going to the Knox family vineyard over the weekend and you should have seen her face." Mason reached for his camera. "Actually you *can* see her face. I snapped a few shots of her reaction."

"You did tell her I needed her to be a plus-one to a wedding, didn't you?"

"And do all the legwork for you? Absolutely not. Natasha!" Mason called over his shoulder.

Her trailer door opened a crack. "More photos?"

"No photos. Cooper has something to ask you." Mas slapped Jay's shoulder as Natasha came out of the trailer and wiggled her way across the sand. "No time like the present."

Mason vanished inside and shut the door behind him.

Natasha, still in her see-through robe, peered up at Jayson expectantly. "What's up, Coop?"

Palming the back of his neck, Jayson smiled down at the supermodel. Here went nothing. "Are you busy on Saturday?"

Four

Denver drove separately to the wedding, which left Gia wringing her hands. She assumed he knew better than to wear a baggy T-shirt, jeans and Converse to a formal Knox event but...*did he?*

Her own attire was a blush pink bridesmaid's dress, short but flowy. The dress was higher in the front than the back, the spaghetti straps showing off her shoulders. The narrow bodice gave her a bit too much cleavage, but it wasn't as if she could help it.

Turned out there was no need to worry. Denver showed up for the wedding in head-to-toe Armani so it wasn't hard to forgive his windblown hair with sunglasses perched in it. He turned plenty of heads upon his arrival, mostly other men at the party who knew sports.

She hadn't spotted Jayson yet, but no matter. She'd achieved her goal. She was at Royce and Taylor's wedding with a date, which meant she wasn't going to trip over Jayson after she drank too much champagne and then try to take his pants off.

Denver made his way to the white folding chairs set up on the hill overlooking a stunning vineyard and Gia readied herself with the other bridesmaid, her very pregnant sister-in-law Addison.

Addi blew out a breath and gave Gia a steady smile. "I'm fine."

"It'd serve Taylor right if you went into labor right here, right now," Gia joked. After all it was Taylor who'd gone into labor after Addison's wedding.

"I'll see what I can do," Addi said with a laugh.

The violinist started playing. As maid of honor Gia began the procession of two. She stepped onto the white runner, smiling for the photographer. She winked at her brother Royce who looked uncharacteristically nervous, before her eyes tracked to Brannon who gave her a nod.

When her gaze naturally reached the final groomsman, her heart thundered. Of course she knew that Jayson was a groomsman and would be standing with her brothers, but she wasn't ready for the gut-punch vision of him at the end of an aisle she was walking. They'd been married outside as well, though their wedding was beachfront instead of among a backdrop of grapevines.

Her smile tightened along with her grip on the bouquet of lilacs. She could do this. She would. For her brother.

Positioned up front, she scanned the crowd for her date, finding Denver sitting in full man-spread in the second row. Before she could decide how she felt about that, Addison took her place next to Gia and Taylor began her descent.

Taylor made an ethereal bride in white, the short beaded train of her dress shimmering in the midday sunshine. Tears pricked Gia's eyes as she watched her best friend take Royce's hand, and they rolled down her cheeks as she considered that her best friend was about to become her *sister*.

Once Royce had kissed his bride, and Addison and Gia had gone through several tissues, the crowd cheered for the latest Mr. and Mrs. Knox. The exit music began, which meant Gia was officially off the hook.

Or so she thought.

Brannon bypassed her to take Addi's arm. "Sorry for the bait and switch, sis, but my wife needs me."

"You wish," Gia teased. Addison chuckled.

Addison, her hand bracing her very pregnant belly, beamed up at her husband before looping her arm in his. Bran mumbled something to her and she nodded, assuring him she was "still fine."

"Stuck with me, then," Jay commented as he offered Gia his arm.

"The sacrifices we make for those we love," she mumbled before pausing to smile for the photographer. "I didn't see your date."

"She's seated behind your date."

Gia turned her head to find her date leaning over a chair and chatting up a gorgeous brunette. She had to blink twice to be sure she was seeing correctly. "Is that—"

"Natasha Tovar. Supermodel."

Yes, that's what Gia thought. She let out a noncommittal hum. "Did Mason hook you up with Miss *Sports Illustrated*?"

"He introduced us. She likes my accent." He leaned down when he spoke. Whenever he was close, she had trouble thinking clearly.

"You don't have an accent."

"To Natasha I do. She's Russian."

"Good for her," Gia grumbled.

The guests meandered to the tent next and Gia and Jayson waited for their dates. As the supermodel approached, Gia felt her lip curl.

It'd have made her day if Natasha Tovar had been airbrushed within an inch of her life in her photos, but the gorgeous brunette was every bit as tantalizing in person as on a glossy magazine page. She was tall and leggy with high cheekbones and big eyes. Every other step she took revealed one supple thigh through the slit in her short black dress.

"What about your guy?" Jay rumbled, his voice low. "Does he own a hairbrush or is that how the kids are wearing it these days?"

Jerking her attention to Denver, who she honestly hadn't been watching, Gia retorted, "I admit, it's nice to date someone younger after having been with an older man for so long."

Jay smirked, his confidence unwavering. "Aged to perfection, sweetheart."

Goose bumps cropped up on her forearms the way they did whenever her ex-husband was accidentally sexy. Which happened more than she'd dare admit. Thankfully their dates reached them before he noticed her reaction.

"Dude, do you know who this is?" Denver asked Gia, his thumb pointing at Natasha.

"Ms. Tovar, is it?" Gia extended a hand. "It's lovely to meet you. I didn't know you were dating our Jayson."

"Coop and I met a few days ago and we hit it off. He's not gay like his brother so it worked out."

Gia pressed her lips together to smother a laugh and turned to Jayson. "Such high praise."

"Looks like Denver has all of his teeth," Jayson said under his breath. "Good for you."

Gia leered at him but he still wore that infuriatingly handsome smirk. He swept Natasha away and Gia groused in their wake, wishing they didn't look good together. They did. Dammit.

"She's hot," Denver put in as he placed his hand on her lower back.

"Not all of us are built like giraffes," she said, noting that she was being catty but not really caring.

"No, baby, not you." Denver bent his knees to come eye to eye with her, his hands gripping her biceps while he looked straight into her eyes. "You are gorgeous in another way. A different league. Beneath this package of curvaceous goodness, you deliver a totally gnarly experience."

Judging by his smile that was a compliment. "Um. Thanks?"

"You're welcome. Let's find some grub." She and Denver walked to the reception tent overlooking the vineyard. Where Addi and Bran's wedding had been contained to the immediate backyard, Taylor and Royce's was more sprawling. There were easily three times the number of guests here than at Bran and Addi's. Maybe Gia would be lucky and she wouldn't run into Jayson and Natasha again tonight.

Alas, when Denver and Gia approached the bar, Jayson was there, handing off a slim glass of clear bubbly liquid with a lime wedge in it to Natasha.

"What do you think, baby? Shots?" Denver asked Gia. Jayson turned and frowned. No, not a frown. There was an entire lightning storm forming behind his eyes.

Ignoring them both, she ordered for herself. "Dirty martini, up with three olives. Blue cheese stuffed if you have them."

"Shot of rum and a bitter IPA. Something local if ya got it." Denver seemed none the wiser to Jayson's disapproving presence.

Well, her ex could just deal with it. She didn't like his date any more than he liked hers.

The bartender made their drinks and Jayson, one hand wrapped around a glass of red wine, the other around Natasha's waist, gestured to a table.

"Dirty martini," Natasha laughed before she walked off with Jayson.

"What the hell was that supposed to mean?" Gia whispered to herself.

"It means she knows you got it going on, baby," her date answered.

"Gia," she snapped, shooting lasers from her eyes at Denver. "My name is Gia."

"Jee-ahh." His grin widened.

She sighed. She guessed that was better than "baby."

Five

"The guest rooms are on the second floor," Gia was saying to Denver as they crested the stairs. It was getting late, most of the guests filtering off. As part of the bridal party, it was her duty to oversee that the guests who were staying the night had everything they needed.

"Cool. I'll grab my stuff." He dropped a kiss on her mouth—one that startled her since they hadn't kissed yet. The night they'd enjoyed their first drink together had ended the way it'd started: with a demure brush of his lips on her cheek. "Yo, Natasha," Denver called before jogging up the stairs.

Gia's eyes sank closed. *Of course* the Russian goddess had witnessed that kiss. She turned, unsurprised to find Jayson there as well.

"We are staying, too," Natasha informed Gia.

"Yippee."

"Yes, it's very exciting," Natasha said, missing Gia's sarcasm. "I'll freshen up, but not done yet. More dancing." She gave Jayson a limp shove on the chest and then glided up the stairs.

"Enjoying yourselves?" Gia asked him, her tone flat.

"I love a good wedding." He pushed his hands into his pants pockets. He'd lost the jacket and bowtie from earlier, which left him in a white button-down shirt with the sleeves pushed to his elbows.

He looked good.

He rarely didn't.

He cleared his throat. "Where's your room?"

"Far end of the hallway." Denver's room was catty-corner to hers, not that she volunteered that information. "What about yours?"

"We're in the middle." He shot her a heated look and she could've sworn it was because he was thinking of the room they'd stayed in when they'd last visited her parents' mansion. The master guest suite. At least neither of them had been stationed there tonight.

Still, the "we" niggled at her. "We" meant that he'd be crawling into bed with *Miss Russia* tonight.

"She's not your type." Gia worked to sound curious. To be fair, she *was* curious. She hadn't seen him with anyone since they divorced and then he came out of the gate with a thoroughbred.

His shrug was infuriatingly blasé. "I don't have a type."

Her type used to be broad, dark and handsome with a protective streak a mile and a half wide. Five o'clock shadow and short-cropped dark hair. Eyes so blue she'd felt as if her soul was being inspected by a fallen angel…

But that was when she was in love with Jayson. She wasn't in love with him anymore.

When she'd married him she thought he understood her; that he'd allow her to be herself and forge her own way. Instead he'd attempted to corral and protect her, a lot like her father and brothers had done.

She twisted her lips in thought. "I don't have a type either."

"Coop! I found these in our room!" Natasha jogged down the stairs waving a pair of maracas from a Knox family trip to Puerto Rico. A keepsake. Gia felt the slow burn of anger broil her hairline. This woman needed to learn keep her hands off what didn't belong to her.

"Hey!" Gia lifted her voice, "Those are—"

"Going right back to where they came from." Jayson removed the maracas from Natasha's hands and gave them to Gia. As he walked off with his date, Gia heard him assure Natasha that they'd find some other way to entertain themselves on the dance floor.

And probably, Gia thought as she stomped upstairs, they'd find a way to entertain themselves in their shared bed, too.

Ugh.

"Cool digs." Denver shut his bedroom door and met her in the hallway Then he rubbed his hands together. "What are those for?"

"Nothing." Gia shoved the maracas into his chest and bypassed him to walk into his room. "Change of plans. We're staying in my room."

She exited carrying his duffel bag and opened the door to her room next. He followed behind her, a confused expression on his face.

"Together?" he asked.

"Yeah." She dropped his bag onto the down comforter. "Together."

Denver gave her one of his wide, carefree grins. "Sweet."

"But dancing is my *favorite*."

It wasn't Natasha's enunciation of favorite (fave-oh-right) that annoyed Jayson so much as the whine that accompanied it.

She was a beautiful woman with scads of confidence. She was educated and outgoing. She didn't drink alcohol. She was polite to everyone she met.

But.

She was needy and clingy and driving him up the wall. He'd danced with her. And danced. *And danced.*

He unwound his date's fingers from his forearm. "Natasha. No means no."

She thrust out her bottom lip. It didn't make her any less attractive.

He offered a tolerant smile and gentled his voice. "If I don't have a cigar with Brannon, he's going to kick my ass."

She let out a sharp gasp. "Cigars cannot touch this mouth."

"It's just one," he said, instead of *so, what?* There wasn't a single spark of attraction between them, though sleeping with her had crossed his mind. If for no other reason than to take his mind off his ex-wife, who was swishing around here in a short dress with enough cleavage to fall into.

He'd bet Denver noticed. Jayson sawed his teeth together.

"No kissing," Natasha hissed before she scampered off. The band played a fast song and she grabbed hold of a geriatric gentleman and started dancing with him. Jayson seemed to remember that guy from a board meeting. Anyway, the old guy looked happier than Jay was about the dancing, so they could have at it.

Outside, he found Bran standing in a half circle with a few other guys from work.

"There he is." Bran handed over a cigar and cutter. "Where's your supermodel date? Did she finally realize what a loser you were and ditch you?"

"She's dancing." *Some more.*

"Gia and Denver Pippen?" Bran asked around the cigar between his teeth. "What's that about?"

Jayson cut and lit his own cigar. He took a long puff and blew out his answer. "Wish I knew."

"Haven't seen them in a while. Did they leave?"

Jayson welded his back teeth together. "I think they're staying."

More like he *knew* they were staying. At the end of the hall. He saw her go upstairs earlier. If she'd met Denver in that room, Jayson had a good idea what they were doing right now.

He shouldn't care, but when it came to Gia, married or not, he'd always had the fierce desire to protect her. Denver seemed harmless—the sports star probably did more damage to himself than he'd ever do to another person—but she might need a reminder that she didn't have to wander that far down the evolutionary scale to rummage up a date.

"Huh." Bran sent a derisive look at the second floor of the house where a few bedroom lights were on. Gia's brother didn't go on a rant about her and Denver, and Jayson understood. Bran was close friends with Jay, had been for years, but if he had to choose sides, Bran would choose Gia. That was the way it should be.

"How's Addi? She holding on to that baby a while longer?" Jayson asked, segueing as seamlessly as possible.

"She's taking it easy tonight. Other than a few kicks to the beat of the music, she says the baby is content to wait." Bran's smile was contagious. "God, I can't wait to meet her. My daughter."

"Me too." Jay slapped him heartily on the shoulder. Brannon and Royce were family. Being divorced from Gia hadn't changed that. After they'd split, she'd insisted no one treat Jayson differently. The only one unable to follow that request was Gia herself. She'd been aloof and cool for the most part. Exception being at this very house about six months ago…

"Gentlemen," Royce greeted them upon his approach.

He was still dressed in his tux, the formality suiting him. Taylor, in her formfitting lace wedding gown, a scooped V in the front and back, wore a tired smile.

"Cigar?" Bran offered Taylor.

"Shut up." She gave her brother-in-law a playful slap before fussing with a drooping ring of flowers in her hair. "I'm falling apart."

"You're not," Jayson assured her.

"Thanks, Coop." She smiled genuinely before turning her attention to Bran. "Say the word and we'll delay the honeymoon. Royce and I want to be home when Addi has the baby."

Jayson was surprised to see Royce nod his agreement. "It's not a problem, Bran. Really."

"Go." Bran waved a hand. "The baby will be here when you come back."

"But I want to be there." Taylor appeared as unsatisfied by this decision as her new husband. "The *moment* it happens."

"Guys. Go to the Bahamas. Any excuse to delay and neither of you will ever go. You work too much."

Jayson regarded the ground and smiled to himself. Bran was as dedicated to their family's company as Royce and Taylor, even though he played down his commitment.

"He's right," Taylor told Royce. "Plus, if we stay here, your mom and dad will insist on keeping their granddaughter anyway. They've been looking forward to our honeymoon as much as we have."

"Not as much," Royce told his bride.

"We have things under control here," Jayson assured her. He was happy for them. Not every marriage ended in catastrophe.

Though a lot of them do, murmured the cynic inside.

"*Fine.* I'll go to the Bahamas," she said with a surly huff. "Where is Gia, anyway? I wanted to say goodbye."

This again? "I believe she went to bed."

"Oh." Taylor's brow crinkled. Jayson was an inch away from encouraging her to go upstairs and interrupt whatever might be happening, but he managed to keep that request to himself.

Progress. He was growing.

Royce shook Jayson's then Brannon's hands. "Call us the second Addi's in the hospital," he instructed his brother. "Day or night."

"Honeymoon, Royce," Bran told him. "You have to relax."

"I don't relax." Royce dipped his chin at Jayson, his tone firmer than before. "Coop. Keep an eye on our girl."

"What was that about?" Bran asked once they'd gone.

"No idea," Jayson lied, lifting his cigar to his lips.

Royce wasn't referring to his daughter, but Gia.

It wasn't so long ago that Gia's father, Jack Knox, had given Jayson a similar command. Her family had always wanted to protect her.

It'd taken Jayson a while to learn it, but he now knew what Gia wanted more than anything. And that was to take care of herself.

Six

Last January, the ThomKnox parking garage

"Thanks for the help," Gia said, chasing after Jayson. "Even though I told you I'd carry that."

"Not happening, G." Like he'd let her carry a thirty-six-inch screen from the executive floor down to the parking garage. "Why are you in the garage, anyway? You should be parked up front in the space with your name on it."

She beeped a key fob. "My interior is black leather. It'd soak up the heat from the sun and then when I climbed in I'd suffocate and die."

"Well, we can't have that." The black Mercedes Benz C-Class was a beauty. He should know. He'd picked it out. At the time he hadn't imagined he'd be leaving it with her because they were divorcing.

Five days from now they'd finalize their split on paper. Officially.

He'd already secured an apartment. Most of what he was

taking there was already in storage. He'd moved out gradually, thinking it would hurt less. Turned out there was no way for divorce to hurt less. It hurt. That's all there was to it.

He slid the large screen, in its factory box, into the trunk and shut it. She went around to the driver's seat and climbed inside, turning over the engine. The sound echoed in the garage. Not a soul was parked on the third level. Other than a guard and few brown-nosers, Jay guessed the first floor was just as empty.

Gia rolled down the window. "Guess I'll see you later."

He locked onto her brown eyes, stuck on what to say about any of it. All of the arguments he wished could have been simple misunderstandings. All of the accusations said in the heat of the moment that he should have taken back.

Too late now.

"I'm sorry," he said, the words exiting his throat like broken glass. Not because he didn't mean it. He was sorry, sorry that their marriage was ending in a stalemate.

"Don't be." Her smile was forced. "We did our best."

"Did we?"

She watched him, chewing on her lip. He hadn't meant to ask, but now that he had...*did they* do their best? Or were they giving up?

She shut off the engine and stepped out, folding her arms and leaning on the door. Eyes on his, she said, "Yes. We did."

"I'm not a quitter. Neither are you," he offered. "This feels like quitting."

"We can't change the past, Jay." She shrugged. "And the future is unknown. Besides, we're not quitting. We're deciding to be apart. Our love for this company, and my family, isn't going anywhere. The only difference in our lives will be that you no longer live in the house."

He rested a hand on the car's roof and hovered over her. "I'll also no longer be in your bed."

Heat warmed her caramel-colored eyes to deep, chocolate brown. He brushed her soft cheek with the back of his fingers.

"I'll no longer kiss these lips good-night." He touched her mouth with his thumb. That would be the hardest transition—for both of them, he'd bet.

"We have a few days," she whispered, arching her back and brushing her breasts against his chest.

He didn't need more of an invitation than that. Lowering his face, he captured her lips with his. She wrapped her arms around his neck and kissed him back.

Her entire body participated, from her fingernails scratching his scalp to her leg wrapping around his hip. Hand beneath her thigh, he hiked her leg higher and deepened their kiss. His erection raged as a contradicting voice inside yelled for him to both stop and go faster.

"Point of no return," he breathed into her ear before nipping her earlobe. If they slept together, it'd change everything. He knew it in his bones.

He wasn't sure if that was wise, or infinitely stupid.

She pulled away, her tongue swiping her bottom lip. When her teeth came down to capture it, he knew her answer.

"One more time," she answered.

He didn't think, he only acted.

Cigar enjoyed, time killed, Jayson trudged upstairs to his date.

He'd waited until the band packed up, sitting up and talking to Bran and a few of his friends to further stall the inevitable. He knew Gia was upstairs with Denver. Neither of them had reappeared. Jayson hadn't been in a big hurry to run upstairs and corroborate that suspicion.

He turned down the hallway to walk to his room when Denver clomped up the stairs behind him, a glass of brown liquid in hand. "One for the road, bro," he said, his speech wobbly.

Jayson welded his jaw together as Denver disappeared into Gia's room. Fists balled, he considered his options. Bust into the room and demand his ex-wife stay away from that harebrained, brick-headed dolt, or stand idly by.

There would be consequences if he banged on that door and checked up on her. She didn't like him undermining her. That was the word she'd often used. *Undermining*. As if protecting someone he loved was an insult.

Then again, making sure she was safe was worth any consequence, big or small. He'd started toward the bedroom door when her laugh floated out from under it.

He froze in place, at once disgusted and resigned. She sounded fine. Happy, even.

That sucked.

On heavy legs he turned back toward his own room and walked in. Natasha was waiting for him.

"Fix it." She pointed at the dresser, where one drawer was opened at a weird slant. "I can't live like this."

"Can't have you roughing it," he said, sarcasm thick, as he fixed the drawer with a quick wiggle. Forget that she was in a Knox mansion overlooking a vineyard, majestic mountains as a backdrop.

All he wanted to do was close his eyes and wake up in the morning.

"You are not nice," she said. Arguably she was right. He hadn't been very nice. "I am showering. Don't join me." She closed herself into the bathroom. And locked the door.

"No problem, lady." He sat on the edge of the bed and scrubbed his face with both hands.

He was beat, but he couldn't sleep knowing what was going on at the end of the hallway. He decided to head downstairs. The bar was closed, but he knew where Jack kept the good scotch. Jayson needed a nip after the day he'd had. Hell, he needed a *bottle*.

When he exited his room, Gia was tiptoeing out of hers. They shut the doors to their rooms simultaneously. He smiled and she smiled back at him, each amused by the unintentional choreography.

She'd changed from her bridesmaid's dress into a short pair of cutoff shorts and an oversize pink T-shirt. She looked cute. Relaxed. Warm and sleepy.

The thought of Denver touching her made Jayson want to howl.

She shoved her hands into her back pockets. "Hey."

"Hi." Still in his trousers and white shirt from the wedding, he was overdressed for this chance meeting. "Couldn't sleep."

"Yeah. My roommate is, ah, he finally fell asleep."

After what?

He didn't dare ask.

"Is the party winding down?" She folded her arms over her stomach and shifted on her feet. Fidgeting, the way she did when she was nervous.

"Royce and Taylor took off for the honeymoon. Addi and Bran are in their room. Your mom and dad left a little while ago with the baby. Just catering staff and house staff tidying up downstairs."

She nodded, glancing away before looking back at him. "I was going to grab a snack. Want to join me?"

"I was heading for the bar, but I never turn down a meal."

She joined him at the top of the stairs and they walked down side by side. "I didn't mean to take you from your *date*."

If it wasn't for the way she pronounced that hard *T*, he wouldn't have had any idea his ex-wife was jealous. He wasn't proud of it, but he liked knowing he wasn't the only one entertaining the green-eyed monster tonight.

Downstairs in the kitchen, she weaved between the house staff, greeting them by name while pulling out containers of leftovers from the fridge.

She handed him a large plate and filled it with a variety of salads and pasta, meats and cheeses, and on another plate served up a large slice of cake. When she started to put the containers back into the fridge, one of the house staff shooed her away.

She walked outside and on the way Jayson grabbed a pair of sparkling-water bottles. They stopped at a picnic table beneath a broad tree overlooking the vineyards. The house glowed warmly in the background, looking as homey as a thirty-something-room mansion could.

They dug into their shared snack in silence.

"Mmm. God. This is better than…" She trailed off before rephrasing her statement. "This is better than it was the first time."

"Did you do something to work up an appetite?" He narrowed his eyes.

She popped a square of cheese into her mouth and raised an eyebrow. "Did *you*?"

He reached for his water bottle and unscrewed the cap before taking a long guzzle. Not as good as scotch, but it would do. Patience shot, he said what was on his mind. "What the hell are you doing with that clown?"

"Excuse me?"

"Denver Pippen. *That's* who you're choosing to be seen with?"

"How is that any of your business?" She let out an incredulous laugh.

"I refuse to stand by while you waste your time with an idiot like Denver Pippen."

"Oh, you're one to talk! You brought a runway model to my brother's wedding."

"She's a *swimsuit* model."

Even in the dim light he could make out the redness of his ex-wife's cheeks. "You're a hypocrite. You're allowed to sleep with whoever you want, but I can't? Who the hell do you think you are?"

"I didn't sleep with Natasha," he blurted out before he thought better of it.

"Not yet," Gia said, but her voice was small. She hadn't expected him to say that.

"Not ever," he answered with finality.

Seven

Jayson took a bite of the cake and licked his fork. Gia crossed her legs beneath the table, memories of his mouth—and how good he was with it—assaulting her.

So he hadn't slept with Natasha? Gia had to chew on that for a while. She did so with a slice of brie.

He scooped up another large bite of leftover wedding cake. "Is it about sex? Is that the appeal?"

Unwilling to confess anything, she claimed her own fork and ate a bite of cake. She was still sort of in shock that Jayson hadn't slept with the beautiful woman he'd brought to the wedding.

"If it's about sex, you can do better," he pressed.

She met his eyes and in their blue depths recalled the way he used to look at her. Heated. Down to her very soul. Sex with Jayson had been exquisite. Unparalleled.

Too long ago.

"Who am I supposed to sleep with? *You*?" Her heart

thundered while she held her breath. Waiting. Daring him to answer. He didn't disappoint.

"Yes. If what you're after is a physical release, I'm a sure thing. But not with some random guy who isn't worthy of you." The words were gravel dragged over concrete. Jayson was pissed. Which also made him *hot*.

If temptation was a grain of sand, she'd be standing on an island. He could deliver on a physical release—tenfold. And if any proof was needed, she had it. Her body had come alive the second he'd said the word *yes*.

But they'd learned that lesson, hadn't they?

"We tried that already," she said. "We're good in bed but not outside of it. Look at us now. We should be in our separate rooms and yet…"

"And yet." He let the words hang.

She had a heart to protect. Unraveling her marriage had been the hardest thing she'd ever done in her life. Away from him she'd finally felt like an adult who was in charge of her own life. She loved her family, but they had a way of coddling her that she didn't appreciate. She understood that she was the youngest, but her reaching the pinnacle of adulthood should have quelled everyone's urge to protect her.

The freedom of being married was eye-opening…until she'd realized Jayson trying to take care of her much like her father and brothers.

There was a certain amount of freedom that came with being single. She could eat dinner whenever she liked without having to take a vote about whether to order out or dine in. She could stay up too late, fall asleep on the couch, enjoy the shower all to herself…

Although that part had its downsides.

Jayson had washed her back *and* her front when they'd lived together. In the moments she was romantic with herself, she used some of those memories as motivation.

But.

Going backward was never the best way forward. Wasn't that what all the memes on Pinterest said?

"It's too late." She stood from the picnic table.

He stood and blocked her path, hulking and dark, brooding and beautiful. "Too late for what?"

She put a hand on his chest to push him away but it settled there, content to touch him even as her brain urged against it. "It's too late to get back together."

He leaned in, the clean scent of his aftershave mingling with the crisp air from the vineyard. Lips close to hers, but still not touching, he muttered, "Who said anything about getting back together?"

Time stopped.

The only sounds came from the catering staff packing up the truck and the rustling of the leaves overhead. Chaotic thoughts dipped and weaved inside her head while she debated the very thing she shouldn't be debating.

Was she delaying the inevitable? Or was she too tired to think clearly?

Too *excited* to think clearly…

"You're right, G." He dragged in a sigh and blew it out, his breath dusting her cheek as he moved his lips to her cheek. "It's too late for this conversation."

She didn't know if he meant it was too late tonight or too late overall but either way she supposed he was right.

"Good night."

"Good night." She watched him go even though part of her wanted to chase after him. The stupid part of her that forgot what life was like when they'd been married.

He'd been opinionated and stubborn. He didn't listen when she spoke. He thought he knew best. He made decisions for her instead of with her. What made her think he'd changed?

Upstairs the light in his bedroom window turned on and

then off. He was in there now, with Natasha. He hadn't slept with her. Not yet. But like with their marriage, Gia was out of time. She'd had her chance to have him for herself. And it would have been amazing.

But then what?

Inside, a staff member rushed to take the dishes from her hands. Gia headed upstairs to her date, bypassing Jayson's bedroom door and doing her best to shut out what might or might not be happening beyond it.

Denver was sprawled out and snoring, where she'd left him. She crept through the darkness and bumped into his foot hanging off the end of the bed. Grabbing her pillow, she snagged a quilt off the footboard and went to the armchair in the corner.

Looked like she'd be sleeping here tonight while Prince Charming hogged the covers.

Natasha turned pouting into an art form.

Jayson had never seen anything like it. He'd gone back to the room last night and had tried to negotiate for one of the pillows. She'd kept all four. He could see the argument forming in midair between them, so he'd smiled and assured her he was good on the floor. Which was where he slept, his tuxedo balled up into a makeshift pillow while he slept in his shorts.

Now morning, he was feeling every inch of that hardwood floor on his aching lower back. He needed a cup of coffee more than a shark needed seawater. The outdoor patio was bustling with wedding guests who'd stayed over. They were making their way through the breakfast buffet and from the looks of it, the food supply was nearing depletion.

He squinted through the windows against the bright sunshine, his eyes adjusting and catching sight of Natasha in a royal blue dress. Her plate was piled with fruit and she was carrying a glass of green liquid.

Yeah, he'd skip socializing outside, thank you very much.

He tipped the last of the coffee into a mug, grateful not to have to mingle to acquire a much-needed caffeine fix. He couldn't talk to Natasha without at least being mildly alert. He raised the mug to his lips, but before the blessed moment that first hot drop hit his tongue, Gia appeared out of the ether.

"Is that the last cup?"

She wore the same cutoff frayed shorts and pink top from last night, only today she'd strapped on open-toed sandals. They added to her height, which brought her lips closer to his. At least the sandals were what he was blaming on his inability to look away from her mouth.

"You look like you slept better than me," he told her. She looked rested. Damned good. A little too rumpled for his pleasure, like Denver had slid his busted fingers through her hair this morning.

"There's more coffee outside." Jayson scowled and lifted the mug to his lips again. This time she wrapped her fingers around his at the handle.

"Then go outside and fetch yourself a cup. This is my house." A feral spark lit her dark eyes as she tugged on the mug.

"This is your *parents'* house. My employers. Plus, I was here first." He pulled up on the mug while she pulled down, each of them careful not to spill the precious liquid that would deliver morning pep.

"I can't go out there," she said with a frown.

"Why not?"

But then he turned his head and saw Denver lounging at the carafe, chatting to a couple Jayson didn't recognize.

"Did you two have a spat?" Jayson's smile was incurable at the idea.

"If by *spat* you mean did I sneak back into our shared room on tiptoes so I wouldn't have to wake him and have an awkward conversation this morning about how I wasn't going to sleep with him, then yes. We had a spat."

Shocked by that, he temporarily forgot to hold on to the mug. She easily removed it from his hand, doctored it with some half-and-half from the fridge and leaned on the wide, stainless steel doors. She took the first coveted sip, closed her eyes and hummed.

"You mean have an awkward conversation about how you weren't going to sleep with him *again*?" Jayson asked, fairly sure that's not what she meant. Sounded like she hadn't slept with Pip at all. If so, *that* was good news.

"I didn't sleep with him. Do you think I'd sleep with a guy on our first date or something?"

He tilted his head and watched her with his eyebrows raised.

Cheeks blushing, she mumbled at the edge of the mug, "You don't count."

"I don't?" Hand on her waist, he leaned over her to say into her ear, "As I recall it was right in this house." Her turn to be too shocked to hold on to the coffee. He reclaimed the mug and took a heavenly drink.

"That bathroom, if memory serves." He pointed across the hall at the staircase, beyond which was a half bath where they'd sneaked off after excusing themselves from the dinner table.

"That wasn't our first date. It was a work function." Her lips lifted at the corners. Good memory for both of them, that night.

"Tomato, potato."

Smiling, she shook her head at his bad joke.

"In all seriousness—" he moved the mug when she reached for it "—I'm glad you didn't sleep with him."

"I'm glad you didn't sleep with *her*." She snatched the mug. "You didn't, right?"

He shook his head. "I didn't."

"Good. She's too beautiful. It's unfair to us mortals."

Oh, Gia. He managed a sad smile. Tipping her chin, he peered down into her coffee-colored eyes, took in the riot of deep brown waves surrounding a face he'd stared at many a night while watching her sleep. Without makeup, freckles dotted the bridge of her nose—too faint to see unless you were really looking.

He was really looking.

"She's got nothin' on you, G."

They were in a holding pattern, her hands wrapped around the mug, and one of his hands on her face, the other flattened on the refrigerator next to her shoulder. The rest of the world might as well have crumbled to dust. All his reasons for not sleeping with her were harder to grasp when he was this close to her.

If they slept together she'd throw up a wall. They'd argue. This would end as badly, if not worse, than it had when they'd divorced.

And still…

"Jay…" She was poised to say something really undesirable. Maybe a "we can't" or "we shouldn't." She would have been right.

So he did what he had to do to prevent hearing it—and kissed her before she was able to speak.

Eight

Gia wasn't sure who leaned in first and erased the gap between them, but before she knew it, the sexual tension that had been roaring inside her like a five-alarm fire in the dry season *ignited*.

Jayson's warm lips pressed against hers as her back flattened on the cool steel door of the refrigerator.

His mouth was still fused with hers when he took the coffee mug from her hands and set it on the counter. He pulled her away from the fridge and, still kissing her, walked her out of the kitchen. Had anyone seen them? Had their dates seen them? She didn't know.

She didn't *care*.

When they reached the staircase, he came up for air and craned his neck toward the voices coming from the top.

There was a moment of hesitancy that gave her enough time to reconsider, but she only laughed. He took that as a yes, when in reality it was a *hell yes*, before eagerly steering her into the bathroom on the other side of the stairs.

Having sex back where it'd all started was risky territory, but by the time he shut them into the small room, she only cared that they were finally—*blessedly*—alone. He didn't bother with the switch, so the yellow glow of a night light barely illuminated the space—if it could even be called that. His big body added to the necessary bathroom accoutrements, the only place left for her was where he put her next.

On top of the sink.

"Oh!" Hand to her mouth, she stifled her surprised reaction as the people who owned those upstairs voices passed by the bathroom door. Once they were gone, Jay moved her hand away.

Mouth ravaging hers, his hands moved to her T-shirt and stripped it over her head. He didn't hesitate, didn't ask, didn't wait. He simply read her body language and right now—with her own hands pawing at his T-shirt—it was fairly obvious what she wanted.

Him.

Her fingertips raked over his abdominal muscles, still defined the way she remembered. So much of him was the way she remembered—which was both good and bad—but at the moment she focused on the parts of him she craved.

His seeking mouth over hers.

His diving tongue, hot and insistent.

His big hands, making her delicate by comparison.

She unbuttoned his jeans and slipped her hand inside. Both of them moaned their approval when she found what she was looking for. Long and broad, he was a sight to behold. She couldn't resist sneaking a peek of her stroking hand in the meager light.

"This is a bad idea," she couldn't help pointing out. She was out of breath from excitement, no longer able to call up *why* this was a bad idea. She only knew that it was.

"The worst," he agreed. "Some things never change."

A crooked, cocky smile crested his firm mouth, his eyes at half-mast while his erection was at full tilt. "That was verbatim what you said the last time we were in here about to do this for the first time."

"You remember that?" she asked as he divested her of her shorts. She had to let go of him to support herself on the edge of the sink but once her lower half was naked, she put her hands on him again.

"Are you kidding?" There was something tender in his voice, even as he wrestled with her shoes and shorts. Something about his tone reminded her of how in love they once were. Before he became the Fixer of All Things.

"I—I don't have a condom," she said since that was the first unromantic comment that popped into her head.

"I do." He frowned. "In my room."

She shook her head. "We're not risking that again."

Being busted by Addison at her wedding last year had been embarrassing. Gia had been walking around telling anyone who would listen that hers and Jay's split was amicable and that they were better off apart. And then she'd been caught with her pants down—well, not really. But when Addi had busted them, Jay's zipper was *open*.

Resting his forehead on hers while her hand worked on him, he blew out a slow breath. "I have to be inside you."

She gripped his face, feeling the stubble on his jaw. His next exhalation brushed over the tender skin on her neck. His desperation matched her own.

"Are you still on birth control?" he asked.

"Yes."

He lifted his head, his blue eyes going stormy gray with lust. With need. With want.

"No condom," she decided, because that was the only decision.

He wasted no time lining up her entrance with the swollen head of his cock, pulling her flush to the edge of the sink. She held his neck, her fingers eagerly bunching his T-shirt while he slid in deeper. *Deeper.*

Seated to the hilt, he blew out a tortured breath that fanned her hair and tickled her ear.

Against that delicate shell, he growled, "God *damn.*"

No one had been inside her since he had, and sex in the Mercedes, while that back seat had been a tight fit, had been similar to this time. Out of control with want, they hadn't considered the future.

They hadn't considered the past, either. The years of arguing and misunderstandings. The sadness over their crumbling marriage with each of them helpless to stop it.

Now, though. Ahh, the blessed *now.*

Now was about the physical. About his ability to turn her on and know what she liked. He displayed that next, by tucking his wide palms around the globes of her ass and pulling her down on top of him. Impaling her while his arms shook with the effort of moving her on and off him. Her breath sawed from her lungs in soft high-pitched sighs.

This was Jayson Cooper at his best.

The first time they'd had sex had been in this very bathroom, in this *very* position. She'd joked then that she was going to marry him "if only to have sex like this on demand whenever I need it."

He must have noticed her mind wandering. He stopped long enough to remind her, "Stay with me. You have an orgasm for me. I know it."

An orgasm for me.

He'd always phrased it that way, as if her having an earth-shattering, bone-rending orgasm was a gift *to him.* Another reason she'd vowed to marry him.

She shut out all other thoughts and concentrated on the sensations in her body. On the soft rub of her nipples on her bra each time he pulled her flush against his chest. On the way he tasted on her tongue, the salt on his skin, the rough scrape of whiskers from where he hadn't shaved yet…

He gripped her hair, balling it in his fist while she explored his neck with her mouth. He loved that.

Scraping her teeth along his jugular, she suckled his earlobe next. "Did Natasha treat you this well, Jay?"

His agonized "no" made her believe that was true.

"Did your skateboarder friend handle you the way I do?"

"Never." She shook her head, feeling naughty that their dates were still here. Couldn't be helped. Jayson and Gia hadn't been great at avoiding each other even when they'd tried.

They exchanged grins briefly and then they stopped talking. The only sounds were the heated slap of their bodies interspersed with labored breaths until her orgasm rolled over her like a cresting wave, crashing down and taking her mind with it.

For this finite moment, any issues between them were nonexistent. There was only right now—only him coming, the growl in his throat, the stiffening of the muscles in his arms. He filled her, both with his essence and with the deep, guttural moan of completion in her ear.

Eventually, after they'd managed to calm their breathing, he pulled out of her and rested her limp body onto the sink. He braced the sides of the counter, his forehead conking onto her shoulder.

"That—" he said between a deep breath "—was better than the last time we had sex."

In the parking garage. Five days before their divorce.

He wasn't wrong. It *was* better, and on that long-ago day it had been pretty damned incredible.

"When you got it, you got it." She kissed his temple.

He raised his head and his smile nearly took her breath away—as if she needed any help with that. He lowered his mouth to hers for a kiss when the doorknob jiggled.

"Someone in there?" came Addison's voice from the other side of the door.

It occurred to Gia suddenly, alarmingly that she'd ducked into a bathroom to have sex with her ex at yet another wedding. Only this time, she'd succeeded.

And she'd done it with their dates outside. With the possibility of being caught, she felt more shamed than naughty. She and Jayson had no business carrying on with each other anywhere, let alone *here*, where she might have to explain their behavior to her sister-in-law...

"One second!" she called out then whispered to him, "I can't believe it. Addi's going to bust us *again*."

"Like I said—" He zipped and buttoned his jeans and laid a succinct kiss on her forehead "—some things never change."

Nine

"It's a good thing Royce and Taylor aren't here," Brannon said from the head of the conference room table.

"Agreed," Jayson said. Those two deserved to enjoy their honeymoon and their time together *without* worrying about problems at the office.

"We'll solve the issue before they come home," Gia chimed in from his left. Her eyes flashed quickly from Jayson to Brannon.

As Jayson had expected, she'd been as cool as a cliché cucumber this week. He'd seen her react that way before—after the car sex and the almost-sex last year. She'd let herself go with him, but when they were done, she acted like it'd never happened.

That morning after Royce and Taylor's wedding, Jayson exited the bathroom first with Gia behind him. Addison had given them a wide-eyed blink followed by a sideways smirk. There was no need to explain. He guessed Addison

Abrams had overheard enough to answer any lingering questions she might've had.

Natasha, on the other hand, hadn't noticed he was missing. He'd driven her home, admittedly awkward after their tense date, but she hadn't said much. Though she did make sure and tell him, "It was a nice wedding, but we will not be seeing each other again, Coop."

Fine by him.

He'd called Mason after the drop-off to apologize for potentially ruining his stepbrother's working relationship with Natasha, but Mason assured Jay that his prize supermodel was under contract.

That left Jayson to wonder what the hell he'd been thinking bringing a stranger to a Knox wedding. And further wondering why the hell Gia had done the same thing. But he knew. They'd been trying to fireproof from exactly what had ended up happening anyway.

Jayson couldn't regret it, even if Gia was still giving him the cold shoulder. He, for one, wanted to do it again. No sense in letting perfectly incredible sex rot on the vine.

He wasn't sure where she stood. If she was regretful or reliving the afternoon on a loop in her head the way he was. She was a good actor when she needed to be. And at ThomKnox, under the watching eyes of her brothers, she did some of her best work. He understood why she didn't want to broadcast what happened, but he saw no need in pretending. Addison knew what had happened, so there was a ninety-nine-point-nine percent chance that Brannon knew, too.

He glanced at his ex-wife while her brother pecked at the T13 tablet in his hand. She held Jayson's gaze for an extra beat, licking her top lip before pressing it against her bottom one.

He'd expected an unreadable expression, but hers wasn't

unreadable. Her eyes were heated and slightly vulnerable, and the way she jerked her gaze from his gave her away.

She wanted him again. He knew it in his balls. Not such a good actor after all, it seemed.

"I see what you mean." Brannon frowned at the tablet in his hands. "It shuts down."

"That's the bug," Jayson said, his mind returning to the task at hand. The tablet launch last year had been smooth and since then, the sales were above where they'd projected. The software update that was due to go out next month, however, was a hot wad of WTF. "It ran fine last week and now it's not. I have no idea what's transpired since then to screw it up."

Unless Jayson and Gia having sex caused a tear in space and the working part of the software was sucked into a black hole.

Unlikely.

"We'll find the glitch," she reassured all of them, her expression shifting back to calm and collected. "We have the best tech team is the country."

"Damn straight," Jayson agreed. He didn't realize that he and Gia were smiling at each other until Brannon cleared his throat.

"No need to mention this to Taylor or Royce until they're back to work. This issue could go away in a matter of hours." Bran handed the tablet back to Jayson.

Also unlikely. Jayson had complete faith in their tech team, himself included, but he wasn't sure this problem would be resolved that quickly.

"I'll clear my desk and make myself available," Gia said. "You could use the extra brainpower." She smirked at her brother and Jayson and then left the conference room.

"You two seem to be getting along well," Brannon said, his tone droll.

"Yeah." Jayson wasn't giving him any more than that, just in case.

"Guess her and Pip didn't work out."

"Guess not." Jayson smiled.

"How's it going with Natasha?"

"That didn't work out, either. Which I'm assuming you already know."

"It wasn't like you two pulled off a supersecret heist." Bran appeared more amused than angry. "What the hell were you thinking? Your dates were outside having coffee and you and Gia were—" He shook his head.

"My brain wasn't doing any of the thinking."

"I do *not* want to hear details. What Ad told me she heard outside that bathroom door was already too much information." Brannon pushed his hand through his hair.

"Is there an 'if you hurt my baby sister' speech forthcoming?"

"If anyone hurts you," he told Jayson, "it'll be Gia. She's been taking kickboxing, you know."

Jayson frowned. He hadn't known that, actually. He didn't know a lot about what she did outside of work these days.

"Probably to protect herself from the morons she's contented to date."

"Pip." Bran shook his head. "Why *did* she bring that halfwit to Royce's wedding, anyway?"

"Got me," Jayson said, though he suspected he knew.

"Clock's ticking. Find the mysterious bug that's killing our tablet before Royce returns from his honeymoon," Bran said, obviously glad to change the subject.

"We'll run at it with everything we have. I'll pair everyone up to run code."

"Let me know if you need any monetary support for the venture." Bran slapped Jayson's back as he exited the conference room.

Downstairs, Jayson entered his department and clapped his hands together to get his team's attention. Gia, standing in her office doorway, paused to listen.

"I have a project for you that's going to take precedence over whatever you're currently working on," he announced. The room fell silent as all eyes turned to him. "The good news is I'm paying for overtime and carryout."

"And the bad news?" Gia asked.

"There'll be a lot of both," Jayson answered with a smile.

Jayson stepped into Gia's office and shut the door. He was suited, his jacket in place and his tie knotted.

Each time she'd seen him since last weekend she was reminded of their midnight snack outside, the sexual tension that had been strung so tight she could have played it like a harp. Of course, they both knew where that'd led.

Even though she'd been trying for the last few days to pretend the morning in the bathroom hadn't happened. That she hadn't had sex with the last man on the planet she should've had sex with.

She wrinkled her nose and considered Denver Pippen.

Fine. Jayson was the *second to last* man on the planet she should have sex with.

She'd done a damn good job of keeping her attraction to him in the "There but Unacknowledged" category since they nearly tore each other's clothes off last year. Now she wasn't sure she was hiding it as well.

Shutting her office door behind him, he stalked toward her desk. "I need you."

Because she had sex on the brain, she imagined him throwing her onto her desk and searing her lips with his specific brand of kiss. Instead, he sank into the guest chair.

He crossed his legs ankle-to-knee style and rested one broad palm on his knee. His posture was strong and sure. Nothing new there, but now it served as a reminder that he'd made love to her while standing and supporting her weight using nothing but his arm strength.

"More accurately," he continued. "I need your hardware."

I need your hardware.

"Oh?" she said instead of what she was thinking, which was admittedly half as interesting.

"Big Ben," he answered.

Big Ben was her computer system at home—formerly hers and Jay's home. It had multiple screens, the newest, latest bells and whistles, plus an encrypted cloud back-up system and crazy-fast internet connection set up in the family room. Ben was the Ferrari of home computers. Of course Jay wanted to use it.

"And your software." He tapped his temple with one finger. "I paired everyone off to investigate the bug wreaking havoc on the update. Hell, there could be several bugs for all I know." His eyebrows jumped. "Winner gets a pizza party."

She chuckled. The winner would get more than that—whoever solved this conundrum would attain superhero status.

"If we can fix that bug, it will increase speed and update security on every ThomKnox tablet out there. Our reputation is at stake," he said, serious now.

She felt the same way he did. Despite the casual way he'd asked to borrow her hard-and-software, they both knew that ThomKnox's future was nothing to laugh about. Could their company hang with the behemoths, or would ThomKnox forever be second in the technology world?

"Whatever you need," she answered.

"You're the most technically savvy human being in this company." He stood. "Apart from your father."

"And Jack's retired." She used to be shy about flaunting her brains or know-how until she went to college. Leaving for school had given her a freedom she hadn't been able to attain when she'd lived at home. College was the first time she could date without worrying about her father and brothers stating their opinions for the record. As she'd grown up, her family had loosened up, but at times she still felt like a little girl around them.

She'd say this for Jayson: For all his flaws and their incompatibility, he never let her play down her accomplishments. He'd always told her she was smart and to use that to her advantage. *Hell, G, abuse it,* he used to say.

What'd torn them apart ultimately, and a little at a time, was his overprotective nature and need to control every aspect of their shared lives. Now, though, while he was acutely focused on fixing the tablet issue, he didn't seem overbearing at all.

Was she seeing him through sex-colored glasses since their last encounter, or had he really changed?

She shook her head to jar loose that dangerous thought. Jayson had said it himself—they weren't getting back together. And if they weren't getting back together, then there was no reason to wonder if he had changed.

If she kept that front of mind, it would make being alone in the same house alone with him a lot easier. Anything could happen, true, but if they were on the same page, they could solve this issue swiftly and then be done with it. And with each other.

But when he stood and gripped the doorknob to leave, her gaze lingered on his capable hands and strong body.

"I'll bring Thai," he said.

"Okay," she said, even though she wasn't sure it was going to be.

Ten

It'd been a long day.

Gia left her hunchback of Notre Dame posture at the desk in her home office and walked to the sofa to collapse on it.

The square plastic black containers holding the remnants of their Thai dinner were strewn about the coffee table. They'd eaten before and during reviewing the complicated update code but somehow she was hungry again.

She reached for one of the containers and her plastic spoon, slumping back on the couch again. She scooped the tofu green curry on rice and vegetables into her mouth and chewed forlornly.

Jayson joined her, forking a bite of his leftover dinner, Thai Basil Beef, into his mouth. "I don't feel any closer to figuring it out," he said between mouthfuls.

"Me neither. I love lemongrass," she said before her next bite. No sense in talking about their abject failure.

"Someone at work could've had some luck." But they

knew better. If any of their team at ThomKnox had found the solution they'd have called Jay immediately. "We'll figure it out."

"Hell yes we will." She set aside her food and straightened her spine. She refused to be felled by one little error. The T13 had been wildly successful and the update would only improve its usage. She wouldn't—couldn't—let her team fail. Er, Jay's team. *Their* team.

The tech department was as close to having kids as they'd come.

"Don't despair." Food container empty, he rested his palm on her knee. Her bare knee thanks to her changing into shorts and a T-shirt. He still wore his pants from work, his sleeves shoved up, his top two buttons open and revealing the bit of dark chest hair she'd always liked. That masculine thatch reminded her that he was capable. And even an independent girl like herself could appreciate his trustworthy side.

Speaking of…

"I owe you for the food. We'll split it." She stood from the couch and walked to her purse, resting on a chair in the corner of the room.

"I got it."

"Jayson. I ate my weight in Thai food tonight."

"So?"

"So, I can pay for my own dinner." She dug some cash from her purse.

"ThomKnox is paying for dinner."

"Well…you picked it up." She waved the bills.

"*No.*" He enunciated the word slowly.

"It's important to have boundaries. And this is a good way to establish them."

"Boundaries? The sex on Saturday *established our boundaries.*"

"I thought we weren't going to bring that up."

"I thought you would have by now." He walked to where she stood and bracketed her hips with his hands. Before she could lecture herself about kissing him, he'd leaned temptingly close. "Why don't you want to have sex with me?"

She did, but damned if she would admit that. She choked on a laugh and said, "I can think of approximately a million reasons."

But really, there was just one.

Sex with Jayson made her remember being married to him and remembering being married to him made her remember divorcing him and that hurt.

When he lowered his lips to hers each of those million reasons disintegrated into a million pieces. He erased the inch and a half between them and kissed her gently.

She drank in his spicy kiss before she could argue with herself about it. He banded his arms around her waist like he did the last time they were together. When he'd lifted her into his strong arms and held her like she was the only woman on the planet who mattered.

A long time ago, she *was* the only woman who mattered to him. He had taken his duties as husband seriously. Some days too seriously. He'd ruled this house, or had tried anyway. So many of their arguments came from his inability to be flexible on a decision, or his tendency not to include her in the decision at all, and her own insistence that she could take care of herself without him.

Her urge to be independent was a constant refrain she'd grown tired of thinking about. Her whole life she'd been fighting for every inch of independence gained. By the time she was married to Jayson, a man who'd championed her more than any before him, she'd expected to have plenty of that much-needed space.

She pulled her lips from his. How could she expect space from a man who was constantly, and welcomingly, invading hers?

He was breathing heavy, his pupils wide and black. His eyes were her favorite shade of smoky blue. Judging by the state of his pants, he was as turned on as she was.

"We can't," she managed, half expecting him to lean in and prove her wrong.

He didn't.

"You always do this," he said instead. His nostrils flared.

"Do what?" Her blood pressure spiked at his tone, and at losing out on what they both wanted, and she didn't know what he was talking about yet.

"Retreat," he answered. "I don't remember you giving up this easily when we were married."

The reminder that they used to stand in this very room and argue about who knew what was a shadow she couldn't escape.

"Lucky for us we don't have to dig in our heels any longer, Cooper." She stuffed two twenty-dollar bills, now sweaty in her palm, into his shirt. "Thank you for dinner."

"What the hell did you call me?"

Since he'd just challenged her on retreating, she decided to stay for this battle.

"Everyone calls you Coop or Cooper," she said with a shrug.

His hulking dark presence was less intimidating than it was downright hot. "You're not everyone."

Like a stripper in reverse, he pulled the money from his shirt and dropped it onto the coffee table. "I don't need more reminders that you don't need me, Gia. You've made that perfectly clear."

She was frozen in shock until he turned to leave.

"You are so arrogant!" she called after him. "You only care about getting your way, don't you?"

"Getting my way? You think I'd rather leave than give you an orgasm with this mouth?"

He gestured to his mouth, tempting her since she still

felt the imprint of his kiss on her lips. Her knees literally went gooey. Jayson was good with his hands but he was very, very good with his mouth.

"I can take care of myself." But her response was automated. She'd been trying to convince everyone in her life of that for so long, the words came out robotic.

"No, you don't need anyone, do you? Least of all me." His tone was angry, but there was a dose of pain in those words—one she didn't like hearing. Part of her wanted to correct him. To tell him that she'd missed him when they'd split. That his presence in and around the house was what had made this pile of bricks and siding feel like home.

She'd missed him, but she hadn't known how to find her way back to him, either. Not when she'd said so many hurtful things she couldn't take back. She hadn't wanted Jayson's protection and service. She'd wanted to stand as his equal. To experience life with him, not apart from him.

But it was too late for those sorts of observations.

Their standoff lasted several seconds. He stood, silently daring her to give in to her wants—her *need*. But they'd already given in to the temptation and sex hadn't solved anything. Worse, their at-work conversations had been laced with hidden innuendo. Her mind wasn't on her work, it was in his pants. And as long as that was the case, they'd never fix this damned update.

"We have an important job to do," she said, leaning on her old friend, Pragmatism. "We shouldn't let ourselves be distracted."

"Yeah," was all he said before he gathered his bag and walked out of the room. She stood and listened to him go, closing her eyes against the finality of the front door quietly shutting.

Eleven

"**I** should let you two rest."

Jayson meant to hand back Addison and Brannon's daughter right away, but he delayed. Quinn Marie Knox was nestled in his arms and cooing up at him. A series of gurgles and grunts came from the precious bundle, her big eyes taking in as much of the world around her as they could. Tiny fingers clutched and released the air and he was fairly certain he'd lost his heart to her.

Finally, he was able to release baby Quinn in her mother's arms. "Sorry it took me so long to stop by."

Addison had gone into labor the night he and Gia had eaten Thai food and argued. The same night he'd kissed her and had hoped to end up in her bed, or hell, at least on the couch.

But, no.

In spite of the desire surging within and between them, Gia had retreated. Once again he'd found himself surrounding her with the protection and love he thought she needed, only to watch her retreat.

He stepped in, she stepped back. The dance continued. He wondered if he'd ever learn.

Addison adjusted her baby girl against her chest, who was nuzzling to be breastfed. "That's okay, Coop. I know you're busy."

"Say bye to Uncle Jayson." She waved her daughter's closed fist.

He smiled and waved back. Uncle Jayson. He liked that.

Family had always been important to him. Losing his marriage with Gia had been the ultimate failure. He didn't know what he would've done if he lost his work and his in-laws, too. The Knoxes stitched everyone into their family quilt—and once you were there, you didn't want to leave.

Jayson exited the sitting room and wandered through the kitchen. Bran was at the back door, pulling on a pair of boxing gloves. Once they were on, he punched them together. "Ready?"

"As I'll ever be." Jayson hadn't been through training Bran had, but he knew how to scrap. *Without* gloves. He'd gone a round or two with his own father and had lost. Badly. At age twelve he'd stepped between his abusive father and his mother, and had taken hits for her. He'd never been prouder of a black eye in his life.

Since then he'd developed a penchant for protecting those he loved, made easier when his mother remarried a good man and in turn gave Jayson a brother. He smiled as he considered Bran's and Addi's daughter. That little girl would never have to wonder if she was loved or safe a day in her life.

"She's great, your daughter," he told Bran.

"Those Knox genes." Bran grinned. "Although she inherited all the beauty from my wife."

Not all of it. Jayson found himself thinking of Gia. Again.

After stepping into the ring and receiving some basic instruction, Jayson was throwing punches comfortably at his ex-brother-in-law. Bran's backyard was lush with green grass and flowers and trees. It was a strange setup for trying to kick the other man's ass.

Not that there was any animosity lingering between them. Throwing punches at the middle Knox sibling was more about technique than working through a problem.

Jayson was frustrated with the way things *hadn't* gone with Gia, but there was no need for him to exercise that frustration physically. He preferred to funnel that irritation into his work—namely solving the problem with the tablet before Royce and Taylor arrived home from their honeymoon.

Jayson finally landed a hit on Bran's ribs and earned a satisfying grunt from his opponent. Bran caught his breath against the ropes, nodding that he was done.

"You're a fast learner," he praised as he and Jayson stepped from the ring.

A pair of loungers was set up in the grass, a cooler of ice-cold beer bottles between them.

"And I thought your daughter was beautiful. That cooler is a sight." Jayson accepted a beer and sat down, spinning off the cap and taking a long, refreshing slug.

Bran let out a beer commercial–worthy "Ahhhh."

After Bran reminded Jayson to keep his face protected in the ring, he paused, stared into his beer bottle and asked, "You and Gia avoiding each other?"

Here we go.

"Why?"

"You two arrive separately to meetings. I thought at first you were trying to make it look like you weren't dating by avoiding each other, but since Quinn was born, it seems like things went south."

"Well. Well. Look who's become observant."

"Very funny."

"I was being serious." This was the same man who, last year, hadn't had a single clue that Addison was madly in love with him. If it hadn't been for Bran and Addi's road trip to Lake Tahoe, Jayson wondered if Bran would have ever figured it out.

"So am I," Bran said, studying Jayson closely. "What's going on? Gia and Addi were talking when Gia was here yesterday, but Addi told me she's sworn to secrecy." Bran took a swig from his bottle. "Can you believe that?"

"Yeah, I believe it." Jayson sighed. "Nothing happened. Not really. We worked. She insisted on paying me for her half of dinner. We fell into old patterns of arguing like we did when we were married." He shrugged, unsure how else to explain it to someone who had been married for about two minutes. "It's hard after a while. The arguments become tiresome. And they're never about what they're about."

"Meaning Gia's paying for dinner was about more than money." Bran, his gaze unfocused on the yard, shook his head. "She always wanted to be treated like one of the guys. I suspect it's because of having two older brothers. And of course, we have this adorable kid sister who is a smart-ass, but loves so fiercely it's undeniable. All we wanted to do was protect her from anything—or anyone—that might make her cry."

Jayson stared at Bran's profile in deep thought. He could relate to that. How many times had he stepped in to protect Gia the way he'd stepped in to protect his mother? Only Gia hadn't really needed that sort of protection. There was no dragon to slay where his ex-wife was concerned.

But for the first time he considered how Bran and

Royce, and Jack, too, had handled Gia with kid gloves. She wouldn't have seen their efforts as protection, but as them stunting her growth. She'd wanted to flourish on her own, without their involvement.

And, he reasoned, without his as well.

"She's not weak," Jayson said, and wondered if his protectiveness made her feel like he thought she was. Then he remembered a bunch of other arguments that had ended with her accusing him of being "controlling" and he didn't have to wonder any longer.

"I overstepped," Jayson admitted for the first time in his life.

"By buying her dinner?" Bran asked, dubious.

"In the past. By telling her what she needs. By making decisions without her. By refusing to let her stand on her own two feet."

"You were trying to take care of her. We all saw that." Bran sipped his beer. "Plus you know how much she loves to win. She'll do anything to make you see her point of view."

"She stuffed the money down my shirt."

"'Course she did," Bran laughed. "Listen, whatever stuff you and G have going on is your business. I care about you both, but I also know you're capable of working things out. I just wanted to make sure I wasn't going to lose the dream team when it came to fixing this tablet issue."

"Gia and I are pros at dancing around each other," Jayson assured his friend.

That was the truth. They knew how to button down and focus on work. No matter what had happened between them since their divorce, they would prioritize ThomKnox and fix the tablet because nothing was more important than that.

Almost nothing… but there was no fixing what had been broken between him and Gia.

Twelve

The motivation to succeed was an attribute Jayson and Gia shared. Which was why they'd agreed that on Saturday, he'd return to the house and fire up Big Ben, and the three of them would make a decent bit of headway.

He'd been working for four hours straight without coming up for air when Gia interrupted.

"How's it going?" She was carrying her own T13 while his was being used as a coaster for his coffee cup. Without a solution for the update, "coaster" was the only purpose the tablet would serve. She moved the empty mug, clucking her tongue.

She didn't need to say anything. That small gesture spoke volumes.

It spoke of mini arguments about using a coaster or a napkin, about not resting his shoes on the coffee table. All insignificant, but they had a way of becoming bigger and bigger over time—the way individual grains of sand eventually became an island.

That's what he and Gia had between them. An island of misunderstandings and assumptions.

"I thought I had a breakthrough, but it turned out to be nothing." He might as well be talking about them. He'd had an inkling of the part he'd played in the deterioration of their marriage, but hell if he knew what to do about it now.

She seemed content to keep her distance. She'd worked by the pool today rather than inside the house, and when she did venture into the house, she grabbed whatever was fastest to eat before returning to the pool again.

"We'll find it." She sounded tired, as if she might not believe that.

He understood how hard it was to admit something was unfixable. Admitting as much about their marriage had been the most difficult thing he'd ever done.

"I'm going to run a few errands. I can't look at a screen any longer." She started to leave the room but he wasn't ready to let her go yet. In an attempt to keep her attention, he dealt a low blow.

"Finally met our niece," he said, receiving the smile he'd expected.

She crossed her arms over a simple sundress that looked anything but simple on his ex-wife. Her curves tantalizingly stretched every seam.

"I love that both Addison and Taylor have baby girls. Serves my male-dominated family right."

Remembering what Bran had told him, Jayson said, "They were overprotective."

"Men tend to treat me like fine china."

"Not a bad thing to be cared for." He still didn't fully understand why she didn't like her family looking out for her. He'd have given anything for a father who wanted to protect him at all costs.

"I had to run off to MIT for my brothers to admit I grew up. Jack didn't catch on ever, I don't think."

Yeah. Jayson didn't think so, either. Gia's father had stepped in time and again to make sure she was taken care of. Including with her husband. Whenever he thought of Jack's conversation with him before he and Gia married, Jayson bristled. Mistakes were definitely made.

"I'm not fragile," she stated now, and just stubbornly as she had in the past. "And I don't give up. On anything."

He thought of something else he and Bran talked about—how competitive she was, and suddenly had a great idea.

"Except you're going shopping. So you sort of are giving up."

She made a disgusted sound. "I'm taking a break. Breaks are good for the brain."

So was sex.

"I'll bet you I find and fix the bug before you do." She was smart, but so was he. "We've been stuck on this for far too long. Maybe what we need is a little friendly competition to motivate us."

"I'm plenty motivated." But her eyebrow arched high on her forehead, a sure sign she'd been properly provoked. "I know I'll find the problem before you do."

"If you're so sure, then why not bet?" he goaded.

"What do you have that I could possibly want?"

When he held out his arms, she rolled her eyes, but her smile was worth it. "Be serious."

"Okay." He thought for a second, and then landed on the one offer she couldn't refuse. "If you win, I'll cook for you."

She snorted.

"My grandmother's homemade pasta."

Her mouth dropped open.

He grinned, knowing he had her. He didn't make his grandmother's homemade pasta recipe often, but he had made it for Gia when they were married—for their anniversaries. Both of them.

"I can guess what you want if you win." She folded her arms. "I'm not having sex with you again."

"You're sure you'll win. What are you worried about?"

"Hmm. Well I *was* sure. You're pretty motivated by sex." Her smile held. She didn't hate this idea. Not even a little.

"I admit, that's a good motivator." Especially sex with her. "But this time we're not doing it on a bathroom counter. We'll be in bed."

He tipped his head and walked closer, daring her to say no. To admit that she was afraid of losing, and therefore sleeping with him. Or worse, to refuse the bet because she didn't *want* to sleep with him.

She did neither.

Because she'd sooner die than admit she didn't think she could win. Plus, as he'd suspected, she wanted to sleep with him again.

She folded her arms over her breasts. "This is bribery. I love that pasta more than anything."

"I know." He loved every second of this exchange. He slid by her and headed for the kitchen. "Have fun shopping. I'll be here toiling away on a solution."

"Shopping can wait," she said. "If I'm going to win, I may as well do it. Also, I expect the works for my meal. Candles. Music. I want to walk in and mistake my kitchen for a fancy Italian restaurant."

Yep. He had her. Now all he had to do was win.

"Sounds like you're taking the bet." He pulled open the refrigerator and pretended to search for something to eat.

"Okay, Jay." She faced him. "We have a deal."

She picked up her tablet and walked through the kitchen, sliding her sunglasses onto her nose. She took her place outside on the lounger by the pool.

The clock was officially ticking. He no longer cared

whether or not he found the problem before Royce and Taylor came home.

All he had to do was find it before Gia did.

Gia justified her decision not to shop since she had something to wear to her date tomorrow. Nothing new, but still.

She'd spent the remainder of the day hunched over her notes and her tablet, though sadly didn't feel much closer to the answer than before.

The stakes were high. Jayson's grandmother's pasta recipe was nothing to joke about. Plus, while sex with him was off the charts fantastic, she also knew the repercussions of falling into bed with him again.

She didn't need to feel any more for him than she already did. Letting her heart be involved after she'd put their marriage *and* divorce to bed could be disastrous. She was supposed to be moving on, but here she was a year and a half later and not only had she had sex with him already, he was inside their former shared house right now.

Which was why she didn't cancel her date.

She'd paused from her work by the pool to check her messages on the Divinely Yours app. She had several, including one from Denver Pippen. He mentioned he'd be out of the country for a skateboarding competition in Germany. He let her down easy, telling her know that while he'd had fun at the wedding, he didn't see them going further.

She agreed, but appreciated his candor. He could've ghosted her, but chose to lay out the facts. Pip wasn't a bad guy, he just wasn't right for her.

She'd scrolled down through a few seriously gross offers in her inbox before coming across a message from a name she recognized. Elias Hill.

Elias was the founder/owner of Hill Yacht Company.

He'd praised her work at ThomKnox and then invited her out on the maiden voyage of his latest model before it hit the showroom floor. He'd sealed the deal at the end: "No pressure, Gia. Just a day on the water."

She *so* needed a day without pressure.

She didn't expect a relationship to bloom from a yacht-date with Elias Hill. But if the unthinkable happened and Jayson won this bet, she could lean on the excuse of dating Elias and avoid going to bed with Jayson. That was cheating, she supposed, but didn't they say that all was fair in love and war?

Yawning, she gathered her things and headed inside. She was done for today and looking forward to curling up with a cup of tea and a good book. It was time for Jayson to head home, too. He'd been tireless, but he had to give up at some point.

Plus, she needed to tell him about the date—which he wouldn't like—and let him know that the house was off-limits while she was away. They could resume their investigation on Monday when they were both working.

But halfway through those thoughts, she found her ex-husband, the heels of his sneakers resting on the arm of the sofa, fast asleep.

"Jayson." A familiar frustration bubbled up at the sight of him sprawled out, his shoes on the furniture. Irritation was easy to come by when she spotted his empty coffee cup and a plate with crumbs on it left on the table.

And yet, she didn't have the heart to wake him. He had to be exhausted. He'd admitted earlier today that he hadn't slept well this week, too worried about this update fix. There was something so vulnerable about the way his long eyelashes shadowed his cheeks. And something so animal about the way his dark scruff decorated his jaw. She remembered the last time he'd kissed her, his whiskers abrading her chin. How hard it'd been to stop kissing him. To put up her guard and turn him down when her body had begged her to continue...

She tossed a blanket over him rather than wake him, reassured that the date tomorrow was exactly what she needed. There was a time when she would've kissed the corner of Jayson's mouth and told him it was time for bed. A time when he would've pulled her down into his arms and said, "Lie with me a while."

No longer.

Their passion and sexual need for each other was alive and well, but their ability to be vulnerable had vanished. She mourned that briefly as she flipped off the lamp. But by the time she locked the front and back doors and headed upstairs to bed, she justified that her mourning period was well and truly over.

Already she could feel herself softening toward her ex-husband, those old feelings lurking around in her head and, if she wasn't careful, in her heart.

That was one risk she wasn't willing to take.

Thirteen

Jayson exited the downstairs bathroom and wandered into the kitchen. He'd fallen asleep in his former house. Being here this early in the morning, and stumbling into the kitchen in search of coffee, was so familiar it was bizarre.

He didn't know if he was more surprised he'd slept through the night or that Gia had let him stay.

He could hear her moving around upstairs, but evidently she'd been in here earlier. Coffee was made, most of the pot gone. He poured what was left into a mug and took a long draw.

"Morning." Gia breezed into the kitchen dressed in a bright pair of shorts and a shimmery shirt. Her shoes were tall. Her toenails painted the same color pink as her shorts.

"You look nice," he said, unable to keep from running his eyes over those tanned, smooth legs. Her hair was wavy and draped over her shoulders, the way he liked it.

"Thanks," she replied.

"I'm making more coffee," he told her as she gathered

her purse and stuck a pair of sunglasses on top of her head. "Sorry I crashed on the couch. I was beat."

"No big deal." She flashed him a quick smile.

"Where are you off to?" Apparently, he was going to have to ask.

"Oh, I have a thing." She waved a hand like she wasn't going to say more but then she did. "A date."

"A date." What the hell?

"Yes. It's a casual day on a yacht."

"With who?"

"Jayson. This isn't any of your business."

He knew that. He forced a smile, hoping it'd gain him an inch. "Just curious if you and Pip ended up working everything out."

"No." She said it with enough finality that he believed her. "I met today's date on the same app where I met Denver, though. His name is Elias Hill."

"You're still on the dating app?" He blinked down at his coffee, wondering if he was still asleep. Or hallucinating. After what had happened between them at the wedding, he hadn't expected her to be *dating*.

She started for the front door and he chased after her, careful not to spill his coffee. "Is that safe?"

"Is what safe?" she asked, grabbing her keys.

"Going on a boat with a guy who could be a serial killer."

"Jay." She gave him a bland look. "Elias Hill is the CEO of a billion-dollar yacht company. I doubt he has murder on the high seas at the front of his mind."

Jealousy roared to life inside him at the same time he had the realization that even though this setup felt familiar—them waking up in the same house and chatting over coffee—there was one big difference.

They were no longer married.

If she wanted to go on a date, she could. Still, he couldn't help saying, "I don't like it."

"You don't have to." She patted his cheek with one hand.

Then she was out the door, leaving him in need of a shower, a second cup of coffee and an excuse to stick around. Any good friend would make sure she returned home safely from her date.

Elias Hill had been perfectly nice. Perfectly casual. Perfectly polite and perfectly suited for someone like her. He liked talking business but knew when to relax. He didn't have any dumb come-on lines and he didn't call her "baby" or "Jee-ahh" the way Denver Pippen had.

Elias was…well, perfect.

He was also perfectly *boring*.

By the time they'd had lunch, she was yawning behind her hand. She tried to convince herself it was because she'd stayed up late working. Because she'd had trouble sleeping knowing her ex-husband was downstairs—the man was majorly throwing off her chi. But all that line of thinking did was bring Jayson back to the forefront of her thoughts and then she'd ended up comparing him to Elias.

Elias's muscles beneath his white shirt looked nice enough, but he somehow lacked the roundness through the shoulders that Jayson had. His forearms were fine, but she doubted he had the strength to lift her up so she could wrap her ankles at his waist. His face was pleasant, but too clean-cut. His lips were too narrow. His hair, wavy in the breeze, was thinner than Jay's full, thick, but short locks.

Elias was as boring as his stale, white outfit—a literal blank slate—and his personality barely appeared. He spoke carefully and evenly, but his stories droned on, and the last one about the investors' party meandered and looped but in the end had no point.

He wasn't witty. He wasn't stubborn. He wasn't challenging.

He isn't Jayson, her mind offered and she told it promptly to shut up.

She didn't want Jayson. That was her mantra after they docked, after she'd allowed Elias to kiss her cheek and as she drove home. So intent on making that her new truth, she decided that working side by side with Jayson was probably a bad idea. Bet or no bet, she needed to put some distance between them.

When she stepped into the kitchen of her house and looked out the window, instead of finding peace in being alone she found Jayson Cooper in her pool.

He was naked save for a pair of board shorts, and floating on a yellow raft shaped like a lemon slice. He should have looked ridiculous, especially wearing a pair of pink sunglasses that belonged to her, but he didn't.

He looked damned tempting with a solid tan and a five o'clock shadow darkening his jaw. He was cradling a can of sparkling water in one hand, his head leaning back, showcasing the column of his strong neck. Beads of water danced along his body, glistening in the waning sun.

Her mouth watered.

How dare her body react to him? He ruined everything—including her date. If not for sleeping with Jayson so recently, she might have found Elias Hill perfectly pleasant.

Perfect. *Yuck.*

She replayed that dumb story about the family dog he'd told her and cringed. How was it that a billionaire yacht CEO wasn't more interesting?

"What the hell are you doing here?" she growled, tossing her beach bag onto an empty lounger. She was still wearing her new bikini beneath her shorts and top and had been planning on coming home and swimming off her frustration.

"You're back. Didn't expect you for a while." He finished off his water and crunched the can with one hand before tossing it to the side of the pool. "I was going to leave, but I was caught up in working and decided to take a dip. I was planning to be gone by the time you came home."

"Sure you were." But him being here didn't piss her off as much as she wanted it to.

Especially when concern leaked into his tone when he asked, "Didn't go well?"

She crossed her arms and shrugged.

A frown bisected his eyebrows. "What the hell did that bastard do?"

She dropped her arms. "Nothing. I'm not mad about my date. I'm mad because you're here and I want to swim."

"I have to leave so you can swim?" When he said it out loud it did sound silly.

"Whatever. It's hot and I'm frustrated and I'm coming in."

Hands in her hair, she pulled her waves into a ponytail and stripped out of her clothes. She was aware of Jayson watching her from behind those pink sunglasses. Especially since this bikini was gorgeous. The hot pink suit covered what it needed to, but the peekaboo mesh at the neckline hinted at what she was hiding.

She stepped to the zero-entry side and started down the ramp, the warm water lapping at her ankles, then calves, then knees. She commented about how the water was colder than she'd expected and he grinned.

"Don't." She warned, sealing her fate.

He was off the raft in a shot, tossing the sunglasses to the side of the pool and then…he was gone.

"I just washed my hair!" she shouted as he cut through the water. Before she could turn to walk up the ramp, he'd surfaced and scooped her into his arms like Swamp Thing.

"You know better than to tell me the water's cold, G," he said, his eyelids lowering ominously.

She kicked her legs uselessly and wiggled in his grip. "I take it back!" she said through breathless laughter.

"You can't take it back." He laid a hard kiss on her mouth and walked her toward the deep end. Before she could beg him not to throw her in, he'd already tossed her into the air.

Fourteen

What was more fun? Kissing and then throwing Gia into the deep end or watching her try and catch him while he swam left then right in a zigzag?

Kissing her, definitely. With or without the throwing. Though throwing her in had been fun, and something he'd done time and time again after they'd bought this house.

"Dammit, Jay!" she sputtered after she surfaced.

"You know better than to step into the water with me. You'll end up wet." Letting the double entendre hang, he gave her a wicked smile and added, "In *or* out of the water."

"You're an ass." She launched herself at him but this time he didn't move, catching her instead. He wrapped her legs around his waist and walked her into deeper water.

"I have a very nice ass. Or so I've been told."

She rolled her eyes. "Is that what *Natasha* told you?"

"Natasha didn't think of anyone but herself most of the time. Care to share about Elias?"

She pouted, but didn't move to escape his grip. "No comment."

"Were you trying to make me jealous by going on a date?"

"I was trying to take my mind off of you!" She jerked her gaze away like she hadn't meant to admit that.

"Oh, really." He gave her a squeeze. "Did it work?"

She tightened her arms around his neck. In this position every one of her curves lined up with his body perfectly. What he wouldn't give to have a taste of her mouth, or feel her ride him, those thighs locked tight...

"I'm not seeing Elias again."

That was evasive, but some damn good news.

"Why'd you go out with him in the first place?"

"Because sleeping with you is a really, really bad idea."

"Ouch." That hurt.

The divorce had been hard on both of them—he knew that. But he'd also figured out that they hadn't had their fill of each other yet. A marriage was more than attraction, but that didn't mean they couldn't have fun together while in each other's immediate proximity.

"You already slept with me."

She sighed. "I know. I don't think we should do it again."

He felt the corners of his mouth pull down. "Why the hell not?"

"How's this going to work, Jay? We give in to our physical attraction, and then what? Walk away?"

That was the gist. But she sounded as wounded as he felt at the idea.

"What's the alternative? You've made it clear you don't want me in your space permanently."

"That's not fair."

"No, but it's true."

She quirked her lips, and he guessed it was because he'd made a good point.

"We tried to repair our marriage and work together. We failed. I'm not sure much has changed since then."

They were the same people, he couldn't argue that. "Yes, but we know what it costs to be together. We know better than make the same mistakes we made before. That has to count for something."

She watched him and he watched her. The water lapped against his waist and her thighs, which were still cradled in his hands.

"Gia. If you don't want—"

She kissed him and cut off the offer he hadn't wanted to make. He'd been about to reassure her that if she didn't want to sleep with him, she didn't have to—bet or no bet.

Turned out she put his tongue to better use. Her mouth moved on his. Softly. *Slowly.* This was nothing like the day in her parents' vacation house kitchen—or the bathroom interlude that followed. They explored each other carefully, like neither of them wanted to spook the other away.

Her hand vanished into the water and next he felt her tender grip on his erection.

He grunted, hardly able to breathe now that she was handling him with long, even strokes. She smoothed her lips over his open mouth, tempting him, turning him on so much his brain wasn't operating at full capacity.

But he couldn't keep from replaying her words—and the wave of regret they'd arrived on.

He ended the kiss and looked his ex-wife in the eyes. "I don't want to fail with you again, G."

Damn. That was honest. More honest than he'd meant to be.

She released him, untwined her legs from his hips and swam for the ladder. He thought that was it, that she'd changed her mind and, hell, maybe that was for the better. For them to cut their losses and let go of the idea of *them* altogether.

But then she turned and looked over her shoulder before climbing out and said, "Well. Come on."

He followed obediently, his eyes feasting on the vision of his ex-wife climbing the ladder. She pulled herself from the water, her long, soaking hair arrowing down her back, a trickle of water flowing over her tanned skin. Her plush bottom in that hot pink bikini. God, he could take a bite out of her—she looked that damn delicious.

Even if this was a bad idea, he wasn't as future focused as Gia. He didn't give a damn what happened in a day or a week or a month from now. Whenever he was with her physically, the world was suddenly right. Everything made sense for the time they were together and that was enough for him.

She toweled off and he did the same, quickly. Unlike his apartment where everyone could see everyone, they didn't have to worry about privacy in this backyard.

The house was in a neighborhood but not the tightly packed suburbia that he'd grown up in. Here, the houses were spaced out enough that no one could peer over at them from an upstairs window. That fact, and the tall white privacy fence around the entire backyard, was probably why Gia let him take off her bikini top.

He released her gorgeous breasts into his hands, stroking the chilled buds. The sun was receding fast, the cooler air blowing in, but he didn't want to suggest they go inside. He was afraid she'd have second thoughts. They had momentum, and if they lost it, they might never find it again.

She shivered as she slipped her bikini bottoms off her legs. He followed suit, kicking off his shorts in record time. Then he stared.

He loved Gia's body. He always had. And now he was going to love her body from head to toe—for as long as she could stand it.

She'd always loved foreplay and he'd been more than

willing to take his time with her. They hadn't had the chance for foreplay the last time they were together. He intended on remedying that.

He backed her to the rattan chaise lounger and laid her down. "Are you—"

She hushed him with her finger against his lips. Clearly she didn't want to give herself a chance to have second thoughts either. She ran that same finger down his chest, belly button and lower as she sat on the lounger.

When she navigated his favorite part of his body into her mouth, whatever thoughts had been bouncing around in his head vanished. There was only the feel of her heated mouth suctioned onto him.

He rested his hand on the back of her head while she worked, admiring her grace and beauty while she took him on her tongue. She was the best. He hadn't been a saint while they were divorced, so he knew of what he spoke.

Gia blew his mind. Thoroughly. She didn't try to impress him; she simply enjoyed herself. Pleased with herself for pleasing him. So focused on him, she must not have noticed when he gently cupped her jaw to stop her. She took him to the hilt again, one long, slick slide that had him welding his molars together.

He forced himself from her mouth, bending at the waist while he waited for the spots to clear from his vision. He wanted to finish inside her tonight.

She peered up at him, eyes wide. When she licked the corner of her mouth, he worried he might come right then. He was a grown man, in charge of his faculties most of the time, but this was his weak point.

She was his weak point. His ultimate Achilles heel.

He was starting to see what she meant about this being a bad idea, but damned if he'd stop now. He tossed his beach towel on the concrete and lowered to his own knees in front of the lounger.

Pushing her shoulders, he encouraged her to lie back. He didn't have to convince her much. Propped up, arms draped over her head, she was a goddess. The purple-pink sky intensified the surreal moment, the water droplets still clinging to her skin sparkling in the fading light.

He bent and licked a drop off her nipple, then the side of her breast. He repeated the action on the other side, not wanting to give one breast an unfair amount of attention. Then he ran his tongue down her middle to her belly button while her hands sank into his hair and gave a little tug.

"Someone's excited," he murmured against her damp flesh.

"It's been a while," she breathed.

He liked hearing that way too much.

"I'll be down here awhile to make up for it."

Promise made, he tugged her so she was flat on her back, and then rested her knees on his shoulders. Her open before him was a gift. She trusted him with her pleasure. It hadn't been enough to save their marriage, but he was proud she was willing to give herself to him.

He kissed the insides of her knees and worked higher and higher up her thigh. Her breaths tightened, and he drank in her anticipation. It gave him strength to know that she needed this—not only the orgasm, but an orgasm that only he could deliver.

Wedging a space for his shoulders, he dipped his head and tasted her, dragging his tongue in one slow line.

She shivered.

He did it again, this time flattening his tongue.

She shuddered.

With a proud smile to himself, he renewed his efforts and dove in, this time not letting up until her cries of completion were echoing across the nighttime sky.

Fifteen

Julia and Albert Robinson's patio was a work of art. The built-in stone grill sat in the center, the matching tiled bar top wrapping around each side. It took up at least half the space available, the other half filled with an oversize square outdoor dining table and eight chairs. Overkill for their modest house, but his mom wouldn't let Jayson buy her a house. He had to be happy with what they'd accept—in this case a brand new back patio design for her for a Mother's Day gift. Next year he'd talk her into an in-ground pool.

His mother deserved to be spoiled, though he would admit his stepdad did a good job of spoiling her in all the ways he could. Albert had padded their retirement fund, made sure she felt safe and loved. But Albert couldn't afford the extras that Jayson could provide. Jay made a hell of a lot of money and without a family of his own to support, figured he could afford to spoil them.

The glass patio door slid open and Chester, Mason's

husband, stepped outside with a tray of burgers and brats, the vegetarian versions for himself. "Mas, hon, bring me a beer," he called over his shoulder.

"Can I help?" Jayson held out a hand.

"Yes, occupy your brother so he doesn't get in my way," Chester said with a good-natured eye roll.

While Chester and Albert decided what grill arrangement was optimum for the burgers and brats, being careful not to "contaminate" Chester's veggie fare, Mason and Jayson sat at the far side of the newly built bar. Their mother was inside finishing up her famous deviled potato salad.

"I like this dining set," Mason said before sipping his beer.

"Glad they let me do it."

"You're a good son. If you're trying to win, you've done it."

Jayson knew his brother was kidding. Mason was driven, ambitious—one didn't accidentally become a standout photographer in the fashion industry—but he was also laid-back. When the topic of conversation rounded to Natasha, Jayson shook his head.

"I should have warned you," Mason said. "She's a diva. Gorgeous, but a diva."

"Gia's prettier," Jayson muttered.

Mason's silence was deafening. He smirked. "What is going on?"

"Nothing's going on. It was just an observation." Jay took a swig of his own beer.

"I noticed you were in a better mood than usual and I couldn't figure out why. Now I know. Sex with the ex."

"Don't be crass," Chester called out before addressing Jayson. "I would love it if you two found your way back to each other."

"He's a romantic," Mason chided.

"Romance is a tall order for Gia and me," Jayson said,

meaning it. They'd tried the happily-ever-after route, went off-road and ended up in a ditch.

He considered Albert, and his mother who joined him at the grill, and Mason and Chester. Maybe romance wasn't a tall order for his family, but it seemed an insurmountable leap for Jayson.

"I'm going to check the garden." Jayson stood abruptly and left his family on the patio. He stepped around the side yard to where his mother kept a small herb garden. Over the fence, the neighbor's squatty bulldog barked hello.

"Hey, Ollie." He grinned down at the portly dog who wagged the entire back half of his body since his nub of a tail was incapable of the action. Jayson bent over the top half of the fence and gave Ollie a scratch before settling on the stone bench next to the garden.

He'd always wanted this sort of peace for his mother. This house, this neighborhood was a huge step up from where he'd grown up with a father who made their lives a living hell for far too long.

Only a boy at the time, Jayson had vowed to save his mom from the adult man who wasn't man enough to pick on someone his own size. Thankfully his mother had friends. The first—and only—time Eric Cooper had hit Jayson in the face, she'd left with Jayson in tow and had run straight to those friends.

By the time they'd returned home two days later, Eric was gone. Julia changed the locks and began looking for a new apartment immediately—even before the house was listed on the market.

She'd picked up a second job, and then a third, and Jayson grew up fending for himself. He'd seen his role as the protector, until Albert stepped into their lives and took over. Albert, a nerdy type who at first didn't seem capable of slaying a butterfly let alone a dragon, had been adamant about their boys being kids and not worrying about adult problems. He assigned household duties, relegating Jayson to trash duty and Mason to lawn mowing.

Jayson grew up the rest of the way like a normal kid, and would be forever grateful to Albert for giving him a good childhood. He hadn't known at the time that Albert was saving him, though. There'd been moments where he'd argued and yelled, but Albert seemed to understand that Jayson had been raised by a man with no boundaries. Boundaries that Albert set gently, but firmly.

Once grown, Jayson was determined to provide his mother and stepfather with the sorts of things they'd done without on their quest of raising two teenagers—one of them angry thanks in part to DNA and past trauma, the other struggling with his sexuality.

Jayson had been lucky. Some kids didn't make it out of a dark past as cleanly.

When he'd met Gia, his world had stopped. Honest to God, it'd been like a movie. He'd spotted her across the room, the soundtrack of a cheesy ballad playing in the background.

When he'd gone to her father to ask for his daughter's hand in marriage, Jack replied, "As long as you take care of her." Jack had gone on to explain that he knew he couldn't always be there for his daughter, and now that was Jayson's duty.

Jayson had taken that duty seriously. He knew how to take care of a woman, knew what she needed.

Or so he thought.

Each time he tried to do his *husbandly duty*, Gia had shut him down. Now that they were divorced she needed him less than ever.

In his efforts to be a good man, a good husband and nothing like his father, had he gone about being a husband the wrong way? He'd never laid a hand on Gia—he'd sooner die—but he'd strong-armed her in other ways, hadn't he?

He'd tried corralling her the way Jack had—protecting her the way Royce and Bran had. And like she'd done with each of those other men, she'd pulled away from Jayson, too.

Flubbing a marriage was a big failure for him. He'd never intended on divorcing. He'd planned on being married one time, for forever. But as their communication deteriorated, he found himself swallowing arguments instead of having them. He'd opted for silence over involvement. He should have told her what he was thinking. What he was *feeling*.

At the time he hadn't wanted to be wrong.

Stupid.

"You two aren't related, but you're a lot alike." Chester appeared around the corner, gave Ollie the bulldog a scratch on the head and then sat next to Jayson. "I have a thing for the strong, silent type. I can't help it. If you need to talk, I'm a good listener."

Jayson debated before giving in. He could use a second opinion on the thoughts ricocheting off the inside of his skull.

"Gia and I have a complicated past, but I think a future would be even more complicated."

"Possibly. It's hard not to go back to that familiarity, though. Been there. My ex before Mason." Chester shook his head. "It didn't end well, but we weren't anything like you and Gia."

Jayson turned his head. "Meaning?"

"You two are good for each other, but you're each holding on to your pride with both hands. Vulnerability is the key to any good relationship."

"Gia and I have been naked together, Ches. *Recently.* How much more vulnerable can you get?"

Chester patted Jayson's shoulder. "Jayson, Jayson. Sometime you should try admitting you made a mistake. That goes a long way."

"She's the one pushing me away." Jayson stood. It hurt to admit that out loud. He assumed that hurt was the vulnerability Ches had been referring to.

"I'll stay out of it," Chester vowed as he stood, also. "After I say one more thing."

Jayson could have guessed his brother-in-law wouldn't keep completely silent.

"Even if you don't ride off into the sunset together, if spending time together helps you and Gia over a hump— no pun intended—then go for it."

"That doesn't exactly sound like you," Jayson narrowed his eyes in suspicion. "I thought you were rooting for us to get back together."

"Always." Chester smoothed a finger over one manicured eyebrow. "I also recognize that you are happier when you're talking about her, and I like seeing you happy. Don't beat yourself up so much about the past. These things have a way of working themselves out."

He patted Jayson's leg and then walked off.

Jayson stood for a solid minute and watched a honeybee visit flower after flower at the edge of his mother's garden.

He *was* happier with Gia in his life. He couldn't argue that. He was happier sleeping with her, too. He thought about her happiness, then and wondered…

Had he prioritized his own happiness over hers in the past? Had she been telling him what she needed this whole time but he hadn't listened?

Ollie barked, interrupting his thoughts.

"Yeah, yeah. I know," he told the dog.

The answer was a resounding *yes*. To both.

Sixteen

"I've never been so tired in my life," Addison said, rocking the car seat on the chair next to her. "I'm not sure how it happened but she's completely nocturnal. Do you think Bran is secretly a vampire?"

Gia laughed. She invited Addi out of the house for lunch, knowing that Bran's wife was climbing the walls. Work was Addison's favorite pastime, which she'd swapped for staying home with her daughter during her maternity leave.

The day was sunny and beautiful so they'd opted to sit outside at the swanky café midway between their houses. Soft jazz music played in the background interspersed with the light tinkling of silverware on plates.

"At least Quinn sleeps when you're out of the house." Her niece's eyelashes cast shadows on her chubby cheeks, causing Gia to smile again. "And you know I can come over and help whenever you need me."

"I know. You're kind of awesome like that."

"Best aunt ever." Gia pressed her fingertips to her collarbone. She'd loved both her nieces on sight, couldn't get enough of them.

She and Jayson hadn't seriously discussed children when they were married. They were always waiting for work to slow down, or for things between them to settle. But now with two of the most beautiful babies on the planet in her immediate circle, she could admit she'd been thinking a lot more about the family she might have some day.

The problem was she couldn't picture a man in the role of father to her children—save one.

Guess who that was?

Now that they'd had slept together twice, she wasn't sure what she should be doing. Breaking up with him to search for Mr. Forever, who she was seriously doubting she'd find on that dating app? Or continuing with Jayson knowing that they wouldn't work permanently?

"I feel like Royce and Taylor have been on their honeymoon for a hundred years." Addison stopped rocking her daughter and ate a bite of her strawberry spinach salad.

"Right? He becomes CEO and then turns into a big slacker." Which wasn't true at all. Her oldest brother deserved a break.

"How is the tablet thing going?" Addi asked. "Have you and Jayson cracked the code?"

"Not yet. We've been working on it, though."

"Must be hard to work that closely with him and not want to strangle each other. Or, you know, have sex in the bathroom." Addi smirked.

Gia shook her head. "Knew that was coming."

"Come on! Give me something. You have sex for the first time since your divorce and you're not going to dish even a little?" Addi tilted her head. "Wait—that *was* the first time, wasn't it?"

"That was the first time," Gia confirmed, then offered

a coy smile. "Though we did do it in the car five days before the divorce."

Addi laughed, pure glee as she stabbed her salad.

"You're enjoying this."

"I really am. I haven't been out much," Addi said. "So, what else can you tell me? Now you're working together and having sex all over the house?"

Gia lifted one half of her club sandwich. "Only once. By the pool. And it wasn't a good idea. Especially after my date with Elias."

"You went on a date?" Addi gaped at her. "Who's Elias?"

"A guy I met on the app." Gia bit the corner of her sandwich. "He was..." *Not Jay.* "Nice but boring."

"Well, one thing's for sure. With you and Jayson, things are *never* boring."

Gia ate a french fry. Things between her and Jayson were never boring because they were unresolved. It was like there were arguments floating in the air between them. Things they'd never said as well as things that had been said way too much.

"I'm not sure what we're doing," Gia admitted. "Jayson and I. We've done this already—the whole shebang. Wedding. House."

"You don't have to figure that out now," Addi said practically. Quinn cooed and Addi rocked the car seat.

"No, but we'll have to figure things out eventually."

"This is where your big brain gets you into trouble. Sometimes you just have to go for it and see what happens next."

"You mean like you did with Bran." Gia folded her arms on the table and lifted one eyebrow. Addison had leaped before she looked with Bran and they'd suffered a setback because of it.

"Just like that." Addi nodded, surprising Gia with her reaction. "It worked out in the end. There's no right way to do what you're doing. And you don't have to protect yourself with Jayson. He's the safest bet you have."

Yes, in some ways he was safe. He wouldn't hurt her. He respected her. He'd give her the best time of her life in bed.

But he was also unsafe—because every time he was around her, she couldn't seem to separate the man who'd broken her heart while they were married from the man who'd won it early on.

She didn't want to dive in headfirst again only to discover they were still in the shallows. Any attempt at a long-term relationship could land them back in the same situation they were in before.

And she couldn't stomach ending things with him again. It hurt too much the first time.

The conversation with Addison looped in Gia's head when she returned to work, crashed into her when she climbed into her car to drive home, and arrived on a silver platter when Jayson showed up at her house twenty minutes later.

The front door opened and her heart zoomed to her toes. He walked in, a leather shoulder bag in his hand. "It's just me" might as well have been a "Honey, I'm home."

She was in the kitchen, the makings for a sandwich spread out on the countertop.

"No takeout tonight?" He examined the countertop: mayo jar, bakery-fresh whole wheat bread, leaf lettuce, a freshly sliced tomato, smoked turkey breast and a jar of pickles.

"You're welcome to have one."

"Thought you'd never ask." He hesitated, his eyes lingering on her mouth. She licked her lips self-consciously, knowing she shouldn't want the casual peck hello but wanting it anyway.

In the end, his mouth flinched into a tight smile and he leaned past her to pluck a pickle slice from the jar.

As homey as this scene felt, they were still separated. She'd do well to remember that.

He set his bag down on a bar chair and rubbed his hands together. "I need chips."

"On top of the fridge," she answered automatically. But he knew where the chips were in this house. He'd been the one to store them there to begin with. Why she'd kept them there when she had to grab a footstool to reach them was beyond her.

He was right. Some things never changed.

"Before you met me you crammed them into a cabinet and broke half the chips in the bag." He sliced open the bag with a pair of scissors from a drawer he was also familiar with. The entire scene was eerily familiar. As if they'd time-traveled back to when they were married and this was a typical day after work.

And yet it was utterly and totally different.

What was it that Jayson had said the last time they'd slept together? *I don't want to fail with you again.*

He hadn't said, "I don't want to fail you" nor had he said, "I don't want to fail." He'd said, "I don't want to fail *with* you," as if they'd both had blame in what happened between them.

She couldn't remember a time when he wasn't justifying his position and his actions. When he wasn't and expecting her to go along with what he'd decided should happen. He never listened, and she never felt heard.

Had he changed in the year and a half they were apart? Or was that dangerous and hopeful thinking?

They made their sandwiches side by side in silence.

"Why did we buy such a big house?" she asked as she traversed the wide layout of the kitchen to the trashcan.

"You love this house."

"I do but it's too much—" Especially now that it was just her.

He navigated a huge bite of his stacked turkey sandwich before speaking. "You loved it and I wanted you to have it."

Both true. She'd stepped into this very kitchen and had done a twirl reminiscent of *The Sound of Music* on the marble tile. "I did love it."

"You talked about huge Christmas dinners prepared in this oven," he reminded her. "And kids running through the halls. You wanted a dog at one point. Remember?"

A dog. That's right. She remembered.

Remembering hurt.

And now she couldn't begin to picture another man—like Denver or Elias—in the kitchen eating over the counter. One who didn't smash potato chips between his sandwich before taking a bite.

"We've had some pretty late nights." She needed to tell him what she'd been thinking. Establish some boundaries for both their sakes. "If you don't want to drive home, you don't have to."

His eyebrows lifted in interest. "Oh, yeah?"

"The pool house is all yours," she said, before he had the very wrong idea of what she was offering.

No matter what fun with Jayson she could have, Gia knew what was at stake. Being with him in this familiar environment was chipping away at her resolve. She didn't need the constant reminder of what they could have had—of what they'd once naively dreamed they could have.

"The pool house," he repeated, his tone flat.

"Sure. There's a lot of unused space out there. I still have that bed out there."

He watched her, his eyes darkening to navy blue. "I know that bed, G."

She couldn't look away even though she should. She knew that bed, too. While the house was filled with decorators for nearly a month, she and Jay had stayed in the pool house. They'd made love on that small double bed, woke to a view of the pool and their backyard. He would rise before her and make coffee in the cheap four-cup coffee maker and deliver her the first cup.

Simpler, better times.

It seemed no matter where she looked she couldn't escape memories of them together. How was she supposed to make a life on her own for herself when she couldn't leave *them* behind?

Seventeen

He'd nearly cracked the code by nightfall.

Gia had gone to bed before him, leaving him in the family room to work. He apparently now had two options. Drive home or sleep in the pool house.

It irritated him that she wanted to kick him out. They'd been close lately. Why the sudden line in the sand?

He shut down Big Ben and pulled his keys from his pocket, frowning down at them. He didn't want to go home. He wanted to stay here—and *not* in the damn pool house. He couldn't escape the idea that Gia needed him here, in the *actual* house.

Not to protect her—the gated community was safe. And the security system he'd insisted she install after he moved out was top-of-the-line. But to just…*be here*. She'd seemed sad after telling him he could stay in the pool house, and he didn't want her to be sad and alone.

So, he laid down on the couch anyway, his arm thrown over his head, eyes on the ceiling. He slept a little and thought a lot. About the arguments they'd had behind these walls. Those once impassioned disagreements that turned into apathetic silence, which then led them to split in the first place.

Around six thirty in the morning, he heard her shuffle into the kitchen. He was already at the desk, bleary-eyed and tired, since he'd thought a lot more than he'd slept.

"Morning," he croaked, to let her know he was there.

"Morning." Her dark hair was scooped into a topknot and she wore a short silk robe, white with big black flowers on it. She looked soft and approachable and adorable, and his hands itched to touch her.

"You're wearing glasses," he observed as he stood to stretch.

"They're new." She touched the frames. "I usually wear contacts at work."

"Oh." So much had changed, and yet whenever he was here he was somehow frozen in time.

She scooped coffee grounds into a filter basket. "Coffee?"

"Sure."

She pressed the button on the machine and propped her fist on her hip. She was cute and sleepy and damned sexy. Especially in those dark-framed glasses. "You didn't sleep in the pool house did you?"

"How did you—I didn't feel right leaving you." He lifted a hand to his hair, feeling strangely uncomfortable.

"And you in my house when I told you to leave felt *right*?"

"What are you trying to avoid by kicking me out, G?"

He could feel the sexual tension between them right now. She was likely trying to avoid this very situation. Them, together, wearing very little.

"You never listen. I have been sleeping alone for a while now. I don't need a guard downstairs."

He opened his mouth to tell her he wasn't guarding her, he wanted to be here for her in case she needed him. But old patterns threatened. If he said that, she'd tell him that he could let go of the need to take care of her since they were divorced.

He didn't want the conversation to go that way. Time to try something new.

Vulnerability.

Hadn't that been what Chester recommended?

Jayson didn't have a good track record with vulnerability. His father had seen it as a weakness to exploit, and his mother felt guilty that she'd caused Jay to feel unsafe. He'd shored up his emotions for a damn good reason—to protect himself and the people he loved. Only now he wondered if opening up to Gia might be the what they needed to bury their past once and for all. Still, opening up could be the ultimate humiliation for him if she rejected him—totally possible.

He needed her closer for this conversation. Tucking a finger into the silky belt at her waist, he pulled her to him. "You like to remind me how much you don't need me, which makes me feel rejected."

She blinked up at him. Now that he'd admitted what he was feeling, what he was *feeling* was exposed. Might as well have loaded a gun and handed it to her. Rather than backtrack, he decided to lean in a bit more. "When we were together I went about protecting you in the wrong way."

Her eyes widened. She stared as if shocked by his words. For good reason. He'd rarely if ever admitted as his mistakes in the past. He'd always thought he knew best.

"I care about you," he said. "I never meant to hobble or limit you. I never intended for you to feel like you were a child I was looking after. Despite not wanting to be like my dad, I guess I had a heavy hand after all."

No, he'd never physically harmed her, but trying to stifle

her when she should be wild and free hadn't been much better.

She reached up and placed her hand on his cheek. "No, Jayson. You're nothing like your father. I heard the stories from both you and your mom, and I believed then what I believe now."

He stayed silent, as if part of him knew how badly he needed to hear what came next.

"You're overprotective at times, but you're also kind. And sweet."

He grumbled.

She laughed and patted his cheek. "It's okay to be sweet. You're not your dad. You could never be that small of a man."

The moment called for a kiss, so he bent his head. She inclined her chin to meet him in the middle.

Maybe vulnerability had its merits.

She tasted like Gia. Like the woman he hadn't seen at this ungodly hour since he'd awoken next to her in the bed they shared. It was a bed he'd like to share with her again... say, right now.

She surprised him by reaching up and clinging to his neck, kissing him deeper. He untied her robe, slipping his palms over her warm skin. Beneath he found a simple white tank top and black panties. This outfit was one of his all-time favorites. No fancy lingerie needed, his ex-wife was sexiest when she wore cotton.

He sucked in a breath as he lifted the edge of her tank and tickled her skin. "So soft."

Her own breathing sped as her hands roamed over his T-shirt. "We have to go to work," she cautioned, but there was no conviction in her words.

"And if we don't?" He wrapped his arms around her and pulled her flush against him. He was already hard from that kiss. "When was the last time you did something you weren't supposed to, Gia?"

She laughed, the sound husky and sexy, and turned those dark eyes up to him. Her grin held. "It's been frequent since we've been hanging out more often."

He liked that.

He lifted and deposited her on the countertop, content to use the momentum they had to spend some serious quality time with her. Just as his mouth stamped hers and his hand closed over her breast, a sharp knock came from the front door.

"It's us!" Taylor Knox called out. She hadn't made it into the kitchen yet, but she would soon enough.

"Crap! I forgot." Gia shoved away from him and hopped off the counter.

"What the hell…?" He adjusted the part of himself that had recently become large enough to be a distraction.

"Royce and Taylor asked if they could swing by on the way to work today to drop off something."

"What something?" It'd better be important, that was for damn sure.

She waved him off. "Go hide."

"Hide?"

"Jayson, it's seven in the morning and neither of us are dressed."

"Last I checked we're not teenagers. You have nothing to explain." He folded his arms. He wasn't going anywhere. "You're a grown woman." As a grown woman she could sleep with Jayson—or *almost* sleep with him—anytime she liked.

"At least act casual?" she pleaded.

"Casual went out the window with that kiss."

She glared, a sure sign she agreed, and then walked out of sight.

A moment later, Taylor was chattering her way excitedly through the house. Royce's low murmur followed. Jayson poured himself a cup of coffee and leaned against the countertop. When Taylor entered the kitchen, her sentence trailed off into an ellipsis.

"Hi, Coop," she said carefully, exchanging glances with Royce before swapping a lengthier one with Gia.

"Morning." Jayson sipped his coffee.

"Cooper." Royce's expression was harder to read than his wife's.

"Coffee?" Jayson offered.

"No, thanks," Taylor said. "We brought a few souvenirs and I wanted to drop them off before Gia took off for work. We have something for you, too, but it didn't occur to me to bring it."

"For good reason," Royce murmured. "We didn't expect to find you here." He didn't often play the big, bad brother card with Jayson—or at least he hadn't in a while. If he thought he was intimidating… Hell, Jayson was older than Royce.

"Why don't we have our coffee outside," Royce added.

"I'll have mine right here, thanks, but you can go outside if you like." Jayson grinned.

Royce glowered for a beat before Taylor interrupted the short standoff.

"We should go. Don't you have to be in the office soon?" Taylor asked her husband.

"Nope."

"What's the matter, Royce? Afraid to admit your feelings in front of your sister? She's an adult, you know." Jayson informed him.

"Afraid has nothing to do with it." Royce faced his sister. "Are you being careful with him? In *every way imaginable*?"

"Royce!" Taylor shot him a peeved look.

"Gia knows what she wants," Jayson said. "She also

knows what she doesn't want. She'd never allow me, or anyone, to trample her wishes. You know that better than anyone. She's damned well capable of making decisions for herself regardless of what you or I want her to do."

Royce's nostrils flared.

Gia took a step closer to Jayson and he instantly realized what he'd done. He'd spoken for her instead of giving her the space to speak for herself. Dammit, would he ever learn?

"Thank you, Jayson."

Wait. Did she just *thank him*?

"I'm not interested in your advice when it comes to Jayson," she told her brother." She winked at Taylor. "Yours I'd consider."

"Aw, thanks, G." Taylor smiled. Royce did not. She gave her husband's arm a light slap. "Oh, stop being so overbearing. Jayson's right. Gia can take care of herself." Taylor set the gift bag on the counter before curling her arms around one of Royce's. "We'll be leaving now. See you at the office."

Once they'd gone, Jayson turned to his ex-wife. "Did I have a stroke or did both you and Taylor admit that I was right?"

"Don't ruin this moment by being arrogant." But Gia was smiling when she said it. She pulled the coffee cup from his hand and set it on the counter. "Now, where were we? We have a few minutes to continue what we started before going in to work."

He didn't hesitate, setting her on the countertop next to his coffee and kissing her.

They didn't end up having sex, but second base wasn't bad.

Eighteen

The moment Gia sat down at her desk later that morning and opened her laptop Taylor appeared as if a magician had *abracadabraed* her there.

"I leave for my honeymoon and apparently miss a really big development between you and Jayson! Did you not each bring your own dates—the first time I've ever seen that happen, by the way—to my wedding? Tell me everything. Every last thing." She dragged a chair over and sat, elbows propped on the desk's surface, chin in her hands.

"Well—"

"Addison told me you had sex after the wedding, but I thought she was mistaken. I mean it was the morning after and there were still guests mingling at the breakfast bar."

"Well—"

"I never believed you with that skateboarder for a second. Or Cooper with that model." Taylor rolled her eyes. "Give me a break."

"Yeah, um… Our dates weren't really doing it for us."

"So you did it to each other?" Taylor giggled at her own joke. "Sorry about busting in on you two this morning."

"It's okay. He wasn't supposed to be there, actually. I asked him to sleep in the pool house."

"Boundaries are important," Taylor said carefully.

About that… The second Taylor and Royce left, Gia happily made out with Jayson. He'd admitted he handled things poorly when they were married and then defended Gia to her brother. It was beyond sexy hearing him say she could handle herself. She'd wanted to see that change in him for so long. Now that she had, she was having trouble trusting it.

"Sex is a normal, natural thing," Taylor said. "If that's where you and Cooper are, enjoy it."

"You, too? Addi told me to go for it. It's not that easy, you know. Jayson and I are divorced."

"Yeah, and you're still human. Plus, you two have a very unique relationship, even with a marriage behind you. Mistakes are always made in relationships. Sometimes you have to grow and learn. Maybe your timing was off the first time around."

"Or maybe I'm going to lose my heart to the one man I should know better than to hand it to." Jayson was a wonderful person and hotter than Hades in the summertime but him admitting he'd overstepped one time wasn't going to fix everything.

"Oh, honey." Taylor patted her best friend's hand. "I love you. I wish you every happiness in life, whether you end up sharing a life with Jayson or not. But sometimes you have to take a leap of faith even if you're not sure it's going to work out. Look at me. After all the mistakes I made, I have Royce. I have Emmaline. Can't blame me for wanting you to have that same happiness."

"No. I can't blame you." Gia smiled. What Taylor and Royce had was beautiful and everlasting.

"It's okay to screw up." Taylor stood. "I know you think

you have to be bulletproof—to hold your own and make sure you do everything for yourself, but in the end it's not worth it. It's okay to admit you messed up. Messing up is a sign that you tried."

Gia *had* tried in her marriage, but she was haunted by the worry that she hadn't tried *enough*. If she and Jayson were to realize they'd made a mistake divorcing, would she ever be able to forgive herself for causing them so much pain? After all, she was the one who'd offered divorce as a solution.

Rather than say any of that, she nodded at her friend. "Thanks, Tay."

"You bet, doll." Taylor slipped out of Gia's office at the same time Jay passed by the door. He stopped and leaned in, both hands on the door frame. He looked good. Somehow better than he had a few hours ago. She was struck with the overwhelming need to touch him.

"Brainstorming sesh tonight at the house?" he asked.

The house. He'd worded that carefully. "Sure."

"Wine?"

Maybe she'd been overthinking—a hobby she was intimately familiar with. Maybe she should take her sisters-in-law's advice and enjoy the moment. "Sure."

"Red? White?"

"Chardonnay would be lovely."

"Consider it done." He tapped the door frame and walked away. She watched him go, admiring his strong, straight back, dark wavy hair and long legs.

That night Gia was propped up on her sofa, tablet in her lap. Jayson sat at the desk on the other side of the room.

She thought about her conversation with Taylor when she should have been focusing on solving the tablet issue. No one on their team had made headway. When she suggested to Jayson they should scrap the update, he nearly blew his stack.

We can't let this beat us, G. Those improvements are vital to the survival of this tablet. If we give up now, we're signing its death warrant.

That made her think of them, their marriage. Had they given up rather than improve?

The longer she sat in the same room with him, the more irresistible he became. That same old familiarity smacked between them, here in their former shared house. Even when they weren't having sex, she felt the sizzle of attraction. Even with the unromantic pizza box on the coffee table, what was left of their dinner having congealed into a rock-hard mass of cheese and olives.

It was important for her to define boundaries not only for Jay, but for herself. She shouldn't have continued kissing him this morning. She should have marched upstairs and dressed for work, and kept her cool. That lengthy physical interaction with him made it harder for her to bury those thoughts about their marriage and the mistakes that were made. In short, it'd made it harder for her to continue moving *forward*.

She was stuck. On the damn tablet issue, and on Jayson.

With a sigh, she restarted the tablet for the nine-hundredth time and began poking around. As expected, it powered down before she'd had a chance to—

"Oh my God," she muttered. While part of her mind had been turning over her current situation, the processing part had shoved two puzzle pieces together. She knew *exactly* what to do to fix this update.

Jay swiveled in his chair, barely reined-in excitement in his eyes. "That sounded promising."

She had to smile. He knew her *Eureka!* voice.

She rushed to the desk, physically moved his hand from the mouse, and clicked out of what he was working on. A few clicks and keystrokes later, she knew she had it. A zap of intuition told her that she'd tripped upon exactly the right code.

She was a superhero.

"That's it. The fix. I know it. I know it, I know it…" Heart racing, she stood over the desk staring down at Jayson, her chest rising and falling with each truncated breath.

"Why am I not surprised?" His slow blink communicated that he was proud. His approval, while dangerous to covet, was oh-so welcome.

"Hand it over. I'll update the software and we'll do a test. We'll see if you just won the bet. Or if I have another shot at winning it myself."

Right. The bet. She hadn't been thinking about that. Her thoughts had narrowed to fixating on him and finding the glitch.

What felt like years later, but was more like fifteen minutes, she chewed on the side of her thumb and paced from kitchen to living room.

Finally, she heard the telltale chime of the tablet firing up. She raced over to watch as his blunt fingers tapped from screen to screen. He powered down and glanced up at her, warmth in his blue eyes. While her breath stalled in her lungs, he powered up the tablet one more time and tapped on the screen.

"It didn't crash. *Yet*." His lips curved. "The shutdown typically occurs immediately. Just to make sure, have at it." He handed over the tablet and instructed her to test it for herself. "I'll do the same with mine."

Jayson opened one webpage and another, and then another. He opened a social media app. He uploaded a game, played it for a few minutes, and then closed it and opened a documents file.

No crashing. Not a whisper that anything hadn't been operating before.

She did it. *She did it!*

He was thrilled and awed by her brilliant mind. He was also disappointed for not discovering the fix himself. Had it been his stroke of genius that fixed the tablet, they'd be naked by now, her under him, moaning his name.

Not that he was giving up.

"Anything bad happen yet?" he asked.

"Not yet." She showed him her screen. "Other than a new addiction to Candy Blaster. I'm on level thirteen already. You know what that means?"

"You can blast candy with the best of them?"

"Har-har. It *means* I am owed a homemade pasta dinner." Her grin was contagious. Once upon a time she'd called that recipe a "panty dropper."

No, he wasn't giving up on getting her into bed yet.

He rose and walked to the sofa. "You should be proud. An issue that stumped the best minds at ThomKnox didn't stand a chance against yours."

"Thanks." She gave him a sheepish smile. He loved her humility, even though he'd argued with her to own her smarts on more than one occasion.

"I'll let everyone know the race is over, then I'll head to the office." He grabbed his tablet and bag and slung it over his shoulder.

"Now?" She stood and fidgeted with her own tablet. "I mean. We should at least soak in the win."

She didn't want him to go? Interesting.

While he would be the first to admit that a celebration was in order, he also knew she'd been hard at work on this for long enough. Once the adrenaline wore off she was going to be exhausted and grouchy. He could handle both, but he wasn't sure she could handle both with him around.

"I don't want to wait another second to input this fix in

the system. Good job, Gia. Killed it." Rubbing her biceps with his palm, he leaned down to kiss her on the cheek. When he pulled back she turned her head, her dark eyes seeking his with so much want he could feel it in his bones.

He thought for a second she might kiss him. Thought that her lingering gaze might lead to more. If that was the case, he'd have a hard time making himself leave, no matter what needed to be done at work.

"Okay." She blinked, at that dash of errant lust dissipated. "You owe me dinner."

"I do," he agreed. One panty-dropper dinner, coming right up. Once upon a time he'd had his sights set on wooing her. How interesting to find himself back in that same boat now. "How's Saturday? Six o'clock?"

She nodded. "What do you want me to do?"

"Enjoy the spoils that come with winning." He headed for the door and she called out good-night. He glanced at his hand on the doorknob, all but forcing himself to leave the house and her behind tonight.

"Good night, G," he said to himself once he was outside.

Nineteen

Jayson sat on the corner of his desk in the center of the tech department, addressing his team. Everyone was sitting at their surrounding desks, eyes on him while he delivered the very good news that the software glitch had been *unglitched*.

Gia lingered at the threshold of her office, arms folded, hip propped on the doorway. In case anyone was watching her, she needed to appear both supportive and comfortable. The supportive part was easy. Jayson was amazingly adept at work and was a respected and admired leader.

The comfortable part took some doing.

Watching him sit there, one foot on the floor, the other dangling off the corner of the desk, his hands folded between the spread of his thick thighs made her want him. The way she'd wanted him last night.

He hadn't tried anything and she kept telling herself she was glad. After all she'd been trying to establish boundaries.

And now, voilà. *Boundaries*.

His team laughed at something he said and Jayson smiled. He had an easy way of wielding power. Like a gladiator in the ring who knew he was in charge of the crowd. Even the standard office attire of a gray-blue button-down shirt and dark tie, dark gray pants and leather shoes didn't distract from that power.

She had been surrounded by powerful men all her life. Men, this one included, who thought they knew what was best for her. She'd never been intimidated or afraid to stick up for herself. She'd never been afraid to speak her mind.

She recalled his moment of vulnerability, when he'd admitted he'd been heavy-handed while they were married. He had, but their problems weren't only caused by him. He'd been trying to help, which made her wonder… Had she been so concerned with asserting herself that she'd trampled on his efforts to care for her?

That was an uncomfortable thought. Almost as uncomfortable as her cheeks going warm the moment he turned his head and focused on her.

Oh, how she'd been tempted to keep him at the house a little longer. To talk him into a glass of wine and some kissing on the couch. It would have been playing with fire, she knew. So why was she so disappointed that he'd left instead?

He'd confused her lately.

She'd thought she knew him. Knew his tendency to steamroll her, and that he hadn't been the best listener, but lately she was beginning to think he'd changed. Not only had he admitted he didn't handle things best while they were married, but he'd also argued with Royce that she could handle things on her own.

She'd been unable to believe what she was hearing.

While she'd been hyperfocused on their *inability* to work things out in the past, she couldn't help thinking that fixing the unfixable tablet issue was a symbol of how much she and Jayson had grown since they'd divorced.

Her body wasn't helping matters.

Every nonsexual thing he said now grew wings and flapped low in her belly. The phrase *integrated software analysis* shouldn't make her want him.

"I appreciate the team's attention to detail," Jayson's voice dipped into an unintentionally sexy husk. "You should be proud of how hard you've worked. I know you've been sweating over the details in search of that magical sweet spot…"

As she absently twirled a few strands of her hair, her eyes feasted on the broadness of his chest. The hardness of his body. She'd stayed up past dark working up a different kind of sweat with him when they were married… And she recalled with clarity how tirelessly he'd searched for her magical sweet spot…

"Now the confession," he said, his gaze arrowing straight to her. "Gia solved the problem. We had a bet going, too. I lost."

After applause, and her demure curtsy, one of their tech gurus, Ric, called out, "What'd you lose, Coop?"

"I have to spend several hours in a hot kitchen making my grandmother's homemade pasta recipe." One eyebrow rose in an insanely sexy way. With a heated glance toward her he added, "If I would have won—"

"I would've had to cook for him," she blurted out. "Great work everyone. It was a team effort, no matter who found the glitch. Sometimes finding what doesn't work can be just as important as what does."

Jayson gave her an approving smile. "Well said, Gia." He turned back to the group. "We're going to celebrate with a party here at ThomKnox for our department. Champagne will flow, but not yet. First we have to finish the corrections that I started, coordinate our efforts with Marketing, and then put the update back on the calendar. Thanks, everyone. You know what to do."

The team turned around in their chairs, opened computers or laptops, reached for their tablets and did as Jayson asked. He stood from his desk and followed her inside her office.

"Champagne?" She asked when he shut the door. "That was nice of you."

"Nice, huh?" He took another step closer to her and she tightened her arms over her chest, refusing to let him in on the fact that her nipples were desperately trying to get his attention. "I didn't know you were going to cook for me if I won."

"Well… I couldn't tell them the truth," she whispered.

"Which was what, again?"

She ignored his devilish, tempting grin, which wasn't easy. "I have work to do too, you know."

"Yeah, yeah. So do I." Before he left, he turned. She felt his eyes raking over her black pencil skirt and red silk button-down shirt. "Proud of you, G. I mean it."

"Thank you." She meant that, too.

His lips pulled into a quick, tight-lipped smile, and then he left the office, and left her to wonder if maybe they had both changed over the last few years after all.

After promising champagne to the staff, Jayson considered that he and Gia hadn't yet properly celebrated their win. Yes, it was a team effort, blah, blah, blah, but she deserved to toast to her accomplishments in private, and without having to put on her work face.

Outside her house, he rang the doorbell, which felt odd considering he used to live here. But as they'd established recently, they were no longer the same people who used to live here. She'd changed since then, and so had he. Now they were somewhere in the middle, and he wasn't sure if that was a good or a bad thing.

The door opened and there stood his ex-wife, in that same scintillating red shirt that hugged her breasts. She'd kicked off her shoes in favor of bare feet, which he liked even more.

"Did I black out? Is it Saturday already?" Her eyes went to the champagne bottle, tied with a gold bow—the biggest one he'd been able to find at the convenience store. "What's this?"

"It's a bow." He flicked the fringed ribbon. "I was going to go with red to match your shirt, but this one matches the label." He spun the bottle to show her a familiar gold label.

"My favorite."

"It's the same brand I chose for the party for the team. It got me thinking that you and I never celebrated."

She chewed on her lip, considering.

"Can I come in?"

"Only because it's my favorite champagne and I could never turn it down. Which I'm sure you knew."

"Guilty." He smiled.

"*One* glass." She stepped aside for him to come in. There was a candle lit in the kitchen, soft music playing from a speaker in the living room.

"Feels different in here." Like it used to, he thought, but didn't say. She had a way of putting her feminine stamp on everything. He hadn't been able to achieve this sort of warm, welcoming vibe at his apartment. It still felt stale and drab.

"I had to air out the stench of defeat." She sent him a feisty smile as she reached for the handle on a tall cabinet. "You didn't have to give me credit for fixing the glitch, by the way." Her T-shirt rode up and exposed her flat, tan belly.

He set the champagne aside, the bottle sweating from

the ride over in the car, and placed a chilly hand on the side of her waist.

"Your hands are freezing!" she shrieked. She swatted him away but there was a playful glint in her eyes.

"Never could resist that move." He eased her to one side and pulled down the pair of fluted glasses.

"I could've done that," she mumbled.

"Yes, but I'm here so you didn't have to." He handed the stemware over, upside down. When she took them in her hands, she brushed his fingers. An innocent touch, but his heart mule-kicked his chest in response.

"They don't get a lot of use. That cabinet is high." That was her way of saying thank you, he guessed. Or avoiding mentioning that those were the very champagne flutes they'd toasted with at their wedding.

Had Gia been anyone else he might have been surprised that she hadn't thrown out every item that had anything to do with them, but she'd never been petty.

She rinsed out the glasses and took her time drying them while he unwrapped the foil from the neck of the bottle. When he moved to twist off the cork she stopped him with one hand.

"Wait! Don't you want to…" She gestured outside.

"Risky." He pretended to deliberate.

"Worth it," she said before dashing outside.

In the backyard, he angled the bottle so the cork would shoot into the privacy fence rather than into the sky—a mistake he'd made once before with near disastrous consequences. He twisted the cork so that it was halfway out and then popped it with his thumb. It sailed over the pool and hit the privacy fence with a soft *thump*.

"I love that noise. Smart aim," she praised. "Remember that time when you shot the cork over the fence? It must've gone a mile."

"How could I forget? It was the shot of a lifetime. If I was trying to hit Neil's lit grill, I never could have done it."

"Not for a million dollars," she agreed with a laugh. He laughed with her, enjoying the memory and the ease between them—a rarity over the last couple of years. "Guess it wasn't all bad. Our marriage."

"No. It wasn't." She took the bottle from his hand and tilted it to her mouth, swallowing a fizzy mouthful of the very expensive champagne. He followed her lead, taking a slug from the bottle next before settling onto the chaise lounger. He patted the cushion next to him, remembering what they'd done the last time they were on this piece of furniture.

"No funny business," she warned as she sat down, proving her memory was as good as his.

"Just an innocent bottle of champagne shared between two ex-spouses. What could possibly go wrong?"

She took a drink, this time holding on to the bottle while she stared off into the distance.

He wondered if, like him, her mind returned to the last bottle of champagne they'd shared out here.

It was one of the worst nights of his life...

Twenty

Two months before the divorce

"I thought you'd be happy," Jayson growled, equal parts confused and pissed off.

Making Gia happy was a target he couldn't hit. God knew he'd tried. It made him feel like a failure when she was unhappy and lately that'd been more often than not.

"Happy?" she asked, her tone filled with accusation.

"Yes." He glugged a few inches of champagne into her glass and then into his. "You had a problem. I fixed it."

She threw her hands up. "Without talking to me!"

"What was there to talk about?"

She snatched the bottle from him, nearly knocking over her glass. He snatched the glass before it hit the newly installed ceramic tile, sloshing champagne onto his hand in the process.

"Unbelievable," she grumbled, sliding the patio door aside and stomping outside.

With a sigh, he followed.

"You making a decision without me, on something as large as a vehicle parked in our shared garage does *not* make me happy. You should have asked my opinion."

"All you do is complain about my truck!" He'd bought the exact Mercedes she'd cooed over when they saw it advertised the other day. "You wanted something classier. You said so yourself."

"I didn't mean I wanted you to go out and buy it for me!"

"Why? Because you can buy it for yourself? I am aware of the Knox family fortune you're sitting on, Gia. You don't have to rub my nose in it."

She set the champagne bottle on the ground next to her and crossed her arms over her chest. "You're never going to understand, Jay."

He was beginning to think she was right.

"I love the car," she said. Cryptically. "But I would rather you have included me in the decision to buy it. Stop assuming you know what I want and *ask me*."

Blinded by anger, and embarrassment, he didn't hear what she was really saying. So, of course, he continued to defend himself. "All I do is cater to what you want. It'd be nice if you appreciated it once in a while."

"You want me to *thank you* for bypassing me and doing what you feel is best?"

He'd dug in then, a mistake, but he was too pissed off to change course. "That'd be a nice change of pace."

Jayson sat next to her now on the lounge, the starry sky black above them, the water in the pool still and dark.

He hadn't handled that night well. He hadn't handled much well when they were married. He constantly felt insulted. Like a failure. He'd been trying to be her hero. How was a guy like him supposed to out-hero Jack and Brannon and Royce Knox, the three giants in her life?

He couldn't.

And so, he'd attempted to prove himself over and over. But he hadn't known what she'd wanted. Finally, he thought he knew what that was.

She wanted to be heard. To be considered.

That night's argument wasn't about the Mercedes. It was about her wanting to be included in the decisions and choices in their shared marriage. He saw that now. As crystal clear as the glassware they didn't bother using.

"You're thinking about the night you bought the car," she said.

"Yes."

"So am I."

"It was the last time I saw you drink champagne from the bottle."

"It was the last time I did it." She took another swig and then handed him the bottle.

He set the champagne aside and rested his elbows on his knees, watching the water on the surface of the pool ripple in the evening breeze. "I should have talked to you before I bought it."

He sensed more than saw her shake her head. "I should've accepted it for what it was. A gift. Instead I accused you of making choices for me."

"That evening didn't go the way I wanted," he said, remembering what came next. She'd been the one to point out that if they couldn't relate on a basic level they were better off apart. He'd asked her if she cared to clarify that, and she'd said divorce wasn't out of the question.

"I told you that night I'd be better off without you." She winced.

"No, you didn't. You said we'd be better off apart. Where we couldn't hurt each other any longer. That was my opportunity to promise you I wouldn't hurt you again. Instead, I refused to back down."

He'd agreed with her. Said that if she wanted a divorce, that was fine by him. He'd been hurt, his pride bruised. His ego had taken a beating. "I thought I couldn't please you."

"In your defense, I can be difficult," she said now, but with a kind smile.

"You were being *you*. Which is exactly why I fell in love with you in the first place." He reached for her hand and intertwined their fingers. As he'd realized previously, vulnerability wasn't his strong suit—or hers. The inability for them to let their guard down with each other was probably to blame for their splitting more than anything. "It'd be so easy to lean in and kiss you."

She licked her lips and dipped her chin. Not a nod exactly, but she leaned the slightest bit closer and peered up at him. Tenderly, he stroked her jaw with his thumb. Once he saw his future in those deep brown eyes. Now he only saw his past.

A past littered with failure and regret. A past he couldn't undo.

"But I promised no funny stuff," he murmured.

Time to stop doing what he wanted, or what he decided was right for her. Gia had gone on not one date but two in order to put distance between them. It was time for him to stop pushing so damn hard.

Pulling his hand away, he stood. She watched him, longing emanating from her like heat off the desert floor. Then she armored up.

"Drive safe." She plucked up the bottle as she stood. "Thank you for the champagne."

That's my girl.

"You're welcome."

He walked inside and she followed, abandoning the bottle in the kitchen to see him to the door. He fought the urge to turn and kiss her one last time. That would've felt too final. Like admitting he couldn't live without her.

And he could.

He'd been doing it for years.

Twenty-One

Saturday afternoon came and he showed up at the house, apron in hand. No, really. The black canvas apron read "Pasta la Vista, baby" in bold stencil print.

Gia bought it for him last Christmas. Got a big kick out of herself for being so clever. But amidst the joking and ribbing, she also went on and on about how he'd made the best homemade pasta she'd ever eaten. And that even the best local Italian place in River Grove, Garlíc, couldn't best his skills. It'd made him proud, truth be told.

He'd gone home that night and made pasta by hand, no pasta maker to be seen since he'd left that piece of equipment with Gia. He'd made enough to feed an army but hadn't taken her any of the leftovers. It seemed too personal. Too much of a throwback to the last time he'd made her pasta—on their wedding anniversary. And after they'd nearly slept together at Addison and Brannon's wedding, he hadn't wanted to risk sending the wrong message.

He found said pasta maker now, an item his ex-wife had

insisted having on the gift registry, exactly where they'd put it after they moved in. Bottom cabinet on the island and all the way in the back. As he wrestled it from behind baking dishes and a large stand mixer, he wondered if she'd forgotten about it or if she kept it on purpose. If she'd been planning on learning to make pasta herself—unlikely—or if she couldn't part with the piece of machinery because it reminded her of him.

That seemed even more unlikely.

He'd ask her why she kept it, but she wasn't home. She'd told him to let himself in, that she had errands to run.

The last time she'd left him on his own, she'd gone on a date with a billionaire yacht owner. It still chapped Jayson's ass, even though he supposed it shouldn't. She was as single as he was and allowed to date whomever she chose. Lately that'd been a bitter pill to swallow.

She didn't disclose where she was going or who she was going with so those feelings of jealousy threatened to rise. He ignored them as he piled flour and dug a well, hand mixed in eggs and slowly folded that into a dough.

He was beginning to see that letting go was an art. One he hadn't mastered yet, but he hadn't been trying until now. Not really.

Over the last eighteen months he'd seen and talked to Gia almost every day. She was part of the fabric of his existence. That he no longer climbed into bed with her was a disappointment he'd managed because he had to. Then the morning after Royce's and Taylor's wedding, he'd realized something important.

Gia wanted him, too.

In the heat of the moment, they'd been caught up, time traveling back to their very first encounter, in the same damn bathroom. Which wasn't that surprising given how lackluster their wedding dates had been. But expecting to be able to continue forward without repercussions or emotions was a fool's dream.

When he'd brought the champagne over, he'd learned just how much of that baggage existed for both of them. The memories, the arguments. Sex—even really great sex *twice*—wasn't going to be the magic wand that erased their past.

He'd admitted his faults to her, but that was also too little too late. If he'd been a man who'd recognized in the moment what she needed, maybe they'd still be together.

He punched the dough, more frustrated with himself for being a dumbass than anything and decided that while he couldn't change the past, he could change the future.

Jayson and Gia weren't going to live happily-ever-after, but they could find joy together right now. Even briefly.

"Hey, Siri," he called to his phone. She answered, in an Australian accent, because why not, and he requested what he'd nicknamed his "Badass" playlist. His favorite song, and Gia's for that matter, was the theme song for *Rocky*.

The drumbeats started playing, those initial first few beats reminding him who he was and what he was capable of. He was going to move forward from here, as he was in this moment. He knew how to treat Gia and what she liked, and regardless of the future—whether they had one or not—they had this moment.

And this moment was what mattered.

After a shopping excursion that had yielded zero shopping bags, Gia walked into her foyer and into a wall of music. Jayson's singing voice was on point. She'd always admired his ability to carry a tune, her own talent having ended up somewhere between Brannon and Royce. Bran was an abysmal singer and Royce wasn't half-bad. She guessed that made her about a quarter good.

Jay must not have heard her walk in. Lingering at the

mouth of the living room/kitchen area she watched as he shook his ass at the stove. A black apron was tied at his waist—the one she'd bought for him last Christmas, she'd bet.

A drum solo lifted on the air and he raised the wooden spoon in his hand and pounded the invisible drum set. Upon spinning around, presumably for a final cymbal crash, he spotted her.

"Hey." He dropped his arms, wooden spoon still in hand, steaming pot behind him on the stove. "I didn't hear you come in."

"You don't say." She allowed herself a laugh, because how charmingly taken aback was he, and stepped into the kitchen. Her senses went wild. "Oh my God, it smells incredible in here."

Looked pretty incredible too: her hunky ex-husband, forearms bared, scruff decorating his jaw, wearing that silly apron.

"Homemade sauce." He gestured to a pot on the back of the stove, lid on, and then to the pot he'd been stirring. "Pasta's almost done. Made-from-scratch garlic bread is in the oven."

"You went all out." She was touched. The last time he'd done that they were celebrating an anniversary. Their last, as it turned out.

"I lost fair and square. You didn't expect a jar of Prego sauce and a box of frozen garlic rolls, did you?"

"No. I didn't." His attention to detail was one of the main reasons she'd fallen in love with him. He didn't miss a thing. And he'd wanted to give her *everything*. When they were married, his attention felt smothering. Once he'd moved out, she thought she'd feel free. Instead she found herself struggling to befriend the man she'd vowed to love until the end of time.

Since that thought was a touch heavy for this homey

scene, she decided to lighten the mood. "You know if you'd have cooked like this more often…"

"Don't say it," he warned, pointing at her with the wooden spoon before giving his pasta another swirl.

"I was going to say I'd be a lot fatter."

"That is not what you were going to say." Sliding her a glance, his mouth hitched into a half smile, he set the spoon aside. He grabbed an open bottle of red wine and the empty glass next to his half-full one, and sloshed in a few inches of wine before handing it to her. "Unless you'd rather chug it out of the bottle."

"Us being apart certainly didn't make you any funnier."

He grinned—full out—and she thought to herself that while he hadn't become funnier, he'd somehow become *sexier*. She eyed his backside as she sipped the fruity, deep-colored wine, recognizing it the moment the flavors burst onto her tongue.

"Is this—"

"One and the same. I wasn't going to, but then I remembered that whenever I made pasta we had this vintage."

The same wine they'd drunk on their anniversary, and their favorite from their trip to wine country that first Christmas they'd spent together. She hadn't had it in too long, fearing bad memories. But here they were, and the wine was delicious, her ex-husband was in her house shaking his great ass, and she didn't have any bad memories. Only good ones.

She'd been overthinking the night he'd delivered her champagne. She should have leaned in and kissed him—even if they'd ended up in bed together, it would have been better than soaking in the tub by herself, wishing he was there.

Regardless of the consequences.

It wasn't as if they'd end up *accidentally* remarried. They each knew the score. Their marriage didn't work because of their needs to guard their own space. They couldn't be together while also being apart.

She'd loved him, but that hadn't made them bulletproof. Admiration, friendship and sexual compatibility was one thing. Wedded bliss? Another altogether.

He lifted a noodle from the pot with a pair of tongs and gingerly ate it. Nodding, he lifted his eyebrows before slurping the rest of the noodle down and Gia pressed her thighs together. *Soooo. Sexy.*

"Done," he announced with a nod.

"I'll go change."

"Why? You look great."

She supposed her dark blue skirt and red-striped tank and flats were suitable for a dinner at home, but she wanted to honor his efforts by stepping it up.

"I just want to. You're dressed up." she told him.

"Am I?" He glanced down at his charcoal gray pants and short-sleeved gray utility shirt—the one she'd always liked, with the black buttons.

"Give me five minutes."

"Okay." He held her eyes for a prolonged beat. His gaze was a touch daring, more playful than aloof, almost... tender. Open.

Shutting out thoughts about how she wished he would have been this open and irresistible when they were married, she climbed the stairs to change for her dinner date.

Twenty-Two

Jayson wished she wouldn't have changed. Seeing her in the low-cut navy blue dress that showcased her gorgeous breasts was torture. Also, *incredible*. He was gifted an eyeful whenever she bent over her plate.

Plus, she moaned while she ate.

Literally. *Moaned.*

He'd already been distracted by her bare legs and a pair of sexy high-heeled shoes. When she reentered the kitchen he'd nearly fumbled the bread basket. The moaning thing? Not helping matters.

"You should've been a chef," she proclaimed before taking a giant bite out of a wedge of toasted garlic bread. He'd mixed minced garlic and fresh herbs with butter and slathered it onto the bread before baking. The result?

"Ohhhhh, God." Her eyes slid shut and she tilted her head back.

Orgasmic. That was the result.

He adjusted his pants and drank down more wine.

Maybe if he was super drunk he'd pass out and not be tempted to sleep with his ex-wife.

Again.

"If I were a chef, who would run your tech department?" Work. Talking about work wasn't sexy.

She swiped her mouth with a cloth napkin. "Duh. Me."

"Then who would run Marketing?" Fork hovering, he waited for her to answer but instead she twisted her lips to one side.

"We'd find someone." She shrugged one petite bare shoulder. A shoulder he wanted to kiss.

"Someone better than you?"

"I'd rather be in tech, anyway."

"You were. Before we split."

"You were there first," she argued.

She'd left the department—while not *physically* leaving the department. Her office was the same as it'd been back then. He'd originally given her the space since he felt as if he'd taken the job that should have been hers.

He wound pasta on his fork. "I would have thought you'd jump at the chance to be CEO when your father retired."

"I was too busy putting out marketing fires to even think about it."

He knew that. She worked hard.

"And now?" He leaned in, interested to hear her plans.

"I'm happy for Royce. And I'm relieved that the position of CEO didn't come between him and Brannon."

"What about you, G? What do you want?"

She blinked at him as if she was stunned that he'd asked. Had he ever asked her? Had anyone?

Damn. He'd been an ass.

"I want world peace." She gave him a disingenuous smile and then ate a bite of garlic bread. "What's wrong, do you want me out of your department?"

"You know I don't." He liked her there. "I need your brains."

"Finally, a man who loves me for my brains." She chuckled before going quiet. Probably because she'd mentioned the *L*-word. Love seemed to be tangled up between them and whatever they were to each other now. It was easier to compartmentalize before they'd had sex. Before he'd been sleeping over. Before he'd made her pasta and brought anniversary wine.

"I always appreciated how smart you were," he admitted. "I also appreciate how kind you are. How giving. Admit it, you wanted to kick my ass out of the tech department but you didn't want me to be exiled."

"My family never would have let that happen." A dodge for sure, but he felt justified that he was right.

"But you're doing well without me," he said.

"Without you! You won't leave!"

"You went on a date after we slept together, G. I can take a hint."

"This again?" She dropped her fork. "Elias and I didn't connect. He was as boring as plain oatmeal."

Jayson sat up taller. He liked hearing that.

"Plus you can't be mad about it since I returned home and had sex with you right away."

"You were the one who stripped down to a bikini."

"And you were powerless to stop yourself?" Her smile held and he didn't look away this time. Despite her trying to be blasé about this entire interaction, sexual tension was strung between them, power cable thick.

"I can stop myself." His voice was a low growl. "What do you think I'm doing right now?"

"What if…" She lifted and dropped one shoulder and studied her plate. "I don't want you to stop yourself? What if…" She met his gaze and batted her thick dark eyelashes. "I want to cut dinner short and take you upstairs?"

His entire body screamed *yes*, from his head to his lap. His grip on his fork tightened. He said nothing. Seemed the wisest course of action since he wasn't sure if he was being pranked.

"What if—" she stood from her chair and reached behind her to unzip her dress "—I want to have sex with you right now? On the kitchen floor." She dropped the front of her dress and exposed a strapless bra, the cups pushing her breasts up and together. That's what had been teasing him during dinner. That damn bra.

"I'd say no," he bit out.

She pushed out her bottom lip into a pout and he nearly let loose the feral grin he'd been hiding. Standing from his chair he reached her in two steps and crushed her body against his. With one hand he gripped the material of her dress and tugged it down until it was on the floor.

"Upstairs. In bed. With the lights *on*."

Excitement crowded out the worry in her eyes. "Sounds good to me."

Wasting no time, he lifted her into the cradle of his arms and carried her upstairs. With every step he ascended he stomped out the warnings in his head. They were crossing a lot of very dangerous lines. This time when she retreated, would she avoid him for good?

He didn't know.

But if this was their last time, he was going to make sure she never forgot it.

She kissed his neck when he crested the top of the stairs. Softly. Gently. Her lips on his skin caused his blood to heat.

"Which room is it again?" He smiled down at her before kissing her briefly on that beautiful mouth. So precious, his Gia.

No. Not precious. Just satisfy her needs and yours.

He'd make tonight worth it for both of them.

In the room he deposited her not-so-gracefully onto the rumpled blankets.

"Still don't make your bed?" he asked as he unbuttoned his shirt.

She sat on her knees, those luscious breasts spilling over her bra and giving him a peek of nipple. "Why bother? When I'll only mess it up again?"

She reached for his belt and while she worked at unbuckling it, he took off her bra and thumbed each of her nipples until she was squirming where she sat. She let out a moan.

"Thought you only made that sound while you ate pasta."

"Pasta and sex." She shoved his pants past his hips and he left her to kick off the remainder of his clothes.

"The two things I'm good for," he said, to let her know that he knew the score tonight. He knew she wasn't asking for a reunion. She didn't want to relive anniversaries past.

Tonight was about physical need. Sex for sex's sake.

Knee to the bed, he positioned himself over her. One side of her mouth lifted as she touched his chest and scooted herself back to accommodate him. He liked being accommodated. By this woman especially.

"Kiss me, Jayson Cooper."

"You got it, Gia Knox-Cooper." The air grew suddenly heavy. As he tasted her mouth and she wrapped her arms around his neck, he pushed out any thoughts about how she used to be his—how she still had his name. How he'd blown it over and over again and this could be yet another in a great line of mistakes he'd made with her.

Instead he focused on the tight, high breaths coming from her throat. On the feel of her fingernails tracing the lines of his back while he stroked into her. On the nip of her teeth on his earlobe.

Soon, to the crescendo of her hoarse cries in his ears, he followed her over.

And his world went blissfully black.

* * *

Unwilling to move from her spot on the bed, Gia stretched like a languid cat before curling into a ball again. Jayson had come out of the bathroom and stepped into their formerly shared walk-in closet, rummaging for what he called "those sexy gold shoes."

He was talking about a pair of Greek goddess, strappy heels she'd purchased for a Cleopatra costume one Halloween. She'd kept them, even though they were the most impractical purchase ever, because that night he requested that she wear *only* the shoes. They'd had fantastic sex, which was apparently par for course, and she'd fallen asleep wearing those shoes. She woken with strap marks crisscrossing up her legs. He'd removed her shoes and kissed every inch of her body before bringing her a very strong cup of coffee while she was still in bed.

That'd been a great morning.

He emerged with a white shoebox and shook it. "What's this?"

"I don't know. What is it?" But as he came closer and began digging through the box, she knew exactly what was in it. He lowered himself to the edge of the bed and she sat up and pulled the sheets over her naked body to peer inside.

He held up a birthday card with a dog holding a pair of false teeth in his mouth. "You kept this?"

"I like it." She snatched the card and read the inside. The inscription read "Love you, wife. J."

"The front is funny," she amended, tossing it back into the box. She stuck her hand in and came out with a refrigerator magnet from their trip to wine country that read "Let it merlot, let it merlot, let it merlot."

"I should put this on the fridge." She set it aside.

"You have a lot of random things in here." He held up a new pair of shoe strings that were knotted together.

"They were the extra pair that came with my Sauconys. I don't have those shoes anymore."

Jayson plucked out a laminated tag. "My old ID badge from the office."

"You look like a serial killer in that photo." His hair was longer, and messy, and he had that goatee. His expression was bland and morose.

"Must have been a bad day." He held the badge next to his face and mimicked his old self. "Before. After."

"After is better." She snatched the tag and studied the slightly out-of-focus mug shot. "I liked that goatee though. Why'd you shave it?"

"I got lazy."

She scraped a fingernail along his cheek. "I like it now though. Sometimes scruffy. Sometimes smooth. You keep me guessing."

"So do you." He held her eyes for an uncomfortable beat, one that reminded her more of their past than this shoebox of paraphernalia.

"You rose through the ranks faster than anyone I'd ever seen," she said to change the subject.

"Oh yeah?" he said distractedly, pulling out her old gym pass.

"Yeah. Even Royce didn't become chief financial officer as quickly as you became chief technology officer." She'd never thought about that, actually. One minute Jayson was a web designer with talent to burn and the next running the entire technology department. It'd impressed her. She'd been so elated over his raise, she'd wanted to throw a party but he wouldn't let her.

She'd forgotten that until now.

He was frowning, sifting through the random collect-ibles. She took the box from his hands and set it aside, wrapping her arms around his neck.

"Guess I forgot how talented you are outside of the bedroom and kitchen."

His cocky smirk returned. "Is this your way of asking for seconds?"

"Do you mean of pasta?" She tried to sound innocent.

"I mean sex. Are you kicking me out tonight?"

She bit her lip, considering. She'd sort of forgotten about that part—the leaving part.

"I mean, whatever you want," she hedged.

"Are you asking me to stay?" He cocked his head. "Or saying I don't have to leave?"

"Is there a difference?" Her smile shook. There was a *big* difference.

"Let's discuss it at length after." He removed the sheet covering her breasts and kissed a path down to her belly.

"After what?"

"Don't play dumb with me. You and I both know you're not."

She sighed and fell back into bed, the shoebox forgotten as well as the discussion about him staying or leaving.

The next morning, she woke to find him next to her. They never had discussed it. And she tried not to think about how much she liked rolling over and bumping into his solid, warm back.

Twenty-Three

Gia had planned the pool party with her family a month ago and since she didn't have the heart to disinvite Jayson, he was in attendance as well. Not that anyone present batted an eyelid. Her ex was part of the crew.

Only after the night he'd cooked for her, made love to her multiple times, and slept over, she was regretting him being there, and not because she wanted him out of her life.

She was beginning to want him back *in* and that was infinitely more dangerous.

Despite her trying not to soften around him, somehow he'd wedged into her heart.

She'd loved him when they were married, but now she loved him in a different way. What she felt for him was deep with understanding and nothing she could shrug off easily. They'd grown since their divorce, and she was fairly certain them splitting had a lot to do with that growth.

There were only so many flippant responses and sarcastic jokes she could trot out before the truth was evident to her—and everyone in her family.

She'd fallen in love with her ex-husband.

Doomed. That's what she was. *Doomed.*

How could she be brave enough to try again? After she'd failed so completely the first time? And after he'd summarily dismissed her the morning after he'd cooked for her and made love to her. He'd left, calm, cool and collected. As if he *hadn't* felt the earth shake the night before.

"I know what this was, G," he said, lingering at the front door. She had dressed in her robe and panties while he'd pulled on his trousers and shirt from last night. When she'd asked him to stay for coffee, he'd refused.

"Oh?" Her heart pounded. She was afraid to ask what he meant and afraid not to. She couldn't very well tell him she loved him, could she?

"There is a lot between us that is unforgivable. I know that a few good moments aren't enough to erase the past. Reconnecting with you was worth whatever happens next."

"Jay—"

"Hear me out. I have zero regrets on my end. I don't want you to have any on yours." He leaned down and kissed her. It felt final. Too final. "You don't have to find ways to avoid me, either. I won't come around unless asked."

Then he'd walked out the door and she hadn't seen him until they were both at work, their office faces on. When Bran had asked Jayson if he'd see him at the pool party this weekend, the three of them had been standing in her office. To avoid awkwardness, Jayson had swiftly agreed. Once Bran left, Jayson told her that he didn't have to come, but she'd lapsed into her "no big deal" self and told him to show up anyway.

Now he was here and splashing in the pool with her niece and Gia feared she'd made a colossal mistake.

"Meeting in the kitchen," Taylor announced. They were

seated around the patio table, snacks in the center. Bran and
Jayson were in the water with Quinn while Jack and Royce
were enjoying a beer on the loungers.

"Girls only," Taylor added as she handed over baby Emmaline to Royce and gestured for Addi to follow. She nodded at Gia and then at Gia's mother. "You too, Macy."

Gia, feeling as if there was a boulder in the pit of her
stomach, followed her sisters-in-law and mother into the
house. They stood around the kitchen island and every pair
of eyes homed in on her.

"What?" Gia asked, growing more nervous.

"Did something happen?" Taylor asked.

"Like what?"

"Like you're madly in love with Jayson?" Addison filled
in.

"Honey, it's all over your face." Macy, apparently, hadn't
missed a thing.

"Did you tell him? Did he shoot you down? Did you two
break up?" Taylor asked.

"No and no. And...not really."

Taylor, unsatisfied with those answers, narrowed her
eyes.

"After we—" Gia's gaze trickled over to her mom and
decided to be vague "—ate pasta, he said he didn't expect
anything from me."

"Only because you run like a startled deer each and
every time he gets close," Addi said. "Sorry. I know it's
not my business, and I don't want to argue with you, but
I'm right."

Taylor and Macy nodded in agreement.

Unable to defend herself when she was outnumbered,
Gia threw up her hands. "Fine! I love him. What am I supposed to do about it?"

"Go out there and tell him!" Taylor whisper-shouted.

"We're tired of you guys skirting each other. Just lay it out there. Let 'er rip."

"How much sangria have you had?" Gia asked.

"A lot," Taylor said, "but that doesn't mean I'm wrong."

"I have so much to lose," Gia announced miserably. She could be shot down. And then her carefully constructed façade that she'd erected—the one where she pretended not to miss him and that she'd moved on with her life—would come tumbling down. Only this time she had a feeling she'd be buried beneath the rubble.

"Hell yeah you do," Taylor agreed. "But he might surprise you. We're going to leave soon. You should talk to him once we're gone."

"So are we. Quinn needs a nap and so does her mom." Addison smiled warmly. "Go for it, Gia. If the worst happens, we'll be there for you."

"I'll corral your father out of here, too," Macy promised.

A second later, Gia was enveloped into a hug from all three women. Feeling excited, nervous and…yeah, mostly nervous, she wondered what Jayson would say. She wondered what she *wanted* him to say.

She wasn't expecting a proposal, but was it too much to hope for a reunion? Even one where they continued on the path they were on would be better than nothing. Though she was risking *nothing* as well, wasn't she?

Admitting to him that she loved him could push him away completely. He seemed so *done* the other morning when he'd pragmatically explained she didn't need to worry about him being in her space. And when Bran had asked if he'd be at the pool party, Jayson had been quick to tell her she could disinvite him.

He could revert to form and tell her how she *should* feel. But she held out hope that he'd listen to her this time around. That he'd be the man she continued to want and need.

The what-ifs were killing her. There was no way to know for sure which outcome to expect... She'd just have to confess, and hope for the best.

The next hour passed easily. Her family made no more mention of love or whether or not Gia talked to Jayson yet. As promised, Taylor and Royce filtered out, Addi and Bran right behind them.

Macy still hadn't managed to corral Gia's dad, but everyone knew that Jack Knox was almost as hard to corral as his daughter.

"I'm not leaving until I have ice cream cake," he declared with a white-toothed smile.

"I'll get it," Jayson offered but Macy pushed him back onto the lounger.

"You keep Jack company. Gia and I will get it."

Gia found herself back in the kitchen at the same countertop, facing a similar firing squad as before, only now there was only one gunner.

"How are you? Are you losing your nerve?" Macy asked as she pulled the cake from the freezer and opened the box.

"There's a lot at stake, Mom."

"Marriage isn't easy. Whether you've tried it once or four times."

"How would you know if you're in the *once* club?" Gia pulled a knife from the drawer and began cutting the cake.

"Because husbands and wives change each decade so it feels like multiple marriages," her mom joked. "Everyone makes mistakes. Jayson has made his, you've made yours. The trick is being able to admit them and forgive each other."

"He's different," Gia said, thinking of how Jayson had behaved lately. "He talks differently. I know it's dangerous to think people change, but—"

"But they do. That means you've changed, too. Have you

been honest with yourself about that? Have you showed *him* you're different?"

Gia felt the sting of tears in her nose. "Of course not. It's all his fault, remember?"

"Don't be glib with me, Gia Knox-Cooper. You have been gracious and poised about this divorce. You've also been an insufferable smart-ass."

"Mom."

"I love you, but if you don't start going after what you want in life, you'll forever accept what you're given instead. You've been trying for years to escape the shadow of your father and brothers. Now you have a chance to make your own choices, and you should choose what *you* want for a change." Her mother plated the slices of cake. "Deliver these. The sooner your father eats, the sooner we'll leave."

Before Gia picked up the plates, she hugged her mom.

Macy patted her daughter's back. "Go on."

Outside, Gia maneuvered two plates through the open sliding door. Jayson and her dad sat, their backs to her. There were having a quiet, and she guessed by the low hush of male voices a somewhat intense, conversation. She should interrupt but she was too intrigued by what Jayson was saying.

"Gia deserves it more than I do."

"It's not about *deserve*, Jayson," Jack replied. "It's about want. You want it. The same way you wanted chief technology officer."

Jayson's back stiffened. "That was a mistake."

"I promised you the tech department when you asked for my daughter's hand. You seemed excited about it then."

She blinked in surprise. Had she heard that correctly? She stayed out of sight, content to listen a little longer.

"I never should have accepted it." Jayson sounded as frustrated as he looked. "She graduated MIT with honors,

Jack. She's overqualified for tech and her current marketing position."

"Hell, I know she's smart. I tell everyone that."

"Yes, you do, but you say it as if it's your accomplishment. Then you treat her as if she can't handle the world on her own. When you asked me to take care of her, I thought you were being fatherly. I didn't know you meant for her to settle for a lesser role in your company."

"You didn't take care of her, though, did you? Instead she shows up with that idiot skateboarder at a family wedding. You failed me," Jack snapped, his face going red. "Don't think I haven't forgotten it."

"I failed *her*," Jayson bit out. "Not you. Our marriage had nothing to do with *you*. And since you're retired neither does ThomKnox."

"But you are seeing each other again. That might lead to more. Vice president would be a good position for you, if that were the case."

"Our marriage ended a long time ago," Jayson announced.

Upon hearing that, Gia felt as if someone had plunged a knife into her chest.

"You can't bait me with the promise of VP," Jayson added. "You can't bait me, period."

"I should have fired you the second you divorced my baby girl," Jack growled.

Macy stepped outside, two plates in hand. "*Jack*. What is the meaning of this?"

Jack turned to face his wife, spotted his daughter and promptly pasted on a smile. "There are my girls."

Stunned, Gia was still frozen in place when Jayson turned and met her eyes.

"The ID badge," she muttered. "I thought it was odd how quickly you'd advanced to CTO."

"Because I gave it to him." Jack scowled. "No daughter

of mine was going to be married to a man who couldn't provide."

"Jack!" Macy gasped.

"You underestimate her," Jayson told her father. "And so did I. But at least I had the hindsight to pull my head out of my ass."

Jack opened his mouth to retort but Macy stepped in. "Not another word. Jayson, Gia. We'll be going now. Thank you for the lovely afternoon."

"This isn't over," Jack promised Jayson. Then he turned to Gia, having the decency to look guilty. "I can explain."

"Not now, Daddy." She put up a hand and kept her eyes on her ex-husband. She had issues with both of them right now, but the one with Jayson was paramount.

Her father silently followed Macy into the house. Jayson folded his arms over his chest and waited until they heard the Knox family car leave the driveway.

"I wanted to run tech," she told him.

Jayson's mouth was a grim line. "I know."

"And my father gave to it to you like…some sort of dowry?" Gross. That's what this was. "You never told me. And you had an opportunity to do so the other night."

"I only wanted to protect and care for you. I—"

"I only wanted you to love me!" she shouted, tears rolling down her cheeks. Damn him. He hadn't changed at all.

"I tried! Do you know how hard it is to want to be everything to the woman who needs nothing from you?"

She shook her head, but he kept talking.

"You could make a career out of pushing me away."

"What about the last time we were together?" she asked. "What about you leaving and telling me where we stood? That was you pushing *me* away."

"I know your pattern. The second we get close you back away. I was giving you an out."

"You were protecting yourself!"

"Oh, really?" His expression shifted from disbelief to anger in a snap. "And what about now, when your dad offered me the vice president position on a silver platter? Was I *protecting myself*?"

No.

He wasn't.

"I don't want a pity job, Jayson." She put the cake on the table, the melting ice cream pooling onto the plates in the warm night air.

"It's not pity." Exasperated, he threw up his hands. "I'm damned if I do and damned if I don't. You don't want me to give you anything, but you don't want me to take anything for myself either. And by the way, I *did* love you. So much I was stupid with it. Can you say the same?"

Yes. And she could say that right now, in fact. Judging by everything he'd just said, though, he wouldn't want to hear it. She found herself guilty of doing what she'd accused Jayson of doing—protecting herself.

"You don't have to answer that," he said. "That's the benefit to being divorced. We don't have to answer to each other anymore."

He walked around her to the patio door but before he disappeared inside, he had more parting wisdom. "Being in the role of vice president is your destiny, Gia. You wanted to be involved with tech, marketing? The entire damn company? Here's your chance. Take the VP position and step into your role at ThomKnox. For a change, claim what you deserve."

Then he was gone.

She slumped onto the lounger, her eyes clouded with tears and her mind racing. Her emotions were battling each other. She wanted him, but was afraid to tell him. She wanted to step into a greater position at ThomKnox, but didn't want to risk failing. She'd crowed about wanting a shot at making her own decisions and mistakes. Now she had the opportunity and she was too scared to do either.

And, possibly the most depressing of all… She'd wanted to tell Jayson that she loved him but she couldn't.

He didn't love her. Not anymore.

Chester filled a small shot glass with golden liquid and pushed it under Jayson's nose.

"I fucked up," Jayson said, his speech slurred thanks to the three tequila shots that had preceded this one. He'd come here straight from Gia's. Too pissed off to drive home and stew in his own juices, and maybe a little bit needing the comfort only Chester's empanadas could provide.

As it turned out, Jayson couldn't eat.

Ches, a bartender, had taken one look at him and asked what was wrong and Jay had spilled his guts.

"It happens to the best of us," Ches said. "Now drink."

"I don't want it." But Jay took it anyway. Drinking until he forgot what an idiot he was wasn't a great plan, but it was the only one he had. After downing the liquor that'd done a good job of making his head swim already, he lay back on the uncomfortable outdoor couch. The palm trees overhead canted at an awkward angle and his stomach flopped. He was horribly uncomfortable without a pillow—as if the cushions were built out of the same hard material as the frame. He sat up as quickly as he'd lay down, his head spinning in protest. "I hate this couch."

"So do I," Mason said, stepping outside to deliver a tray of beers in pilsner glasses. "And he paid five grand for it."

Jay sent Chester an appalled look. "Seriously?"

"Shut up. This is not about my couch." Chester moved to sit on the overpriced piece of furniture next to Jayson. "You know I adore you. But, Jay, honey, why didn't you tell her you let her dad give you that position *while* you were married?"

"Secrets like that tend to grow hair." Mason sat across

from them in a chair that matched the couch, but at least he had a pillow that looked squishy.

"Tell me about it. Before I had the chance, we were talking about divorce and then… I dunno." Jay felt his mouth pull into a miserable frown. He knew why he'd procrastinated telling Gia. He didn't want her to hate him and she'd seemed to be heading there at a fast clip already. And if she hated him he couldn't live with himself. Which was where they'd ended up, even though he'd tried his damndest to prevent it. "She hates me."

"She doesn't hate you," Mason argued. "She's pissed off. There's a difference. And by the way, she has a right to be. Probably feels like she was swapped for a flock of sheep or something."

"Thanks, Mas." Jay reached for his beer. Not needing it, but wanting it.

"Don't be mean to your brother," Ches warned his husband as he patted Jayson's back. "He's going through a tough time. Jay, you can stay here tonight."

"Yeah, you can sleep on our five-thousand-dollar patio couch," Mason said with a smile.

Jay surprised himself by laughing. "Pass."

"You were supposed to move on," Mason reminded him unnecessarily. "That's why you took Natasha to the wedding, right? You weren't supposed to sleep with Gia at said wedding. And you weren't supposed to sleep with her over and over again. Especially since she didn't know her own father bribed you."

"Not helping," he grumbled at his brother. Jayson's arms felt like cement. He let them lay heavy on his legs when he leaned back on the couch that might as well have been crafted of that same cement. "I do *not* like this couch, Ches."

Like that, he lost his only ally. "You two hash it out. I'm done helping."

Once his husband was gone, Mas lifted an eyebrow in judgment.

"Like if you lost the love of your life you wouldn't do anything in the world to be close to him again? Even temporarily?" Jay gestured to the house behind him where Chester had disappeared.

Mason blinked. "I didn't realize you were still in love with her."

"It's a moot point, dontcha think?" Jayson lay on the couch anyway, his spine screaming in protest.

"I don't know. Did you tell her that?"

He let out a morose laugh. "Are you kidding?"

"No. I'm not." Mason sounded scarily serious. "If you're in love with her why not tell her?"

"Um, hello? How much have you been drinking? We've said everything we needed to say and most of that was said too many times and the wrong way." Jay took a hearty gulp from his own beer glass. "And she just found out I've been trying to control her for my own gain."

"Have you?"

"Jesus, Mason. No! But that's how she sees it. And if you know Gia—and *I* know Gia—you know that the only thing that matters on this planet is her perspective." He lifted the glass again then set it aside, an idea sparking. "I know. I could quit."

"You're not going to quit. You love ThomKnox."

He did.

"I could step down," Jayson said anyway. "Give her my position. Work in the mail room or something."

"Are you high?"

"No. Drunk." But he didn't feel all that drunk. Sure, the earth was moving under his feet, but he couldn't say he wasn't thinking clearly.

"Tell her how you feel," his brother said. "Man up. Grow some balls."

"Weren't you just banging the don't-date-your-ex drum?"

"That was before I knew you were a goner for her. How long have you been in love with her, anyway? And how much longer are you going to let your bravado stand in the way of what you really want?"

"Jack offered me vice president."

"What?"

"He said ThomKnox is adding a VP position and I was in the running. He said that my being with Gia, and seeing through my promise to take care of her, would stack the deck in my favor."

"What an asshole."

"That's Jack." But that wasn't all Jack was. He was also eccentric and grossly friendly. He loved his family with a fierceness that was hard to understand, especially when Jayson's own father couldn't have given two shits about him. But Jack also had a way of undermining his family when he had his own plans in mind.

"You weren't seriously considering his offer, though."

"No, I wasn't." Jayson shook his head. "Gia deserves it. She deserves the best. That's not me."

"That's not you?" Mason let out a sharp laugh. "Give me a break. You know I know both of you, right?"

A frown pleated Jayson's forehead.

"You'd break your own back trying to prove yourself worthy—trying to prove you're not your asshole dad. Then when Gia doesn't need you to handle her, you sulk."

"Fuck you." Jayson was aware he was sulking now, though, which pissed him off more.

"Listen, man. You chose a strong woman. That's not a bad thing. Give her what she really, truly needs, though. Don't just try and shine in her eyes. Okay?"

What she really, truly needs.

Jayson turned that over long after Mason went inside. Long after the air grew cold and his beer was gone.

Sometime during the night he came to a conclusion about what she needed. It had nothing to do with him or what he wanted.

He was going to have to give up what he wanted more than anything.

And he'd do it. For her.

Twenty-Four

By the next afternoon, Gia couldn't stand her own company any longer. She'd spent the entire morning cleaning the house. She'd thrown out the float shaped like a giant lemon slice because it reminded her of Jayson whenever she saw it. She'd even hauled the big-ass pasta maker out from under the cabinet and put it into a box bound for Goodwill.

She'd stripped the bed and washed the sheets, before going online to order a new bed so she wouldn't have to sleep in the same bed where she'd slept *with* Jayson.

What a mess. What a big, fat, stupid mess.

Her anger had spread beyond the boundaries of her person and her house, which was how she found herself at her parents' home without an invitation.

When her mother opened the front door, Gia stormed in. "Where is he?"

"Enjoying his afternoon iced tea," Macy answered as Gia blew by. "On the balcony."

Shoulders squared, Gia rerouted to the stairs.

"Don't throw him over!" Macy called up to her.

Her father's office led out onto a wide balcony outfitted with chairs, a table and an awning. She stepped into the room, rich with red leather and brass accents. Her father's *lair*.

She'd never before pictured him in here scheming. Until recently.

The French doors were open and she found her father reading the *Wall Street Journal*, a glass of whiskey and the carafe within reach.

"Gia." He smiled. The crinkles around his eyes and his puff of white hair used to be comforting. Not today.

"You owe me an explanation." She stood over him. "And an apology."

"I had my reasons."

"I'm listening."

He gestured to the chair across from his and folded his paper. "Sit. Please?"

She did, because he said *please*. She still vibrated with anger and while she wasn't going to toss him off the balcony she thought emptying his whiskey bottle over the edge might make her feel better.

"You gave Jayson the position of CTO because you didn't think I could handle it. You completely overlooked me." She'd come here for his explanation, but she had a point to make, too.

"I wanted him to feel worthy of you," her father told her. His legs where crossed, and he rested his folded hands on one knee. "I didn't overlook you, Gia. I know exactly what you're capable of. World domination, I imagine."

She didn't smile at his joke.

"You're a powerful woman. I couldn't be prouder of who you've become. But, honey, Jayson isn't from the same world we are."

"This is about image," she said. "You were embarrassed of him."

"No." Her father's voice was firm, unyielding. "It was about him feeling as if he belonged and not like he was limping behind the rest of you. He's a good man. I care about him. I can tell you're in love with him. Still."

She slumped in her chair. "Is it that obvious?"

"I know you're mad at me. I do. And… I'm sorry."

She lifted her eyes to her father's to see if he meant it. He looked like he did.

"I was trying to make up for my mistake. I was trying to offer him vice president so you could finally have the position you want. Then he went on about you taking VP and I started talking out of my hat. You know I don't like to be challenged."

"Pretty sure I inherited that same instinct." She gave him a wan smile.

"Jayson was right. You're the worthiest candidate for vice president. I just didn't want him to leave the company, especially since you two have been…close lately."

"You were bribing him to keep seeing me?" Ugh. That was horrible.

"Incentivizing," Jack corrected. He took her hand in both of his. She tugged it away. "I was wrong to interfere. Then your mother told me you two were, uh, dating."

Gia winced.

"I wanted to make you happy again," he continued. "You've been unhappy. I only ever wanted you to smile."

"Well, giving my job away wasn't the best tactic. I thought he'd earned that position."

"He did. He's fantastic in that capacity. I care too much about my company to hire anyone who didn't make us shine. Honestly, Gia, I thought you'd have given your brothers a run for their money when I announced my retirement. And yet you never wanted CEO."

"No." She shook her head. She had ambitions and aspi-rations but running ThomKnox wasn't for her.

"And after that, I didn't think you'd want the vice presi-dent position."

"I don't know what I want." But she did. She wanted her ex-husband.

"Jayson cares for you."

"He does," she admitted. "But not in the way you were hoping. Not in the way I was hoping."

Her father hummed and released her hand. "I've made my fair share of mistakes in the past—in the recent past. I'll call him and apologize. I owe him that."

"Yes, you do."

"But don't blame him for taking the tech position back then. I practically forced him into it," Jack said. "He took it for you."

"How was taking CTO from me done *for* me?"

"I told him you didn't want it. That you'd…asked me to give it to him."

"Daddy!"

"You were compensated well and I thought you would find your way to a higher rank. I never doubted you. I was trying to make sure Cooper had a place in our family en-terprise."

"And he does." Jayson was a big part of the reason ThomKnox was so successful.

"How are things between you two now?" Jack asked carefully.

She shook her head. "They didn't end well. This after-noon there's a party happening at work, so I'm sure that won't be awkward at all."

Her father stood. "This is my fault."

As tempting as it was to let her father shoulder the blame, she couldn't.

"No, you only managed to tip the already leaky boat."

She stood from her chair and touched his arm. "I understand why you did what you did. It was noble, in a way. I wish you would have talked to me, though. I wish Jayson would have talked to me. It would have saved a lot of misunderstanding over the years."

"Would it?" Jack frowned.

She shrugged. "I don't know. I tend to be as stubborn as you are, Daddy."

"Stubbornness is a good quality when you want to graduate with honors." He offered a half smile.

"Not so much in marriage," she said. "Compromising, I hear, is a thing."

"Stop blaming yourself. You did what you knew how to do. You guarded your life and your choices. I'm sorry I didn't honor your union and keep my nose out of it. I'm learning, too." He held out his arms. "Forgive me?"

"Yes." She embraced him, understanding better why he'd done what he'd done. It seemed Jack had believed in her strength after all. Even though he'd gone about showing it in a way she didn't agree with.

"Off you go to claim that VP position, then?" He held her at arm's length.

"I'll talk to the executive team about it," she said. "Taylor. Royce. Brannon." She poked him in the chest. "Not you. You're retired, remember?"

"Trying to," he admitted.

Downstairs, she found her mother in the sitting room on a gray sofa, a blush pink pillow tucked at her back. Macy's charity work often spilled over into this room from her attached office. Gia took in the spread of papers on the coffee table and smiled.

"How'd it go?" Macy asked.

"He was surprisingly open. And he apologized." She sat next to her mother. "I'm assuming you two talked."

"Your father and I might have had a long talk wherein

he agreed he had no right to interfere in your marriage." Macy sipped from her teacup. "Lord knows marriage is hard enough with the two people it involves."

True story.

"Did you and Jayson talk through it?"

"We argued. He left." Gia poured herself a cup of tea.

"I'm sorry."

"I'll see him at work later today. I'm still not sure what I'll say. Daddy's calling to apologize to him."

"Good."

"What are you working on, anyway?" Gia leaned forward and lifted a sheet of paper off the pile.

"A charity for abused women. It's called HeartReach. They help women who are trapped in abusive marriages with children to create an exit plan. You might recognize the chairwoman's name."

Gia's eyes went to a familiar name. Julia Robinson. Aka—"Jayson's mother."

"HeartReach was where she went for support when Jayson was younger—to help her escape Jay's father. I can't imagine."

Neither could Gia. "Daddy said he wanted Jayson to feel worthy. To feel like he fit in."

"Jayson had a father who didn't honor him. Jack wanted to cheer him on."

"The way he always cheered me on." Gia had always been loved. Had always been wanted.

"You championed Jayson, too, dear. When you announced your divorce, you were adamant about us not shunning him from the family. You didn't want him to lose us. Even if you were losing him in the process." Macy patted Gia's leg. "You have a great big misguided heart, like your father."

Gia hummed, finally seeing the big picture. This argument wasn't about roles at ThomKnox or Jayson having a job she'd wanted at one point. Life was about love and what really mattered. Family.

"Remarkable how Jayson turned out nothing like his father, isn't it?" Macy said thoughtfully as she took the flyer out of Gia's hands.

"I used to accuse him of being controlling." Gia shook her head. "He was trying to be accommodating."

"Well, he could have communicated better. Men assume they know what's best. It's our job to correct them. Frequently, it seems."

Gia smiled, then sighed as the gravity of what had happened weighed on her anew. "I don't know what to do. I love him. I don't want to lose him, and I feel like I already have."

"Being brave is hard. Speak your mind. And your heart. Leave nothing on the table."

Gia blew out a breath as she swiped fresh tears from her cheeks. "Easy for you to say."

"Yes. It is." Her mother tipped her head and swiped a stray tear from Gia's face. "Can I do anything to help?"

"You already have. It's my turn to make a few decisions involving what I want. You were right. I need to step out of Daddy's and my brothers' shadows. I've been trying, but I've been going about it the wrong way. That changes right now."

"Good girl."

Gia stood to leave and then turned back to ask, "What if…he doesn't love me back?"

"I don't know how that's possible." Her mother shook her head. "Royce, Brannon, Jack and now Jayson. The men in your life fall all over themselves to protect and care for you."

For the first time in her life, Gia thought about being cared for by the men in her life. Maybe that wasn't so bad after all.

Twenty-Five

When Jayson walked into the ThomKnox building, a cup of strong coffee in hand, he didn't go straight to his desk. Instead, he entered the elevator and pressed a button for the top floor.

The executive floor was humming as per usual. He heard the quiet purr of office landline telephones interspersed with the delicate tapping of high-end keyboards. Like in the tech department, everyone had the sleekest, newest equipment and the flattest screens. Unlike tech, the desks weren't littered with candy bar wrappers or several paper cups that used to hold coffee. It was as if everyone up here knew they were in the presence of greatness. ThomKnox royalty.

Gia belonged up here.

She'd been working closely with Jayson throughout their marriage and after, and now he saw that for what it was. He was holding her back.

As long as he remained closely intertwined with her, she'd continue to vehemently deny herself and give him favor. He knew that was because she loved him—maybe not as a husband any longer, but she couldn't turn off her emotions like a switch.

Neither could he.

He'd fallen in love with his ex-wife, against his better judgment or any iota of common sense. He'd always loved her, even when he'd been trying to bury his feelings for the sake of saving face during their rocky divorce. But since they'd reconnected, he'd felt that love on a deeper level.

No longer was he focused on gaining ground or being right. He wanted to give her what she deserved because she deserved it. Sacrifice, and vulnerability, evidently went hand in hand.

Ultimately, no matter how much money he made, no matter what kind of luxe lifestyle he lived, he didn't belong in the same category with Royce or Bran, and especially not with Gia. He'd been fooling himself. He didn't know if today's sacrifice would make up for years of treading where he didn't belong, but it was a start.

He crossed the room and silence fell. Fingers stopped tapping on keys and interested eyeballs landed on him. He felt Taylor's burning gaze as he stepped past her office and angled straight for Royce's.

They must have heard what happened after they left the house. Gia told them, or maybe Macy. It'd saved Jayson the trouble, he supposed.

He let himself into Royce's office after a brief knock. Gia's oldest brother sat up tall at his desk, his face a mask of anger. He looked as though he had something to say, so Jayson let him.

"Gia always wanted what was best for you," Royce said. "She was brokenhearted and sad after the divorce and still she insisted that nothing change between us. I honored that."

"I know you did." The Knox family had been incredibly accommodating.

"And you repay my family's loyalty by allowing my father to concoct this ridiculous plan? When you'd already accepted the CTO seat because you married Gia. If you think I'll place you in the role of vice president—"

"I don't want to be vice president. I never should have accepted the role I have now. At the time I wanted to please your father and I thought that would help Gia see me as worthy of her."

Some of the fire went out of Royce's expression. He let out a long sigh. "She always saw you as worthy, Coop."

"Sure about that?" Jayson asked. Royce didn't answer. "I was a guy from a broken home who built websites. It was crazy to imagine myself worthy of marrying into the great and powerful Knox family."

"We never made that distinction."

"You never had to. Gia loved me and Jack validated me. You accepted their approval at face value." Jayson took a breath. "I was never going to accept a VP position. Jack was being Jack. He steers his children's lives into the direction he believes is right. He was orchestrating a Jayson-and-Gia reunion."

Jack had called early this morning. He'd apologized for the things he'd said at the party. Jayson told his ex-father-in-law that he wouldn't have to worry any longer. Jayson had a way to fix everything that had happened. To set things right again.

"And now?" Royce asked.

"Now what?"

"You and Gia have been…" Royce closed his eyes as if he couldn't bear saying it aloud. "Spending time together."

"Not anymore." Admitting that aloud hurt worse than he could have imagined.

"Was it only physical for you?" Royce shifted in his chair like he was uncomfortable asking.

"Why else?" Jayson lied. He'd been close. So damn

close. Before Gia had overheard that conversation and learned the secret he'd been keeping—before he'd blown everything, he'd been planning on telling her exactly how he felt about her.

That he loved her. He'd fallen in love with her again, only this time he believed himself incapable of screwing up. He'd committed to honoring her needs—her actual needs—and meeting them.

Then his past had bitten him in the ass and he realized he wasn't incapable of screwing up. He *was* a screw-up. No amount of time could fix that.

"Are you coming to the party this afternoon?" Jayson asked. "It's in celebration of the tablet fix. Gia singlehandedly saving your company and all."

"I'm planning on it."

"Good. I have an important announcement to make."

"I look forward to it," Royce said with a curt nod. Jayson couldn't tell if the other man was lying or not.

Gia arrived at the start of the party, only to bump into the party planner on her way in. "Looks fantastic in here, Joanna."

"Thank you. Everything is in place, Ms. Knox."

Gia didn't correct her by saying that her name was *Knox-Cooper*. She was too tender after everything that had happened to go there. "Wonderful. Thank you."

"You're welcome. My staff and I will be in the background making sure everything runs smoothly." Joanna, her hair pulled back in a smart tight ponytail, turned to straighten the platters of catered sushi.

Music was playing in the background and Gia walked to a bucket of ice to grab a soda for herself. Taylor and Addison were there, smiles bright.

"We're here for you no matter what happens." Taylor offered. "I'm really excited for you."

"Thank you." Gia hugged Taylor and then Addi. "I appreciate your both showing up."

"And miss the action?" Addi asked as she straightened from the hug. "Never."

"Photo booth, ladies!" The photographer interrupted.

"Not me, thanks." Gia waved them off. "You two go ahead."

The photographer shooed Taylor and Addison over to the booth and handed them each masks on sticks. Taylor, halfway to the booth mouthed the words "you owe me."

Gia wiggled her fingers in a wave, relieved at having avoided the embarrassing photo booth.

"If I could have your attention." The low sound of her ex-husband's voice came from the front of the room.

Jayson, dressed in black trousers and a slate-gray shirt, climbed onto a sturdy chair. Not that he needed to. His presence was so commanding he didn't need the chair to establish that he was in charge. His power was as undeniable as her admiration of it. She'd spent years guarding herself from that power, but now she saw the truth. That was simply *Jayson*.

"Not that anyone asked for a speech, but I have one." His eyes flicked to the back of the room and Gia turned to see her brothers enter. Bran gave her a wave, his mouth flinching into a half smile. Royce wore a frown as usual, but when he walked by, he briefly cupped her neck in a supportive gesture.

"I've been a part of ThomKnox for going on seven years," Jayson continued. "I was named chief technology officer almost five years ago, the same year I married one Miss Gia Knox-Cooper."

Smiles around the room were soft, careful. More than a few heads swiveled in her direction.

"Our marriage did not outlast the role, and I've been telling myself for nearly two years that I was okay with that. That relationships work but sometimes they don't, and Gia and I fell into that latter category. It was a lie I've been content with until recently, when I realized that not only was I in love with Gia when we were married, I have been for the entire time we were divorced."

Those soft smiles melted into gasps, Gia's own gasp among them.

"Gia is a gracious, beautiful, incredibly lovable woman," Jay went on. "She's giving. She's tough. She's strong. She's a certified genius mastermind." Nods of support came from several of their coworkers. "She's been in the role of running Marketing, and I know she loves this company with her whole heart, but Marketing isn't where she belongs. She's an MIT grad with a nerdy brain in that gorgeous noggin of hers. She loves code more than any one person has a right to. She found the glitch we're all celebrating." He cleared his throat and added, "Not me. She doesn't need me."

Her chest tightened as those words. That wasn't true. She *did* need him. More than he knew. She thought about her family members who had tried to take care of her over the years. Not because they thought she was incapable or weak, but because they loved her so very much. She'd recently learned that it was okay to lean on others; that it would have been okay to lean on Jayson while they were married.

Needing someone didn't make her unworthy. It made her *human*. Beautifully human, flaws and all.

"And yet I'm the one who's chief technology officer of this company. Or well, I was," Jayson finished. "*Was* CTO."

"No," Gia whispered. She'd made a decision about what she wanted after talking with her mother. She finally knew her goals and dreams and wasn't afraid to claim them. Jayson in the role of CTO was the *right* place for him to be. It had been all along. Her father, while he'd fumbled, wasn't wrong about that promotion.

"I love this department. I love ThomKnox as a whole,"

Jayson was saying. "I love Royce and Taylor, Brannon and Addison, and Jack and Macy like they're my own family." He then locked his gaze on Gia's. "I love my ex-wife enough that I refuse to stand in the way of her living the life she should be living. I should have done this years ago, G," he said, his eyes on her. "I never should have taken the position that was destined to be yours. I should have walked out the door and not looked back when you said you wanted the divorce. I should have left you at ThomKnox with your family to claim what was rightfully yours. No matter how badly I wanted to be in your orbit."

Oh, Jayson.

"I'm leaving ThomKnox, effective immediately," he said as the room erupted in excited chatter. "Gia will take over where I left off, and your upper management is more than capable of filling in the gaps. If there are any."

He stepped off the chair and that chatter grew louder. Panic laced through her stomach until she realized that she could take her power back rather than stand idly by.

"Jayson Cooper!" she shouted. No way would she allow him to make this huge of a mistake.

"My mind is made up, Gia," he said as he walked for the exit.

"And what makes you think you have the final say?" she asked his back.

He turned. Slowly. His face was a beautiful shadow of confusion and hope. She loved his face. She loved *him*.

The room grew eerily quiet. She felt every eyeball snap to her as she closed the gap between her and Jayson, her arms folded at her chest.

"As the newly named vice president of this company," she told him, her voice firm. "I don't accept your resignation."

Twenty-Six

Earlier today

"Thank you all for coming." Gia stood at the head of the conference table and addressed the upper management team of ThomKnox. "I have a proposition for you."

Brannon, tapping a pencil, eraser side down, on the table, shot her an easy wink. Royce, on Gia's left, wore a muted smile. Taylor was grinning like she'd gleaned what was coming next.

"We've been in discussion about adding a vice president position for a while now," Gia began. "And then at the pool party, Daddy decided to offer that position to Jayson."

Brannon frowned. Taylor mimicked his expression. Royce curled his lip.

"Jayson didn't accept it."

"But he had no problem claiming chief technology officer for himself," Royce grumbled.

She blinked. Royce knew plenty.

"Daddy called you."

"He called me, too," Brannon said. "We each received a Jack Knox speech about how he's failed and won't fail us again."

"He does love his grandstanding." Gia shook her head, but smiled to herself. "Jayson would make an excellent vice president. But I'd make a better one."

Taylor elbowed her husband and then bounced in her seat. "I knew it. You owe me twenty bucks."

Royce's smile came out of hiding. "I don't need twenty bucks, but we can negotiate terms later."

"Anyway," Gia said with an eye roll in the direction of her besotted oldest brother, "I want to earn the position of VP on my merits, not based on what Jack or anyone else says. I want this position. I want it to include Marketing and Tech, and then I can oversee both my passions. *And* I want Jayson to stay exactly where he is—in charge of the department he built."

"I had a meeting with the CEO, COO and president of this company this morning," she told Jayson now, aware of many onlookers, said CEO, COO and president included. "I specified that while I'll be overseeing both Marketing and Technology, I would only do it if you were involved. I need you exactly where you are."

"You don't need me, Gia. You never did."

"ThomKnox needs you." She reached down, way down, and found her bravery. Jayson had been brave enough to stand in front of everyone and tell her how he felt. She knew she could do the same. "And *I* need you," she added on a broken voice.

"Gia—"

"I never had the courage to admit that. I never wanted to appear weak in our family of titans." She glanced over at Royce and then Brannon, who each wore compressed smiles of pride. She turned back to Jayson. "Marriage is about admitting you need someone else. It's about being someone's other half."

The lines on Jayson's forehead softened as he tilted her chin gently. "I'm leaving so that you don't feel compelled to take care of me. I'm supposed to be taking care of you."

"I guess we're just going to have to take care of each other." She shrugged, vulnerable and unsure. "I mean, if that's what you want. I don't want you to feel like I'm controlling you."

A slow grin spread his mouth. "How ironic."

She grinned back at him.

"I love you, Gia. I've made so many mistakes. I've been holding on to you without realizing it."

"We both made mistakes." She gently touched his hand, still cradling her face. "And hey, I've been holding on, too. Have you checked my last name lately?"

"You never dropped the Cooper."

"I couldn't let go. Not all the way. Letting go's not the answer and you know it. We screwed up, Jay."

"Yeah. We did."

"I have a better idea of how you can make it up to me and it doesn't involve you leaving ThomKnox. You can't leave me in a lurch and force me to find a good executive to run this department with no notice at all." She affected a stern expression. "Do we understand each other?"

"Yes, boss."

She quirked her lips. "I like that."

He leaned in to whisper into her ear, his voice a low rasp, "Only here. In the bedroom you know who's in charge."

When he pulled away, she felt her cheeks grow bright pink. "Jay," she whispered. "We have an audience."

"Right." He winked. "We'll talk about that later."

Taylor broke the silence. "To our CTO and new vice president!" She held up her plastic cup.

Addison cranked up the music.

The crowd cheered.

By the time the dancing started and everyone had dispersed, Gia and Jayson still hadn't moved from where they stood in front of each other.

"What are you doing tonight?" he asked.

"Oh, the usual." She shrugged. "Making dinner. Having a glass of wine with my laptop. Meeting the installers who are delivering the new bed."

"You ordered a new bed?"

"Yeah. I thought I wanted a different one since that other one was ours."

"And now?"

She tipped her head. "Now I'm thinking we should break in the new one. It'd be a crime to let a brand-new bed go to waste."

"Hell yes it would." He stepped closer and muttered, "Kiss me, Gia."

"No. *You* kiss *me*."

His smirk was one for the books. "Meet me halfway?"

"From here on out."

Epilogue

Laptop aglow in front of her, Gia was curled into the corner of the sofa, her eyes heavy. She just wanted to finish this one last part…

In a flash, the screen vanished, swept up by Jayson, who swapped the laptop for a glass of wine.

"I was busy!" she argued, but took the proffered glass before she ended up wearing it.

"You're always busy. You'd work until your eyeballs rolled out of your head if I let you."

"That's a charming mental picture."

"Can this wait?" He held up the laptop. Then he glanced at the screen. "Candy Blaster?"

"It's strangely addicting."

He sat next to her, his hand wrapped around her waist. "You, Gia Knox-Cooper, are strangely addicting."

She accepted his kiss, her eyes sinking closed. Since she'd taken the vice president position, she'd moved her office from the tech department to the executive floor. Jayson took her former office and she was glad that he finally had his own space.

He was a man in charge, an executive as much as she was, and he deserved more than open office seating.

He'd been sure to remind her that *she* deserved to be at the top of her namesake company. She was a Knox and thereby "royalty" and, he'd also mentioned, again, that vice president was her destiny.

She was beginning to accept he was right. She'd done a lot of sidestepping over the years around taking what she wanted. For all her fighting for her own independence, she'd had a hard time accepting it.

As vice president she could make her mark at the company she loved. Plus, she worked closely with Taylor and her brothers, and Jayson, and that was the best part.

"I was going to ask you about that new—"

He pressed a finger to her lips and shook his head.

"Unless you were going to finish that sentence with the words *sexual position*, I'm not interested."

"Jayson!" She giggled when his fingers tickled her bare skin under her shirt.

"All work and no play, G. Don't you want a break?"

She set the wineglass aside and wrapped her arms around his neck, kissing him rather than answering. He was a lot more fun to kiss than he was to spar with, even though they were both really good at that, too.

He'd moved out of his apartment and back into the house they'd once shared. They had enjoyed plenty of sunbathing in the heated in-ground pool, and they were enjoying their new *and* old beds. Though the new bed had been relegated to a guest room. They preferred their former marriage bed for their room.

"I have a toast." He slipped away from her and grabbed his own glass.

"Now? That was just getting good." She pouted.

"I know but I have something to say. It's your favorite Chardonnay."

The crisp white Chardonnay was hard to turn down. It was her favorite autumn wine. She reached for her glass.

"To our anniversary," he said, clanging his glass with hers.

"Today isn't our anniversary."

"Not our wedding anniversary. The anniversary of the first time I saw you."

"That was New Year's Eve."

"I don't mean then, either. I'm talking about when I first saw you at ThomKnox. I was addressing my staff and stopped midsentence when you walked by. Stevens called me on it, gave me shit for a week about how I couldn't keep my tongue in my mouth."

"No! I've never heard this story before."

He set his glass aside and dropped to his knees in front of her. "Marry me, Gia." He took her free hand—her left hand. "Again."

"Why? I already have your name. You already live in my house."

"Our house."

She barely held back her smile. Her heart lifted, her mind whirred. She wanted to marry him again.

He'd learned he didn't have to prove his worth to her. She'd learned that him taking care of her was how he showed love. Being gracious was her challenge, while his was realizing he could let his guard down.

Nothing would come between them again. She knew it in her soul.

They had already agreed to communicate better, to stop trying to guess what the other one wanted, and ask instead. They understood how to give and take in equal measures. No one had to carve out their own corner. They met in the middle. Always.

"I need a new pasta maker since you threw the old one out. Figured we could register for one." He gave her a half smile.

"I do love your homemade pasta. Can we break tradition and have you make it for Christmas?"

"Gia, I asked you a question."

"I know. I'm thinking!"

"You have to think?"

"Not about the yes I'm going to give you. About which anniversary we'll celebrate in the future. Our old anniversary or our new one? Can we celebrate both?"

Grinning, probably because she'd sneaked her *yes* in those sentences, he said, "We'll celebrate today. The day we decided to make forever official. The day we decided that nothing matters more in this world than each other. The day we went in one hundred-one hundred."

"Because fifty-fifty is for losers," she whispered.

"Exactly." He rested his elbows on the couch cushions and pressed his big body against hers. Heat engulfed her whenever he was near and he was promising never to be far again. "The rings, the license, the ceremony are details. I don't care how it happens, so long as it does. Let's make a real go of it this time, G."

She put her hand into his hair and looked into his earnest, blue eyes. She was grateful, so grateful to have this time with him—to have this chance again. "I love you, Jay."

"I love you, gorgeous. Always and forever."

"Always and forever is a big commitment."

"You think of something bigger than that, you let me know." He kissed her softly and then reached into his pocket to pull out her original engagement ring…only the stone was a hell of a lot bigger than it was the first time around.

She pretended to shield her eyes from the glare.

"I won't do anything with you halfway—not ever again." He slid the band onto her left ring finger.

"How did you—"

"Your jewelry box isn't that vast," he answered. "I stole it and took it to the jeweler for the upgrade."

She admired the chunk of diamond on her finger, glittering in the lamplight. "It's *massive*."

"It's the biggest I could buy without you needing a stroller to push it around in." She laughed and he continued, "Though I'm not opposed to a stroller for you to push something else around in."

"You mean like a toy dog?"

Jayson didn't balk. "Dog. Baby. Your collection of Funko Pop! character dolls. Whatever you want, *wife*."

She put her hand on his cheek and touched his nose with hers. "I like the sound of that, *husband*. I'm willing to give you what you want, too. That's how much I love you."

"Honey," he said in that low, growly sexy way of his, "You've already given me everything I want. Anything else from here on is the cherry on top."

* * * * *

LET'S TALK
Romance

For exclusive extracts, competitions
and special offers, find us online:

f facebook.com/millsandboon

🐦 @MillsandBoon

📷 @MillsandBoonUK

Get in touch on 01413 063232

For all the latest titles coming soon, visit
millsandboon.co.uk/nextmonth

MILLS & BOON

THE HEART OF ROMANCE

A ROMANCE FOR EVERY KIND OF READER

ODERN

Prepare to be swept off your feet by sophisticated, sexy and seductive heroes, in some of the world's most glamourous and romantic locations, where power and passion collide.
8 stories per month.

ISTORICAL

Escape with historical heroes from time gone by. Whether your passion is for wicked Regency Rakes, muscled Vikings or rugged Highlanders, awaken the romance of the past.
6 stories per month.

EDICAL

Set your pulse racing with dedicated, delectable doctors in the high-pressure world of medicine, where emotions run high and passion, comfort and love are the best medicine.
6 stories per month.

rue Love

Celebrate true love with tender stories of heartfelt romance, from the rush of falling in love to the joy a new baby can bring, and a focus on the emotional heart of a relationship.
8 stories per month.

Desire

Indulge in secrets and scandal, intense drama and plenty of sizzling hot action with powerful and passionate heroes who have it all: wealth, status, good looks…everything but the right woman.
6 stories per month.

EROES

Experience all the excitement of a gripping thriller, with an intense romance at its heart. Resourceful, true-to-life women and strong, fearless men face danger and desire - a killer combination!
8 stories per month.

DARE

Sensual love stories featuring smart, sassy heroines you'd want as a best friend, and compelling intense heroes who are worthy of them.
4 stories per month.

To see which titles are coming soon, please visit

millsandboon.co.uk/nextmonth

MILLS & BOON

HEROES

At Your Service

Experience all the excitement of a gripping thriller, with an intense romance at its heart. Resourceful, true-to-life women and strong, fearless men face danger and desire - a killer combination!

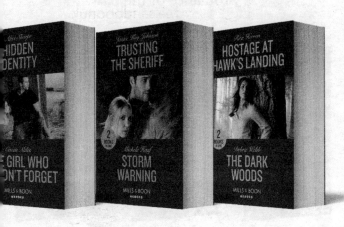

MILLS & BOON

HISTORICAL

Awaken the romance of the past

Escape with historical heroes from time gone by. Whether your passion is for wicked Regency Rakes, muscled Viking warriors or rugged Highlanders, indulge your fantasies and awaken the romance of the past.

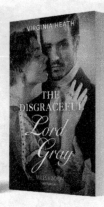